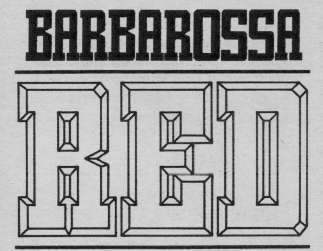

BARBAROSSA RED

DENNIS JONES

General PAPERBACKS

Toronto, Canada

Stoddart Publishing edition 1985

General Paperbacks edition 1986

ISBN 0-7736-7126-9

Cover design: Brant Cowie/Artplus
Cover illustration: Peter Mossman

Printed in Canada

Schoenbrunn Palace, Vienna
March 1

THE SKY was stone-gray, drawn in and cold. Out in the great park to the south of the palace, the trees shed heavy beads of frozen rain, and in the Fountains of the Naiads the drops congealed on the shoulders and breasts of the nymphs half sunk in the cold basins. Nearer the palace the intricate whorls of the flowerbeds lay dormant and sodden, earthen brown.

Because the wind was from the southeast, the palace's rear facade, especially under the balconies and on the sills of the tall arched windows, was rimed with ice; on the rooftops rain froze in the cornices and encrusted the balustrades and the marble sculptures in pebbled glassy sheaths. Occasional gusts of wind drove the sleet against the green louvered shutters and the windowpanes where the drops, because of the warmth of the palace's interior, were unable to freeze. Except for those on the very topmost story, Schoenbrunn's windows were all alight, yellow and warm as they had been when the great palace was home to the emperors of Austria-Hungary, before the monstrous watershed of the First World War. It was in Schoenbrunn in 1914 that Emperor Franz-Joseph decided to order his armies into the tiny rebellious state of Serbia, and by doing so had precipitated the long horror of trench warfare in France, the human and military disasters of Verdun and the Somme and Passchendaele, the ruin of Germany, the collapse of his own dynasty, and the bloody end to a thousand years of Czarist rule in Imperial Russia.

Perhaps luckily for his peace of mind, Franz-Joseph did not live to see the end of the war he had so inadvertently begun. He died in a simple iron bedstead in his private apartments in Schoenbrunn, in the third year of the war. He was succeeded by the last of the Austrian emperors, Klaus, who abdicated the throne in the Chinese-wallpapered Blue Room in the palace at the war's end in November, 1918. The emperors were gone, but Schoenbrunn remained: a reminder.

The palace was badly damaged by Allied bombing and Nazi vandalism during the Second World War, another legacy of Franz-Joseph's miscalculation. After the Russian occupation ended in 1955, Schoenbrunn was lovingly restored, the Guglielmi paintings above the long galleries renewed, the gilding reapplied, the delicate Baroque furniture brought from storage and the chandeliers hung again. Had he been present in the renewed white and gold of the Grand Gallery, Franz-Joseph would have noticed nothing out of place, except for the curiously altered fashions of the men and women gathered there in the glow of the wall sconces and vast chandeliers.

At the exact center of the forty-two meter length of the Grand Gallery, and perhaps two meters from the north wall, a low dais covered in red silk carpeting had been erected. On the dais stood a gilt-legged Baroque table with a green marble top; behind it were two precisely placed chairs with high backs carved with clusters of fruit and wreaths of acanthus leaves. On the table in front of each chair was a maroon leather folder, and two pens in gold trays. A pair of tiny wireless microphones sat on the table before the chairs.

It was three minutes to four; almost time. Ernst Rudel, chancellor of the Federal Republic of West Germany, turned away from the tall window through which he had been watching the rain and said to his companion, "A great day." He spoke in moderately accented French; the chancellor was known as a cultured man.

"One hopes that it is a new beginning," said the man beside him. Francois de Lespinasse, president of France, nodded towards the throng in the Grand Gallery. The photographers and television crews were being admitted. "Everyone is here, hoping."

"Yes," Rudel said. He could see his own foreign minister, Franz Diercks, in animated conversation with the Austrian chancellor, near another grouping that consisted of the British prime minister, the president of Belgium, the Italian premier, and senior diplomats and cabinet members of assorted nationalities. Even the Russians were mixing in well. An air of euphoria hung over the gathering; as de Lespinasse had said, perhaps a new beginning, a durable peace in Europe for the first time in nearly seventy-five years.

"I speak unofficially and only for myself," de Lespinasse said, losing interest for the moment in the diplomatic minuet, "but may I take it that you've reconsidered your reservations about the treaty? You were, shall we say, more than a little opposed to the withdrawal of the Pershings and the cruise missiles before you formed the new government. And even after that, until the Americans and the Russians ratified the agreement. Has Bonn now decided on a more conciliatory stance?"

"We've elected not to pursue the matter any further for the moment," Rudel said, almost absently, as though he were thinking of something else. De Lespinasse, after nearly half a century in politics and diplomacy, had developed a keen ear for the unsaid. He studied the German chancellor for perhaps three seconds, searching for a glimpse into the man's mind. But Rudel's face was urbane, composed, unreadable, the startlingly intense blue eyes attentive but revealing nothing. De Lespinasse, no stranger to power and the ways of the men and women who held it, thought: This man has the magnetism and the intensity of the great. No wonder he was able to salvage his party from ruin after the scandals under Kohl. How did he manage it? In France it would have meant the political wilderness for a decade. But in Germany people believe in him more than anyone since . . . since who? Willy Brandt, say, or Adenauer. Perhaps he is believed in even more than either of those.

Perhaps as much as the Austrian corporal with the mustache?

The image had come unbidden. De Lespinasse shook it off with disgust, thinking: But I do not think he will let the matter of the arms treaty rest here.

Rudel gestured towards the doors at the west end of the gallery. De Lespinasse noted for a brief moment how small and slender the hand was, like that of a woman's. But strong, wiry. "I think they are coming," Rudel said.

"Ah," said de Lespinasse. "Now we see history revealing itself." He injected a trace of Gallic irony into the words, but Rudel did not respond. He too was looking down the length of the gallery to the two white doors, which were now opening. The voices in the great room fell silent.

Through each door walked a man; from the north, President James Hood of the United States, and from the south, General Secretary of the Communist Party of the Soviet Union, Alexei Sergeyevitch Nikolayev. A brief flurry of applause broke the silence. Side by side the two leaders walked sedately to the dais, mounted it, and simultaneously sat down in the chairs behind the table. The American secretary of state and the Soviet foreign minister took up stations just to the right of their respective leaders. Camera flashes illuminated the gallery for a moment, like summer lightning; videotape recorders whined softly. After a pause, Secretary Nikolayev opened the maroon folder before him, and began to read in Russian. He did not read long. When he had finished, he nodded and smiled at the American president. James Hood opened his own folder and repeated the Russian's words, in English.

"We are here today," he said, "to sign the first Intermediate Arms Limitation Treaty, as ratified by our respective governments. We hope and trust that this agreement, by removing all intermediate-range missiles from both Western and Eastern Europe, will be the first of a series of treaties which will provide for the peace and security of the peoples of this continent, and for that of all humankind, for all future generations. We also commit ourselves to the tearing down of the barriers of mistrust and fear between our two nations, recognizing that although in an imperfect world our interests will from time to time conflict, our differences can be resolved openly and by peaceful means. We are determined upon these things so that our children, and the children of their children, may be free of the devastation of war, and so that we may better spend the great energies of our two nations in the service of humankind."

More flashbulbs. Aides stepped forward and turned the pages of the treaty bound into the maroon folders. Nikolayev and Hood began signing the multiple copies, their respective foreign service heads witnessing the signatures.

The signing required less than five minutes. When they had finished the two leaders stood up, shook hands, and then embraced in the Russian manner. A couple of minutes after that they were gone, for the predicted "informal chat" before the state dinner that evening.

Rudel had been watching Hood and Nikolayev so intently that he had not noticed de Lespinasse drift away for the company of the Italian premier. Alone for a moment, he looked around. Waiters in white jackets were beginning to circulate with silver trays of champagne and Austrian wines; a long table at the west end of the Grand Gallery was being laden with food.

"Ernst?"

It was Franz Diercks, Rudel's foreign minister. He was carrying two glasses of champagne, one in each hand. He gave one to Rudel. The chancellor sipped at it, wishing it were good cold German beer.

"It's done, then," Diercks said. "Signed and sealed."

"Yes. The Americans truly have lost their minds. They have handed us to the Russians on a platter."

Diercks pursed his lips. "Hardly that just yet," he said. "Begging your pardon, Ernst, but the removal of the Pershings and the cruise missiles does not really indicate that the Americans are abdicating their responsibilities for the defense of Europe."

"It's the first slice at the sausage," Rudel said. The two men had had this argument before; Diercks, while he agreed officially that the missiles were needed to counter the enormous conventional-arms superiority the Warsaw Pact had achieved over NATO, was still not convinced that the IALT I treaty was a preliminary to Washington's disengagement from Europe. "They may not have thought it out for themselves," Rudel went on, "but I think that sooner or later they will leave us to sink or swim. No matter that political and military logic dictates otherwise."

"Well," Diercks said judiciously, and sipped some champagne. He began to speak again, but halted on the approach of the French president. De Lespinasse held a full glass of some kind of still pale wine, but he did not appear to be drinking it.

"What do *you* think?" Rudel asked with some exasperation, turning to de Lespinasse. "Are the Americans going to leave us to fend for ourselves, fifteen years down the road?"

A shadow crossed de Lespinasse's face. "The thought has occurred to us. One can never tell what the Americans will do next. It drives the Russians mad, and the British. And Bonn as well, I imagine." He paused and added, eyes not quite looking into Rudel's, "Although Paris is disengaged from NATO, we still feel the tremors periodically."

"There is something to be said for your position," Rudel commented with an easy warm smile. He looked up to the ceiling of the gallery, at the vast blue and gray and pink Guglielmi paintings, and then down again. "Your freedom of decision is certainly less circumscribed than ours."

"It brings its own difficulties," said de Lespinasse blandly. "I would not bore you with the details." Diercks, he noted, was studying the bubbles in his champagne glass with great attention. De Lespinasse recalled that the German foreign minister spoke good, if stilted, French.

"I can imagine," said Rudel. "Well, perhaps we do have the beginning of a new era of trust, as you put it so aptly earlier."

Germans should not attempt irony, de Lespinasse thought, even if they are possessed of the talents of Rudel. "One can always hope," he said. "If you will forgive me, I have some business to attend to with my staff. I shall see you this evening, at the dinner?"

"Yes. Of course."

De Lespinasse moved away from the two Germans, sparing a passing glance for the weather outside as he did so. The sky had become much darker, and on the tall windows of Schoenbrunn the rain was at last beginning to freeze.

East Germany
April 30

COLONEL JOACHIM HARPE, in the front seat of the Volga staff car, winced as Lieutenant-Colonel Vedenin swerved to avoid a pothole and nearly put their vehicle under the tracks of the T72 tank in the right-hand lane of the road. The T72's enormous toothed drive sprocket spun like a saw not fifty centimeters from Harpe's right ear. High above the staff car, like a figure in a prop-aganda poster, Harpe glimpsed the captain of the T72 hunched over the hatch rim of the low curved turret; because of the din of the tank's engine and running gear, he hadn't heard the Volga as it came up on the wrong side of the road.

After an interminable moment, the slab-sided muddy hulk of the tank drew away and the staff car slid past its bow into the open road ahead of the armored column. Beyond the Volga's hood the road, lined with tall hedges and overarched by oaks and beeches, gleamed wet and black in the dawnlight. It was still very early, and occasional pale strata of mist hung over the road and in the shallow ditches along its shoulders.

"This low ceiling is going to screw up the air support," Vedenin said, in Russian. "Regimental HQ's going to be frothing at the chops by now."

"How much farther?" Harpe asked, also in Russian. He preferred to speak the foreigner's language; Colonel Vedenin's German was just a little more than adequate.

"About two kilometers."

The wood and the hedgerows came to an end. The mist had thinned enough to reveal pastureland sloping up to the north and south, away from the road. The Volga was in a shallow valley; the surrounding hillsides were still obscured by fog. In the strengthening light the woods on the crests took on definition; the yellow facings on Harpe's tunic and the insignia of the East German Army's Signals Branch were no longer a pale gray.

"Startline's just ahead," said Vedenin.

The mist thinned as they drove; a breeze had risen in the east and the air smelled of spring. The staff car began to pass military vehicles halted at the roadside and in the pastureland beyond. Then, without warning, the fighting machines of the first assault echelon loomed out of the mist: T80 tanks, BMP armored troop carriers, gun tractors towing field artillery, self-propelled howitzers, gasoline tankers, supply trucks, all spread out in apparent confusion. Most of the vehicles' engines were shut down, to reduce noise and conserve fuel.

A lane branched off the road to the north. Colonel Vedenin turned the staff car along it, the machine shuddering over the tread-corrugated earth. A BMP bearing a commander's pennant on its radio antenna was just ahead, the commander leaning against the hatch rim.

"Where's the specialist OP?" called Vedenin.

Without speaking, the officer pointed up the lane. His face was drawn with strain. Vedenin drove on.

"Bad enough to have to jump off in the first echelon," he said. "Being delayed makes it a fuck of a lot worse. Better to get it over with."

Harpe nodded.

The lane began to slope upwards as it climbed the side of the valley. Where it levelled out at the top there was a grove of beech trees.

"There's the OP," Vedenin said.

The German and the Russian got out of the staff car and walked past the generator vehicle and the Gaz trucks with their direction-finding antennas to the observation post. It was a concrete-walled bunker, but despite its proximity to the startline of the attack it was roofed only with rusted sheets of corrugated iron, barely solid enough to keep out the rain. Inside the bunker were two Russian majors and four specialists manning a bank of electronic support measures equipment. They all jumped up and saluted. One of the majors said briskly, "Comrade Colonel Vedenin, everything's in order. All the frequencies are carrying normal radio traffic."

Vedenin waved at the specialists to sit down. "Good," he said. "No breaks in the command network radio silence? Even with the fog delay?"

"No, Colonel. Regimental HQ's been using runners. And the telephone."

As if prompted, the field telephone chirred. The major picked it up quickly and said, "Bullfinch." He listened a moment and then re-hooked the receiver. "The regiment's attacking in ten minutes," he said. "The fog's lifting."

"They hope," Vedenin said.

Harpe peered out one of the bunker's vision slits. "It's lifting, alright," he said. "There's a wind getting up."

The men in the bunker listened for a moment. Outside the bunker the bud-swollen branches of the trees were rustling fitfully.

"That's that, then," Vedenin said to the other Russians. "Look sharp." He turned to Harpe. "Let's go outside and see how they start off."

They left the bunker and walked ten meters through the wet undergrowth to the crest of the hill above the valley. The mist was dissipating rapidly under the combined pressures of the sun and the wind. Harpe could begin to see the organization of the Russian startline now: a row of tanks, eight of them abreast, and behind these a rank of BMP armored troop carriers. Farther back, about 750 meters, was the battalion headquarters' BMP and the mortar platoon and behind these again the tanks and BMPs of the second echelon. The fighting line spanned nearly the kilometer width of the valley floor. On the far ridge Harpe could just make out the artillery batteries assigned to the battalion's breakthrough.

So much committed to this, he thought, wrinkling his pale forehead. He was a thin dark man of thirty-four, fit and wiry, full of nervous energy. Short of sleep, he rubbed his eyes and thought: So much committed to war.

What Harpe was seeing on the valley floor was a scrap, a tiny fragment of the Warsaw Pact war machine. There were three infantry battalions — like the one below — in each regiment, plus the tank battalion; Harpe was looking at perhaps a quarter of the regiment's combat strength. And there were three infantry regiments and a tank regiment to each division, and in East Germany alone there stood something like twenty Russian divisions, and six East German ones: nearly a third of a million men.

Harpe occasionally asked himself, in moments of doubt, whether these great masses of fighting men would do what they were supposed to do when training ceased and fighting began. Control of modern military formations and weapons systems depended largely on electronics, but to rely too much on radar and radio was dangerous; if the enemy disrupted communications and target location by jamming, or worse, began issuing false orders, an army could collapse into a collection af armed bands, undirectable and worse than useless. A whole military specialization had evolved to deal with the problem; Harpe and Vedenin were such specialists.

"There," Vedenin said.

An orange flare blazed above the far ridgeline, trailing pale smoke as it rose. Down in the valley the tanks and BMPs started their engines. The sound rolled up the slope to beat at Harpe's eardrums. The line of fighting vehicles at the battalion's cutting edge began to move west.

"Now it gets interesting," Vedenin said. "Looks as though the Migs were delayed. Fog."

The enemy positions west of the valley were supposed to be attacked by ground-strike aircraft at first light. So far there was nothing above the eastern horizon but the early sun and scraps of cloud.

"Wait," Harpe said, hearing a crashing in the brush behind them.

It was one of the OP majors. "Colonel Vedenin," he said, "we've picked up an enemy alert. They've spotted an incoming airstrike."

"Ah," Vedenin said. "Our lucky day. Go on back."

"Neat," Vedenin said when the major had gone. "This is what makes wars interesting. The ground troops are delayed, the planes are delayed, everything works out. This time, anyway. The poor bastards on the other side don't even know the tanks are coming. All they know about is the planes. So far," he added.

Harpe, intent on the sky to the east, wasn't listening. He could just make out half a dozen dark specks above the throat of the valley. The specks were expanding rapidly.

"They're here," he said. "Couldn't have timed it better."

It was a flight of Mig-27 ground-attack aircraft. To Harpe and Vedenin the planes' approach, as they swept low into the valley, was almost noiseless. Only as they passed, their undersides jagged with bombs and rockets, did the faint hiss of their flight explode into a long rolling boom, the shockwaves of the engines' afterburners battering at the face and stirring the viscera.

"Noisy bastards," said Vedenin when they could hear again.

"It'll be noisier at the other end," said Harpe.

Vedenin chuckled. "Much noisier," he agreed. "You stay put and watch if you want to. I'm going back to the OP to see how good we are at our job."

"Alright," Harpe said.

"You may as well have the binoculars," Vedenin said, handing him the case. "See you shortly."

When the Russian had gone Harpe undid the case and put the binoculars to his eyes. The optics were good German ones, not the garbage the Russians produced; the valley floor leapt up at him. The tank line leading the battalion's BMP infantry carriers was already well to the west, where the valley opened into the plain beyond. Out there Harpe could see the rise of the first smoke columns from the airstrikes. The battalion's attack was undisturbed, as he had expected; the enemy had been caught too much off guard to start artillery counterfire yet.

Everything seems to be working, Harpe thought, lowering the binoculars and turning to go back to the bunker. We'll know better in a few hours, maybe less, depending on how long it takes for the other side to pull its communications back into shape. If they can do it.

In the bunker, Vedenin was leaning over the shoulders of the ESM personnel. "We've got them by the short and curlies," he announced to Harpe, with some satisfaction. "They're running around like headless chickens."

"Any countermeasures?"

"Some. Nothing effective. According to the umpires, so far, the airstrikes put out some of their jammers."

Harpe felt a certain amount of professional pleasure at the success of the exercise. The troops simulating the American defense were obviously confused and distracted, exactly as he and Vedenin and their staff had planned it back at the Zossen headquarters. Harpe and Vedenin were very senior specialists in what the Americans, with their love of acronyms, termed C3CM: Command, Control and Communications Countermeasures. It was the technology of wrecking an opponent's command structure through a careful mixture of deception, electronic warfare and physical attack. Vedenin belonged to the GRU, Soviet military intelligence, and specifically to Department B of the GRU Sixth Directorate. The Sixth Directorate was responsible for electronic intelligence and warfare, and its Department B was a specialist unit paying particular attention to the intelligence needs of the Group of Soviet Forces, Germany, and its East German allies. Department B worked out of Zossen, the GSFG headquarters, and Vedenin's subsection was responsible for electronic warfare and countermeasures for 20th Guards Army, the big Russian formation earmarked to overrun the NATO garrison of West Berlin if war came. East German army units would support the Guards in such an attack and so had to be included in the planning; Harpe was the electronic support and countermeasures liaison officer responsible for ensuring that East German preparations linked properly with the Russians'.

"When do you have to be back?" asked Vedenin.

The bunker's iron roof buzzed as another flight of aircraft passed low overhead. The specialists pressed their headphones to their ears. "Two o'clock," Harpe said. "I've got a meeting." Now that the planes had gone he could hear gunfire off to the west.

"We've seen enough here," Vedenin said. "I'll take you back to Zossen. You'll have plenty of time to get to Berlin." He didn't ask what the meeting was about; he never did.

"Thanks," Harpe said. It was was quite possible that Vedenin knew more about Harpe's work with the East German Trade Ministry than he let on; but although the Russian knew Harpe to be unusually well informed about Western microelectronics — an invaluable asset in this line of work— he never probed. This could be either politeness, or an indication that the Russian knew all he needed to. Harpe thought the latter. The links that joined East German military intelligence to the GRU, and to the KGB and its German equivalent, the SSD, were many. Not all of them were formal or committed to paper.

As they got into the staff car, Harpe wondered if he would have time both to eat lunch and change into civilian clothes before the Technological Trade Bureau sat down with the American to refine the details of the import contract. Brand would drive a tough bargain, but it was plain that he wanted the deal, so there was room for maneuver. Over drinks afterwards, Harpe would read through the specification sheets and trade journals the American had brought with him. It was amazing what Western businessmen would disclose to someone interested in their field; they didn't seem to realize how much a fragment of information could reveal when placed in the context of other such scraps. The Pentagon would be appalled at what the Soviet and East German electronic deception directorates had found out through the services of apparent trade bureaucrats like Harpe.

And a good thing, Harpe thought as the staff car bumped down the lane to the main road. As long as Brand's got things we'd like to know about, General Stollenberg will keep me as close to him as a pair of dirty underwear. Maybe I'll get to the West again, maybe Brand could set up a trade mission to America. . . .

The daydream was interrupted as Vedenin said, "We may see less of this in a few years, you know."

"Of what?" They were near the main road, which was still clogged with support vehicles moving up to the simulated front line. Vedenin maneuvered around a BMP which was about to run them down and said, "This." He waved a hand at the fighting machines surrounding them. "Exercises. Maybe some peace for a change."

"Watch that tank," Harpe said nervously, wishing Vedenin would put his hand back on the steering wheel. The Russian, like most of his countrymen, was a terrible driver. "What have you heard?"

"Well, I've *heard*," Vedenin said judiciously, "that the Americans are serious about getting some of their ground forces out of Europe. They're withdrawing some of those Pershings next month, and that's a fact."

"I'll believe it when I see it," Harpe said carefully.

"It must be true," Vedenin said. "About the Pershing missiles, anyway. *Red Star* and *Pravda* both had articles on it this week. We promised to move the SS20s first, of course, so the Americans had to do something, even if they'd rather keep threatening us. But we're so strong we don't really need the SS20s, anyway. And somebody had to take some positive action to preserve peace."

"That's what *Pravda* and *Red Star* said?"

"That's what they said."

"Well, it must be true, then," said Harpe. He was never quite sure how seriously Vedenin took his own government's pronouncements.

"I don't suppose they'll let us all go home, though," Vedenin said with a trace of gloom, after they had driven another half kilometer. The staff car was now entering the stretch of road bordered by the hedges and the military traffic was thinning out. In a full exercise or real attack it would have stretched nose to tail for dozens of kilometers eastward. "The West Germans are still armed to the teeth. You know what the capitalist Germans like to say?"

"No."

" 'We did not lose the Second World War, we are only resting.' "

Harpe laughed dutifully, feeling the old resentment of the Russians bite at him like heartburn. Whatever faults the Federal Republic to the west had, it wasn't the slave of the Americans, no matter what the Party line blathered. And its people spoke German, not this Slavic aberration of a language that sounded to Harpe like pigs farting in a mud wallow.

There was a smear of damp earth on the right knee of Harpe's trousers. Absentmindedly, he brushed at the cloth. It was the *steingrau* color, close enough in shade to the traditional field gray of the wartime German army as to make no difference. It was an oddity that East German soldiers wore a uniform almost indistinguishable from that of the old Wehrmacht of Hitler's Third Reich, right down to the *Waffenfarben*, the colored facings that denoted the arm of service: pink for armor, red for artillery, white for infantry, assorted hues for the other specializations. Harpe's yellow Signal Branch facings were actually a convenience; he in fact worked for the Directorate of Military Intelligence. He had been assigned the Signals cover since so much of his work dealt with communications of one kind or another.

It's a *German* uniform, Harpe thought. It's part of us, even if a few in the Party call us Red Prussians, even if we can't wear medals from before 1945, like the West Germans can.

He had not always thought this way; the change had begun eight years earlier. At that time Harpe had already been assigned to the Trade Bureau for three years, prying nuggets of information out of Western businessmen, and General Stollenberg had finally decided that he was trustworthy enough to visit the West. As an intelligence officer, Harpe had even had a hotel room to himself, in Kassel, where the trade delegation he was using for cover was meeting with Tantek Corporation representatives.

He had dropped his cigarette lighter, a Bic he had bought in the hotel that day, and it had rolled under the bed in his room. He searched for the lighter. Beneath the bed, right at the back and awaiting him like a land mine, was a thick paperback book some earlier guest had forgotten: a copy of Paul Carrel's *Scorched Earth*, a history of the Wehrmacht's doomed battle against the Russians on the Eastern Front. Harpe spent the next two nights reading it, all 652 pages including the index, ignoring the opportunities Stollenberg had arranged for his testing against the temptations of the West. This earned him a favorable report to the SSD on his return; the report concluded that he could be exposed to Western influences without serious security risk, and this had accelerated his rise in the East German military intelligence hierarchy. The report would have reached rather different conclusions had Harpe's observers known what he was reading with such intense fascination. For Harpe it had been two nights of revelation: the great tank battle of Kursk, where the Russians were savaged and the best of the German Panzer divisions destroyed; the stand of Combat Group Huehner against the Red onslaught in the Sinyavino Hills near Leningrad; the Demyansk Pocket, the Bukhrin Bridgehead, the Wotan Line, the Cherkassy Cauldron, the disaster of the Khersun Peninsula. And the greatest disaster of all, the collapse and destruction of Army Group Center in the spring of 1945, that laid the road to Berlin open to the avalanche of the Red Army.

All the submerged resentment Harpe bore the Russians became conscious during those two days in Kassel, especially when he saw that his own government had lied to him about conditions in the Federal Republic. The workers were neither starving nor ripe for revolution, and behaved in ways — like striking — that would have earned them swift retribution in the East.

We could have won, Harpe thought, picking at the mud on his knee. If only Hitler had left the war to the generals, to von Manstein.

Harpe had not dared bring the book home, but its contents had lived in his imagination, slowly being embroidered with the passage of eight years. We could have won, he repeated to himself. *If only.*

"What's going on up there?" said Vedenin.

Harpe looked up from the patch of mud on his trousers, surprised at how little ground they had covered since Vedenin had made his joke. Ahead, pulled right up to the hedge on the north side of the road, stood a T72 tank. A Gaz light truck was parked just ahead of the huge vehicle. Several men were standing by the roadside tracks of the T72, studying something on the ground. They looked up apprehensively as Vedenin halted the staff car on the road's far side.

"Accident," Vedenin said to Harpe. "Let's take a look."

They got out of the staff car and crossed the road to the group of soldiers by the T72. Harpe saw what they had been looking at. On the ground lay a young tank crewman; he was about nineteen and his right arm was missing just above the elbow. A rough tourniquet had been applied to the stump. The soldier's face was wan with shock.

"Those fucking automatic loaders," Vedenin said. He turned to the soldier wearing tank commander's badges. "Were you ordered to use the loader?"

"No, Comrade Colonel. We decided to try it out before we reached the startline. To be ready."

"Ah, shit," said Vedenin. The automatic shell loading mechanism of the T72 was notorious for jamming the gunner's arm into the breech ahead of the shell. "You're not very ready now, are you?"

"No, Comrade Colonel."

"Did you give him permission to do it?"

The tank captain swallowed. "We all wanted to test it, Comrade Colonel. To be as ready as possible."

"You did, did you?" said Vedenin. He knelt and felt under the injured man's jaw for a pulse. After a moment he stood up. "Have you given him morphia?"

"Yes, sir. He was yelling his head off."

"He's still alive, anyway. Have you radioed for medics?"

"No, sir. Radio silence."

"At least you got *that* right," Vedenin barked. "I'll send someone for him. Stay here until they arrive. Then try to rejoin your unit. You've fouled up but good, you idiots, you'll be in the glasshouse for this, the lot of you." Vedenin turned and looked at the light truck. "What the devil is that Gaz doing here?"

"We stopped to help, Comrade Colonel," said the soldier wearing transport command flashes.

"Where are you supposed to be?"

"Front, Comrade Colonel. We were just — "

"Name, unit, serial number," Vedenin yelled at him. "You know you're not supposed to stop. You're ending up in the glasshouse too for this, you moron, you syphilitic halfwit. Don't you know you're *supposed to keep moving?*"

Harpe walked away from it, around the great armored bulk of the tank. There was perhaps a meter of shallow ditch between the fighting vehicle's tracks and the hedgerow. A few centimeters from the T72's treads a rabbit lay dead in the spring grass, bright blood at its throat. I wonder what killed it, Harpe thought. It wasn't long ago. He stooped and peered into the thicket of the hedge.

Among the twigs and branches and dried leaves there was a flash of russet and a sudden rustling. Startled, Harpe recoiled momentarily. Then he peered through the hedge again, this time glimpsing the animal dart into a pile of brush a few meters beyond.

Stoat, he thought. Of course. Waiting for us to go before it comes out for its rabbit.

He heard the Gaz start up and pull away. Vedenin was saying, "You lot stay put. While you're waiting do something about that mantlet cover, it's a disgrace. Colonel Harpe?"

"Coming," Harpe called. He picked the rabbit up by the hind legs. The animal had not yet stiffened and its fur was soft against his fingers. Harpe tossed the rabbit over the hedge in the direction of the brushpile and waited for a moment, but the stoat didn't come out.

"Colonel *Harpe*," said Vedenin, with an irritable rising tone.

"Yes," Harpe said, and went around the tank to the staff car. Vedenin was already inside it, starting the engine. "Those loaders," he said angrily as they pulled away. "They'll cause us more casualties than the enemy."

"They're dangerous, alright," agreed Harpe absently. He turned in his seat to look back at the tank crew standing disconsolately by their vehicle, with the injured man lying at their feet in the early sun. He wondered how long the stoat would wait before it came out of the brushpile for its rabbit.

West Berlin
May 2

THE LONG GRAY ROOM was already quite full when Brand entered it. He stood uncertainly just inside the double oak doors for a moment, a slender man of average height, in his late thirties, with dark brown hair and hazel eyes. In the few seconds he stood there his hostess detected a new presence in the room, although she was standing with her back to him, talking with a small group of consular-level diplomats and city councillors.

"Paul!" she said, not quite hurrying over to him. She spoke the rapid Berlin patois, although she was capable of formidably correct High German when the occasion demanded it. "I'm so glad you're here." She took a glass of champagne from the tray of a passing waiter and presented it to him. "Jenny couldn't come?"

"She's got some kind of flu," Brand said. "She really did want to be here."

"The children? Do they have it too?"

"Not yet," said Brand, smiling down at her. Lotte von Veltheim, the first woman Mayor of West Berlin, was only five foot four, but she packed into her stocky frame more energy and determination than most of her fellow politicians. The mayor's opponents and supporters alike referred to her (not in her hearing) as *Die Eisenfräulein,* the Iron Maiden. She was fifty and had never married, preferring to direct her energies to a long climb up the hierarchy of West German politics and to the strengthening of the Christian Socialist-Christian Democrat coalition that had so decisively defeated the Social Democrats a few months previously. From time to time, speculation appeared in the press that if West Germany ever had a female chancellor, it would likely be Lotte von Veltheim; although the present chancellor, Ernst Rudel, showed every sign of remaining the coalition leader until death or political mischance claimed him. Lotte von Veltheim could have a long wait; Rudel was only five years older than she.

"Chancellor Rudel has been delayed," she said. "He should be here quite soon, though. Oh. I have something I'd like to show you. Come over here."

Brand obediently followed her through the clusters of her guests towards the end of the big room, which was painted in severe tones of gray, blue and white with groupings of velvet-covered settees and armchairs spotted here and there. On the walls near the ceiling was a delicate plaster frieze picked out in white. Beneath the frieze hung dozens of paintings and old photographs. As he followed Lotte, Brand nodded to a number of the guests, most of them businessmen; he had been drawn into the mayor's circle almost as soon as he arrived in West Berlin, partly because of the industry he represented, but more because of the bloodline that connected him to the mayor herself.

"There," Lotte said, gesturing at a framed photograph on the wall. "I came across it a couple of weeks ago while I was going through some old papers."

The photograph was sepia-tinted in the early fashion. In it a dozen soldiers stared rigidly into the camera's eye, stiff as their creaseless uniforms. Brand leaned forward to look more closely. The uniforms bore the lieutenants' insignia of the old German Imperial Army.

"The one at the left of the front row," Lotte said.

Brand looked, and shook his head. "I don't recognize him."

Lotte reached out and removed the picture from the wall. She turned it over and gently removed the backing to withdraw the photograph itself, handing it to Brand. On the photograph's reverse were two signatures and the date: August 1917. The signatures were faded and brown in the old Fraktur script. Brand made them out with difficulty.

"Klaus von Veltheim," he said, "and Wilhelm Brendel."

"My grandfather," she said. "And yours, next to him."

Brand turned the photograph over to look at the two young faces, long since gone under the earth. "I didn't know they served together," he said.

"It was only for a few months," she told him. "In the 1918 offensives they went to different units. This must have been taken just after your grandfather married Klaus' sister. Klaus was already married, my father was born that year, 1917."

"I've never been able to figure out exactly how we're related," Brand confessed. "Third cousins several times removed, or whatever."

"I find it hard to think of you as an American," she told him. "I hope that's not an insult. But you have fitted in so well. Your German is perfect."

"My father made sure it was," Brand said, remembering the long lessons. "He didn't want me to forget who we were. My brothers got off a little more easily."

"It's curious," she said, replacing the photograph carefully in its frame. "Those two young men. If they could have foreseen."

"Perhaps it's as well they didn't," Brand said, looking at his grandfather's stiff face as Lotte hung the photograph back on the wall. What would you have thought, he wondered, if you could have known your three grandsons? The middle one an American electronics industrialist, the youngest an officer in the United States army, me, the oldest, no longer an American colonel, just a salesman for the family firm.

Perhaps not too ill a record. The army and industry: Germany's tradition for its children, even transplanted grandsons.

"You can have a copy if you like," Lotte said, making final adjustments to the hang of the picture. "I can have one made."

"Thank you," Brand said, meaning it. "I'd like that."

"Colonel Brand?" someone said at his elbow.

Brand turned. The speaker was a man of about sixty, marginally overweight with a receding chin and hairline to match. "Colonel's something of a misnomer," Brand said. "I've been out of the military for several years."

"Ah," said the man. "Well. My name is Egon Spring. I have the good fortune to be head of Bavaria Electronics. You're with Mitex, unless I've been misinformed."

"I've heard of your firm," Brand said. "You produce some rather advanced test equipment, I believe."

"You're very well informed," Spring said. "That is our major line. I gather that Mitex has developed a number of specialized electronic components that we might find very useful. This is not the place to discuss business, perhaps, but I'd like to meet with you while I'm in Berlin. We are in a position to buy in quantity, if our specifications are met."

"Military specs?" asked Brand.

"Yes. We supply equipment to the Bundeswehr, among others."

The Bundeswehr, the West German armed forces, would be a source of fat contracts. Mitex had never managed to crack that market directly; Spring might be worth doing business with. Brand had a vested interest in expanding Mitex's export sales. The company, which his father had started in the late 1940s after emigrating to Boston from the shattered rubble of the Third Reich, had gone public in 1983, but Brand and his two brothers still held the controlling interest. On their father's death Alex had taken over management of the corporation, and Brand had become its European representative in 1986 after leaving the army. Charles, the youngest of the brothers, still preferred the military life and was a lieutenant-colonel with the American forces in West Germany.

"Perhaps we can come to some arrangement," Brand said, giving Spring his business card. "Would you care to drop around to my office about three tomorrow?"

"Delighted. Until tomorrow, then."

Brand watched him move away among the clusters of Lotte's guests. Lotte herself had disappeared. Spring, Brand thought, had to have political as well as economic importance to the new government; Lotte was judicious in her bestowal of social as well as political favors. Spring was no doubt one of the nationalist, neoconservative businessmen who had supported Rudel in his bid for leadership of the CDU-CSU coalition that ruled West Germany. Now that Rudel was chancellor, Spring and others like him would be expecting their rewards. One of these, for Spring, was likely the invitation to Lotte's reception for the chancellor.

The room stilled abruptly. He's here, Brand thought.

Through the big double oak doors walked two security men in unobtrusive dark blue suits. They scanned the room quickly and professionally. Behind them came a third man, slim, perhaps a few centimeters less than average height. His movements were quick and assured, as though directed by great inner energy deftly controlled. He stood for a moment, surveying the men and women before him. Brand studied the man's face. Like his body it was thin, perhaps just short of gaunt, but even in repose implying the same energy displayed in his movements. Rudel's skin was unusually pale, the hair a deep brown, not graying; but it was the eyes that caught Brand. They were a startling intense blue, magnetic. Brand had seen the chancellor half a dozen times on television, but even that notorious synthesizer of charisma paled beside Rudel's physical presence. He dominated the room without moving.

Lotte von Veltheim came forward to greet the chancellor and the moment ended. Brand grabbed another glass of champagne from a passing waiter; for no obvious cause he felt mildly shaken. He looked about for someone he knew. Raoul de Sartines was about three meters away, standing next to the mantelpiece on which stood a collection of small clocks. Brand made his way to the Frenchman and raised his glass. De Sartines returned the salute with a sardonic air. He was a cultural attaché with the French consulate in West Berlin.

"He certainly knows how to make an entrance," Brand said, trying to define the peculiar sensation Rudel had aroused in him.

"Ha," said de Sartines. "He makes an entrance even when he is not making an entrance. It is a gift I believed only we French were born with, and not many of us at that. The chancellor, however, is blessed with good fortune beyond that common to his race. You've never seen him before?"

"Magazine pictures. Television."

"He has a gift of drawing people to him," de Sartines said. "I gather there is a certain type of woman whose ovaries can be heard to rattle faintly in his presence. However, as far as is known, he has remained excruciatingly faithful to his Anna-Marie. She has some French in her, of course."

"Of course," Brand said. De Sartines' speech was even more ornate than usual. Brand realized that the Frenchman was ever so slightly drunk. "He's going to need it. The charisma, I mean. They say it's going to be another long hot summer. Politically."

De Sartines hiccuped and placed his half-empty wineglass meticulously on the mantelpiece. "I had better not have any more of *that*," he said. "Yes. A hot summer. The foreign workers, the unemployed, the leftists, the neoconservatives, the unionists, the nationalists, not to mention the collections of thugs that are pleased to call themselves sports clubs. They don't quite dare wear the old SS lightning bolts and the swastikas, but they'd like to. And there is this *peculiar* behavior of your President Hood. Withdrawing forces from Europe. Does he really believe the Kremlin will do the same?"

"The agreements have been signed," Brand pointed out.

"So were the agreements in Helsinki, on human rights. I recollect that unrestricted freedom to travel was among them. How many busloads of Russian tourists did you see in the Kudamm this week, all clicking Japanese cameras and complaining that the hotel didn't serve sturgeon the way it's done in Chelyabinsk?"

"None," admitted Brand.

De Sartines took his glass from the mantelpiece, drained it at a gulp, and replaced it. "Exactly. And another thing. Chancellor Rudel, while I have the greatest regard for his enthusiasm for European unity, and so on, and so on, is *not happy* about the American withdrawal. When Germans are unhappy, they do peculiar things. I for one would not be surprised if Rudel's government decided to take more control of its military affairs. The West Germans field more divisions for NATO than anybody else, but they're shackled to the Americans. They'd like to change that, I think."

"You're being paranoid," Brand told him.

"We have a right to be paranoid," said de Sartines. "They've invaded us three times in the last twelve decades."

"They're just upset at you because of Napoleon," Brand said reassuringly. "They'll get over it."

De Sartines snorted and said, "Excuse me. German wines have an unfortunate effect on my kidneys."

Brand nodded and watched the Frenchman maneuver carefully through the crowd. Rudel was moving among Lotte's guests, exchanging greetings, brief conversations.

Mending fences, Brand thought. Preparing. For what? De Sartines' speculations had lodged unpleasantly in Brand's mind, like a grain of sand in an oyster shell.

The chancellor, Lotte on one arm, was now only a meter off. Brand hesitated, debating whether to slip away or waylay de Sartines on his return from the bathroom and try to pry more information out of him.

He hesitated too long. Lotte had seen him and was gesturing him to approach. "Chancellor Rudel," she said. "This is Paul Brand. He works here in Berlin." Brand noticed that she had dropped the Berlin patois. "Paul spent several years in the United States armed forces. He is also," she added with a smile, "a relative of mine."

Interest quickened in Rudel's face. The blue eyes gave Brand their total attention, as though Brand and the German chancellor were the only two people in the room. "Ah," he said. "How so?"

"His grandfather married my grandfather's sister," Lotte said.

"And you're American," said Rudel, still with that strange focussed gaze. His voice was soft but very clear.

"My father came to the United States in 1946," Brand said. "His name was actually Brendel, but they made a mistake on his immigration papers. It was easier not to correct the mistake." He paused, feeling slightly foolish at uttering such inconsequential details. He did not normally volunteer personal information.

Rudel seemed interested; no, Rudel *was* interested. "You speak German like a native. What sort of work do you do here in Berlin?"

"I'm the European representative of a microelectronics firm. I handle exporting arrangements."

"Ah. I gather our East German brethren are quite interested in that sort of thing. Have you found them a fruitful source of business?"

"Yes, within my government's export restrictions. I visit East Berlin quite regularly."

"That's very good. Anyone who helps strengthen the ties of

East and West is welcome here. Perhaps we'll be able to speak again, Mr. Brand."

"Yes, Chancellor. I hope so."

Rudel and Lotte continued their circuit of the room. Brand realized that his glass was empty. He went in search of another. De Sartines, returned from the bathroom, had already acquired one and was standing by the double doors, as far away from Rudel as he could arrange.

"Christ," Brand said. "That man's got *something*."

"That," de Sartines told him with a humorless smile, "is the smell of power. Not just political. The kind that comes from inside."

"Whatever it is," Brand said, "Rudel's got more than his fair share of it."

"Yes," said de Sartines. "That is why I am so frightened of him."

It was an hour later. The reception was officially over, and all the guests except a half dozen of the inner circle around Rudel and Lotte von Veltheim were leaving, including Brand. He had had to park three blocks away from the mayor's residence, and as he unlocked the BMW 320i a light drizzle was beginning to fall. He got into the car and drove northeast through the Grunewald District past Tegel Airport towards the city center. Near the Technical Institute he parked in a side street, locked the BMW, and strolled slowly away from it. Around the corner a brown Opel was drawn up to the curb, its dome light on. The driver was reading a newspaper.

Brand walked nearer the curb, clasping his hands behind his back. The man in the Opel laid his newspaper against the steering wheel and picked at his teeth with a fingernail. Brand relaxed and opened the passenger door.

"Evening," he said.

"Evening," said the man with the newspaper. He folded it unevenly and tossed it into the rear seat. Under the dome light the skin over his cheekbones was pitted and rough, from old acne and childhood malnutrition. He was wearing a seedy green sweater with leather patches at the elbows. His name was Erich

Kastner and he was head of cross-border operations for the West Berlin station of the BND, the West German foreign intelligence service.

"What's up at the mayor's?" Kastner asked as he started the Opel and pulled away from the curb.

"Rudel's mending fences," Brand said in English, without thinking.

"What?"

"Sorry. The chancellor is making his presence known among people that matter."

"Well he should," Kastner observed. The Opel was passing the Kaiser Wilhelm Memorial Church, the bombed-out ruin to which a further memorial in the form of a glass tower had been added in the 1960s. Berliners referred to the tower as "The Egg-crate." Brand had to agree with them; Berlin was not an architectural delight.

The drizzle was turning to rain. Kastner turned on the windshield wipers. One of them was defective and made an unpleasant juddering sound as it swept the glass. "What's happening out at Zossen?" asked the BND man.

"They had that exercise," Brand said. "Testing ESM and deception, we think."

"Any details?"

The professional relationship between Brand and Kastner had its awkward moments, and this was one of them. When Colonel Joachim Harpe had made his initial approach to the CIA the year before, he had specified that the BND was *not* to be involved in his handling in any way, shape, or form. The West German security service had been penetrated too many times by East Bloc agents, among the worst of which was the case of a BND counterintelligence colonel who was found to be in fact working for the HVA, the East German equivalent of the Central Intelligence Agency. The CIA, by reputation at least, had never been penetrated, and to obtain Harpe's cooperation Langley had instructed its West Berlin station that the West Germans were not to know Harpe's identity. The BND would receive sanitized versions of Harpe's reports, but would never know their exact source.

However, since Langley's people were operating in territory

under BND jurisdiction, some form of cooperation was required — hence the irregular meetings between Kastner and Harpe's control agent, Brand. Kastner had been given the impression that the agent Brand controlled was actually a disaffected Russian colonel somewhere in the Soviet HQ at Zossen-Wunsdorf. Whether Kastner in fact believed this, Brand had no idea. He himself almost never saw any of the documents Harpe was clandestinely supplying to the West, and absolutely never carried anything incriminating through the Berlin Wall. Brand supposed there was a system of dead drops to pass the information through to the CIA's Berlin station, but he did not know where they were and never would. His role was to supply money (only occasionally, and not very much at a time), keep Harpe loyal and in good spirits, communicate instructions, and carry any urgent verbal messages back to the West. For the most part it was humdrum work, carried out in the context of business meetings with the East German Bureau of High Technology. If Bureau officials noted that Harpe spent time now and again alone with Brand, lunching or having a drink after a meeting, they would assume that Harpe was operating in his own field, trying to extract capitalist secrets from the American. It was good cover, overall. Harpe ran ninety-five percent of the risk.

Still, there was the delicate nature of Brand's relationship to Kastner and the BND. The West Berlin BND station was annoyed at being excluded from direct contact with the supposed Zossen source, and Kastner no doubt had instructions to probe as much as he could without irritating the Americans. There was something of an uneasy truce between the two men in the Opel.

"Details?" Brand said. "Are your people after anything in particular?"

"Reactions to Rudel."

The Kremlin was known to be uncomfortable with the new German chancellor, who in one of his pre-election speeches had spoken (perhaps too loudly) of the "tragic and unnecessary division of Germany." The support Rudel had found, whether he had intended it or not, among the more conservative elements in West Germany, had aggravated Soviet discomfort. After his election *Pravda* had muttered darkly about the "distressing reluctance of the West German government to support the peace initiatives of the Soviet Union" in reference to Rudel's well-known opposition to the withdrawal of American Pershing II missiles from Europe.

"No reactions to Rudel," Brand said. "Zossen's worried about losing the SS20 missiles, of course, but they're going to have to live with it."

"Like us," Kastner said as he halted the Opel at a red light at Hofjagerallee. The rain had petered out and the wipers scrubbed noisily. Kastner switched them off. "Remember all the hair-tearing when the Pershings were put in here? Now they're being taken out. Washington and Moscow could have saved everybody a lot of trouble if they'd come to an agreement in the first place."

"That was Reagan," Brand pointed out. "And Andropov and Chernenko on the other side. They're all dead. Now that Nikolayev's running things over there, maybe we can all get down off our high horses."

"Maybe," Kastner said reluctantly, letting out the Opel's clutch as the light turned green. "If I were your President Hood, I wouldn't trust Nikolayev's good intentions a millimeter."

"We'll have to see," Brand said noncommittally.

"Business," Kastner said, changing the subject. "Any problems in your travels?"

"No." The BND could have found out for themselves about Brand's comings and goings, but there was a standing order that Brand's movements were not to be under BND surveillance. This was to ensure that anyone watching him was readily identifiable as hostile. "Anything bothering your people?"

"They'd like reports sooner that they're getting them. Two weeks stales some of it."

"Alright. I'll mention it. I'd better get on home."

They followed a circuitous route back to Brand's BMW. Kastner glanced regularly in the rearview mirror. One of the chinks in Brand's cover was the need for meetings with the BND man; if the East German HVA noted such a contact, Colonel Harpe would sooner or later come under suspicion. Brand and Kastner met irregularly, and carefully.

"Here you are," Kastner said, pulling up to the curb around

the corner from the BMW. The American would walk the rest of the way.

"Thanks," Brand said. Then, pausing with his hand on the door, he asked: "What do *you* think of Chancellor Rudel?"

Kastner looked at him, his pitted face sombre in the illumination of the dashboard instruments. "Do you really want to know?"

"Really."

"Well," said Kastner, "I think that if Hitler had been sane, he would have been like Rudel."

"Thanks," Brand said. "That's what I was trying to figure out."

West Berlin
Late Evening, May 2

ON THE SECOND FLOOR of Lotte von Veltheim's home was a small sitting room, four meters by five, into which were crammed a beige corduroy sofa, two leather wing chairs, a wicker coffee table, a pair of brass floor lamps, and a real fireplace. The walls were dotted with old pictures: a daguerrotype of the original Reichstag building; an early photo of the Alexanderplatz at the turn of the century, showing the Grand Hotel and the long vanished statue of Berolina, the symbol of the city; a picture of the stiff, mustachioed patrons of the Treptow Beer Garden of 1913; and over the small fireplace mantel, a group photograph of the Berlin garrison of 1897. The images on the wall produced a curious effect: they seemed to project the room into an earlier year, as though on the far side of the polished oak door the time was still August 1913, in the last full summer of peace before the great disaster. Before Verdun and the Somme, before the starvation and defeat of 1918, before the Austrian madman with his lank hair and Swastika banners, before Stalingrad and the firestorms of Hamburg and Dresden. Before the Russians came.

"Germany," said Rudel.

"I beg your pardon?" Lotte von Veltheim said. She was pouring a freshly opened bottle of Krug.

"I was just thinking," Rudel said, "looking at these pictures of yours. What we might have been. If Kaiser Wilhelm hadn't gone to war, that is. It would have been just another year, 1914, like 1909. Who knows anything about 1909, except the historians? If only Wilhelm had ignored the generals, refused to mobilize."

"History is a long list of *if onlies*," Lotte said, handing him the glass of wine and settling herself on the sofa. Rudel sat in one of the wing chairs by the fireplace, in which a low fire burned. The flames fluttered gently.

"That's true enough," Rudel said. "Unfortunately." He lapsed into silence, staring at the fire.

"What's going to happen now?" she asked. She had known Rudel for many years, but by some trick of chemistry she was immune to the powerful charm he exerted on most men and women. Rudel had discovered this immunity early on; it was a measure of his character that rather than resent her autonomy he had made use of it, relying on her for advice and insight unclouded by any inordinate desire to please him. She had repaid his confidences with consistent loyalty, at least partly because of the formidable political strength the relationship afforded her. Allied with her own political astuteness, it had given her the mayoralty of West Berlin, and a mayor of West Berlin had become chancellor once before.

"Now?" Rudel asked, rotating the stem of his wineglass slowly between his fingertips. "Now life is going to become very complicated indeed. If we succeed, Germany will have a chance to control at least some of her own destiny again."

"If we fail?" she asked.

"Then I'm thrown out of office and the Social Democrats win the next election and trot back to the Americans to have their noses wiped."

"There is the little matter of the Russians," Lotte said dryly.

"If it is presented properly," Rudel said, "the Russians will have nothing to complain about. They have always wanted NATO to fall apart. They were delighted when de Gaulle pulled France out in 1966. They could hardly complain over our withdrawal. The ones who will scream will be the Americans and the rest of NATO."

"The Russians may not see it that way. The French haven't

invaded Russia since Napoleon took Moscow in 1812. We're the ones they're afraid of, even now. An armed West Germany under American domination they can live with. One with an independent military policy may be another matter."

"I have been thinking this over for some time," Rudel said. "The Soviet-American treaty to withdraw the SS20s and the Pershings may or may not have been to Moscow's advantage, but it was certainly none to Europe's. The Social Democrats were asleep when they acquiesced to it so easily."

"It would have been political suicide to do otherwise," she pointed out. "All Europe breathed a sigh of relief when that treaty was signed. In public, anyway. You took a considerable risk in making your doubts about it known."

"It didn't make any difference to the election," Rudel said. "The Social Democrats lost anyway. In any case, I wasn't alone. Paris and London and the Benelux capitals see the treaty for what it is, no matter what they say publicly. The Americans are backing out of their military commitment to Europe." He paused for a moment, studying the bubbles in his champagne as they winked in the firelight and were extinguished. "And Chalmers, the American secretary of state. Remember what he said in January?"

"Yes," Lotte said. "That if Europe wanted better protection against the Warsaw Pact, we should start paying more attention to such measures ourselves."

"It's part of the American move towards disengagement in Europe," Rudel said. "If we strengthen our armies, the Americans can withdraw some of the divisions they've had here since Hitler lost the war. They think it will reduce the tension between themselves and the Russians. So it may. At our expense. The Americans will sit behind their moat of the Atlantic, and leave us to take our chances."

"It's possible," she admitted. "One can never tell what the Americans will do from one administration to the next." In the fireplace a log popped and hissed.

"If we are to be responsible for our own defense," he said, "we are going to have to do it properly and we have to begin now. We will never be able to plan or build rationally if we remain in

the NATO command structure. That means withdrawal. Also —"
He paused, looking at the photograph of the garrison officers over the mantelpiece.

"Also what?" she prompted.

"We will have to reestablish the General Staff."

"Ah," she said, with a slight intake of breath. There had been no German General Staff since the collapse of the Third Reich. The victors had not permitted the Bundeswehr to maintain one, reasoning that it was this cadre of highly trained officers that had sustained Germany's resistance in both world wars, even after she had no hope of victory. "This will frighten even our friends," she said, "let alone the Russians. They have long memories."

"It has to be done," Rudel said. "We can't mount an effective defense otherwise. We will have to delare ourselves neutral in the East-West conflict, as Austria has done. That will alleviate the Russians' worst fears. And there is a strong neutralist sentiment in the country just now. From a domestic viewpoint the timing is good."

"I think you're being too optimistic," she said. "The Russians will react badly to your military plans, and the Americans to your neutralist ones."

"There will have to be diplomatic preparations," Rudel admitted. "But even the Kremlin must know that we're no real danger any more. What could we do? Invade them again? It's in their interest that we detach ourselves from NATO. The Americans will grumble, but what else? They can't threaten to withdraw military support, they're doing that already."

She spread her palms. "Alright. It's not me you have to convince. What does Foreign Minister Diercks think?"

"He's not comfortable with the NATO disengagement," Rudel said. "He argues both for it and against it, as though he can't make up his mind. I haven't told him about the General Staff, yet. The next cabinet meeting's Tuesday, I'll tell him then. The defense minister's been informed. You're the only other one who knows."

Lotte reached for the bottle of Krug and refilled their

glasses. The wine was half gone. From the walls the Germans of the lost generations stared down.

"We have earned the right, I think," Rudel said finally. "For decades we have done as we were asked, or told. It is time that ended."

"Be careful," she said. "You will be accused of speaking like the Austrian corporal."

"There was a little truth mixed in with his lies," Rudel said, "but I'll be careful."

"I have one other question," she said. A log shifted in the fireplace, sending up a rush of sparks and a bright tongue of flame. "Will we arm ourselves with the bomb?"

"Better not to," said Rudel, "unless the decision were forced upon us."

"Could it be?"

"Anything is possible," Rudel said, with a tiny smile. "Anything at all."

Bonn
May 4

DARKNESS WAS FALLING. Through the windows of the Federal Chancellery building Maria Lamberz could look a few hundred meters up the lighted prospect of Reuterstrasse until it disappeared over the hump of the railway overpass. Momentarily the clack of her electric typewriter stilled, leaving only its motor's hum and the distant whisper of traffic beyond the window's nearly soundproof glass. Maria was in her mid-thirties, dark and, in certain lights (which the fluorescents above her did not provide), attractive.

The door to the inner office opened and Foreign Minister Franz Diercks came out to her desk. With some care he placed a file folder beside the typewriter. "You're working very late, Fraulein Lamberz. It's past seven."

"Herr Minister, there is a great deal to catch up on," she said placatingly. Diercks had betrayed signs of tension ever since the cabinet meeting that morning; he was normally even-tempered, but this afternoon he had snapped at a staff aide who had chatted too long at Maria's desk. "I'm nearly done."

"Before you go, would you please make one copy of that file and bring it and the copy back to me."

"Yes, Herr Minister."

Diercks went back into his office and closed the door. She finished the typing and put the cover on her typewriter. Many of the other secretarial staff used word processors but Maria had never liked them. Neither did Diercks; he felt that putting a document in a computer was like posting it on the facade of the Bundestag for all to see. Maria had been his personal secretary for some five years; when Rudel won the election and Diercks became foreign minister he had installed her, and her electric typewriter, in the outer office.

She slipped the document out of its folder and began to run it through the copier. She made two copies of each page, collated them, and put the original and one copy back in the folder. The other copy she rolled into a tight cylinder and placed in the bottom drawer of her desk, next to her purse. Then she took the file into Diercks' office. He was standing at the window, looking out at the lights of the German capital. It was now just dark.

"Your copy, Herr Minister."

"Good. Leave it on the desk. Good night, Fraulein Lamberz."

"Good night, Herr Minister."

In the outer office she put her coat on, slipped the cylinder of paper into her purse, and let herself quietly out into the corridor.

She left the U-Bahn at the University station and strolled south along one of the avenues leading through the Hofgarten, towards the museum. About halfway she saw him coming towards her. He was smoking a pipe and had a raincoat draped over one arm. A few meters away from her he took the pipe out of his mouth and stopped to relight it. Maria transferred her purse from her left to her right shoulder.

"Good," he said, as she came up to him. Then, "This is irregular. What is so urgent?" She was supposed to request meetings only in emergencies.

"It's in my bag," she said. They resumed walking towards the avenue's south end, her purse brushing his raincoat.

"There's a dark patch ahead," he said. "Open your purse a little."

She did so. In the diffused light between two streetlamps he deftly removed the roll of paper and arranged the raincoat over it. "What urgency?" he repeated.

"They're the confidential minutes of this morning's cabinet

meeting," she said. "Rudel is going to leave NATO and bring back the General Staff."

"Shit," the man said. "Are you sure?"

"Of course I'm sure," she snapped, but in a low voice. You were supposed to trust your case officer, and she did hers, but he was sometimes irritatingly obtuse. She also hated unscheduled meetings. She always observed the precautions the HVA instructors had drummed into her in East Berlin, but once the BND suspected you, you could be under constant surveillance and never know it. "It's all in there," she went on. "Diercks was upset all day."

"Alright," said her control. "I'll let you know what to do next, as soon as I can. This is going to cause worries back home."

"Good night, then," she said, relieved that it was over, again.

"Wait," her control said. "One other thing. There's a message to pass along when you have the chance. It's this: 'The work you have begun will be of inestimable value. With what you have already given us you have earned our deepest respect and our total support.' "

"Wonderful," she said after she had memorized it. A sardonic tone crept into her voice. "I'm sure that will cheer Comrade Diercks up immensely."

Sochi, Union of Soviet
Socialist Republics
May 9

TO THE WEST, the Black Sea lay as flat and blue and clean as hot steel. The villa, partly obscured by plane trees and poplars, stood on a low rise overlooking the beach, which was composed of stone-dotted white sand sloping down to the rough shingle at the water's edge where the sea-wrack lay: wreaths of weed, broken shells, worn chips of glass like rough diamonds, small dead fish served up by the patient waves. The waves were low today, the fish and shells and shards of glass barely stirring in their hammocks of weed.

Ten meters from the waterline, sitting in a striped beach chair under a sun umbrella, was Alexei Sergeyevitch Nikolayev, general secretary of the Communist Party of the Soviet Union. He was reading a book, which had been translated from the original German under the auspices of the Soviet Academy of Sciences. The book was called *The Psychology of Political Crises*. Nikolayev was perhaps a third of the way through the volume, and had followed it with some interest, but this morning he found himself drowsing off as he read. This was partly because of an excessive intake of alcohol the previous evening, on the occasion of his daughter's twenty-fifth birthday. Nikolayev didn't particularly regret the overindulgence; he rarely drank, and four days remained before he was due to return to the capital. Still, he had a headache and his eyes felt gritty. He placed the book carefully across his somewhat rounded stomach (he was wearing trousers and a light shirt against sunburn) and put his balding head against the back of the chair.

Behind the indefinite reddish cast of his eyelids he thought idly: What a pleasure to have so little business for ninety-six hours. The treaty tidied up with the Americans, even the General Staff fairly content with it, now we can take some time to develop inside the country, deal with the mismanagement we've had under Andropov and Chernenko. Some security at last; remember, though, we can never be *too* secure; the Americans have their troubles but let them solve them, they'll be back, grinding away at us, always trying to tighten the ring. It's just a breathing space, but we can make the most of it. It may even go on for a long time. Who knows what then? Russia secure. The Czars, even they never had that, not even Lenin, nor Stalin, despite the blood. Perhaps I will. He half turned in the chair, drifting off.

Nikolayev had been sleeping for perhaps twenty minutes when a man wearing a dark blue suit and carrying a briefcase left the poplars along the villa's western facade and started down the flagged path to the beach. The suit was painfully out of place, as were the shoes the man was wearing; when he stepped off the path onto the beach, they promptly filled with sand. He muttered and went on, with the tentative gait of one unsure of his footing. A meter from Nikolayev's beach chair he cleared his throat and said: "Secretary Nikolayev?"

Nikolayev grunted and half awoke. The book nearly fell off his stomach and he caught it by the cover. Looking up against the sun's glare he said, "What?"

"I'm sorry to wake you, Secretary."

"Baturin? What are you doing here?"

Baturin looked about for somewhere to sit, and finding nothing, squatted wearily on the sand, setting the briefcase down beside him. He was far from his preferred environment; as Party secretary for relations with communist countries, he spent most of his time in Moscow or the Warsaw Pact capitals. Always just within reach of full Politburo membership, he had never quite achieved it.

"KGB Chairman Minkov asked me to bring this to you," he said, tapping the briefcase.

Nikolayev looked at the case and felt an apprehensive stir.

His mouth was dry and sour from sleeping. He leaned over and groped under the beach chair for the thermos. It contained ice and vodka; Nikolayev poured a cup and both he and Baturin drank from it.

"What is it?" Nikolayev asked, taking the cup back. Baturin had nearly finished the contents.

Baturin extracted a sheaf of papers from the case. "The pages at the front are the original document," he said. "The ones behind the divider are the KGB appreciation."

Nikolayev took the sheaf and began to read. Five minutes later he finished, and then sat looking out at the sea for several moments, his broad peasant features still and composed. Then he said:

"Rudel's really going to do all these things?"

"According to the documents, Comrade Secretary. And the KGB appreciation says he's capable of it."

"What about nuclear weapons? Has there been anything about that since this was prepared?"

"No. This is the latest data. Rudel hasn't spoken of nuclear weapons. To our knowledge."

"This is a thorough fuckup," Nikolayev said mildly, as though he had been served cold tea. "We get the Americans nicely disengaged from Europe and then the Germans pick up their stick. How could the Americans be so *stupid?*"

"Maybe the Americans don't know," Baturin suggested, with some diffidence. "They wouldn't like it either, I don't think. German neutrality, I mean."

"The Germans have *never* been neutral," Nikolayev snapped. "They can't be, they're slap in the middle of Europe. Rudel's playing his own game. Neutral, my eye. Germans are either at your feet or at your throat." He stopped, looking out over the sea, thinking: Ivanov and the others who were against the treaty with the Americans will be making hay out of this in Moscow. I have to get home.

"Go up to the house," he told Baturin. "Find Agayan; he's head of the domestic staff. Have him get me a plane at Sochi airfield within two hours. I'm going back to Moscow. Leave the briefcase here."

Baturin nodded, got up hastily, and scurried away up the

beach. Nikolayev stuffed the papers back into the case and then poured the remainder of the vodka into the cup. The ice had melted and the spirit had become warm and sickly.

The Politburo is going to be in knots over this, he thought furiously. And I was so close. Rudel. Always the fucking Germans.

He drank the vodka and stood up. *The Psychology of Political Crises* slid onto the sand. Nikolayev picked up the German book and hurled it as far as he could out into the sea.

Moscow
May 10

"I CANNOT SEE," Nikolayev observed, "that there is immediate cause for alarm. In the medium term, perhaps; in the longer quite possibly, but not this year or next."

Gregori Ivanov, secretary for Party Administration, reversed his pencil and tapped it on the lined pad in front of him. His mouth was pursed with annoyance. "Quite possibly, Comrade General Secretary. But that doesn't prevent us from taking precautionary actions. In any case, Chancellor Rudel should not be allowed to continue what he's doing. It is in no one's interest, not even that of the West Germans."

Nikolayev sighed inwardly. The Politburo had been in session for two hours and the long narrow conference room in the Central Committee building in Staraya Square was becoming overwarm and stuffy. They had been wrangling most of the two hours and a consensus on measures regarding the German chancellor was no nearer.

"If the Americans can't stop him," pointed out Boris Kamenev, the foreign minister, "I don't see that we would be any more successful, at least not immediately. I—"

"Begging the Minister's pardon," Yuri Minkov said.

"What?" Kamenev half turned in his chair to stare, with suppressed irritation, at the KGB chairman.

"There's no evidence," Minkov said, "that the Americans know anything about Rudel's intentions. *We* wouldn't if—"

"If the KGB weren't so far-seeing," Kamenev finished for him. "So we know, and the Americans don't. Very good. I *thought* this agent of influence of yours was supposed to prevent exactly this sort of German adventurism. You don't seem to have been far-seeing enough to have picked the right man. You might better," he finished sardonically, "have recruited Chancellor Rudel himself."

Minkov gestured with a thin hand, his expression as opaque as usual. Before he could speak, Nikolayev cut in. "This is taking us nowhere," he said. "We could talk until this time next year, but unless the talk results in some kind of action we might as well save our breath to cool our porridge."

"What," asked Ivanov, "would the General Secretary propose?"

Nikolayev paused for thought. Ivanov represented the conservative elements of the Party and its primary organs, as well as the hardline ideologues of the Politburo and Secretariat; he had numerous sympathizers in all of those organizations. He also, as secretary for Party Administration, had access to a great many of the personal files on Party members, and as a result knew where a goodly number of bodies — literally and otherwise — were buried, and which closets might be inhabited by skeletons. So far he had shown no particular animosity towards Nikolayev or to the mildly reformist policies the general secretary represented, but he had to be handled carefully; it was quite possible that Ivanov merely awaited some opportune time to assist in Nikolayev's political demise. The IALT I agreement with the Americans was the only one of Nikolayev's initiatives he had disagreed with to any extent, and he had curtailed even that reluctance when it became clear that the armed forces, for once, favored at least a partial detente with the West. The General Staff's acceptance of the European disengagement was so far the major policy success of Nikolayev's administration, and would have been impossible had not even the military realized that the prolonged arms buildup of the '70s and '80s was bringing the country to the brink of economic ruin. More practically, the military chiefs wanted breathing room to spend their rubles on some of the more exotic arms technologies, rather than merely adding to their existing inventories of tanks, missiles, ships and aircraft.

Ivanov was looking at him expectantly. Nikolayev said, "I would propose that we take no overt action just now. Rudel's policies may not pass the West German Parliament, and if they were to, the next administration could very well rescind them. With the IALT I agreement we have gained ourselves time for military development, and political maneuvering room. The

Americans are already removing their Pershings, and some of the cruise missiles are to follow in July."

"We *will* reciprocate of course?" said Defense Minister Fedashkin. "Even with the developments represented by Rudel?"

"Yes," Nikolayev said. "Our SS20s have to come out of East Germany. If Rudel does in fact follow the course described in the KGB report, we could replace the weapons and be justified in doing so. And if at that time the West Germans were out of NATO, Bonn could hardly ask the Americans to give them the Pershings back."

"There is also," observed Kamenev, "the possibility of bringing Rudel down by political action."

There was a pause. "That's also a possibility," Nikolayev agreed. The same thought had occurred to him as he was leaving the beach at Sochi. "Comrade KGB Chairman Minkov, what are the possibilities in that area?"

Minkov studied the wall opposite his chair for a second, as if wondering whether the portrait of Lenin would lend him inspiration. "We're studying the options," he said. "I would prefer not to present them until they are in a more comprehensive form."

"No action without Politburo authorization," Ivanov said as a warning. If he and Nikolayev were united in anything, it was to preserve the Party's control of the KGB.

"Absolutely not," Minkov said. "At this point the plan is no more than a draft."

For a moment Nikolayev studied the KGB chairman, the swarthy face, the black hair combed straight back above the thin eyebrows, the arched blade of the nose betraying a remote ancestor from the south. Stalin was from the south, he thought.

"Good," he said. "Present it as soon as possible." He turned to Kamenev. "Do you think Rudel can actually do what the KGB report suggests?"

Kamenev took a sip of water and refilled his glass from the carafe. The ice cubes tinkled gently. "If they really are his intentions," he said, "and not just fantasies of a Fourth Reich for his own entertainment, I would say they have only a marginal chance of passing in the Bundestag. Under the right conditions, the reaction could cost him the chancellorship and bring down his government. He is also making Paris nervous. This business of the General Staff will aggravate that. On balance, I think we needn't overly concern ourselves just now."

"They're *Germans*," said Ivanov, his jowls flushed and wobbling, his gray hair disarrayed where he had run his fingers through it. "They haven't forgotten what they did to us, or what we did to them. Bonn has been itching to reunite the country since the day it was divided. Have you forgotten the effect West Germany's independence from the Americans might have on East Germany? Scratch that socialist veneer we've put on the East and you'll find Prussians with Iron Crosses and armbands. We—"

"Use your head, Gregori," Nikolayev said, the heat and his temper momentarily getting the better of him. "What do you think you're going to be reading in *Pravda* this time next year? 'Leningrad besieged by Fascist hordes'? 'Workers unite to halt invaders at gates of Moscow'? They can't do it again. They might like to, but they can't."

"And if they develop their own nuclear weapons?"

There was a long pause. "They won't do that," said the foreign minister.

"Are you so sure? What would we do if they did?" Ivanov looked at the defense minister. "What are our contingency plans for *that?*"

Fedashkin said, "Military pre-emptive action. That's always been the planned response."

"I'm glad *something's* decided," Ivanov said.

"Enough," said Nikolayev. He looked around the table. "Can we at least agree to take no action for the present, pending further developments?"

An indecisive stir among the other ten Politburo members, even the ones normally supporting Nikolayev. Nikolayev felt tired. He was going to have to give them something. "Not that, then. What?"

Ivanov said, "At the very least we should make some of our displeasure clear to Rudel. Simply as a matter of course, we must react to the stories that have been in the West German press this week. I'd suggest a carefully worded note to Bonn, regarding the need for proper recognition of spheres of interest. Coupled with a small military demonstration."

Nikolayev looked at the foreign minister. Kamenev nodded. The minister of defense said, "We could carry out an unscheduled exercise near the border. If we used two divisions or less it would be unnecessary to inform NATO."

"Is that sufficient?" asked Nikolayev. "For a consensus?"

This time the stir was one of agreement.

"Then," said Nikolayev. "that's what we'll do."

West Berlin
May 16

ON SUNDAY, Brand took his family to the Grunewald for the first picnic of the year. They often spent weekend afternoons in the great park which lay in the western part of the city along the Havel River. Occasionally Walter Anderson and his wife Kathleen joined them; Anderson was in the Trade Section of the American consulate in West Berlin. Brand had first met him in professional matters, when Mitex was beginning to open up the East German market, and over the passage of time the two families had become friends.

It was unusually warm even for May. Anderson and Brand were sitting on a grassy bank overlooking the Havel, on whose rippled surface half a dozen dinghies tacked slowly back and forth, sails barely filled by the midafternoon breeze. Brand's two children (the Andersons were childless) were puddling about near the riverbank thirty meters away, under the watchful eye of their mother. The remains of lunch were spread over a blanket near the two men.

Anderson reached out to the blanket and retrieved his beer bottle. He was a tall spare man of about forty, with large brown eyes and a quizzical air accentuated by thick black-rimmed glasses. "Warm," he said after drinking.

"Put it back in the cooler," said Brand. He was leaning back on his elbows, his shirt open.

"Not enough to be worth it," Anderson said, and finished the bottle. He set it back on the blanket and asked, "How is your friend getting along?"

"Alright," Brand said. On Thursday he had signed a delivery contract, a sizeable one, for MPX6483 graphics processor chips. The chip was difficult to fabricate and therefore expensive; it was just sufficiently behind current North American technology to be legally exportable to an East Bloc country. After the contract was signed, Harpe had taken Brand up to the Weinstube in the Hotel Metropol. On the way there the two men had engaged in a highly illegal conversation.

"He seems comfortable," added Brand. "No complaints about drops or delivery."

"Good," said Anderson. "Look, there was an unscheduled Soviet troop exercise up north the same day you saw him, 3rd Shock Army units. Did he say anything about that?"

"No," said Brand. "But he wouldn't have known about it, anyway."

"I know," said Anderson. "He practically lives with the 20th Guards, dammit. Sometimes you get lucky, though."

"Not this time, sorry."

"Want another beer?"

"No, thanks."

Anderson rummaged in the cooler. His work in the consular trade section was the cover for his real profession; he was a CIA case officer with the West Berlin section. He controlled Brand's dealings with Harpe.

"It's the last one, anyway," he said, opening the slender brown bottle. "Look, they want to know back home why that exercise came up all of a sudden. Did Harpe say *anything* last Thursday?"

"He was putting stuff together for a drop," Brand said. "He was nervous. Zossen's been told to be ready for maneuvers at the drop of a hat. No big ones, nothing over divisional size. There aren't to be any special preparatory deception measures, only standard ones."

"Why not?" Anderson said. He was looking past Brand at the children.

"Harpe doesn't know. It doesn't make a lot of sense."

"That kid of yours is going to fall in the creek," said Anderson suddenly.

David was leaning over the riverbank and peering intently into the water, his precarious four-year-old balance at the point of disappearance. Brand's wife was looking away from the river, talking to Kathleen Anderson.

"Jenny," Brand called. "David's going to fall in."

At that moment he did, with an anguished yell at the cold water. Jennifer Brand calmly leaned over the bank — the water was no more than thirty centimeters deep — and fished him out by one arm. His six-year-old sister Alison hopped up and down in an excitement composed of equal parts of glee and consternation.

"That water's damned cold," said Anderson. "Have you spoken to Kastner lately?"

"Tuesday. We went to the safe house. The HVA's been getting busier, as far as anybody tells Kastner anything. Here and in Bonn." The HVA was the foreign arm of the East German intelligence and espionage service, the *Staatssicherheitsdienst* or, more manageably, the SSD. East Germans referred to the men and women who worked for it as the *Stasis*.

"Doing what, exactly?"

"He wouldn't say. He suggested we take extra precautions at the East Berlin drops."

"We're not cutting any corners," Anderson said reassuringly. "I hope you've got some dry clothes for your kid."

Jennifer Brand was lugging David toward them, a hand under each of the child's armpits. David had stopped howling but was wearing an expression of extreme disgust and discomfort. Alison fluttered behind, followed by Kathleen. The two adults were struggling with barely suppressed laughter.

"Your son fell in," Jennifer said, releasing her hold. David promptly subsided into a sodden and miserable heap at the edge of the picnic blanket. His mother knelt beside him and began scrubbing at his hair with a cloth napkin. She was thirty-four, not very tall, with reddish-gold hair and the traditional peaches and cream English complexion. She had a well-developed sense of the ridiculous, which was what had attracted Brand to her in the first place, and a great zest for living. They had met in Washington in 1978, when Brand was a major in US army intelligence and she was working for the British embassy in the commercial attaché's section. They had married a year later. Her father was a retired and widowed British consular official living in southeast England.

"He's my son now, is he?" said Brand. "Whose son was he when he fell in?" He was rummaging in one of the bags for a towel.

"Yours. You should have been watching."

"He'll get chilled in those clothes," Kathleen Anderson said.

"I brought spares for both of them," Jennifer said. "Each of them has to fall into the Havel at least once each summer. Alison just hasn't had an opportunity yet."

Alison, who had her mother's coloring and Brand's wiry build, stood first on one foot and then on the other. "I won't fall in," she said, with outraged dignity. "The last time was an accident." She added something in German; both children were bilingual.

"Your brother is *not* an ass," Brand said sharply. "Come on, short stuff," he said to David. "Let's get some dry clothes on you."

"Can you manage him for a while?" Jennifer asked. "Kathleen and I were going to walk up to the Grunewald Tower."

"Go ahead."

The two women left, trailed by Alison. Brand began changing David, towelling him dry as he went. David had lost the toddler's pot belly and was slimming out into a lean, brown-haired elfin-like child with a delicate pointed chin and blue eyes. Like his sister, he was extremely intelligent; within the limits imposed by their ages they both spoke German as fluently as English. In many ways they were more German children than American. Alison had only been two, and David four months, when Brand took his family to West Berlin. Before they were very much older they would have to spend some time in the United States, if Brand's work permitted it.

And that depends, Brand thought, slipping the dry shirt over his son's narrow head, on how long Harpe keeps clear of the SSD, or when he comes over the Wall. I didn't really think about the effects of all this on the children when I started. Should have. What a profession. In a couple of years somebody else can do Mitex's footwork over here, when I've got things rolling. No more CIA work when I go back to the States. I'll be forty anyway, getting too old for it. But if Harpe's still running, they won't want me to leave. Resign if I have to.

He never, almost never, thought about the other possibility: that the SSD would catch not only Harpe but himself. He occasionally did wonder, though, what Jennifer would say if she knew exactly what his work east of the Wall involved. Perhaps she did know, or guessed. A couple of months after his first meeting with Harpe she had said, thoughtfully:

"If I were to ask you if you did other things than make deals for Mitex, what do you think you'd say?"

He had paused, perhaps too long. The question had come out of the blue as they were driving back from supper with the Andersons, the first supper they had had there.

"I'd say you didn't need to worry about it," he had told her.

"And that's all you'd be able to say?"

"There wouldn't be anything else I could."

"Alright," she had said, as though coming to some kind of final decision. "That's all I wanted to know."

The question had never arisen again. British reserve had its positive aspects.

"Off you go, short stuff," Brand said, swatting David lightly across the seat of his blue corduroys. "If you want another drink, don't get it out of the river."

"Awright," David said, and stamped away, searching the grass for wildlife.

"Bright kid," said Anderson. "By the way, how's Jenny's brother?"

Kevin Drury, two years younger than his sister, was a major in Britain's Berlin Independent Infantry Brigade, part of the NATO garrison of the western sector of the city. "Fine," Brand said. "He was over for supper last week."

"Wasn't he going to get married?"

"It fell through," Brand said. "She had second thoughts about marrying a soldier."

"Hmm. Too bad." Anderson picked up the empty beer bottle and toyed absentmindedly with it. After a moment Brand said, "What are they up to, over there, do you think?"

"I don't know," Anderson said. "It's peculiar. The HVA's got busier, at the same time as those unscheduled Soviet maneuvers. But the White House and the Kremlin are having a honeymoon. The only thing I can think of is that it's some kind of a signal. What are they trying to say?"

"Who are they trying to say it *to?*" Brand asked. "That may be more to the point."

Anderson thought for a moment. "There hasn't been any similar activity anywhere else that I know of," he said finally. "So it looks like they're trying to tell the Germans something, not us. But there shouldn't be any trouble there. Rudel raised hell about the missile pullout before the treaty went through, but he's changed his tune since then. And made a big point about it."

"For somebody of his convictions," Brand said, "that's a pretty drastic change. What's he going to say if there's a force reduction treaty? That'll be the next step, after IALT I."

The Mutual Balanced Force Reduction Treaty discussions had been going on, sporadically, for years. They were an attempt to reduce the tension along the European frontier by withdrawals of troops of both NATO and the Warsaw Pact. Intransigence on both sides had prevented any useful results, but with IALT I prospects had brightened for a military disengagement in Central Europe. However, since even partial withdrawal of American conventional forces would throw more of the burden of defense on the fragile economies of Western Europe, the MBFR talks were not overwhelmingly popular in some European capitals.

Anderson said, "If a force reduction treaty does come along, it'll take two years to implement. There won't be hordes of Soviet and American troops streaming back to their homelands the next day. There'll be some symbolic nonsense to start off with, then it'll be the same old thing. Everybody will have to argue about who's taking advantage of obscure subclauses in the treaty; after that, there'll be a new administration in Washington. Then the Pentagon'll find an excuse to get around the treaty, or the Kremlin will, and it'll be back to business as usual. The more it changes, the more it stays the same."

"I think Rudel's dangerous," Brand said abruptly. David, a comfortable thirty meters from the Havel's banks, was intent on something in the grass. "He's got that charisma they're always babbling about; it sounds like a load of public relations crap, but it's real. Rudel has it."

"So the Germans have a charismatic leader," said Anderson.

"It hardly matters. They won't be allowed to do what they did the last time they had one."

"No," said Brand.

"What's on your mind?" Anderson asked.

"I think the Russians are worried about Rudel. The HVA activity, the exercises. A message, like we said." He studied Anderson's face for anything more than a polite lack of concern.

"Maybe," Anderson said. "Look, we'll check it out, okay? Hey!"

Brand turned quickly back to the riverbank, much too late. David was in the process of toppling into the Havel.

"Ah, shit," Brand said. "Not again."

Camp David
May 17

HIS NAME WAS JAMES HOOD, and he was president of the United States. He was sitting in his office, reading the Daily Intelligence Brief, the digest of global intelligence matters supplied each morning by the National Foreign Assessment Center. It had come up from Washington by helicopter that morning, and, for a change, reported no new disasters. The world was quieter this May than it had been for a long time; the brief was almost boring. The only noticeable Soviet motions had been the usual to-and-fro-ing in Afghanistan, and a couple of minor Warsaw Pact exercises.

We've done it, maybe, Hood thought, smoothing the papers across his knee. He had avoided the big suede chair behind the desk, choosing instead one of the firmly upholstered settees in front of the fireplace; for some reason its structure eased the pain in his mildly arthritic left hip. The disorder annoyed him from time to time; he knew it was not really a disease of the elderly, but at sixty-two he was still irrationally convinced that he was too young for arthritis. The conviction was, he knew, a vanity; he tried not to have too many.

He closed the covers of the brief, thinking again: Perhaps we've done it, for a while, maybe longer. Drawing back from war, towards some kind of peace. Finally, if we want to survive, we have to trust them, even a little, no matter how they misunderstand us. Perhaps I gave away a little too much, but even so some of the missiles are going home and then perhaps we can get some of the soldiers to follow . . . put the money to better use. What was it that air force general said? By the end of the century the entire defense budget will pay for one fighter aircraft, if the costs keep rising as they have for the past twenty years. What was

Reagan thinking of, with that Star Wars scheme of his? It would have bankrupted the country.

Still, he had taken dreadful political risks to secure the IALT treaty. Hood suspected that the Russian general secretary had taken similar ones; it was perhaps coincidence that the two leaders came onto the scene at about the same time, with similar concerns about the apparently irreversible drift towards war, and about the distortions the dreadfully expensive weapons programs were inflicting on both societies. It was equally coincidental that they had each possessed just enough power to overcome their domestic opposition, both from the ideologues who perceived the slightest compromise as the first step to perdition, and from the timid who were merely terrified of accepting a moderate risk to reduce a monstrous one. Hood was not quite certain, privately, that he believed in any god, but it did occasionally occur to him that there might be something approaching a Providence.

It was ironic that those who had hoped, or feared, that he would cut his political throat with the treaty had both been proven wrong. The country had seemed to heave a sigh of collective relief on its signing, and the few voices in the Congress accusing Hood of being a Communist dupe had been given little attention. Hood was in fact a little concerned about this reaction. It had something of the flavor of the isolationist mood of the 1930s about it, and a substantial proportion of the Congress did seem to favor troop reductions in Europe, on the principle that the West Europeans could shoulder more responsibility for their own defense if they had to. The underlying concern had been most clearly expressed by the senator from Wisconsin, who had recently asked the House whether the United States would risk thermonuclear suicide to protect Western Europe from Soviet aggression. He had brought up an awkward point, one better not publicly discussed: Were the citizens of the United States willing to be incinerated in the defense of German and French cities and villages they had never heard of, and whose existence was to them a matter of profound indifference?

There had never been a satisfactory answer to that; the senator from Wisconsin knew it, and for better or worse the Russians knew it. What the Russians did not know, and what was perhaps the most closely guarded secret of the presidency and the Pentagon, was exactly how far the United States would go in the defense of Europe. Publicly, of course, the commitment was total, as it had to be; if the Kremlin ever had cause to suspect that Washington would prefer the fall of Europe to the risk of thermonuclear war, the Soviets could afford to be substantially more aggressive in their behavior. Their uncertainty was essential to European security, and its preservation had been a key to American foreign policy ever since Kennedy. Hood was determined to preserve that uncertainty.

In any case, he reminded himself, the Kremlin has its own problems. I would rather be here than there.

There was a knock at the door, and the secretary of state put his head around the jamb. His name was Alan Chalmers. "He'll be here in about three minutes," he said.

"I'll come out front," Hood said. Walking sometimes eased the pain in his hip.

He left the office and went slowly out to the front porch to join Chalmers. The meeting was to be a very quiet one, and promised to be awkward. Hood could not see what Bonn hoped to gain by it, but he would listen; it was always worth listening.

Franz Diercks, foreign minister of the Federal Republic of Germany, peered anxiously through the Lincoln's bulletproof windows as the limousine drew up in front of the main lodge. On the porch, next to the secretary of state, stood President Hood, looking thinner than Diercks remembered, the gauntness of his face accentuated by his unusually pale skin and the blackness of his hair. To Diercks, for a moment, he looked a little like Lincoln.

Diercks' palms, uncharacteristically, were sweating. Normally an urbane and self-contained man, he found this meeting to be causing him acute discomfort because of the impossibly conflicting demands that were being placed upon him. His real loyalties were not divided, but what he had been ordered to attempt, and what Rudel had instructed him to say to Hood, were very nearly irreconcilable.

Ask the Americans to find some way to keep their Pershings here, Rudel had said. If they won't do that, then get them to reaffirm their willingness to use nuclear weapons to defend Europe. If they won't do either of those things, don't say anything else. Just come home.

He *knows* they won't do either of those things, he thought, as the secret service men opened the Lincoln's door for him. As for the other things . . .

At least SSD Berlin had been understanding. They didn't want Diercks to endanger his position by exceeding Rudel's instructions. But what he should do, still, if he could . . .

Hood was smiling, stepping off the shaded porch, extending his hand. Diercks shook it, under the careful gaze of the bodyguards. Chalmers beamed. Hood said:

"I believe you wanted to dispense with protocol. If you'd like to come on through the house, we can relax on the terrace. We'll have lunch in about an hour."

"Thank you, Mr. President," Diercks said in his stiff but accurate English. "That would be excellent."

They went through the cool dimness of the lodge to the terrace at its rear. On the terrace were chairs and a round glass table sprouting a large yellow sun umbrella. A wood edged the lawn. It looked, but was not, deserted. Security at Camp David was unobtrusive but impenetrable.

The three men arranged themselves in the chairs. One of the camp staff brought coffee and rolls. Hood and Diercks exchanged amenities. After the first sips of coffee Hood said, while gently replacing his cup in its saucer: "I believe you are here because Chancellor Rudel is still concerned about our withdrawal of the Pershings and the cruise missiles."

Diercks waited, but Hood said nothing more. Chalmers regarded the German foreign minister with an expression of polite interest.

Diercks cleared his throat. "That is correct. He believes the United States is making a grave mistake, that the Russians are not to be trusted. That they will circumvent the treaty in some manner."

"Actually," Chalmers pointed out, "if you look at the Soviet record on previous agreements, they have been very careful to abide by them, to the letter, if not exactly always the spirit."

"Their behavior over the Helsinki agreements hardly falls into either category," Diercks said, to stay in character.

"That's unfortunately true," Chalmers said. "But it was probably a mistake for Carter's administration to insist on coupling human rights with arms accords. The Russians saw that as interference in their internal affairs. By economic blackmail, if you like. But there weren't any such conditions attached to IALT I. There's no reason to think they won't abide by the treaty."

"In other words," said Diercks, "the United States Government intends to carry out the provisions of the IALT I treaty."

"Yes," Hood said. "That's final."

"I congratulate you on your confidence in the Russians," said Diercks. "Such a risk deserves to be rewarded with success." He paused. "Might I ask your intentions for the mutual force reduction talks? There are, naturally, rumors throughout the Foreign Ministry and elsewhere, but it would be preferable if my government were to have some clarifications."

Chalmers and Hood exchanged glances. "The objectives of the force reduction talks are as publicly stated," Hood said. "To reduce tension on the European frontier by lowering the numbers of troops facing each other along the border. Surely the State Department has given Bonn the outlines of the negotiations."

"Yes," Diercks said. "Of course. That is, of course, what we have been told. But there is some concern that there is, what do you call it, a hidden agenda."

"There is not," Chalmers said emphatically.

"I did not really think there was," Diercks said. "There was no distrust intended." He drank a little coffee; it was growing cold in the thin Meissen cup. Somewhere a bird was squalling *jay-jay-jay*. "What sort of bird is that?" he asked. He needed time to think.

"That? Oh, a bluejay," Chalmers said.

"We have none in Europe," Diercks said. After a pause he went on: "The rumor has it that the balanced force reduction treaty is intended to reduce American military expenditures by reducing involvement overseas. Even, it has been said, at the expense of European security."

"That's a rumor," Hood said sharply. "We are trying to reduce the waste in military spending without reducing any of our combat abilities. Any force reductions in Europe will have to be balanced by equivalent Soviet ones. No American troops will leave until European forces are sufficient to European security requirements."

"As defined by the United States?" asked Diercks. "It is the possibility of American unilateral action that discomforts Bonn."

Hood paused, as if weighing what Diercks had said. The morning was growing quite warm. The wood beyond the lawn presented a solid rampart of green, topped by blue sky embossed with cumulus. Finally Hood said, "We will not take any decisions that endanger the interests of the NATO allies."

"Chancellor Rudel," Diercks said bluntly, "wants to know the circumstances under which the United States would retain the presence of the Pershing and cruise missiles in Europe."

"There are no such circumstances," said Hood. "Not as long as the Russians abide by the treaty. They are showing every sign of doing so."

"Cruise missiles are very easy to hide," Diercks said carefully. "The Russians could return a powerful secret force to East Germany without a great deal of difficulty, and it would be very hard to detect. The verification procedures cannot be all that trustworthy."

"Meaning that we could do something similar, if we chose?" said Chalmers, without any particular inflection.

Hood raised a hand. "Minister Diercks is pointing out options," he said evenly. "But if the treaty is to have the remotest chance of success, that particular option isn't available. We could not afford the diplomatic cost of being discovered. In any case, cruise missiles aren't first strike weapons, they're too slow, slower than aircraft. And you can recall an aircraft. Furthermore, we will not be withdrawing all nuclear weapons from Europe, only the cruise and the Pershing delivery systems."

"It would be of assistance," Diercks said, "if the United

States were willing to reaffirm its intention of using nuclear weapons in the defense of Europe. If necessary."

"I don't think that would serve any useful diplomatic purpose just now," Hood said.

"The Russians are paranoid enough as it is," Chalmers cut in. "The more frightened they are, the more unpredictable they are. And we don't want to do anything to undermine Secretary Nikolayev at the moment. We aren't sure how secure he is in the Kremlin. He's the most pragmatic Soviet leader for a long time, maybe ever, and he's preferable to anyone else we know of over there."

Diercks tried his coffee again. It was barely warm but he drank it anyway. His armpits felt sticky. He had to go just one step beyond the brief Rudel had given him.

"Any unilateral actions by the United States might be returned in kind," he said. "If the actions were perceived in a sufficiently negative way in Europe, that is. France withdrew from NATO. There is always a danger of fragmenting the alliance if conflicts of interest go deep enough. Even if there were perceptions of such conflicts."

Both Chalmers and Hood regarded Diercks with a curious absence of expression, as though they had withdrawn for a moment from his presence. Then Chalmers asked:

"Would you be prepared to clarify that statement?"

Diercks picked up the coffee pot and refilled his cup, being very careful not to spill any of the brown liquid into the saucer. As he added a level teaspoon of sugar he said, "In matters like these one should provide for all contingencies. I ask only to discover what your reaction would be to a member of the alliance choosing to, what's the phrase, *go it alone*, if it felt its interests were no longer served by NATO. For instance, as France did." He finished stirring and set his spoon down. The bluejay was calling again.

"The instance would have to be more specific," Chalmers probed.

"There is nothing to be specific *about*," Diercks said. Softly,

softly. "There must be some theoretical reaction to such an event, even an imagined one."

Again the two Americans exchanged glances. "The response would depend on the political, military and economic conditions," Hood said. "Greece left NATO in the 1970s and then rejoined. There was naturally some concern when Athens opted out. A stronger nation in a more sensitive position would cause proportionately more concern."

"There would possibly be military and economic sanctions?"

"That would depend on the stance of the withdrawing nation," Chalmers said.

"There could be many variations," Diercks admitted. He could go no farther. East Berlin had wanted him to find out what the Americans would do if the West Germans went neutral, but clearly the Americans had no suspicion of the chancellor's plans. And Lieutenant-General Ott of the HVA would be mightily displeased if Diercks endangered his cabinet position by betraying them. There was no more he could do.

"I only ask," he said diffidently, "because Bonn is naturally concerned about the solidarity of the alliance. It is curious that this arms treaty causes the strain it does. As though we all secretly preferred the dangers of war to the dangers of peace."

"Quite so," Hood said. For a moment the absent look was there again, and then was gone. "I'm very glad Chancellor Rudel has resolved his earlier . . . doubts about this administration's policies."

"No one's interests are served by pointless bickering," Diercks observed.

They continued on these lines through lunch, which suited the German minister precisely. He left, at two that afternoon, with substantial but perfectly concealed relief.

When he had gone Chalmers said to the president, "What was behind all that? What he said out on the terrace."

"It's hard to be sure. I thought at first it was intimidation, but if it was he covered it perfectly. Bonn is probably worried about the effect of the treaty on NATO. Not surprising."

"Maybe," admitted Chalmers. "Nonetheless . . ."

"Nonetheless what?"

"What *would* we do if the West Germans decided to do what Paris did?"

"It won't come to that," Hood told him. "Bonn's just seeing things under the bed."

Southern Germany
May 21

OVER THE AMERICAN MISSILE BASE the sky was patched with blue and gray, a broken cloud cover driven by a wind from the north. Along the perimeter fence of the base, at intervals of precisely ten meters, stood a cordon of German police. They were young and bored; they had been standing there, except for reliefs, ever since the previous evening when they had been summoned to guard the installation against the civilians.

The civilians, about thirty of them, were scattered on the young grass on both sides of the base access road. Many of them lay on air mattresses or curled in sleeping bags; they had been there all night, the ground was hard, and they were tired. Half a dozen of them, more sustained by passion or conviction, were still on their feet, leaning on the lengths of wood that supported their placards.

To Colonel Charles Brand, as he slowed the staff car on the approach road to the main gate of the base, they resembled the tattered standardbearers of some defeated and long-forgotten army. The last of the children's crusade, he thought, stepping lightly on the brake. The fruits of victory, this. They've won, or think they have.

The car was perhaps fifty meters from the group of demonstrators. One of them waved a placard at the vehicle, but it was a feeble gesture. There was nothing to protest any more; the missiles were going. A woman shouted, *"Raus! Raus!"* as the car went by: "Get out, get out." Probably she did so only by reflex, because of Charles' American uniform. A few years ago they would have been throwing themselves under his wheels. Not any more; with some kind of victory at hand who would risk not being present to enjoy it?

This is victory? Charles wondered, looking sidelong at the

civilians as the staff car slid away from them. They don't *look* as if they enjoy it very much. They've always been willing to risk jail or whatever for their convictions, maybe even concussion or a face full of riot gas, but they've never signed a contract to die defending somebody else. They've always known the worst they could get would be a week in jail, a trespassing fine, maybe have their letters opened or their phones tapped. How many of them would have gone on if the penalties were a labor camp, a psychiatric hospital or a penal battalion, or a hole in the ground and a bullet in the back of the neck?

Well, that's why we're here, he told himself as the staff car drew up to the main gates of the base, where the German policemen and the American soldiers were drinking coffee out of white styrofoam cups. To make sure they can go on enjoying their righteousness.

"Colonel, sir," said the American guard at the car window. "May I please see your identification?" A Carolina accent; the soldier was young and very black.

Charles showed his passes. The guard checked them against some information on his clipboard and said, pointing, "Sir, the meeting's in the main headquarters building, last street before the airfield, on the right. Two stories high, over that way."

"Thanks," Charles said. "I've been here before."

He looked at his watch again as he pulled up in front of the HQ building; he was a good quarter of an hour early. He put the car in one of the parking slots marked VISITORS ONLY and got out, stretching in the warm early sun. Out on the airfield perimeter, towards the Pershing support and storage complex, he could hear the sound of heavy engines.

Getting ready to load, he thought. Sending them back home. I wonder where they'll put them? More to the point, I wonder where the Russians will put their SS20s? Under some handy trees just outside of Leipzig?

"Colonel Brand?"

It was spoken with the *d* turned into a *t*, in the German fashion. Charles turned around. Colonel Uwe Hoth was standing at the corner of the headquarters building, next to a flowerbed planted with red and yellow tulips. His uniform was immaculate, from the tips of the polished shoes to the peaked cap with its oak leaves and crossed swords.

"Hello, Uwe," Charles said, in German. His command of the language wasn't quite as good as his brother's, but it was flawless compared to the bastard mixtures spoken by most of the Americans stationed in Germany. "We're both early."

"It was such a pleasant day," Hoth said, "I decided to get up early. So I am here early. Shall we walk over to the airfield and watch history being manufactured?"

"If that's the way to put it," Charles said. "Alright." The two soldiers fell into step automatically, walking smartly along the base's main street in the direction of the airstrip. The sound of engines waxed and waned on the fitful morning wind.

"When does the first flight leave?" Hoth asked.

"Anytime now, I gather. What did you think of the farewell committee at the gate?"

Hoth made a dismissive gesture. "They had nothing to do with the withdrawal of the Pershings. It pleases them to think so, but they didn't. The missiles would be staying here if it weren't a matter of mutual interest to get them out."

"Mn," Charles said. He could see the hangar roofs looming over the administration buildings on their left. They turned down a side street which ended at the airfield perimeter road. The perimeter road was separated from the airbase proper by a high chainlink fence topped by barbed wire and alarm sensors. The backs of the hangars blocked their view of the loading area.

"Let's walk over towards the gate," Charles said. They turned south.

"I'm surprised they're withdrawing the whole brigade," Hoth said. "I would have thought your people would have left some kind of caretaker formation."

"That's what I'm here about," Charles said. The men who maintained and would have launched the Pershings were going home in company with with their weapons. As interim tenants a battalion of Charles' tank brigade was moving in, and the airbase was being redesignated as an airlift supply depot. Eventually the Germans were to take over the base, which was why Hoth was to be present at this morning's meeting. The diplomatic niceties had to be observed; the base was on German soil, after all, and the meeting was supposed to result in some kind of schedule for Bundeswehr occupation. It would have made more sense for the Germans to take over the installation immediately, but this would have been, Charles supposed, politically sensitive. Removing American men and weapons was redeployment; handing over a base was retreat. By the time the Germans moved in, the media's memory of the Pershing withdrawal would have faded, and with it would go most of the likelihood of embarrassments for the White House and the Pentagon. The presence of such relatively low-ranking officers as Uwe Hoth and Charles Brand at the morning's meeting signified Bonn's and Washington's intention of keeping the handover in as minor a key as possible.

"I was going to ask you," Hoth said, "how much do you like your new tanks?"

Charles scowled. He commanded the 2nd Brigade of the United States First Armored Division, and the modified M1 Abrams tanks were a delicate subject; the first production runs had delivered a vehicle worse than the ones they were supposed to replace. The Abrams Mark One had broken down more often, been harder to repair, and had carried less fuel and ammunition than the M60s, the solid and reliable (if elderly) main battle tank the US army had relied on for nearly twenty years. The Mark Two had removed a good number of the problems, but the ammunition storage was still too restricted.

"The new ones are a lot better," Charles said. "The gunnery computers need attention. They work beautifully, but they're too delicate."

Your Pentagon is perhaps too much in love with high technology," Hoth observed.

"Maybe."

They were passing the last of the hangars. Beyond the perimeter fence, out on the tarmac, stood the great bulk of a Starlifter transport, the aircraft's clamshell doors exposing the dim interior of its cargo hold. Inching up the ramp into the hold was a long shrouded cylinder on a wheeled transporter: a Pershing II intermediate-range ballistic missile. The two soldiers stopped. "There you are," Hoth said. "History being made. The dawn of a new age of peace."

"This age isn't different from any of the others," Charles

said. "What you're looking at is a hiccup in history. It won't go on. It just serves everybody's interests, temporarily."

Hoth adjusted the peak of his cap against the sun. "You're probably right, unfortunately. When the bloom is off this particular rose, we will be back to business as usual. Cheer up, at least it keeps us employed."

"At least," Charles said. They watched the Pershing crawl up the Starlifter's ramp, hardly seeming to move but moving anyway. "What do *you* think of all this?" he asked, at last.

"Of what?"

"The withdrawal. The agreement with the Russians. Chancellor Rudel didn't like it. What does the Bundeswehr think?"

The Pershing was perhaps halfway into the transport aircraft. Hoth said, "I'm an officer, so are you. No matter what the civilians drivel at us, we obey orders. We have to. There is no other way."

"And the *Innere Fuhrung?* " Charles asked.

Hoth hesitated; the American had hit on a sensitive point. *Innere Fuhrung* was the psychological device used by the Bundeswehr to negate any accusations of rampant nationalism; it was intended to foster a questioning attitude in the line soldiers, and could be translated, roughly, as "moral direction from within." The concept supposedly guaranteed that there would be no return to the mob psychology of the Hitler years.

"I think," Hoth said finally, "that the Bundeswehr is more German than anything else. If there were a national crisis, I would hope that *Innere Fuhrung* would go to the winds. There is no place for it in a fighting army. It is a political device, nothing more."

"Yes," Charles said. "It's always seemed peculiar."

Around the corner of the end hangar, out of sight, an aircraft was starting its engines, the first faint keening building into a whine.

"Do you know what this reminds me of?" Hoth asked abruptly.

"What?"

"I studied history at the university in Bonn. Ancient history.

In the year 410 the emperor at Rome recalled his legions from the frontiers, all of them. He needed them for the defense of the Empire. Think of them, marching off down the roads or boarding the ships, always believing they would come back, that civilization would hold. But it didn't, and they never did. Come back, that is."

"No," Charles said. "They didn't."

"The barbarians came after that," Hoth went on, his voice trailing off as though he were embarrassed. "In a few hundred years it was gone, every scrap of civilization. How long can we last here?"

"It's not quite the same," Charles said, refraining from the remark that the barbarians had been German. The whine of jet engines was rising to a shriek. A Starlifter rolled slowly into the line of sight, lumbering along the taxiway towards the long east-west runway. It swung as the two men watched, aligning itself for its run into the sky.

"You're quite right," Hoth said with a half smile. He had to raise his voice to be heard above the scream of the engines. "It's a false analogy. My professors always warned me."

"It's not the same now," Charles repeated.

They watched the Starlifter rise into the warm May sun, far away at the eastern end of the runway, like a moth disappearing into a flame.

Bonn
May 23

THE HVA SAFE HOUSE was in the eastern quarter of Bonn, not far from Konigswinterstrasse. Diercks sat in the living room of the flat. He had been there for twenty minutes, and was becoming steadily more irritated, and frightened, at the delay.

I will give them another quarter hour, he told himself, although he knew that in reality he dared not leave without instructions. He had expected some reaction from the documents he had passed to Maria two days before, but he had not anticipated such an extreme one. He suspected that the information had gone through SSD East Berlin straight to Moscow, at least to KGB headquarters in Dzerzhinsky Square, perhaps all the way to the Politburo. Nothing else could explain his being summoned to a meeting like this one: safe house, passwords. The fundamental principle of his clandestine work was that he was never, under any circumstances, to have contact with field operatives, unless such contacts could be represented, if he were caught, as innocent working relationships (such as that with Maria) into which he had been duped.

He looked at the Cartier watch on his left wrist. Half past nine. The light, what there was of it that filtered through the thick drapes, was fading. The instructions Maria had brought him with the doorkey had forbidden him to turn on any lamps, so he waited in the encroaching darkness and worried. Were they going to ask something of him he could not fulfil except by sacrificing himself? Or was there a reward at hand, something for forty-two years of service, for keeping the doubt always at bay, for believing so long? No, for keeping faith so long? Belief admitted doubt; faith did not.

He could hardly remember, now, when he had not had that faith. Certainly he already possessed it by the time his Communist father had disappeared into one of the Third Reich's extermination camps, in 1938, on the day of Dierck's eighth birthday.

At that time his surname had not been Diercks, but Rau. He and his mother, Diercks realized later, had been lucky not to follow his father when the Nazi purges of the early war years began; she had been quite beautiful and even now he sometimes wondered what arrangements she had made with the local Nazi officials to keep them safe.

When the Russians came to Berlin in 1945, he and his mother, unlike everyone else he knew, had gone out to meet them. His mother had a piece of paper; he had never found out what was written on it. He stood awkwardly behind her in the cleanest of his civilian clothes (he had got rid of the Volkssturm militia uniform the SS had issued him before the last Nazi resistance collapsed) while she presented the folded paper to a filthy, bearded captain leaning on the front glacis plate of a Josef Stalin heavy tank. Half a dozen equally filthy infantrymen were standing beside the great mud-caked treads of the fighting vehicle, studying her. Young Rau had already heard the rape stories. He wondered what he would do if it happened.

It almost did. One of the infantrymen by the rear of the tank took a step forward, grinning, unslinging his submachine gun. The captain looked up from the paper and said something sharp in his own tongue. The infantryman said something back. The captain, in a professional swift movement, was suddenly pointing a pistol at the infantryman's testicles. The soldier grinned placatingly and stepped back, reslinging his gun.

After that it began to be easier. The captain summoned another officer, some kind of political cadre, who gave them a paper written in Russian. The paper kept the Russian soldiers away from their cellar until the city's streets quietened and they could pay some attention to their empty stomachs.

A little while later Berlin was divided by the victors into Soviet, British, French and American zones. The Germans, no matter where they lived, were hungry, cold, threadbare and exhausted. In the capital city of the Third Reich there was nothing left, hardly one stone standing on another.

In their cellar, now that it was safe for the boy to hear, Hanna Rau began telling her son about his father. He listened. He saw the Americans, pinkcheeked and (to his eyes) plump, riding the streets in their long cars and big trucks, occasionally throwing food and gum. Never throwing cigarettes, not after the first few months; by 1946 cigarettes were better than currency.

One evening that year Diercks' mother failed to return from a foraging expedition. After the first thirty-six hours had passed he went looking for her, without result. After three more days he managed to discover that she had been raped and strangled. What was left of her had been thrown into the Havel River. Two American soldiers had been arrested after trying to sell her wedding ring. The day after his mother was buried Diercks went to the East, carrying with him the paper the Russian commissar had given her when the city fell.

Four years later he returned to Western Berlin, this time to the British sector. His name was no longer Rau, but Diercks, and he had a brand new identity to go with the name. He was twenty-two, and utterly dedicated: the East German Socialist Unity Party had promised heaven on earth, and Franz Rau, in the name of his slaughtered parents, believed. He had kept that belief, in a manner that had impressed first his political instructors and later the equally dedicated men who maneuvered him up the political hierarchy of the Federal Republic, until he had reached the cabinet of West Germany.

And here I am, Diercks thought, just as frightened as I was in front of that Russian tank in the Kudamm, with the soldiers watching my mother. Everything asked of me I've done, without question, grinding my way closer to the center of power in this country, making Strauss and then Rudel trust me, even when the things I had to say to them made me want to vomit. But never able to rest. Marrying a flat-chested wife because she was an entry to political power, never liking her, never being able to take a mistress because it would be too dangerous. Years going by, getting tired, getting old. Perhaps that's why I'm so frightened. Berlin and Moscow must be frightened too, or they would never have risked me like this. Why are they so late? Something gone wrong? Has the BND found out? Precautions: perhaps my people are just taking extra precautions.

He looked longingly at the curtains, wanting to part them half a centimeter for a glimpse of the street, although he knew he would see nothing there, nothing he could be sure was surveillance. His field techniques were rusty and obsolete, had been for a quarter of a century.

Still, a glance, no more, a couple of seconds. He began to get to his feet.

There was a metallic *snick* from the flat's vestibule, the sound of a key being inserted into a lock. Diercks sat down.

Light from the hallway spilled into the vestibule, falling across the worn carpet. The doorway itself was not visible from the living room, but Diercks could see the shadow of a man's head against the vestibule wall. After perhaps ten seconds the bar of light narrowed to a thin line and disappeared. The doorlatch clicked home.

I don't think this is how the BND would do it, Diercks thought, waiting.

"Herr Rau?" said a voice from the vestibule. Diercks relaxed a little; only the SSD would know his original name. Unless the BND . . . He dismissed the thought. "Here," he said.

"Ah, good," the voice said, with what sounded to Diercks' ear like a hint of relief. They *are* worried, he thought. Risks.

The man entered the living room, moving carefully in the dimness. As far as Diercks could tell he was in his mid-thirties; he was dressed in dark blue slacks and a powder-blue shortsleeved shirt. In one hand he carried an airline satchel. The white Lufthansa lettering stood out in the gloom.

"I —" said Diercks.

"Hush," the man said. He put the satchel on the chair across from Diercks, opened it, and took out some piece of apparatus studded with switches and small flickering lights. After manipulating the switches he walked slowly around the room, waving the device in some intricate pattern. Apparently satisfied, he then moved the detector carefully over Diercks himself, from head to foot. The lights flickered. When he finished with Diercks, he went into the kitchen. Several minutes went by, punctuated finally by the sound of the bathroom door opening. Another silence, then the spatter of a urine stream. The toilet flushed.

"Fine," the man said, returning to the living room. "No ears or eyes." He put the detector in the flight bag, put the bag on the floor beside the chair, and sat down. "We can have some light now, if you like."

A pink vase with a lightbulb and a white shade stood on the end table next to Diercks. He reached out and switched it on. Pale yellow light flooded the room. Diercks, blinking, saw that he had been wrong about the man's age; by the lines in his face he was nearer fifty than thirty-five. It was the trimness of his body and the thickness of his hair that were deceptive. His cheekbones were rather high.

Russian, Diercks thought. This man is speaking from KGB Center, from Dzerzhinsky Square. They are very worried indeed.

"For convenience," the man said, "you might as well call me Anton. How much time do you have?"

There was no trace of accent in the man's German. How good they are at it, Diercks thought. "An hour, perhaps two. I left no specific destination or time."

"Good," Anton said. "It shouldn't take anything like that." He studied Diercks intently for some moments. The foreign minister looked away uncomfortably.

"Sorry," Anton said. "It's like looking at the hero of a myth, in the flesh. You are without doubt the best we have ever had in the Federal Republic. Perhaps the best anywhere."

So it was not to be punishment. "I am glad," Diercks said carefully, "that there is a good opinion of my work."

"There is . . ." began the Russian. Then, briskly, "We received your documents. They are not as specific as we would have liked, but even so they are very disturbing. Will Rudel put these things before the Bundestag?"

"Yes. He's doing it tomorrow. We — the CDU-CSU coalition, I mean — have the majority. The bills will pass, I think. Rudel has been preparing the political ground since he took the chancellorship, before that, even. The Social Democrats and the Free Democrats won't be able to stop him, unless our own party votes against the legislation. I don't think they will. He's hypnotized them." A thought struck Diercks. "Are you recording this?"

Anton gestured at the Lufthansa bag. "Of course. Can you get me the text of Rudel's speech?"

"Not before it's delivered. I think no one has a copy of the speech but Rudel himself."

"You mean it won't be checked by the public relations people?" Surprise.

"Not this time. He's never liked the kind of media glossiness everybody else's been using for the past ten years. He has tremendous confidence in his own resources."

"Yes," said the Russian. "Look, can you give me more details, more than what was in the documents?"

"A little," Diercks said. "We already knew he was going to withdraw from NATO, phased over five years. There were the increased appropriations for the Bundeswehr, up to three more armored divisions. He's going to deal with the unemployment problem by economic sanctions against the foreign workers, to get them to go home. He'll also reduce unemployment by expanding the size of the armed forces."

Anton whistled tunelessly between his teeth for a moment. "What about this business of reestablishing the German General Staff?"

"I don't know. I don't think it's in the speech. Probably he's just going to do it quietly, later this year I'd think."

"And acquiring nuclear weapons?"

"Nothing. But he's meeting the French president next week. You remember, there was talk of French-German collaboration on nuclear weapons a few years ago. Rudel might be trying that again. The French have the technology, but not enough money to produce bombs and new delivery systems. We have the money."

The Russian digested the idea in silence. Then he said, "What does your defense minister think of this?"

"Von Tebbe is in favor. He has grown disgusted at the behavior of the Americans, in respect to the IALT treaty."

"How does Rudel think he's going to *manage* all this?" the Russian said. "He can't possibly believe the West German people are a collection of unrepentant neofascist warmongers, slavering at the prospect of another Reich. Why is he doing this?"

Diercks gestured helplessly, palms upward. "I don't know.

I've spoken against it, I don't know how many times. But politically he has the *Fingerspitzengefühl*, the craftsman's touch in the fingertips. He believes he knows what the West Germans want, underneath the strikes and the demonstrations against the missiles and against the Americans, and the riots against the foreigners. He thinks they want Germany for Germans again, without the Americans, without the rest of Europe, without having always to dance to a foreign tune."

"*Deutschland erwache*," muttered the Russian.

" 'Germany awake?' Perhaps. But he would never be so rash as to use exactly the words Hitler did. There are too many bad memories."

"It must be tempting to him, from time to time," Anton observed thoughtfully.

"Perhaps. But Hitler was insane. Rudel has many of the qualities Hitler had, except one. He is not mad."

"His behavior suggests the opposite," Anton said.

"I'm afraid that you, that we all, have underestimated him," Diercks said. "He's the most successful leader Germany has known for forty years, and it's because he's succeeded in fragmenting his opposition. The leftist youth movements want the Americans out and their missiles out, want us out of NATO, and a lot of the Bundeswehr wouldn't object to that either. That's fine, they're getting that. On the other hand the unemployed and the poor in the Ruhr and the other industrial centers are afraid of the Russians and want the foreign workers out, but the leftists are more than willing to riot against sending the foreigners home. For every one of Rudel's policies some group doesn't like, he's got another one they do. They can't coalesce into an effective popular opposition. And on top of it all he's appealing to nationalism."

"Germany for the Germans," Anton said. "A new General Staff, and the German military independent of NATO. Germany as the chief economic, political and military power of Western Europe. To say nothing of this possible nuclear arrangement with the French. What kind of disaster is this?"

"I've exhausted every resource I can think of," Diercks said. "The only other thing I can think of doing is to resign, and say publicly why I'm doing so. But Rudel would ignore it. It would be futile."

"There is no chance of your resignation splitting the cabinet?"

"No. He would replace me with someone more malleable. The cabinet would remain intact. He has persuaded all of them."

"We couldn't have you resign, anyway," the Russian said. "You are much too valuable where you are."

"I have been here for a long time," Diercks said. "What are you going to do?"

"That's not your concern at the moment. Now I'd like more political background."

They talked for another hour about Rudel's cabinet, about men and women Diercks knew in the senior civil service, about the Bundeswehr, and about the BND and its political controls; the Russian was searching for weaknesses in the power structure Rudel and his predecessors had built, for some vulnerability in the Federal Republic and its government that would let the Russians bring the German chancellor down. Whether the man from Dzerzhinsky Square found anything to help him, Diercks could not tell; when he let himself out of the flat a quarter of an hour after the Russian had gone, he was left only with Anton's last congratulatory words, and a pervasive feeling of apprehension.

Munich
May 26

"SUPERB," Brand said, folding his napkin and arranging it precisely beside his plate, on which lay the remnants of an excellent lunch. "Truly superb."

"It always is, here," said Egon Spring. The two men were in the back room of Boettner's, at the most private of the eight tables. "The caviar here is the finest in the world," Spring added. "Did you know that Wasily Kandinsky and Thomas Mann used to eat in this room? It probably looked like this even then. Boettner's hasn't changed much in ninety years. Except the prices, of course."

"Unfortunately," Brand said. He had caught a glimpse of the bill before Spring sent it off with the waiter; the caviar alone, which they had eaten as a start to their meal, had been worth a month's rent on a medium-sized Berlin apartment.

"Well, it's on Bavaria Electronics," Spring said. "I believe we have excellent business prospects ahead of us."

"I think that's quite likely," Brand said. He had flown down to Munich from Berlin the previous morning, booked into the Vier Jahreszeiten hotel, and met Spring early in the afternoon. The meeting had evolved from their first encounter at Lotte von Veltheim's reception for Rudel; after a discussion the following day, Spring had invited Brand to the Munich offices of Bavaria Electronics, to go into further details. The upshot was that Bavaria Electronics would negotiate with Mitex for the production rights to three types of microchips, with a royalty agreement to be determined in consultation with Mitex's head office in Boston. Brand and Spring had finished the preliminary negotiations that morning, whereupon the German had decided to take Brand to lunch in the inner city. Since Brand's connecting flight to Berlin wasn't until four, he could not decently decline, although he would have preferred to. He had found Spring to be a competent, knowledgeable and aggressive businessman, but there was a self-satisfied arrogance about the man that put Brand off. At least three times over lunch, while they were talking of Rudel, Spring had said, "But then, you're German, you understand." It was an attitude Brand had encountered more than once in his years in Germany, and it always made him feel more American than usual. The peculiarity was that when he was in the company of most Americans — Anderson was an exception, but then he had lived in Europe for twenty years — Brand felt more German than American. In the company of other nationalities than these, he remained more or less Anglo-Saxon, but occasionally, in moments of depression, it seemed to Brand that he had misplaced his nationality somewhere, and that he would be hard put to identify himself exclusively as either American or German.

"A highly agreeable arrangement," Spring was saying, "provided your Boston office agrees. West Germany fell behind in microelectronics in the mid-eighties, as you doubtless know, and we are only just now beginning to pick up the slack. We much prefer to manufacture here, even from non-German designs, than to import the finished devices. It secures our sources of supply."

"It's always preferable not to depend too much on foreign support," Brand said, to see how Spring would answer. "It makes one extremely vulnerable."

"Exactly," Spring answered, either not noticing the bait or not interested in it. "Do you come to Munich often?"

"No," Brand said. "Two or three times. My wife and I came for the *Fasching* last year."

"Well," Spring said, "you should come more often. Munich has a great deal to offer." He stirred in his chair. "I always like a walk after lunch. Why don't we stroll over to the Marienplatz, it's not far. We can have a beer, then we can get your things from the hotel. I'll be happy to drive you to the airport."

"Thanks," Brand said, with carefully concealed resignation. "Let's walk, then."

They left Boettner's and walked along Theatinerstrasse to the town hall, then around the corner into the Marienplatz. It was very hot; Brand took his jacket off. So, after a few minutes of grim Prussian resistance, did Spring.

The German pointed. "Let's go over to the Glockenspiel and have a beer. They've excellent *Dunkles*."

The cafe's tables, like those of the other cafes around the Marienplatz, spilled out onto the square's flagstones. Brand and Spring were lucky enough to find a pair of vacant chairs at an already occupied table; the Marienplatz was crowded even in the early afternoon with a lot of tourists, even more Germans. After a longish wait they got two *Masskrug,* big liter tankards filled with icy light beer.

"I prefer the *Dunkles* myself," Spring said, after a long pull at the tankard, "but I find a heavy beer interferes with my digestion."

"This is very good," Brand said, eyeing the *Masskrug* dubiously. It seemed an excessive amount of liquid to put into an already full stomach. He leaned back to ease the waistband of his trousers and looked up at the front of the Neues Rathaus, the New Town Hall, with its gray-brown Neo-Gothic facade studded with spires, crenellations and cornices. Spring's gaze followed his. "The Old Hall is much more attractive," he said. "It was restored after the war, probably more . . ."

He went on. Brand was only half listening. There were three other men at the table, lower-middle-class laborers by the look of their hands and their clothes; not yet of the legion of the unemployable, but slowly subsiding into that underclass from the ranks of the unemployed, spending their haphazard days in the squares of the city, doing nothing. They were talking, with the emphatic gestures of semi-drunkenness, about Rudel's latest Bundestag speech.

"Never should have let them in in the first place," one was saying. He was heavyset, about sixty, with broad calloused hands and rough nails. "And they should have been sent back when they got off the trains, or whatever they got off of. Before they started taking the jobs away from *us*. That bunch in Bonn, what a lot of old women, not enough brains to pour pee out of a boot. Until we got Rudel. By God, he'll make them sit up and take notice. No more of that shit about social responsibility, *we* didn't ask the Turks and half the rest of the farmers in Europe to come here. Maybe the companies did, always looking for ways to keep the wage down; fuck them, why should *we* have to put a roof over their heads and food in their brats? They can't even speak German, send them all back where they came from." He buried his nose in his *Masskrug*.

"And the Americans with them," said the man on his left. He was slightly younger, thinner, and drunker than the man with the calloused hands. "Every time you turn around, Turks, Greeks, Yugoslavs, Ami soldiers. My niece started going out with one, an American soldier, I mean. Fine, fine, everybody said, Ilse's got herself a new boyfriend, maybe she'll get to America, so what? Then she brings him home, the dumb bitch. He's black as a miner's fingernails. We put a stop to that in a hurry, I'll tell you."

Spring had stopped talking. Brand met his eyes for a moment. The expression was pained, saying: These aren't my sort of people, please understand.

"Well, anyway," said the third man, who was about thirty, wearing cheap black-framed spectacles over a pink surgical eyepatch, "Rudel's going to send the blacks home. The lot of them. No more NATO, no more Yankees, he'll turn the country around. Get things organized properly, like they should be. Fix those students up at the *Gesamthoshule* in Kassel. Did you hear they rioted yesterday? Calling Rudel a Nazi, because he wanted to chuck out the foreigners?"

"And give us a bigger army," added the second man.

"Fucking students," said the heavyset one. "Half the little assholes are fags and the other half are communists. They'd let the Russians in here in a minute if it were up to them. The country's been screwing up ever since the sixties. Look at those pricks in the Bader-Meinhof gang; Bonn put them away in nice comfortable prisons when the fuckers should have been put up against a wall and shot. There's no discipline any more."

Ah, Christ, Brand thought. The brownshirts are back. Here's 1930 come round again, then it was the Jews, now it's the Turks and Americans.

"Can you—" Brand began, and stopped, looking out into the square past the Mariensaule Column towards the Old Town Hall. Down the Tal some kind of commotion had broken out; he could see a crowd with a nimbus of white placards floating above it. The placards were rapidly approaching the Marienplatz.

The three laborers at the table caught sight of the placards. "It's those fucking blackasses," said the third one in a rush. "They're waving their fucking signs around again."

The crowd, in a rough processional, spilled out into the Marienplatz. The third man was right: they weren't Germans for the most part, but Turks from the city's motor vehicle and machinery industries and their poorer relatives, the dark-skinned men and women from the municipal services. Street cleaners, sewer maintenance crews, collectors of garbage, the developing underclasses of the Federal Republic, the other side of the glitter of Munich's boutiques, the malnutrition and the despair. Among the dark faces rode a few paler ones, leftist German youth taking up the cause of the dispossessed. Brand could make out one of the placards now. It read:

RUDEL = HIMMLER

On another square of white cardboard to its left were scrawled the words, in red marking pen and with the usual lack of originality, DOWN WITH THE BONN FASCISTS!!!!

They were out in the square now, placards bobbing, the column of marchers spreading into a crowd. Near the brass Fischbrunner Fountain a pair of Turkish youths piled wooden boxes one atop the other, and a third man climbed onto them. He had a battery-powered megaphone slung from one shoulder.

"Get off your fucking box and go home!" the heavyset man shouted at him. "Go back to your Turkish pigsty."

The man on the boxes either couldn't hear him, or paid no

attention. He cleared his voice while raising the megaphone; the cough rattled around the square.

"We—" he began.

A raucous singing from up Dienerstrasse drowned out the rest of his words. A mob of German youths, many with heads shaven, stormed out of the sidestreet into the Marienplatz. The singing fragmented into a cacaphony of shouts, but not before Brand recognized the words: the old *Horst Wessel Lied*, the anthem of Hitler's storm troopers. Above the lead rank of the Germans waved a huge red gonfalon bearing the image of a black eagle.

"God in heaven," Spring said, "I thought the police had broken them up."

Brand could barely hear him over the shouts and screams as the brownshirts waded into the Turkish demonstrators. "What?"

"The Eagle Front. A soccer sports club. They were in Frankfurt, now they're here."

The sports clubs had existed in West Germany for years, but in the mid-eighties they had taken on a virulent nationalist cast, beating up referees and shouting the slogans of the Third Reich from stadium bleachers, fighting in the streets with the Turks, serving in some cases as guards for meetings of the radical right National Democratic Party. The clubs were formed mostly from the unemployed youth of the big cities, and in their clubrooms hung portraits of Hitler garlanded with team colors. Often they were fronts for right-wing organizations, or had been taken over by the right to provide a supply of street fighters and counter-demonstrators for the interminable wars with the student left. As a general pastime the clubs made life miserable for West Germany's four million aliens: harassment, beatings, the occasional rape. Soccer was perhaps the least immediate of the clubs' interests.

They're not playing soccer now, Brand thought. A pitched battle had erupted around the fountain. Shouts of *"Sieg Heil"* and "Kill the Turks" mixed with curses and slogans in Turkish. The heavyset man drank off the rest of his beer, turned the *Masskrug* upside down to be sure the drink was gone, got up, and lurched off towards the riot. His two companions followed.

"Let's get out of here," Spring said urgently.

Brand half rose. Around them tourists and Munichers were dispersing rapidly, like a school of frightened fish, hurrying away from the square into the sidestreets and buildings that bordered the Marienplatz. Brand looked at the mob again. Two of the Eagle Front brownshirts had knocked a Turkish youth to the flagstones and were beating him with heavy wooden cudgels. Blood streamed from the Turk's forehead. Suddenly, a slight young woman, blond, German, emerged from the tangle of fighting bodies and tried to drag one of the thugs away. He turned and struck her across the breast with his club. She staggered back, then fell to her knees. The other Eagle Front man stopped beating the Turk and punched her on the side of her head. The first one kicked her in the stomach. She doubled over and toppled onto her face. The Turk tried to get up but couldn't.

"Ah, shit," Brand said. He vaulted over a chair and ran out into the Marienplatz. Behind him Spring shouted, "Idiot! Come back! The police will be here—"

Brand was five meters away from the pair of Eagle Front men when they seemed to decide that the girl had other uses than a target for their fists. One bent over her, tugging at the waistband of her jeans. Brand covered the distance; the tip of his right shoe struck the bending man squarely in the testicles, from behind, and hard. The brownshirt gave a strangled yelp and fell in a heap over the girl, clutching his groin.

Brand was out of practice; the kick had left him off balance. The other brownshirt grabbed him by the left arm, twisting viciously. Brand stiffened the fingers of his right hand and swivelled, driving them like a wedge into the other's midriff, reaching for the solar plexus. He missed. The brownshirt caught Brand's hand and tried to put a knee into his crotch, but couldn't get past Brand's leg. Brand tried to break the hold — uselessly, the man was thin as a steel rail and as strong — and then lowered his head and drove the top of his skull into the man's face. Brand heard a satisfying crunch, punctuated by a scream. His arms were suddenly free. Mildly stunned by the blow he had inflicted, he stepped away, tripped over the Turk's body, and fell flat on his back.

The sun was very bright overhead. He couldn't find his breath. In his peripheral vision he could see the brownshirt whose face he had smashed, kneeling, hands over nose, blood runnelling over his fingers.

Have to breathe, have to get up, Brand thought. The Turk squirmed under his calves.

The sun was obscured suddenly. The other brownshirt, the one he had kicked in the testicles, was standing over him, still bent with pain, mouth open, yelling something incoherent. I should have kicked him harder, Brand thought. Dammit, why didn't I keep in shape? Somewhere in the distance he could hear sirens.

The brownshirt had something bright in his hand. A knife. Leaning close. Words, half-heard, " — cut your — " a scream from the direction of the Mariensaule — "off — "

He wouldn't really, Brand thought, without words. But.

A few reflexes came back. He kicked at the wrist of the knife hand, a little slow, feeling the blade's edge slide into his flesh just above the ankle, not painful, only a sensation of heat. The brownshirt, hand numbed, dropped the knife. Brand swivelled a little on his back and drove his heel into the man's groin again, as hard as he could. The brownshirt collapsed, vomiting. Brand got to his knees, looking around. Green and white police vehicles were wailing into the entrances to the square, police in riot gear leaping out of them as they halted. The Turk was sitting up, bloody but apparently alert. The girl was another matter. She lay motionless, face down on the flagstones, head on arms, blood seeping from under her left elbow.

Oh, God, Brand thought, if she's dead I'll be mixed up in it. Anderson will have a fit.

"Are you alright?" he asked the Turk. He glanced warily at the two brownshirts. One lay on his back, hands over nose, the other on his side clutching at his genitals.

"Who are you?" the Turk asked, in dreadfully accented German, made worse by his smashed mouth. He looked to be about eighteen. "Where's Elise?"

"They hit her," Brand explained, realizing that the man had seen very little. "I came to stop them." The police, he realized, with a mixture of relief and apprehension, were only a few meters away. The riot was breaking up at the edges, dissipating.

The Turk eyed Brand's clothes doubtfully. "You're police."

"No. American. He leaned over the girl. "Look, we have to see if she's—"

"*Up! Up!* Get your hands off her! Get up, you and you. All of you! *Schnell, Schnell!*"

Brand felt a violent prod in the small of the back, as though from a gun butt. A pair of helmeted police stood over him, visors like the faces of huge mutated insects. He stood up, heavily. The *Polizei* behind left of prodding him with the riot stick. The two brownshirts were hauled roughly to their feet.

"What happened here?" said the *Polizei* behind Brand.

"These two were hitting her," Brand said, gesturing at the girl's still form. "I tried to stop them. She needs an ambulance."

"Alright," the *Polizei* said, "all of you. Into the trucks. Now. *Move!*"

"Wait a minute," Brand said, "I was helping—"

"No, he wasn't," said the man Brand had kicked in the testicles. "This Turk was trying to hit her. We came to stop them, then this asshole attacked us, we were trying to help—"

"Stuff your prick in it," said the *Polizei*. A green and white van, followed by an ambulance, was pulling to a halt a dozen meters away. "Get in the truck, *right now,*" the *Polizei* said. "All of you. *Schnell!* Move!"

"*Excuse me,*" said a voice from behind Brand. The *Polizei* turned, ready.

"Excuse me," Spring said again, audible now that the racket in the square was dying. He cupped something small and white in his hand, a card, some kind of paper. "Can you come with me for a moment?"

The man, an officer by the way he gave orders, looked briefly at whatever Spring held in his hand, and then stalked away with him. They stopped a dozen meters away and exchanged words. Then the officer walked back to the group of prisoners around the prone body of the girl and said to Brand, "Alright. You can go. Our apologies."

Brand hesitated. Paramedics were dragging a stretcher out of the ambulance; another was already hovering over the girl's head. Spring called, "Paul. Come now, please."

"She was trying to save the Turk from those two," Brand said to the officer, not knowing what good it would do. "My name is Brand, I'm an American. If you need a statement you can contact me through Herr Spring."

"Just get lost," said the officer. "We don't want to know who you are. Just bugger off."

Brand shrugged, nodded to the Turk, and walked away as the paramedics began sliding the girl onto the low aluminum stretcher.

West Berlin
May 29

MITEX HELD A LEASE on a medium-sized house in southwest Berlin, not far from Wannsee and the long run of the Wall. Brand and his family had lived there ever since arriving in the city; by North American standards the house was a little cramped, but given the geographic limits imposed on the free city it was more spacious than most. It did have a walled back garden with plenty of shrubs and an oak tree, which provided the feeling of privacy, if not the substance. Along the rear of the house lay a small terrace paved with brown brick, on which the Brands ate meals in hot weather. The oak tree supported a swing and there was a sandbox near the garden's rear wall, next to a rosebush.

It was late afternoon. Brand and Kevin Drury, Jennifer's brother, were sitting on the terrace, drinking beer. Alison and David puttered in the sandbox, engaged in some engineering project that involved large quantities of twigs and water. Jennifer had gone shopping.

Kevin Drury was a few years younger than his sister, blonder and less outgoing. With his fine features he looked rather too young to hold the rank of major in the British Berlin Infantry Brigade; the pale mustache he sported made him appear only a little older. At the moment his face bore a morose expression; he was still recovering from his fiancee's decision to end their engagement. Privately Brand was not sure this was a bad thing.

He had met Christina Mellors and had judged her an extremely attractive and extremely critical young woman. Outside his profession of arms, Kevin Drury was an easygoing soul, and Brand thought that Christina, with her determined views on what was and was not acceptable social behavior, would have given him a difficult life.

"How's the headache, by the way?" Kevin said, rousing himself with an effort. He had consumed half a dozen Lowenbrau, on what Brand suspected was an empty stomach.

"Haven't had it since yesterday," Brand said. He had received a mild concussion when the brownshirt knocked him down in the Marienplatz in Munich, and what with Spring's insistence that he see a doctor he had missed his plane and arrived back in Berlin a day late. Jennifer had been furious, not because he was late but because he had put himself at such risk. Brand didn't think the risk had been so great, the police were on their way, after all. It could have been worse . . . that knife. He had not been in such immediate physical danger since . . . when had it been? He felt mild surprise that the date did not spring to mind. He studied the children as they turned their sand into castles.

January twelfth, he thought, that was the day. Just after the new year. On that sweep up into the north. El Salvador, benighted country. Some village or other, so small it didn't even have a name.

At the time of the incident in the village Brand was a colonel and had been in the country for a little over two years, one of a collection of advisors Washington had sent to help the government against the guerillas. He had become an advisor by a somewhat unlikely route; for his first nine years in the military he had specialized, by virtue of his background in software engineering, in developing computer programs for processing military intelligence. Out of this had grown an interest in counterinsurgency techniques, and in 1982 Brand had managed to obtain a transfer to a select task force studying the subject. The task force was using the El Salvador conflict as a test vehicle; the year after his transfer Brand was posted to the country to observe the government's counterinsurgency measures at close hand, and develop more successful methods of dealing with the rebels.

The fieldwork changed him. By the end of the first year in the country he was experiencing a severe emotional reaction to the necessities of the counterinsurgency program, with its random killing, its charred villages with streets dotted with dead dogs, the alleys sheltering children bulge-bellied with *kwashiorkor*, the protein-deficiency disease he had always thought was the special affliction of benighted African nations. The peasants had been brutalized, the Salvadorean army had been brutalized, and the impossibility of either side offering accommodations to the other had left even the new moderate government with no more policy than the massacre of its enemies, real or imagined. The reconciliation plans of the Salvadorean government had failed to obtain the support of the military, and the execution squads of both persuasions were active again. Nothing in the country, except weapons, seemed to work properly.

None of the elaborate computer programs Brand had developed, with their precisely quantified analyses of risks and neat stacks of printouts, had prepared him for El Salvador. Somewhat to his own surprise, however — and certainly to the astonishment of the Special Forces officers with whom he was working — he exhibited a natural flair for small unit tactics and an eye for deception that earned him a substantial amount of respect from the regular combat officers with whom he worked. What he found difficult to bear was the killing, endemic and random: peasants in the fields shot down across their hoes; women head down in wells where the bullets had thrown them; children's legs amputated with machetes; scalpings, crucifixions, castrations, beheadings. There was no purpose he could see to it; he began to wake up in the middle of the hot nights, tangled in his bedding, stinking with sweat.

In January 1985 he was ordered to a nameless village in the north. The insurgents were strong in the region; the Salvadorean army was beginning a series of operations to "collapse the support infrastructure," which amounted to blowing up a dozen or so villages and burning off the fields that fed the villagers.

The Salvadorean army unit to which Brand had been assigned reached the village on the second day of the offensive. The soldiers, half-trained, were angry and frightened. They had been ambushed the first day out and had lost two dead and three wounded without so much as a glimpse of their attackers. Brand had never worked with the captain commanding the unit, but in the past thirty-six hours he had found the man to be short-tempered, unnecessarily hard on his men, and abysmally incompetent at planning any but the simplest tactics.

They had entered the village — a miserable affair of cinder-block huts with roofs of rotting tarpaper-encrusted boards or rust-eaten corrugated iron sheeting — and had begun to search for weapons or food caches when they came under fire. The guerillas were in the village itself; half a dozen government troops were shot down before the remainder even began to think of reacting. After perhaps two minutes the rip of automatic-weapons fire slackened. Brand, not allowed to participate in combat because of his advisor status, went to ground by a stone wall, his M16 clamped firmly under one arm. Next to him the Salvadorean captain lay in the dust and yelled indecipherable orders. The firing slackened further and then stopped. By the time the government troops raised their heads from whatever shelter they had been able to find, the insurgents had slipped out of the village and were disappearing into the treeline to the northwest.

Brand's captain screamed something incomprehensible, jumped to his feet, and ran to a pair of soldiers huddling against a wall on the far side of the street. He started kicking at their legs. The two men got up; others appeared out of doorways. Brand slung his M16 and went over to the captain, who was waving an arm ineffectually in the direction of the treeline where the guerillas had disappeared. "Captain," Brand said, "you should call in—"

The captain rounded on him, flat black killer's eyes, mouth pinched to a slit. "Shut up! Shut up! You stay out of this, you hear, you fucking Yankee. You keep out of this or I'll cut your balls off and feed them to you alive. You, you fuck off, by God I'll kill you—"

Brand retreated to the stone wall. Adrenalin vibrated in his muscles. He unslung the M16 and took off the safety. Surreptitiously, he checked the magazine. It was full and clean.

The government troops were combing the villagers out of

their huts; Indians, most of them. The soldiers herded them towards the center of the village, where the road widened into a narrow version of a town square. There were only about sixty of the villagers left, women and children and old people, no men of fighting age. It was definitely an insurgent village; the rest of the inhabitants had escaped into the forest before the soldiers arrived. Why these few had remained was comprehensible only to them.

Brand stood up suddenly from his seat on the stone wall. Two soldiers were mounting a light machine gun on a bipod near the edge of the square. One of them started feeding in an ammunition belt.

"Hey!" Brand yelled at the captain. "What're you doing?"

The captain swore at him. Brand had a good command of Spanish, but this particular stream of invective escaped him entirely. He stalked over to the captain. In his combat boots Brand overtopped the other officer by a good four inches. "You'd better stop this," Brand said. He had the M16 loosely cradled, but ready. "You remember what happened to the commander at San Joaquin? He—"

The captain yanked his pistol out of its holster and rammed the muzzle into Brand's solar plexus. By some act of mercy it didn't go off. Brand grunted, his grip on the M16 gone with his breath. The captain slashed the pistol barrel across Brand's forehead, splitting the skin open, stunning him. He dropped to his knees, the muzzle of the M16 digging into the road dust. Blood ran into his eyes. The captain yelled and the machine gun on the edge of the square began to fire. The villagers collapsed, the taller ones like telescopes folding, the children resembling kicked dolls. The captain grabbed Brand's rifle, yanked out the ammunition clip, and threw it into an alley. Then he hit Brand over the head, this time with the pistol butt, and it all went away.

Afterwards the captain had Brand's head bandaged, and attempted explanations. Brand, partly because of the concussion that made the events in the village seem no more than half-real, ignored him. That evening they went back south; the operation was being called off. Back in the capital, Brand reported the slaughter, and waited. Nothing happened. The major was not arrested, only transferred to another unit. Brand took his evidence higher, to the American officer in charge of tactical liaison with the Salvadorean forces. It was explained to him that nothing was going to happen to the captain; he was related to the general commanding the Central Region.

Brand's father knew a senator in Washington. Brand wrote a long letter, including all the documents he could find on the operation, to his father. His father gave the letter and the documents to the senator, who raised the issue in the House. The question received no more than three minutes' governmental attention, but a particularly bored reporter on duty that day picked it up and put it on the wire. The story of the massacre made several national newspapers, although it was normally relegated to the fourth or fifth page, in company with columns dealing with psychokinesis frauds or the impregnation difficulties of female pandas.

Brand was recalled, with no explanation. He requested reassignment to his old intelligence position, preferably to a post dealing with East Bloc nations. He was indeed assigned to a study group, in no less a place than the Pentagon. The group was to develop "methods of improved inventory control, preferably employing current computer technology, to rationalize materials procurement methods and systems to effect a fifteen percent saving in resource allocations in the fiscal period 1985-1990."

And he was passed over for promotion. Colonel Brand was to remain a colonel, and like it, until he and his group got materials procurement methods under firm control. This was as likely as total bilateral disarmament. Brand resigned his commission, spent several exhausting months catching up on technological developments in the microelectronics industry, and then took the position his father had offered him as Mitex's European representative in West Berlin.

About two months before he left, a quiet gentleman in a gray suit called at his office, expressed an interest in Mitex's wares, and asked Brand to lunch. Brand accepted. They were joined by another equally subdued gentleman, this one in brown. Colonel Brand had had an unfortunate dislocation in his career, the man in the gray suit had said, but it would be a shame to waste his . . . unique abilities. High-quality intelligence people, especially ones with his technological background, did not grow (so the man said) on trees. Brand agreed with him. They did not grow on trees.

Colonel Brand, the man in brown pointed out, was going to be in a particularly sensitive business, militarily speaking, in a particularly sensitive place, politically speaking. He would merely have to keep his eyes and ears open, talk from time to time with a few carefully selected people.

Would Colonel Brand be interested in putting his talents to full use? the man in gray wanted to know, over coffee and Henessey cognac. They knew his tastes perfectly; it occurred to Brand to wonder how they had found out what he intended to do with the rest of his life. It was, the man in gray admitted, rather a lot to ask, especially when the colonel's personal affairs were in such . . . call it a flux. If Colonel Brand were not interested, then no more would be said. On the other hand, if he were . . .

Brand said he'd think about it. They gave him a telephone number, and a name. He thought about it for three days. Fascinating though Mitex's business was, much as the technology intrigued him, it was still business. Intelligence work, someone had once said to Brand, is a form of addiction for certain people. Especially the ones who are good at it. It's hard to put down, like a crossword puzzle, like a chess problem that wakes you up in the middle of the night and won't go away until you have hit upon an answer.

Brand confessed the addiction to himself, and called the number. He felt mildly guilty at telling Jennifer nothing of the approach, but reasoned (or rationalized, as he told himself in his darker moments) that the work the CIA wanted him to do was little different from that he had done in military intelligence, and he hadn't been able to discuss that with her, either. It was also a great deal less dangerous than El Salvador.

Or rather it had been until Harpe came along. Brand was still uncertain in himself as to why he had been willing to act as the East German's principal contact, just as he had never been certain why he had taken, no, sought out, the posting to El Salvador. Lately, looking back, he had come to the discomforting conclusion that he had done both things because despite himself he enjoyed danger, at least in reasonable doses. In Latin America, at least until the pointlessness of the civil war and the numbed suffering of the people began to wear away at him, he had felt intensely alive. Meetings with Harpe made him feel somewhat the same way.

He pushed El Salvador, Langley, and Harpe out of his mind and said, "How're things in your line of work?"

"Well as can be expected," Drury said. "I expect some of us will be going home soon."

Brand registered surprise. "London's going to pull out the British garrison?"

"Mn, no, not us. At least I don't think so. Even with Bonn packing in NATO there'll have to be some kind of troop presence here. The agreements made after the war are still in effect, for one thing. London'll withdraw some of the units on the lower Rhine, I should think. But the Russians'll never let West German soldiers garrison Berlin. I expect they're brassed off enough with Rudel already, they'd never allow *that*."

"No. Not likely," Brand said. "Maybe life will be a little less tense here, finally," he went on after a moment's thought. "Washington and Moscow seemed determined to kiss and make up."

"I bloody well hope so," Drury said. "The Western garrisons here — French, British, Americans all in one neat little bag — are nothing but a political counter. Maybe we'd be of some military use if the Russians went across the frontier; they'd have to deploy either to take the city or at least to prevent us from interfering with their supply lines. But we'd last four days, a week at the outside. Talk about sacrificial lambs."

Brand heard movement inside the house: Jennifer back from her shopping expedition. "Stay to supper?" he asked Drury.

"Like to," Kevin said. "But I've a raft of paperwork to catch up on."

He left, somewhat unsteadily, half an hour later after consuming another Lowenbrau. Brand felt sorry for him.

* * *

Later that evening, after the children had gone to bed, Jennifer said, "What a muddle. Kevin jilted, you nearly getting yourself killed in a riot, and the Germans rattling their swords again." She was setting the alarm.

"Put it to seven, would you?" Brand said. "I've got some work I want to catch up on before the gruesome twosome wake up. Rudel hasn't been rattling any swords. What makes you say that?"

"You'll be lucky if they sleep past seven," she observed, setting the clock on the bedside table. "I'm sorry, but I *still* don't trust the Germans. Perhaps it's because I'm English. But just look at what he's doing. It could be 1933 all over again."

"Not exactly," Brand said, irritated for no obvious reason. "They're hardly in a position to invade anybody this time around. They just want their sovereignty back."

"That's what they said last time. Look what happened."

"But," said Brand, "that can't happen again."

"Perhaps not. What about something else?"

"Like what?"

"Alright, not like 1933. Try 1914 on for size. Europe at peace, nobody really angry at anybody else in any immediate way, but everybody armed to the teeth, the mobilization and invasion plans all set, and then something goes wrong at Sarajevo in June. Then a month where everybody passes notes around, meanwhile the soldiers are getting all their plans nicely dusted off, then Austria mobilizes, so Russia mobilizes, so Germany mobilizes, so France mobilizes, and *nobody dares stop* because if they do the other side might have them at a disadvantage. An absolutely goddamned pointless war, four years of it. It was there, waiting to happen, and nobody saw it until it was too late."

Brand silently wished his wife's degree in history would go away. "Okay. There are parallels. But we're a long way from that yet."

She was sliding under the covers. "I hope so. Sometimes . . ."

He waited.

"Sometimes lately," she said, "I get the feeling that it's already started."

Dostoyevskovo
June 11

NIKOLAYEV was trying to bring some fresh air, figuratively and literally, to the Politburo meetings. Accordingly, he had called the members to attend at his new dacha out beyond Pushkino, to the north of the older village. Residence in Pushkino was the recognized reward of approved writers and artists; it pleased Nikolayev to live near the place, but beyond, in the new luxury retreat named after Dostoevsky. The author's name had been bestowed on the development in an attempt to associate its residents with the inhabitants of Pushkino, but this had not noticeably succeeded. The writers and artists in their enclaves tended to keep to themselves, despite the tentative blandishments of the bureaucrats and officials up the road.

Nikolayev's dacha was new, smelling still of fresh mortar and sawn pine. It was an L-shaped building set among birch and spruce trees, each of which had been carefully uprooted before the foundations were laid, and then equally carefully replaced, except where the fabric of the house intervened. Unfortunately, several of the birches had been replanted too close to the foundation line and in any wind scraped annoyingly on the dacha's pine siding. Somewhat worse, three of the firs had been dug up too near the roots and were expiring in a shower of brown needles near the curved drive leading to the dacha's front door. They should have been replaced before the weather turned hot, but in the rush to complete the general secretary's new residence they had been forgotten. As it was, the workmen had only just laid the last coat of varnish on the shutters before the day of the Politburo gathering.

The heat was fierce. They endured the first half of the meeting in the dacha's enormous dining room, until Nikolayev called a halt and led them out onto the back lawn where they arranged themselves around three wooden tables on the terrace which, fortunately, were shaded by the bulk of the house. There were just enough chairs. Servants brought iced vodka and wine, and discreetly withdrew. Nikolayev said, after a tiny sip at his glass:

"The business of Rudel. We're agreed he's a danger. What are we going to do about him?" He waited. There would have to be a consensus in a matter like this.

Silence around the table. They are waiting for me, Nikolayev thought. To lead them or to hang myself. Which is it going to be?

"Boris," he said to the foreign minister, "you assured us that Rudel's notions wouldn't get past the German Parliament. They have. Why this miscalculation?"

Boris Kamenev pulled at his nose, a mannerism Nikolayev had found irritating even twenty years previously, when both men had served on the Leningrad Party Committee. Boris had been pulling at his nose, for one reason or another, ever since. The habit had become, in certain circles, as much of a joke as Brezhnev's eyebrows had been, or Chernenko's jowls. There hadn't been any jokes about Andropov, who had served as general secretary between the other two; first, he had been in office only eighteen months; second, his power base was the KGB. There had been an unobtrusive sigh of relief when Andropov died and gave way to that dependable Party hack, Chernenko.

But then they got me, Nikolayev thought, and some of them are wondering whether they made the right decision. Sometimes so do I. There is so much to be done.

"Minister Kamenev?" he said sharply. Kamenev was gazing unhappily into the pine wood that bounded the dacha's lawn to the east.

"Yes," Kamenev said. "I miscalculated." He looked accusingly at KGB Chairman Minkov. "Partly because of the information the KGB supplied. Your contact in Bonn was very confident that Rudel's legislation would be defeated."

Minkov bristled. "May I remind you that he revised his estimates before the legislation was debated?"

"*One day* before," Kamenev snapped. "That can hardly be judged enough time to take diplomatic countermeasures, can it? What were *your* people doing all this time? Rudel paid little more than polite attention to the note we sent him in May, and none to the signals we sent out through those troop exercises. Surely the KGB could have done *something* to cool the Bundestag's ardor for Rudel?"

"We are not supermen," Minkov said. "There are limits to what even the KGB can achieve on such short notice." Minkov, in fact, had reason to be concerned; he had lost some of the confidence the Politburo reposed in him, and his political footing had become slightly unstable. He would have to do something quickly to bolster his authority.

"What are the prospects for military action?" asked Secretary Ivanov.

A small ripple of apprehension went around the three tables. "Begging Secretary Ivanov's pardon," said the chairman of the Council of Ministers, "we can hardly attack the West Germans because they are withdrawing from NATO and talking about expanding the Bundeswehr. The risks of general war are much too great. Even if we were fortunate enough to avoid that, the diplomatic costs would be appalling."

"Suppose it *were* necessary, though," insisted Ivanov. "Marshal Fedashkin, how well prepared are we? We've gone over this before, but I would like to do so again."

The defense minister cleared his throat and said, "The most attractive option is a surprise attack mounted during full-scale Warsaw Pact exercises. This reduces the strength of our forces on the startline, but on balance that is preferable to a buildup of troops and equipment which would inevitably be detected by NATO. The operation aims to seize an objective line well into West Germany within seventy-two hours of the beginning of hostilities. We estimate that this is the maximum safe period before the Americans and NATO can decide whether to use battle-field nuclear weapons. Forty-eight hours would actually be preferable. On the objective line, we halt and negotiate from a position of strength."

"That presupposes nothing going wrong with the military phase," Kamenev pointed out. "I believe that to be a dangerous assumption."

"*Can* the Foreign Ministry handle its responsibilities in the operation?" asked Ivanov acidly.

Kamenev shrugged. "We present the attack to the world as a limited police action to curb resurgent German militarism which is endangering the peace of Europe. We promise to withdraw to our own borders as soon as a West German government accep-table to both East and West, and of course to the West German proletariat, is installed." He repeated the shrug. "All of us know this; why go over the same ground again?"

"Because," Ivanov said in a low voice, looking at the faces around the three tables, "I want each one of us to look this possi-bility in the face and accept that we may have to deal with the Germans once and for all. Before they become too strong. The West German army is our most powerful conventional opponent in Europe, and we must not forget that they are good soldiers. They are probably better than any others on the continent, and I don't exclude our own troops from that judgment. Marshal Fedashkin?"

The defense minister nodded gloomily. "I have to agree. An expanded Bundeswehr would reduce our margin of superiority in conventional warfare to an uncomfortable degree. Even with the Americans gone, even employing the surprise option. We've gamed it out. Almost always we have to use theater nuclear weapons to gain our objective line within seventy-two hours." He paused. "I should add that the August exercises are not far off. If we elect not to act then, we will have to wait at least another nine months, until the May maneuvers at the earliest."

"The Union won't be truly secure until we have reached the English Channel," said Yakov Lensky, secretary for industry and heavy armaments. "Furthermore, we could make good use of the technology and physical plant and natural resources of Western

Europe. Not to mention its population. We are suffering from a labor shortage, and it is not going to get better in the foreseeable future."

Nikolayev listened, letting them go. Despite his views on detente with the Americans, what Ivanov and his faction proposed was indeed tempting, from the points of view both of national security and of economic need. The natural border of the Asian heartland was not the frontier line that ran through the center of Europe, but that great defensive moat of the English Channel and the North Atlantic. Almost unbidden, the thought rose in his mind: *Could we do it?*

And, he had to admit, he was frightened of the Germans. Suppose Bonn managed to obtain nuclear weapons; suppose the Americans' agreement to the disengagement in Europe was only the surface of a much deeper plan, in fact a deception? From West German bases, nuclear-tipped missiles could reach into the Soviet heartland and defense network in minutes, much too quickly for counterstrikes to be launched. The Soviet Union could be decapitated and disarmed in the space of a quarter of an hour, without warning. IALT I could be the foundation of a long-range Amerian plan to destroy the Soviet Union, using the Germans as a proxy; German hatred and fear of Russia might be used to bring the plan to fruition, not next year, perhaps not this decade, but someday.

He had been given warnings like that, when the IALT negotiations began. He had dismissed the warnings as alarmism. Now, with the behavior of Rudel, he was not so sure. Perhaps the sudden American tractableness was only intended to reduce the vigilance of the Soviet Union's leaders.

Could they be so devious? he wondered. Hood, what is he trying to do? I have to remember that Western capitalism is our sworn enemy, if only because our ideology assumes its destruction. In the long run it cannot win, but its leaders will do anything to delay the victory of socialism. Even, perhaps, this.

"What would the Americans do?" he asked suddenly, breaking in on Lensky, who had been expounding on the need for new sources of skilled labor. "They are hardly likely to sit with hands folded like a *babushka* in front of an ikon. Chairman Minkov, what has the KGB to say about the Americans?"

Minkov stirred uneasily in his chair. "There is some reason to believe," he said, "that Hood's administration is less, well, passionate than the last one. We have done psychological studies of the president and his advisors. They seem less willing than Reagan was to cut America's throat for a principle. As long as their heartland was not threatened directly."

"Is that to say," Nikolayev asked, "that they wouldn't react with nuclear weapons if we overran West Germany in the three days we have allowed ourselves?"

Minkov looked troubled. "I can't say that for a surety. But they are more likely to negotiate than the Reagan administration was. The IALT treaty is a case in point. They gave away more than they received."

"But what *would* they do?" Nikolayev insisted.

"If we knew that, we'd have a much stronger hand," said Kamenev. "We have never been able to determine whether they would risk their national existence over a conflict on the periphery of their empire. On balance, I think that good sense would prevail. But the Americans are not always rational."

"If," Nikolayev said, "we decided to move in August—" He stopped, wondering, What has led me to say this? Before Rudel, I would never have countenanced such a proposal. Perhaps I am more frightened than I thought. The Germans, the militarists, and the Americans, the capitalists. A terrifying alliance, if it is an alliance. Perhaps Stalin had reason for his paranoia, after all.

"August is ideal," Ivanov said. "Rudel is making his own bed, let him lie in it. The Americans can't be any too pleased with his direction, either. Look. Washington's missiles will be gone in August. Hood is tractable, and the Americans show signs of being tired of supporting the Europeans. Rudel can be presented as a threat to the peace of Europe. Our presence in West Germany would be temporary. We wouldn't touch France or anyone else. But if we wait another year the Germans will have expanded their army, they may be working on nuclear weapons even, and our best chance will be gone. A year after that there will be another election in the United States, and we might find another Reagan in the White House. The opportunity is about to slip through our fingers. It may never return."

Nikolayev looked across the lawn to the pine wood shimmering in the heat. He wished he were out there, walking among the tall brown trunks. At length he said: "There's a preferable alternative — the political destruction of Rudel. Minkov, can it be done?"

The KGB chairman picked up his glass of wine and drank. "It could," he said, putting the glass down with great care. "But it would be expensive, from the point of view of the KGB."

"How expensive?" Nikolayev asked. "More expensive than a war?"

"Not expensive in that way," Minkov said. "It would involve breaching a trust. Trust is the foundation of KGB foreign operations."

"I understand that," said Nikolayev. "Could it bring Rudel down?"

"Yes."

"Be more specific."

Minkov nodded, leaned over, and opened the briefcase beside his chair. "This is the proposal," he said, extracting a file and straightening up. "We have spent a great deal of time on its preparation. There is an excellent chance of its success."

"Go on," said Nikolayev, thinking: He needs a success now, since the KGB has failed so dismally at undermining Rudel. Too many failures, and Comrade Yuri is out of a job.

Minkov began to read. When he had finished, there was a pensive silence. Fedashkin broke it by saying, "You say the chance of this succeeding is very good."

"There is never any guarantee," Minkov pointed out. "But it is the most direct and feasible way of destroying the German, short of assassination or war."

"Assassinations are too risky," said Kamenev. "We were burnt in that attempt on the Pope — the incompetent Bulgarians. I'm against assassination. And war, for that matter," he added wryly.

The group fell silent in the oppressive heat. Nikolayev was now wishing he had held the meeting at the Central Committee building in Staraya Square. It is all too much, he thought, the chronic bickering of the Politburo, the factionalism of the

Secretariat, the obstructionism of the Council of Ministers, the crop failures, the grumblings of the Warsaw Pact; even my arms agreement has achieved no more, finally, than to permit the military to lay grandiose plans for increased spending in weapons technology. How did my predecessors put up with it?

Easy, he thought. Brezhnev turned his back and made speeches into the air. Andropov tried real change, and it killed him. Chernenko was nearly dead when he took office; he was another Brezhnev anyway. What will I make of it?

"We'll carry out the operation the KGB has prepared," he said. "Unless there are violent objections." Looking around the table, he found it suddenly difficult to care, as though the men with him were actors in some obscure and ancient play.

"We should continue developing plans for military action," Fedashkin said. "If we need to move in August, there is no more than enough time to prepare in detail."

"Yes," said Nikolayev. "Do it."

"How far advanced is the planning?" asked Kamenev.

"Well along," said Fedashkin. He exhibited a faint dry smile. "The operation has been given a code name. We thought it apt. The Nazi plan for the invasion of the Union was Barbarossa, as you know. We have christened ours, since it is going the other way, Barbarossa Red."

"I hope it is less of a joke than its name," said Kamenev coldly.

"Enough," said Nikolayev. "Do we have a consensus?"

There was no dissent.

East Berlin
June 18

HARPE WAS UPSET, more so than Brand had ever seen him. Still under control, though, betraying himself only in the rapid movements of his hands and the brittle quality of his speech. And his laugh, when Brand told him a joke over the excellent cognac that finished their meal, was too abrupt.

They were in the Panorama Restaurant on the 37th floor of the Hotel Stadt Berlin, overlooking the Alexanderplatz. Harpe, as usual after they had finished a meeting with the bland bureaucrats of the Trade Ministry, had taken Brand out for a late lunch. The German tossed off the last of his cognac, a little too quickly; he had drunk three glasses to Brand's one. Brand himself was becoming increasingly edgy, infected by the German's tension. "Well, Joachim," he said, "thanks for an excellent meal. I should be going back soon."

"Yes," said Harpe. He gestured for the bill. It came promptly; something of Harpe's status was obviously known at the Panorama. Brand wondered if there were a microphone under the table; Harpe's restlessness suggested that there might be.

"I'll drive you back to the Ministry," Harpe said.

A few minutes later they were standing outside the hotel in a drizzle so fine it was hardly more than a mist. "I don't need to go back just yet," Brand said. "Shall we take a walk to settle lunch?"

"Good," said Harpe. "Good idea." To Brand's relief he did

not seem worried about surveillance. "Let's stroll over to the Alexanderplatz," Harpe suggested.

"Alright."

The square was thinly populated; its tremendous expanse of paving with the spike of the Television Tower and World Clock that stood on the site of the old Berolina Monument lay gray and damp under the overcast. Near the base of the tower, Brand said, "Joachim, what's wrong?"

Harpe put his hands in his pockets. "I am extremely worried," he said.

Patiently, Brand asked, "What about, exactly?"

"There is something going on out at Zossen."

Brand felt the back of his neck prickle. "What?"

"I've put the details in a drop. But I want this to reach the West today." Harpe paused. The rear facade of the old Marien-kirche was creeping into view around the downswept roof of one of the futuristic buildings around the base of the tower. "There's no single item of major significance," he went on, "but together . . . First, there has been an order to update all deception plans for 20th Guards Army and the German formations that are to fight with it. I've been working twenty-hour days. Second, new jamming and communications equipment for Zossen has been shipped in from Russia. It was supposed to arrive in August, but now there's a big rush to get it installed and operational as soon as the technicians can manage it. Third —" He stopped. Two men wearing beige raincoats were walking towards Harpe and Brand; they seemed to have come out of nowhere. Brand's stomach turned over.

"Have you been under surveillance at all?" he asked in a low voice.

"No. Don't think so. If they were serious about it I wouldn't know, anyway." The German's voice was quite steady. "Let's keep walking."

They did. The two raincoated men drew nearer. They weren't talking to each other, but were looking fixedly ahead, apparently past Brand and Harpe.

They could be SSD, Brand thought. They could be. Why aren't they talking to each other?

The two men were six meters away when one of them said something. His companion laughed and then broke into rapid speech. It was Czech.

"Tourists," Harpe said, when the others were well past. His throat sounded dry. "Just tourists. We shouldn't worry so much."

"Tell me more about Zossen," Brand said. "What was the third thing?"

"Colonel Vedenin, my opposite number, hasn't been available since the day before yesterday. Neither has his superior, Major-General Romanov. I think they have been called back to Moscow."

"Permanently?" They were nearing the fountain, which plashed dismally in the misty air, the bright reds and yellows and blues of the tiles around its basin muted in the afternoon light.

"I think not. If it were permanent, replacement officers would have been sent. That hasn't been done."

"Do you have any idea why they were recalled?"

"Perhaps to receive special orders, briefings." Harpe looked at his watch. "I think we've taken long enough. We'd better go back."

Brand nodded. They walked around the fountain and began to retrace their steps. "Joachim, do you think the Russians are going to do something drastic? Because of Rudel?"

"I really don't know. But these three things together—" He shrugged. "I don't trust the Russians as much as your president Hood seems to."

"Could they be planning to take advantage of the political situation in West Germany and the United States?"

"How should I know?" said Harpe, with a flash of irritation. "I'm a colonel in the People's Army. I don't know what the Kremlin's thinking."

"But you're worried."

"I am always worried. Today I'm just a little more worried than usual. Look," he went on after a moment, as the Television Tower loomed higher and higher above them, "I am beginning to wear out, doing this. We both know I'll inevitably be caught if I go on. I don't think I'm in any immediate danger, but I've been working against the Russians for nearly two years and sooner or later something is going to go wrong. The instant I suspect they're wondering about me, I want you to get me out, no questions asked."

They were back at the great concrete base of the tower. "That's part of the deal," Brand said. "It always has been."

"Yes," said Harpe, "but if I'm on to something, your people would want to keep me in place to the last possible moment. That might be a moment too late, for me. I want a commitment that you'll exfiltrate me, no questions asked, the instant I require it. If I suspect Langley's trying to keep me in place too long, I'll cut off all clandestine contact, no drops, nothing. Tell them that for me, Paul. And I want that commitment."

"Verbally?"

"That would have to do, wouldn't it?" Harpe said dryly. "I can hardly ask for a witnessed document. I have to trust to your honor."

"I'll tell them," Brand said.

"I mean it, Paul. It's nothing personal, but I mean it."

"Yes," Brand repeated. "I'll tell them."

They walked the rest of the way to Harpe's car in silence.

THE NEW YORK TIMES
Bonn Announces New Military Staff, Talks with French

BONN, June 22 (Reuters) — The West German government announced today that it will form a general staff to control its military forces. The new staff is to assume responsibility for West German defense as Bonn's commitment to the North Atlantic Treaty Organization is phased out over the next four years. Chief of the German General Staff is to be General Klaus Freidrich von Sternberg, currently inspector-general of the West German armed forces. General von Sternberg served with the tank forces of the German army in Russia from 1941 to 1944, earning several decorations before being seriously wounded. After the war he went into retirement, but with the reestablishment of the West German armed forces in the 1950s he returned to active duty. He is widely regarded as an expert in mobile warfare.

In a related development, Franz Diercks, the West German foreign minister, announced that mutual defense talks with the French government would begin late next month. While he gave no details, informed sources believe that Bonn will propose an expansion and update of the aging French nuclear force to include the protection of West Germany. Cost of the improvements would be carried at least partly by Bonn, since Paris cannot at present afford a major weapons program. West Germany has renounced the possession of nuclear weapons, but presumably would want some influence over French use of the weapons in the event of war.

THE NEW YORK TIMES
Students, Workers Riot in East Germany

BERLIN, July 5 (Reuters) — The East German city of Leipzig was today reported under tight police and army control following a riot that left at least one dead and dozens injured. The disturbance is said to have begun in the industrial district, and unconfirmed reports indicated that there were also student demonstrations at Karl Marx University, formerly the University of Leipzig. Cause of the factory riot was said to be increased production targets and a cut in wages, part of the East German government's current drive to increase the efficiency of its industrial sector. East Berlin's recent crackdown on politically suspect authors, teachers and artists may have triggered the university disturbances, according to Kurt Hoeppner, a dissident writer exiled from East Germany last year.

Moscow
July 8

THE NOISE WAS DEAFENING. Almost every member of the audience in the Taganka Theater was standing up, clapping in the rhythmic applause that is one of the highest ovations Russian performers can receive. Flowers cascaded onto the stage where the actors and the director smiled out at the audience. The play was a revival of Trifonov's *The House on the Embankment*, a skilfully understated condemnation of the Stalinist Terror. The work had first been performed at the Taganka in the 1970s under the directorship of Lyubimov, but under Chernenko it had been suppressed and Lyubimov sent into exile, whereupon the Taganka had descended into a limbo of officially acceptable and excruciatingly dull productions. Now the theater's management was taking a chance, testing the new regime's tolerance. So far they had gotten away with it, although how long the revival would be allowed to continue was anyone's guess.

"It never should even have gotten into rehearsals," scowled Defense Minister Vitaly Fedashkin. He was sitting in the second row from the back, next to KGB Chairman Minkov. The two men could have been front row center, but had preferred to remain inconspicuous, over the protests of Fedashkin's wife who was sitting in the aisle seat, wearing a sullen expression. She had started to applaud, but Fedashkin had stopped her.

"Yes," said Minkov. "It's stupid to bring up all this old garbage again." He looked down at the stage, where the glass walls of the set gleamed dully under the lights and the flushed actors bowed. "They even used Lyubimov's staging. Too lazy to think up something better."

"Bugger the staging," said Fedashkin. "It shouldn't have been allowed anywhere, with anything at all. Let's get out of here."

"There was something you wanted to discuss," Minkov said. Minister Fedashkin was clearly upset and angry, his pink jowls flushed, gestures abrupt. "Would you prefer to keep it until tomorrow?"

"No. I want to talk to you now. Yevdokia," Fedashkin said to his wife, "take the car and go home. I have some things to do with Yuri. I'll be back later."

"But you said —"

"Go on," Fedashkin interrupted. The actors were leaving the flower bespattered stage and the noise was diminishing. With an angry movement Yevdokia pulled her wrap about her, got out of her seat, and stalked off up the aisle. Minkov glanced over his shoulder at her broad behind as she flounced away, worrying, as he always did, about security. But the Ninth Directorate guards would be in the lobby; she would reach home without incident. For a moment he congratulated himself on his good sense in not remarrying after Irina died these fifteen years ago; even then his wife had shown signs of becoming the petulant nag that Vitaly Fedashkin was saddled with.

"Let's get out of here," Fedashkin repeated.

Escorted not too conspicuously by their bodyguards, they made their way out of the theater. Outside, Taganka Square lay under the last glimmer of sunset, blue-hazed with traces of smog and automobile exhaust, the baroque mass of St. Nicholas Church with its dark red walls and copper-green domes looming over the angular modernity of the theater.

Minkov's Zil was waiting by the curb. Fedashkin and the KGB chairman got in, while the guards hovered. As the Zil pulled away down Narodnaya Street, Fedashkin looked out the limousine's rear window; the Chaika containing the guards was no more than twenty meters behind. He relaxed into the soft leather of the seat. Minkov clicked a switch in his armrest and said, "Just drive." Beyond the thick glass partition separating the front and rear seats the KGB chauffeur nodded and answered, "Yes, Chairman." His voice over the intercom speaker was thin and metallic.

"What's the matter?" Minkov asked.

The minister glanced at his companion. In the dim light of the car's interior the KGB chairman's face looked swarthier than ever. Unlike many Russians, he had not run to fat in middle age, but had retained an almost adolescent lankiness. Except for the deep lines running from the outer curve of his nostrils to the corners of his mouth, he looked younger than his sixty-two years.

"I don't want this taped," Fedashkin said.

"Comrade Minister, it is not being taped." Minkov would have liked to record the conversation, but did not quite dare. Fedashkin was far too dangerous a man to offend. He was a soldier to the core, but remarkably devious for all that.

"Good," Fedashkin said. "What, realistically, are the chances of Rudel losing the chancellorship through this operation of yours?"

"Perhaps less than the general secretary hopes," said Minkov. "As I stated, the KGB is not infallible."

"If it doesn't work," Fedashkin said after a pause, "what's the next option?"

"That's a matter for the Politburo, as you know. As we both know."

"Yes. Nevertheless, what would be a *reasonable* option for Nikolayev to decide on?"

Minkov looked out the Zil's window. The limousine was crossing Krasnocholmsky Bridge. Off to the left he could see the domes of the Novospassky Monastery against the slowly darkening horizon. "Assassination suggests itself," he said. "But it would be very dangerous. And Nikolayev would be very reluctant."

"And if assassination fails?"

The Zil reached the end of the bridge. Minkov turned back to Fedashkin. "Then there would only be Barbarossa Red. Either that or continue as we have, with Rudel continuing as he's done. A waste of opportunity, and of a great deal of effort and preparation. Many risks taken for nothing."

"If Nikolayev knew about this . . ." Fedashkin said, but did not complete the thought.

"Yes, there would be trouble," agreed Minkov. "He is very afraid of military-KGB cooperation. He wants, badly, to strengthen the Party."

"No doubt," agreed Fedashkin. He turned to peer out the rear window again; the Chaika, its headlights on now, kept faithful station behind them. "Do you realize," he went on, turning back to Minkov, "how much easier life would be for everybody if there weren't this constant leakage of capitalist values and Western ideas into the Warsaw Pact allies? Every time we suppress one revisionist sentiment, another worms its way across the frontier to sow doubt and weaken socialist commitment. Some of those governments aren't as vigilant as we are, either. If that flow were cut off . . . You of all people know what I'm talking about."

Minkov nodded. It was not possible to seal the border dividing Eastern and Western Europe; East Germans watched West German television, Hungarians listened to the BBC, tourists from the West, despite all precautions, mixed with the citizens of the Warsaw Pact, trade and cultural delegations flitted to and fro. The KGB and its sister organizations of the Pact were forever cleaning up the ideological droppings of such traffic, and the situation was becoming steadily worse. A recurrent nightmare of the Politburo was that of a coordinated and concerted refusal of the Pact capitals to abide by the political and economic directives issued in Moscow. The East Germans and the Hungarians were the worst offenders, with the Poles, despite the decline of the Solidarity movement, close on their heels. Berlin insisted on closer trade ties with West Germany and had eased travel restrictions between the two states after Bonn established a huge line of credit for the East German government; Budapest continued to expand its economic links to the West, while making it clear that Berlin's activities met with Hungarian approval; and Warsaw went on insisting that Polish internal problems could be solved without reference to Moscow. Until recently only one Pact nation at a time had tried to loosen its ties to the Union, and the Kremlin had been able to orchestrate its other clients to prevent deviance from progressing too far; the police action in Czechoslovakia in 1968 was a case in point. Indeed Prague was now Moscow's staunchest ally, the only one of the Warsaw Pact states to have joined in condemning East Berlin's behavior. Until Rudel became chancellor, Warsaw Pact unrest had been Minkov's primary concern, barring of course the eternal struggle with the Americans.

"Cutting off the flow would reduce the opportunity for deviation," Minkov said. "What people don't know won't hurt them. Or anybody else." He thought, not for the first time: If there were ever a reason for going to war in Europe, that's the one. Rudel is the best opportunity we've ever had.

"You can see what's coming," Fedashkin said, "if we don't bring the Pact governments to heel. Sooner or later they'll try to break away politically as well as economically. We've been able to stop that, so far. But if they ever all tried it at once we'd have our hands full. It could be a catastrophe as great as the war, perhaps greater; this time we haven't a Stalin to lead us. But if we were to act now — our military and political position will never be better, it can only worsen if we don't do something decisive. Bring Western Europe under our control, and we have not only the economic and technological resources we need, we also remove the major source of deviation among our allies. If we go on as we have been . . ." He shrugged. "I am not optimistic."

Minkov nodded. Fedashkin's analysis made a good deal of sense, and the KGB chairman was in fundamental agreement with it; he had gone over the same ground himself, and reached the same conclusions. The stumbling block was the likelihood of full-scale war with the Americans. But if that could be averted, there was little reason not to bring all of Europe under Moscow's rule, especially if it could be done with such speed that minimal damage was done to the physical and human resources of the West.

"I think that the general secretary would prefer to remove Rudel without the risk of a major war," he said. "That could present a problem, if we decide to proceed. Remember, Nikolayev may react badly, afterwards, when he is faced with the results of Barbarossa Red. No matter how fortunate." The darkness was growing rapidly now; ahead Minkov could see the bulk of the Warsaw Hotel, speckled with lights.

Fedashkin snorted. "The general secretary is looking no farther than the end of his nose. He is so concerned with domestic problems that he can't see that they, and many of our external ones, could be solved at a stroke. If he'd just look for a moment at what we could achieve for a moderate risk, he'd have to agree to military action. But he insists on wearing blinkers."

"Politburo opinion is with him," Minkov pointed out.

"Opinions can be changed," said Fedashkin.

And so can general secretaries, Minkov thought, mentally supplying the words Fedashkin had so carefully left unsaid.

"You know what will happen if Rudel falls through political action," Fedashkin said. "With the German chancellor gone, half the Politburo will go back to sleep, and Nikolayev will return to his tinkering with the economy. Meanwhile the Hungarians and the East Germans march nonchalantly off into the West, and we wake up one morning to find ourselves back on our prewar borders."

"I worry about the Americans," Minkov confessed.

"Who doesn't?" asked Fedashkin. "But their political will to use extreme force is weak at the moment. You've read the GRU and the KGB studies. If we acted so quickly they couldn't respond except by destroying Europe and perhaps themselves . . . and if we gave them a way to save face. A way like Rudel. They will have to acquiesce. There won't ever be a better time than now."

"First," Minkov pointed out, "we have to deal with the problem of political action against the chancellor. Nikolayev will want to try that first."

"Yes." Fedashkin looked out the window, at the lights passing. "Are you certain," he said, perhaps mindful of the KGB driver in the front seat, "that the general secretary is unaware of our . . . common interests?"

"I have been unable to determine otherwise," Minkov said. "Andropov knew, but he was KGB. We never informed

Chernenko, it wasn't necessary, he was on his last legs. Nikolayev
. . . you remember, we decided to wait."

"As well we did," said Fedashkin. "One other question. Can
Secretary Ivanov be controlled?"

"I think so," Minkov said. "At the moment he's the only
strong rival Nikolayev has in the Politburo and the Secretariat.
Fundamentally he agrees with us. But he's Party old guard. He
should be left out for now. We can deal with Nikolayev, afterwards, without him."

"Alright," Fedashkin said. "Then we go on."

West Berlin
July 16

ERICH KASTNER was sitting at his desk in his office, which occupied the third floor of a nondescript building half a block from the Criminal Investigation Division headquarters in Gothaerstrasse. The proximity was convenient; in West Berlin the BND and the civilian police, especially the criminal division, made use of each others' resources from time to time. Not as much as they once had done, however; the city was no longer the espionage Mecca it had been in the '50s and '60s. Most of the trade, except for the occasional defector from one of the Pact nations, had gone elsewhere, to Bonn or the various NATO headquarters strewn about Western Europe, or to Geneva. Kastner's section, with its fourteen permanent staff and string of part-time observers of varying degrees of credibility, held little more than a watching brief. There were, of course, a number of highly placed East Berliners who worked with more or less reluctance for the BND, but these were controlled directly from BND headquarters at Pullach, on the outskirts of Munich. Running operations or agents out of Berlin's western sector was now seen as too risky, given the remotely likely but always possible occupation of the city by the Russians. If that happened, there would be no files to incriminate West German agents in the East, and Pullach's espionage assets would have a reasonable prospect of survival.

The policy also concentrated intelligence work in the hands of the BND mandarins in Pullach. Kastner suspected that this was at least part of the reason for the low profile demanded of the Berlin section; for nearly three decades, the city had been known as the espionage capital of Europe, and the tidy minds on the outskirts of Munich had come to look with increasing disfavor on the decentralization of their control. Kastner's trans-border operations section was now reduced to maintaining five safe houses, monitoring delegations and missions from the East, engaging in occasional forays across the Wall to pass urgent messages from the West German capital to some operative or other, and cooperating with the CIA station. This last had always been an aggravation to Kastner and his superiors, but political realities made it impossible to tell the Americans to close up shop and go home. And the information-sharing agreements were next to useless; by the time the Americans had excised any reference to sources and any contextual material that could point to a source, the data was two weeks old and shorn of most of its value. The one exception to this was Kastner's sporadic contact with Brand. The American was willing to provide at least snippets of useful information before the sanitized documents reached Kastner's desk for forwarding to Pullach. By painstaking comparison of these documents with the tapes Kastner made of every meeting with the American, he had come to the conclusion that the high-level source Brand was running was definitely East German, possibly SSD, but more likely a military intelligence man maintaining close contact with Zossen. Kastner had made a mental short list of the possibilities. There were now eight names on the list; slowly reducing the number had become a kind of game, to be pursued whenever he talked with the American. Somewhat to his annoyance, he liked Brand; the man was following his own orders, and appeared to be a thorough professional. Kastner occasionally forgot himself and began thinking of Brand as a fellow German, the man was that good with the language and the background. Under other circumstances, they might have become friends.

Kastner sighed, took his feet off his desk, and adjusted the keyboard on his lap. At the other end of its cord the text of the carefully worded memorandum to Horstmann, the West Berlin BND director, stared back at him from the terminal's screen. The memorandum was another shot in Kastner's battle to prevent the

BND accountants from cutting his section's budget again. Kastner sometimes wondered whether the accounting office weren't in the pay of the KGB, such was its determination to reduce his department's already slender resources to the vanishing point. The idea wasn't quite totally whimsical; the BND had been penetrated again and again by the SSD, and only they, God, and the KGB knew how many East Bloc agents were still tucked away undiscovered in the nooks and crannies of the West German security service. In submitting reports, in the bi-yearly meetings in Pullach, the thought always floated discomfortingly in the back of Kastner's mind: To just how many places are my words going to go?

He tapped out another sentence on the keyboard, the amber characters blinking into existence aross the screen. At the end of the sentence he noticed that the second word was misspelled. Muttering, he keyed back and started to correct it.

The telephone rang. "Shit," Kastner said, and put the keyboard on his desk with unnecessary roughness. He picked up the phone and jammed it between his left ear and his shoulder, so that he could use the keyboard with both hands. "Kastner."

"This is Stechner. Look, there seems to be some delicate property of yours up at the Reuterplatz police station. At least I think it's yours. They seemed pretty certain up there."

Kastner nearly dropped the telephone receiver. He steadied it hastily with one hand, forgetting the memo; Stechner was deputy head of the Criminal Investigation Division, Kastner's liaison to the police, and an unsolicited call from him usually meant trouble. "Are you sure the thing's safe up there?"

"For the moment. It only turned up twenty minutes ago. But I wouldn't waste any time, if I were you."

"Alright," Kastner said. "Thanks."

"Better you than me," said Stechner, and rang off.

Kastner hung up and stabbed at the intercom buttons. "Lammers," he said.

"Yes?"

"Get in here right away. Bring Roth."

"Coming."

Kastner paused for a moment, fingertip on Schneider's call

button, thinking. The Gamma safe house was the most recently established and probably the most secure. He pressed the button. "Schneider. You there?" Thank God there was still half an hour till the end of the work day.

"Sir."

"Get over to the Gamma house immediately and open it up, recorders, cameras, everything. Take anybody you need to help, I don't care what they're doing. Except Lammers and Roth. Be ready in an hour, less than an hour."

"Right away," Schneider said.

Kastner removed his finger from the button and exhaled slowly. Twenty minutes, Stechner had estimated. They could be looking for the man, if it were a man, already, depending on how much preparation he'd had time for. If it were a sloppy defection there could be a solid ring of East Bloc people around the Reuterplatz police station by now. Whoever it was, he or she was high level; Stechner wouldn't trouble Kastner with some customs official or border guard who'd decided to make a run for it.

Maybe we've got an hour, Kastner thought as Lammers and Roth hurried into the office. Maybe just enough time.

Despite the late afternoon traffic, Kastner and Lammers reached the police station in some kind of record time, Lammers driving, Kastner beside him worrying. If the defector had anything to offer they'd have to get him out of the city as quickly as possible, before his people started to make diplomatic noises. Arrangements, all sorts of arrangements. Kastner hoped the defector wasn't Russian; that would make life doubly difficult.

He left Lammers in the car. In the front hall of the station a young and rather nervous policeman met him. Kastner identified himself. "He's in one of the interview rooms," the policeman said. "At the back."

"Let's go," said Kastner. "Did you bring him in?"

"Yes, sir."

"What sort of line did he give you?"

"That he's East German, wants political refugee status. Says he's SSD."

Maybe a big one, Kastner thought. Or a little one pretending to be a big one. "Anything else?"

"No. He said he wouldn't talk to anybody but BND. He showed me some identification, but it was civilian."

"When did this happen?" They turned into a corridor leading towards the rear of the building.

The policeman consulted his watch. "He stopped me forty-five minutes ago, over by the Technical University." They stopped in front of a metal door in which was set a small wire-reinforced window. "We're holding him in there. There's a guard with him."

"Alright. I don't want to take him out the front. Can we get a car up to that exit on the east side?"

"Yes. I can go out and make sure it's clear."

"Please. It's a brown Opel, one man driving." They were using two cars; Lammers in the Opel would make the pickup while Roth watched for any opposition from the VW.

"Right away."

Kastner opened the door of the interview room and went in. The defector was sitting on a wooden chair against the wall, wearing a baggy blue suit and an apprehensive expression. He was about forty, with close-cropped brown hair and rather prominent ears. Except for the ears he had no other distinguishing features, being neither too tall nor too short, with the build of an average male approaching middle age. He looked up anxiously as Kastner closed the door.

"We're going out the east way," Kastner said to the guard. "Would you come with us, please, I don't want any delays." To the defector he said, "I'm from the BND. We're getting you to a safe place."

The defector didn't get up. "I want some identification," he said.

One of the arrogant ones, Kastner thought. "Get up and come with me," he said irritably. "Unless you want to go back where you came from."

The man hesitated, and got up. The guard led them down a hall and then through a cross corridor that ended in a steel door with barred windows at eye level. Outside Lammers was waiting with the Opel.

"Into the back," Kastner said. He got in beside the East German. "Down on the floor, quickly." He picked up the black cloth hood and slid it over the man's head as he hunched awkwardly over the transmission tunnel. "For everybody's protection," Kastner said. "We won't be long." He shook out the army blanket and threw it over the East German. Tapping Lammers on the shoulder, he said, "Let's go."

The Gamma safe house was in the northern quarter of the city, in Reinickendorf. The radio was silent all the way; only if there had been signs of pursuit would Roth, monitoring them in the Volkswagen, have made a brief warning contact. Gamma was actually an aging brick structure that somehow had survived the bombings of 1944 and 1945 and had been converted into two flats, one up, one down, in a neighborhood whose population was heavily foreign and transient. Kastner had taken a lease on it two months previously, when the Beta house had to be vacated to make way for a new residential development. The money for the lease had been approved only with great reluctance by the Pullach accountants; Kastner had almost, before they capitulated, given up on Gamma. He was now extremely glad that he hadn't.

"We're here," he said to the inert bundle on the floor of the Opel. "Take the hood off, and put these glasses on. You won't be able to see through them, so keep a grip on my arm when you get out. Make it as natural as you can."

"Yes," muffled by the hood. The East German surfaced, took the opaque sunglasses from Kastner, and awkwardly put them on. Lammers was already out of the car, unlocking the front door of the building. Kastner unobtrusively guided the defector up the shallow front steps and through the entrance.

"Move the car," he told Lammers. "Then get back here."

Lammers nodded and left, closing the front door gently behind him. "You can take them off now," he said to the East German. "Schneider?"

From the far end of the hall leading to the rear of the flat Schneider called, "I'm back here. Be ready in a minute."

"Alright," Kastner said. To the defector he said, "I'm going to have to search you now."

"The police already did."

"Again, sorry."

The East German shrugged and suffered the indignity. When he had finished Kastner gestured to the stairs leading to the second story. "Up there. Don't open any of the curtains."

They went up the stairs in the gloom. Schneider hadn't turned on any lamps and the sun was westering; because of the narrowness of the street the safe house had little natural light at the best of times. At the top of the stairs the door to what had been the upper flat opened on a short hall, with a tiny kitchen just ahead, the bathroom to the left, and the sitting room and bedroom farther on towards the front of the building. The brownish wallpaper was bubbled in spots and there was a faint odor of mice and boiled cabbage.

"How long will I be here?"

"No longer than necessary," Kastner said. "Depending on what you have to say. Do you need the bathroom?"

"No."

"Then come out here."

They went along the hall to the sitting room. The firmly closed drapes at the window overlooking the street were the most expensive part of the furnishing, thick burlap lined with opaque cloth. There were two old armchairs done in poisonous green corduroy and a cheap settee upholstered in orange vinyl. A beige-shaded aluminum floor lamp and a formica-topped table with a metal ashtray on it completed the decor. It was a profoundly depressing room.

"Sit down," Kastner said. The house had been closed up too long and felt stuffy and airless. "You want to smoke?"

"I don't, often. But now, yes, I would." His voice cracked slightly, tension or dry throat induced by too much adrenalin, probably both. "I'm afraid I have none—"

Kastner gave the man his own pack and lighter, then took off his suit jacket and slouched down in one of the chairs. The other sat on the orange couch and carefully lit a cigarette. Kastner noted that his hands weren't shaking much.

"I'll have one too," Kastner said. Sharing, the first tentative step to some kind of trust. And utterly necessary; Kastner had to find out, and quickly, the defector's status. When he had that he could think about contacting Director Horstmann, and if necessary begin arrangements to get the Easterner out by the morning plane.

"Do you want a drink?" he asked. "There's cognac."

A nod. "Just a minute," Kastner said. "I'll get it."

Downstairs, Schneider was in the rear bedroom, his tape reels already turning. On the left of the monitor screen the defector was visible, smoking nervously.

"Everything works?" Kastner asked. He had a private nightmare of a successful interrogation which failed to be recorded because the machines broke down.

"Yes," Schneider said. "Everything goes."

"When Roth and Lammers turn up tell them to keep quiet and stay down here. Where's that cognac?"

"In the kitchen. Can you get him centered more in the camera? If he goes any farther left he might drift off the screen."

"I'll see." Kastner got the bottle and two glasses from the kitchen and went back upstairs. The defector was sitting hunched over, elbows on knees. He had smoked the cigarette almost down to its filter. Kastner motioned at the pack and poured out two glasses of the cognac before sitting down in one of the poison-green armchairs. He left the bottle open. "It's ten after five," he said. "How long before they know you're gone?"

"They likely know already. We were supposed to eat at five. I'm with — was with — a delegation to the Technical University."

Kastner nodded. He had been routinely informed of the East German delegation's arrival the day before; it was a group of chemical engineers attending a series of seminars on industrial waste management. None of the delegation had been of particular interest to the BND.

Not until now, Kastner corrected himself. "Which one of the engineers are you?"

"Friedrich Ewald. But I'm not an engineer."

Kastner waited. Ewald knocked back his cognac and poured again. "What are you, then?" Kastner asked.

"SSD," said Ewald. "The *Stasis*." He brushed at his eyes; the cognac must have made them water. "Second Directorate. They sent me with the delegation to make sure none of the engineers took a walk." He gave a short humorless laugh. "They really screwed themselves this time."

"How so?" Kastner asked.

"I know things," Ewald said evasively. "Things you'd like to know. Very much like to know." His eyes fixed on Kastner momentarily, then he hurriedly swallowed more cognac.

Kastner sipped at his own glass. "That's true, possibly. If in fact we don't know them already. The value of your information declines a good deal if we already have it."

"You don't have this," Ewald said confidently, perhaps because of the liquor.

"Alright," Kastner said. "Let's leave that alone for a minute. Why did you decide to come across?"

"I used to be HVA," Ewald said. "A year ago I had some trouble with my boss, he made me transfer to the Second Directorate. I went down a grade. I decided I'd get out if I could. So I made sure I was the model officer. Then they needed somebody to babysit this delegation. The man they'd picked out went sick, so they assigned me. I didn't have much time to plan. I grabbed the first chance I could, while the others were in a seminar this afternoon."

"You weren't the only security officer."

"No, there's a major too. Named Golz. He'll have blown the whistle by now. The whole bunch is probably at the checkpoint, going back."

"What did you have in mind as far as an agreement with us?" Kastner asked.

Ewald started in with a long list of demands: money, a lot of it, a new identity, immediate transport out of Berlin to the West, assistance later in setting up a business, a permanent security watch over him, and pressure on East Berlin to let his wife and child emigrate. Kastner was unsurprised; every defector with the meanest scrap of intelligence information to offer had a similar list. Each one seemed to think he was unique. Like most of the lists, this one would be pared down to something financially manageable, depending on Ewald's degree of cooperation and the value of what he was offering.

"I haven't the authority to guarantee you all that," Kastner said, when the East German seemed to have run down. He drank a little cognac, still on his first glass. Ewald downed the rest of his and began work on another, a very full one. "You can imagine how expensive it would be. We can't possibly afford to do that with everyone who comes over."

"The BND's got plenty of money," Ewald said truculently. He was more than a little tipsy. "How often do you get an SSD colonel?"

"You're not the first," Kastner said blandly. "But look, let me make a couple of calls, I'll see what I can do."

"Calling who?" Ewald said apprehensively. "That's another thing, I don't want the whole BND knowing about me. You've got termites, did you know that? Tell too many people and one of them's going to be working for the HVA."

Kastner, half out of his chair, sat down again. "How much information do you have on that?"

"Not yet. I need some guarantees."

"If you can give me an indication," Kastner pointed out reasonably, "I'll have an idea of who to avoid."

"Later," said Ewald. "They're higher —" He stopped.

"Yes?"

"Later. Please make your calls."

"Alright. Have some more cognac."

As he left the room Kastner heard the bottle clink against the rim of Ewald's glass. Bad reaction to stress, he thought, making his way downstairs to the rear bedroom where Schneider hunched over his recorders, Roth next to him on a low stool.

"Where's Lammers?"

"Front room, keeping an eye on the street. Nothing there. Nothing out back, either."

"What do you think? Horst?"

Schneider tapped his chin thoughtfully with an index finger. "I think he's a drinker," he said. "He's putting it away fast and not showing much effect. But he's still a little aggressive. I'm not sure this is the time to put the bite on him. He might turn nasty. He's scared enough to."

"I'd like to put the pressure on," Kastner said. "If he knows anything about Pact people in the BND we'd better get some of it out of him now. Before Horstmann hands him over to Pullach."

"That stuff's tricky," Roth observed.

And dangerous, Kastner thought. A classic method of creating dissension and distrust in an enemy intelligence service was to send over a false defector armed with documentation about purported double agents. Even if you were fairly sure the documents were spurious, you had to pay some attention to them, just in case the defector was exactly what he claimed to be. A great deal of energy would be expended to come to a decision one way or the other, and no matter what happened, there was always the nagging doubt; perhaps I was wrong, perhaps they fooled me this time and the poor bastard was innocent, or, worse: I can't pin a thing on him, it looks like disinformation, but maybe it isn't.

"He's still slugging it back," Schneider said. "He's just about finished the bottle."

"Let him," Kastner said, deciding suddenly. "Let's let him stew another ten minutes, maybe he'll be more tractable when I go back up."

"Call the office?" Roth asked. "Director Horstmann's going to have to know shortly."

"I'll do that. Is there any more to drink around here? If he's on the bottle, he may be willing to cough up something to get another one."

"Brandy over the sink," Schneider mentioned. "It's pretty bad stuff, though."

"It'll have to do."

They watched the monitor. Towards the end of the ten minutes Ewald upended the cognac bottle over his glass and drained the last drops. Then he put the bottle down, an expression of desolation on his face.

"Here we go," Kastner said. He got the brandy and went upstairs to the other kitchen where he left the bottle. Then he rejoined Ewald in the sitting room. The East German was looking the worse for wear, eyes slightly unfocussed.

"Well?" Ewald said, but without the earlier belligerence.

"I couldn't get through," Kastner said. "The people I have to speak to won't be available for a while." He sat down. His own cognac was gone; Ewald must have finished it while Kastner was on his way upstairs. "Look, we've given you something already just by taking you in," Kastner pointed out. "Maybe it's time for something in return."

"Not until I have some guarantees. I—"

"Use your *head*," Kastner snapped. The anger was not quite feigned. "You've got *no* leverage to demand guarantees, or anything else for that matter. For all we know you could be some third-rate chemical engineer from that conference who's got it into his head to get a free ticket out by pretending to be something he's not. I've seen that kind before. I had a check run on you while I was downstairs. Nobody knows anything about you, and nobody thinks you're very important." He stopped momentarily, as if he had revealed something he shouldn't have, and then went on angrily, "I'm not going to waste my time with someone who won't cooperate. You asked *us* for help, we didn't come to you. I've half a mind to kick you out on the street right now and see if you're as important as you think you are. You want civilian refugee status, say so, we'll turn you over to the right people."

"I am *not* a civilian," Ewald hissed back at him, leaning over the coffee table as if he were about to throw himself at Kastner. The East German was fairly drunk. "I've got things you'd give your right arm to know, I—"

"Ah, shut up," Kastner said. He got up and stalked to the head of the stairway. "Roth!"

"Yes?" Muffled, from the back bedroom.

"Come up here a minute."

A few seconds later Roth's head appeared at bannister level. "Anything more on this one?" Kastner asked, with sufficient volume to be heard in the sitting room.

Roth, who had been listening to the exchange over the monitors, said, "Documentation still says no make on an SSD connection. They've come up with a minor agricultural chemist of the same surname. No Christian name yet."

"That's it, then," Kastner said. He imagined Ewald straining his hearing in the front room. "Get the car around. We'll take him over to the refugee center. Maybe the civilians can get some sense out of him."

"Alright," Roth said, and started down.

"Wait," Ewald cried in a slurred voice.

"What for?" said Kastner. Roth stopped his descent.

"I'll give you some things."

Kastner walked back to the sitting room doorway. "You'll give me anything I ask for. Or you're going into the car. I haven't time for this pissing around."

"Alright, *alright.*"

"Wait," Kastner called back to Roth. He went on into the sitting room and was about to sit down when Ewald said, "Is there anything more to drink?"

Kastner eyed the East German. "Don't you think maybe you've had enough?"

"Please. You can undersht . . . imashine what I'm . . ." Ewald's voice trailed off.

"Going through?" suggested Kastner, without much sympathy.

"Yes."

"Very well." Kastner went out to the kitchen and returned with the brandy. Pausing, about to pour, he said, "Tell me something."

Ewald gave a rambling account of the current organizational structure of the SSD's Second Directorate, which among other tasks was responsible for surveillance of East German nationals travelling in the West. The description was disjointed in places, partly because Ewald was speaking so quickly, partly because of the alcohol. Kastner poured Ewald's glass full and let him go; he could be led to more sensitive topics if he were first given a free hand with this one.

After five minutes the East German began to flag. Kastner took advantage of a brief silence and said, "That's all very interesting, but it's hardly anything we didn't know already. I had the impression earlier you had some bigger fish in your basket than this. Let's have a look at one. Then I may be able to make a couple of phone calls."

Ewald looked up for the first time since he had begun to speak; he had been sitting with elbows on knees, gazing intently at his hands which he had clasped tightly together. The knuckles white. Kastner felt a momentary sympathy for the man; taught all his life never to betray any vulnerability to a Westerner, he had now to contradict every value his training had drummed into him.

"You haven't said," Kastner added, "why you decided to come across."

"I lost a grade in rank. I had other problems." Ewald emptied his glass and poured another. "There wasn't anything left over there any more."

There has to be more to it than that, Kastner thought. An SSD colonel doesn't jump because he's been slapped with a reprimand, not even a grade loss. He's in some other kind of trouble, but it hasn't caught up with him yet, otherwise they'd never have let him come over with the delegation. Black market? Political or woman trouble? Given Ewald's behavior so far, it certainly wasn't ideological. Something more devious? Kastner doubted it. Planted defections, enticing as they were in the short run, weren't really popular with the KGB or even with the HVA; if it had been some kind of deception measure Ewald would be carrying a sheaf of documents carefully prepared by KGB headquarters in Dzerzhinsky Square.

"Go on," he said.

The SSD man looked up again from his clenched hands, and then suddenly opened them and buried his face in his palms. His shoulders shook. Kastner pushed the brandy bottle and the cigarettes closer to the far side of the table and watched quietly. "My little boy," Ewald said after a couple of minutes. "They'll never let him out."

"What really happened?" asked Kastner. "It wasn't just the demotion." *If* he's broken this fast, he thought, I can get anything I need. For a little while, at least. Until he starts thinking again.

"No." The fit of weeping seemed to have sobered Ewald. He poured brandy and lit a cigarette. "A girl, like always. Young. Her name's Monika. I met her six months ago, about, my wife and I weren't getting along. I told her I was just an ordinary policeman, not SSD. We started sleeping together. She got pregnant, I found out last week. Two days after that she was picked up for black marketing, jeans, perfume, that sort of stuff. I'd lent her money, I think she was using it on the market. They were going to find out where she got the money, they always do, I'd be implicated. I'd be out of the SSD, no pension, no job, nothing, my wife'd get Pauli, nothing left, I'd rot for the rest of my life. This conference was coming up." He gulped and sniffed, like a child with a cold. "Monika kept her mouth shut for as long as I needed. Or maybe they didn't ask her soon enough." He attempted a smile that died at birth.

"She was using you?" Kastner asked.

"Probably."

"Anything else?"

"No. That's all."

"We could try to get Pauli out. Your wife might have to come too."

"That's alright."

"Could we go back to the other things?"

"Yes. Now. I want some sleep, haven't slept for two nights."

"You'll get sleep soon. Why are you so worried about treason in the BND? We've cleaned house in the last few years."

"Not exactly the BND," Ewald said. "Worse than that."

"Oh," said Kastner. He picked up the brandy bottle, poured some of the spirit into his glass, and drank. Roth had been right; it was dreadful stuff.

"Much worse," Ewald went on. "I know because I was in the SSD when —"

"Which department?"

"Thirteen."

God in heaven, Kastner thought. Why didn't he say that to begin with? "You should have told me you were in Thirteen."

"I wanted guarantees."

"Go on."

"I wasn't supposed to know anything about the operation, it was cosmic security. You know Thirteen."

"Yes," Kastner said. "Records. Everything the SSD has ever done is tucked away in there."

"That's right. I was in Records Security, under Walter Brixius. He's one of Markus Ott's department heads."

"I know about Ott," Kastner said. Ott was head of the HVA. "Who's Brixius?'

"He's in charge of all documentation for HVA operations in the Federal Republic. I had the security responsibility for the Bonn Chancellery dossiers."

"You had access to the *records?* " Kastner asked, showing surprise despite himself. He felt a surge of suspicion. If Ewald had ever seen the contents of even one of those files, the SSD would never have let him put a toe across the border.

"No, no, I only handled physical security, lockup, document traffic control, that sort of thing. I never saw inside any of the dossiers. Not until just after I got on the wrong side of Brixius. That was a year ago now."

"What happened?"

"It was just after your Chancellor Rudel was elected. The day after he won, Ott and Manfred Litke came through the office."

"Minister Litke? The SSD head?"

"Yes. That one. They were very excited, they tried to hide it but you could tell. Just before they went into Ott's office Litke said, 'We've done it, we've finally done it. Not quite the top, but close enough. Now we'll call the tune.' A few minutes later they called for a file. It was one of the high-security ones, that only Reisch was allowed to handle. Reisch is the operations control officer for Bonn. Anyway, he was out. I told Ott that and he said get it anyway, he'd clear it with Reisch. We have a dual-key system in that office, so Brixius and I opened Reisch's safe and got the file. Then one of the clerks came up and told Brixius he had an urgent phone call. Brixius told me to take the file to Ott. It was terrible security. We should have both gone. But Ott's office was only twenty meters down the hall. So I took it there."

"What happened then?"

"I went back to my desk. A couple of minutes later Brixius called me into his office. He said I hadn't been updating the security logs properly. It was true, they were three or four hours behind, but I'd had too much work to do. He gave me shit, said I was going to be transferred if I messed up again. He'd been after me for six months, one thing on top of another. He disliked me, I never found out why. Anyway, when Litke and Ott were done with the file, they called me. I didn't want to see Brixius again, I was too mad, so I went and got it alone. On the way back I looked in it, just the first two or three pages, and the last one, all I had time for."

"Why did you do that?"

"I was already thinking about coming across," Ewald said. "Every time Brixius had me up on the carpet, I thought about it some more."

"And you wanted something valuable to bring with you."

"Yes."

"What was the file about?"

"The names were all coded, of course. But I can tell you who I think the dossier was about." Ewald took a deep breath. "It was a long-term agent. At least twenty years, maybe more. Born in Berlin, left the Russian sector in the early fifties. Political, in the CSU, controlled directly from East Berlin. By Reisch, like I told you. On the last page it said he hadn't been able to influence either the Bundeswehr expansion or the NATO withdrawal."

God in heaven, Kastner thought. "Military or foreign affairs, then," he said. "Where in the government is he?"

"High. Very high."

"*How* high?" Kasner realized that he had clenched his hands. He forced the muscles to relax. If this is true, he thought, it's a catastrophe. I wish I'd never heard of Ewald. Pullach's going to tie itself into knots. For months.

"Maybe cabinet level," Ewald said. "I don't know."

"A ministerial aide?"

"Possibly. It would fit."

"Not a minister."

Ewald slumped back on the settee, looking exhausted and drunk. "It could be. I got the impression from the file that whoever it was was more than an aide. But I can't be sure."

"What happened after you put the file back?"

"Nothing. About a week after that Brixius told me I was being transferred to the Second Directorate. I told you the rest."

"Why did they let you across the border? Somebody with HVA Records background?"

"The man who was supposed to go was in a car accident. They assigned me at the last minute, there wasn't anybody else available. Second Directorate never paid much attention to where I came from, anyway. I got along better there. Until Monika," Ewald added bleakly.

"Second Directorate screwed up, in other words."

"I suppose so. I never thought they'd let me out of the country."

Kastner looked at his watch; half past six. "Alright," he said. "I'm going out for a while. The bedroom's along the hall. Get some sleep if you want."

"If I can."

Kastner went downstairs to the back room. "Well?" he said to Schneider and Roth. "What do you think?"

"It's got to be a plant," Roth said. He looked anguished. "They *can't* have managed something like that."

"No?" said Schneider. "They had that SSD man, Felfe, nearly running our counterespionage bureau a few years ago. If they were able to pull that off . . ." His voice trailed away.

"Look on the bright side," Kastner said. "At least it isn't the chancellor. Maybe we'll be lucky and it's an aide or a secretary. I'm going back to the office. Sit on him until I get back, I might be a while. Don't say anything about this to anyone without my go-ahead. Anyone at all. Even if they're straight from Pullach. Understand?"

Schneider and Roth exchanged glances, remembering the renegade counterespionage colonel. "Yes," Schneider said. "Absolutely."

"How many audio tapes did you run?"

"Three."

"I'll take one with me."

Driving south in the Opel, Kastner worriedly contemplated his next action. He was going to have to tell Horstmann soon, but he needed time to think. First of all, when the HVA woke up to the fact that an ex-records security officer had gone over the Wall they would move heaven and earth either to get him back or silence him permanently. That put Roth, Schneider, Lammers and Kastner in physical danger; Gamma would be safe for another eighteen hours at the most, Kastner estimated. Second, if someone at the ministerial level in Bonn were working for the East, it was quite possible that some of his security was ensured by turncoat BND personnel. If the wrong person found out where Ewald was, where the tapes were, the SSD might simply walk in, dispose of everybody, and worry about the consequences later. That was unlikely, Kastner thought, but he could not dismiss the possibility. More probable, if the agent in Bonn did have allies in the BND and elsewhere in the government, was that any investigation would be blocked, diffused, misdirected, eventually to peter out in a morass of uncertainties. The tapes would be mislaid or accidentally erased or would simply disappear. Kastner and his three colleagues would be assigned to other duties, in Kastner's case perhaps retired early, and his section closed down.

And if those things didn't happen, if the investigation did turn up an agent, there would remain the awkward problem of what to do with him. The damage to Rudel's government, whatever the course of action, would be enormous, perhaps fatal. Kastner reflected bleakly on this as he stopped for a red light. Politicians, he had discovered long ago, would cling to power at almost any cost. Even if the agent wasn't protected by men working for the East, the investigation might be blocked by other men unwilling to risk their careers in the name of national security. After all, they would reason, the man's been with us for years, we know him socially, he's one of us, it must be an SSD deception. Confronted with irrefutable evidence, they would simply retire the agent, if they could. The press, if it could be arranged, would never get within kilometers of the story. And memories would be long. Kastner and anyone else who had pursued the investigation with too much vigor would pay, over the years.

The light turned green. I need help, Kastner thought, letting the Opel roll forward. He felt the onset of one of his depressions. I can't even trust my own people, not the politicians, perhaps not even Horstmann. But I'm going to have to tell them about Ewald. I wish I'd never heard of the man. Where am I going to get some help? Perhaps . . .

No. My head would roll if Horstmann ever found out.

But think of it as an insurance policy. If the worst happened, if it looked as though the investigation were being screwed around by SSD people in Pullach I'd have something to fall back on. It wouldn't have to go any farther than that. Only insurance.

Despite himself, he had already decided. Instead of going on south to Gothaerstrasse, he began looking for a telephone kiosk.

A few kilometers to the east, HVA head Markus Ott was replacing the telephone receiver in its cradle. On the other side of his office, in a chair next to the locked door, sat Voldemar Dmitriev, deputy head of Department 11 of the KGB First Directorate. Department 11 was responsible for KGB liaison with and control of the Warsaw Pact intelligence services; it was an indication of the importance Dzerzhinsky Square attached to the current operation that Dmitriev himself had been sent out from Moscow. The Russian had been smoking incessantly, one Winston after another, while he and Ott waited for the telephone call. The air was blue-gray.

"Well?" Dmitriev said.

Ott, who did not smoke, but who also dared not ask the Russian to stop, coughed pointedly and said, "They've got him. The BND took him away from the Reuterplatz police station at a quarter to five. They went north."

"No one exceeded the orders about surveillance?"

"No, Comrade Dmitriev. There were strict instructions on that, no following to be done. They have a safe house, perhaps in the north, but that's all we know."

"The BND man, Kastner, he's not back at his headquarters yet?"

"No."

"They'll need a while to pry it out of Ewald," Dmitriev said. "Is he going to be able to convince them?"

"He's one of the best we have," Ott said.

Dmitriev grunted. Moscow would have preferred to use a Russian, but the background of the bogus defector had to be so accurate and comprehensive that an East German was the only logical choice. In any case, SSD men had a high reputation for self-discipline and effectiveness. Even when required to get drunk in the line of duty.

"He'd better be the best," Dmitriev observed. "There's a lot hanging on this."

"I hope we can get him back," Ott said. "When it's over."

"Don't worry," the Russian said. "When there's a new government in Bonn, we'll get him back. Your ministry will start making diplomatic protests tomorrow."

West Berlin
Evening, July 16

BRAND WAS PUSHING Alison back and forth on the swing that hung from the oak tree. Four meters away David, in the sandbox, was constructing an elaborate maze of fortifications. A company-sized collection of plastic soldiers manned the ramparts.

"What's that?" Alison asked her brother.

"A city. With a castle."

"Has it got a name?" Brand asked. "Cities and castles usually have names."

"Berlin," David announced. "That's Uncle Kevin there." He pointed. "On top of the castle. Watching out for the Russians."

Brand dropped the beat of the swing. Dammit, he's too young for that, he thought.

The telephone was ringing inside the house. "Push me higher," Alison said. "Please."

"Sure." Brand exerted himself, pressing his palms harder against the warmth of his daughter's back, the delicate ribs. They are so vulnerable, he thought. And they have so little fear, not knowing it. His throat tightened for a moment.

"Paul?" Jennifer was at the back door. "It's for you."

"Coming. You can pump yourself for a while," he told Alison. "I have to go to the phone."

"Can you come back?"

"I'll see."

He entered the house and went into the kitchen. "Who?" he

asked his wife. She was kneading bread; the kitchen was full of the soft smell of yeast.

She was short of breath from the kneading. "A man. Don't know who."

"Hello?" Brand said into the phone.

"Paul. It's Erich."

Brand knew only one Erich who would call him by his first name. He felt his muscles tense, involuntarily. Kastner always called him at the office. "Oh, hello. What can I do for you?" He kept his voice light. Jennifer flipped the dough over, folded it, and started in again.

"I'd like to take up an hour or so of your time. This evening, if you can manage it."

Brand frowned; he had had a difficult day. His senior secretary had resigned because her husband was being transferred to Frankfurt, and the office computer had developed an intermittent bug that was corrupting the accounts payable files. "Okay," he said after a moment. "When?"

"As soon as you can. Listen, there's one other favor. Can you lay hands on an open-reel tape deck? Nine-inch reels, industrial type?"

"I've got one here," Brand said. "But it weighs a ton and it's built into a console."

"Damn." A pause. "I don't want to come over there."

"There's one at the office," Brand said unwillingly. "It's old, though." Brand liked music while he worked; the office recorder gave him long periods of uninterrupted Bach.

Another pause. "You're on the third floor of that building aren't you? A suite."

"That's right."

"That should be safe enough. Nobody working late?"

"No."

"Look, I don't like asking this. But it's important."

"Alright," Brand said. "I can be there in half an hour."

"Fine. I'll meet you fifteen minutes after that."

"See you then," Brand said, and rang off.

"You have to go out?" Jennifer asked in faintly disappointed tones. She began to divide the dough into two loaves. "The bread'll be done inside of two hours."

Brand had a passion for fresh bread. "I shouldn't be any longer than that." He hated lying to her, but said, "One of the clients is having some difficulties."

"Couldn't it wait until tomorrow?"

"He says it's an emergency. Can you get the terrible twosome to bed okay?"

"I've done it before," she said pointedly. "Sometimes this evening work of yours gets on my nerves."

"Mine too," Brand said, and went upstairs to change his shirt.

The Mitex suite was in a relatively new tower block on Bismarckstrasse, a little way from Sophie-Charlotte-Platz. Brand let himself into the outer office and turned on the lights. Renate's desk, as usual, was excruciatingly neat; he regretted again that he was losing her. She was a superb organizer, and kept the noses of the two junior secretaries firmly to the grindstone. The other four staff, all Germans as well, trod warily in her presence, and kept their expense accounts accurate.

He went through the outer office and unlocked the door of his own. The lights were on, although turned low. Brand opened the safe, got the bug tracer out and did a careful sweep. Nothing. He had had trouble with bugs twice, in the first year, but had never been able to find out whether they had been installed for the previous tenants or for Mitex's benefit. He was almost sure that the devices had been intended for industrial espionage, rather than political, although the line dividing the two activities was increasingly hard to draw. In any case, whoever had put them there had apparently lost interest in Mitex's activities, probably because there were no technological secrets in the Berlin office to steal. Occasionally Brand wondered whether the bugs had been installed by the BND to monitor the goings-on of the newly arrived company.

He opened the rosewood cabinet that concealed the tape deck and the liquor supply, rewound the tape that was in the machine, and put it carefully away. According to the digital clock in the deck's fascia Kastner would be arriving within ten minutes. Brand poured himself a short scotch and sat down behind the desk to wait. His computer terminal stared glassily back at him, reflecting the track lighting and a corner of one of the two Miro reproductions on the facing wall. It was a luxurious room, appropriate to the European office of a high-technology American company. Brand, while he enjoyed the room, occasionally found it a little too opulent for his tastes. In some ways he had been more comfortable in the rains and dusts of Central America.

He sipped at his scotch and tapped idly at the computer's keyboard. Damn the machine. He would finally have to make a concerted effort to track down the software problem in the accounts files.

Kastner, he thought. What does he want to play back on my machine that he can't play back on one of his own? Brand knew the BND had its troubles with moles, but he hadn't thought Kastner would be so worried as to ask to play a BND tape on a CIA tape deck.

Unless, he thought suddenly, it's something so big Kastner's scared and wants some support out of left field.

Nonsense. He'd put his ass in a sling with Horstmann and with Pullach if he did that. Stop telling yourself spy stories, do some work.

He had just begun to chase the software fault when he heard a faint double tap on the door of the outer office. He halted the diagnostic program and went to let Kastner in. The lines in the German's face looked deeper than ever, dark patches under the eyes.

"Thanks," he said as Brand led the way to the inner office. "I didn't know if you'd agree to this."

"I almost didn't," Brand said. "Sorry. I'm not trying to tell you your business."

"I'm clean," Kastner said, extracting a flat square tape box from under his sport coat. And then, with some anger, "The East Bloc doesn't pay much attention to us in Berlin here anymore. They know we can't do much across the Wall, thanks to Pullach and Bonn."

"They're not letting you pull your weight," Brand said agreeably. He sensed again Kastner's annoyance that the CIA should be allowed to run an East Bloc agent under the noses of the BND, with the Germans having nothing to show for it but sanitized and out-of-date reports, and, very occasionally, a scrap of useful information or a warning. Pullach probably liked the arrangement even less, but somewhere up in the West German hierarchy American influence had so far prevailed.

If Rudel thinks the same way Kastner does, Brand thought, how long before the BND demands to take over CIA assets here? Langley must be worried. Losing its intelligence nets in West Germany, what a disaster, worse than Iran, even. Much worse.

Kastner sat down on the leather sofa facing Brand's desk and placed the box containing the tape on the cushions beside him, reluctantly, as if he wished he hadn't taken it from under his jacket. He glanced at the screen of Brand's terminal, where the amber diagnostic display still glowed. "Working?"

"Bugs," Brand said noncommitally. "Only in the accounting software, though. The offices are clean. I swept."

Kastner surveyed the office, the Miro paintings, the suede armchairs, the rosewood cabinets and desk, the heavy drapes isolating them from the lights of the Bismarckstrasse. "I must say your working conditions are better than mine," he said ruefully. He displayed a half-hearted grin and said, with an effort at irony, "Capitalist ostentation. Paid for by the sweat of the brows of the proletariat."

"Don't say that into a live microphone," Brand said, attempting to fit in with the mood. "Horstmann'd retire you early."

Instantly, seeing the German's expression, he realized he had said the wrong thing. "Erich," he said, "what's the matter?"

Kastner tapped the box lying on the pale suede beside him. "This," he said. "I want you to hear it."

Brand studied Kastner's pocked, lonely face. "Why?" he asked.

"You'll know when you hear it," Kastner said.

Brand said, "You know if you let me hear the tape, I may have to do something about it."

"Yes," said Kastner. "I know."

"Why, then?"

"Insurance."

"That bad?"

"Yes. Perhaps." A pause. "I might need your help, later on."

"Why?"

"As I said, you'll understand when you hear the tape. I don't want to risk what's on it being suppressed. And it might be. You know the troubles we've had in the BND."

"Are you saying," Brand asked carefully, "that you want my people to know about whatever this is?"

"That's right."

"Erich, the BND could hang you high for this."

"I've already thought about that. But if what's on the tape is true, and Pullach or Bonn won't act on it, somebody else has got to know. It would be disaster to pretend the situation doesn't exist." He paused, and said bluntly, "I work for Germany, not whatever party happens to be in power."

"Very well," Brand said, "I'll listen. How far do you want me to take the information?"

"Just do whatever you would normally. I only ask that your people not take any action unless it's requested."

"By whom?"

"Myself, perhaps. I also have a few friends in Pullach."

"You don't trust your superiors in this?"

"Not all of them" Kastner said. "If the rot's gone as far as the tape says, half the BND could be working for East Berlin." He extended the box to Brand. "We've talked enough. Listen."

Brand accepted the box gingerly, as though the tape inside might erase itself if he handled it too roughly. He loaded it onto the machine in the rosewood cabinet.

"You won't be able to hear the timeline on your deck," Kastner said. "It's encoded. The tape starts at about five-ten this afternoon."

Brand nodded, and pressed the button marked PLAY.

It was finally over. Brand stared at Kastner. "Jesus Christ," he said. "I see why you're so worried. I wish I hadn't heard the goddamned thing." He got up and poured whiskey for both of them.

"I wish Ewald hadn't turned up," Kastner said. "Anything but this." He studied Brand. "Who do you think it is?"

"It's not Rudel," Brand said. Instead of returning to the desk he sat down in one of the suede armchairs. Across the office from him the tape reel rewound itself, the brown mylar coil glinting dully under the track lighting. "An aide in the Foreign Ministry or the Bundeswehr?"

"I don't get that impression," Kastner said. "The implication is that whoever it is, is in a position to shape policy."

"The defense minister? Von Tebbe? That's hard to believe. He's been pressing for larger Bundeswehr appropriations ever since Rudel put him in the cabinet. Not the way an SSD person would behave."

"No. That leaves Diercks, the foreign minister. It's got to be one of those two, unless it's cabinet or parliamentary civil service."

"You don't think it's the civil service."

"No."

"Classic," Brand said grudgingly. "Have the enemy's foreign minister working for you. If the SSD's pulled that off, they deserve congratulations."

"And then a thumb in the eye," Kastner said, savagely. He stood up. "I have to go."

"What are you going to do?"

"I'm going to hold him at the safe house until I can speak to Horstmann. He'll want to fly Ewald to Pullach as soon as possible."

"You've got enough people?"

"A pair of ex-commandos, and a surveillance expert. They'll manage. Horstmann will give me more for the trip to the airport. He'll want to be on this jaunt himself."

Brand got up, dismounted the tape, and gave it back to Kastner. "What're you going to do down there?"

"I'm going to play the tape for the head of counter-intelligence, Anton Schell. If Horstmann will let me."

"You trust them?"

Kastner shrugged. "I have to start somewhere. I can't send Ewald back over the Wall." He was getting up, slipping the tape into its box.

"Good luck tomorrow," Brand said.

"Thanks," said Kastner. "I'll need it."

When he had seen the German into the corridor Brand went back to the inner office and the rosewood cabinet. He pressed the underside of the liquor shelf and an apparently solid panel flipped open. Inside was a small cassette tape recorder. Brand rewound the cassette and played the first ninety seconds. Kastner's voice was very clear. Brand went further into the tape. Ewald had also been clearly recorded. Brand ejected the cassette, replaced it with a blank one, and locked the recording in the office safe.

Washington
July 20

"IT'S AN APPROPRIATE DAY for it, anyway," said the thin tanned man sitting on the damask settee facing the president's desk in the Oval Office. His name was Blake Ormerod, and he was head of the Central Intelligence Agency. On his right, on the same settee, was Thatcher Martin, secretary of defense; in a chair to Ormerod's left slouched Secretary of State Chalmers.

"What?" Hood said absently from behind the desk. He was reading a file, the transcript of the conversation between Brand and Kastner in the office on the Bismarckstrasse.

"July twentieth," Ormerod said. "Anniversary of the bomb plot against Hitler in 1944. Von Stauffenberg did it. He nearly succeeded."

"Yes," said Hood. Unlike his predecessor, he knew what Ormerod was talking about. History and its convolutions had never been Reagan's strong suit. The irony was that Reagan's tremendous defense budgets had made the country, and even the Pentagon, feel so secure that Hood had been able to negotiate IALT agreements with the Russians; the treaty would have been unthinkable in Carter's day.

The old man did do something, Hood thought, squaring the file on the desk. Even if he scared the hell out of us while he was doing it. We got our confidence back. Risks.

"Stauffenberg's *nearly* wasn't good enough," he said. "Not in a situation like that." He prodded the transcript with his index finger. "We'd have to do better than that."

"I suppose you mean this is an opportunity to assassinate Rudel politically," Chalmers said to Ormerod. He arranged himself more comfortably in his chair; he was a very tall man and the low seat made him fold like a jackknife.

"It could be," Ormerod said. "If the allegations are true."

"Are they?" Hood asked. "If they are, who is it?"

"Diercks," said Ormerod. "It is definitely not the defense minister. He fits none of the profiles for an employee of the other side."

Chalmers scratched his chin. "Remember, out at Camp David?" he said to Hood. "When Diercks was there. He kept prodding, to see what we'd do if Bonn went off on its own. Maybe he wasn't asking just for Rudel."

"It could, of course," Ormerod pointed out, "be a Soviet disinformation ploy. Make it look as though Rudel's cabinet has a traitor in it, even if Diercks wouldn't give the SSD the time of day. It could be embarrassing enough to make Rudel resign. Brandt had to do that years ago, when they found that aide of his working for the East."

"Moscow would like that," muttered Thatcher Martin. He was the physical reverse of Chalmers: short and stocky, with a perpetually worried expression. "They can't stand Rudel over there. *Pravda*'s growled about him twice a month since the spring."

"You'd think they'd be ecstatic about West Germany pulling out of NATO," Hood said. He looked at Martin. "Any progress on getting Bonn to change its mind?"

"They're very polite," said the secretary for defense. "But we can't make a dent. Rudel's just as determined to get out of NATO as de Gaulle was back in the sixties. He wants us gone in four years."

"How in hell does he think he's going to stop the Russians from walking into the country whenever they feel like it?" Hood said irritably. "He must know Moscow would like to put an end to the Germans once and for all."

"Neutrality and strong conventional forces," Ormerod said. He gestured at a green file folder on Hood's desk. "Possibly also a mutual assistance treaty with the French. Support for their nuclear weapons program, for instance. That rumor's been floating around, but we haven't been able to determine yet whether or not Paris is seriously interested. They are playing it very close to the chest on that one." He stopped, looked at his shoes for a moment, and said, "The long and the short of it is that the Germans don't trust our defenses any more. They're looking for alternates."

"Rudel has to be hedging his bets on nuclear weapons," Thatcher Martin said. "They have to want some kind of option there, if the French won't cooperate. How long would it take them to build bombs?"

"A couple of years," Ormerod said. "If they put their minds to it."

"*That* would put the Russians' teeth on edge," Chalmers said. "Talks with Paris, the potential to make bombs. And you can bet Moscow knows whatever we know. Thanks to Diercks."

Hood broke in, tapping the transcript. "What are we going to do with this?"

Chalmers stretched his long legs out even farther and steepled his fingers. "Point one: Rudel's damaging the interests of this country, first by pulling out of NATO and then by upsetting the Russians. Like it or not, they still see Bonn as our ally, and I wouldn't put it past even someone as pragmatic as Nikolayev to think we put the Germans up to this. If that happens the IALT treaty will go down the drain, the Kremlin cancels the balanced force reduction talks, and we're back to the Cold War. If that happens the prospects for disengagement in Europe are worse than they've been since 1945, because when you come right down to it we can't really control Rudel, and he seems determined to get the Kremlin's back up. Point two: The Russians are still frightened of the Germans, and I think they see Rudel's behavior as as reversion to prewar patterns. Bonn having any access at all to nuclear weapons outside American control will give Nikolayev and his crew the cold sweats. Point three: Rudel's been very careful to avoid comments on German reunification, but Kohl was muttering about it a few years back when he was chancellor, and East Berlin didn't reject the idea as firmly as Moscow would have liked. Then there's the rapprochement we've been seeing over the last five years — loans from Bonn to Berlin, easing of travel restrictions between the two Germanies, trade agreements. Honecker hasn't been able to stretch Moscow's leash on him far enough for an official visit to Bonn yet, but that's probably coming. In short, the Kremlin's having a hard time keeping the lid on those kinds of developments. They're fighting history and political evolution, and it worries them. Nikolayev doesn't seem as worried as Chernenko was, but the winds can change pretty fast in the Kremlin. Any hint by Rudel that he was seriously going to promote German reunification would give even Nikolayev a case of jitters. Look at it all from his point of view: an independent, strongly armed West Germany, maybe with access to nuclear weapons, allied to the French perhaps, developing closer and closer ties with East Berlin, talking about reunification. Guaranteed to induce paranoia. Even more than the usual level." He stopped.

"That's three points," Hood said. "Is there a fourth?"

Chalmers straightened up in the chair and said, "Yes. Point four: It would be in our best interests, the Russians', and probably Europe's, if Rudel were no longer the German chancellor."

"And that," said Ormerod, indicating the transcript that lay under Hood's fingers, "is possibly a crowbar for prying him out of office. So to speak."

"Suppose we don't do anything?" suggested Hood. "Let Rudel go his merry way until the next German election. Or until the Diercks affair blows up in his face."

Thatcher Martin's expression became even more worried than normal. "I think that's extremely dangerous, from a defense point of view. The man in the street wouldn't guess it from the papers, but the DIA analysts think Europe's been sitting on a powder keg ever since Rudel took office. Whether the fuse is lit or not is open to question, because if anybody lights it it'll be Rudel or Nikolayev." The worried expression was replaced by one of gloom. "It looked so good, a few months ago, at Schoenbrunn. We finally had a breakthrough with Moscow. Now this."

"Accidents of history," Hood said. "They happen. Any way of pulling the fuse out of the keg?"

"The only immediate way is helping the Diercks affair along," Martin said. "Most of the options are on the Soviet side, and you can bet the Kremlin's already figured them out six ways from Sunday. If Rudel put a foot wrong, and if Nikolayev thought for a moment we weren't serious about going all the way in Europe, they'd have a perfect diplomatic and military scenario for overrunning West Germany. If their analysts aren't hashing that over right now, they're all asleep."

"War," said Hood. "European to start, maybe going all the way up." Jesus, he thought, and the Kremlin may read the IALT treaty and the MBFR talks as evidence we've lost our resolve. Goddamn Rudel.

"Maybe," said Martin.

"What about trade sanctions?" asked Hood. "Economic, military ones, anything to simmer Rudel down."

"Our biggest stick was always the military one," Chalmers said. "Rudel's told us to take it home. Trade and economic sanctions wouldn't do anything but screw up the West German economy and worry the other European governments, and we don't want that. For one thing it'd strengthen Rudel's nationalist card, and for another, whatever we think of Bonn, we don't want the West Germans weakened. Fundamentally the country's on the side of the West. But Rudel's endangering us all."

"Blake?" Hood asked.

"I have to agree with Thatcher," Ormerod said. "The Russians have done a couple of odd things, militarily, in the last two months. Sudden small-scale exercises, that sort of thing. We think they're pointed at Rudel. He hasn't paid any attention, as far as we can tell. On the other hand, the Soviets have been pulling out the SS20s, abiding by IALT I, and we're still talking in Geneva. It doesn't look as though they're planning anything drastic, but I think we'd better be on our guard."

"What about the standing start option?" asked Chalmers.

This was the favorite nightmare of NATO war plans staffs: a sudden Russian attack out of East Germany, using the twenty full-strength Soviet divisions stationed there, without any preparation other than the usual ones for routine Warsaw Pact exercises. These usually took place in August. Hood looked at his desk calendar, thinking about that day in 1944 when von Stauffenberg had tried to destroy Hitler to save what was left of Germany. And had failed.

"Can the Diercks affair make Rudel resign?" he asked.

"He'd *almost* have to," Ormerod said. "It'd be politically very bad news."

"But *will* it come out? And how long will it take to do so?" It's almost August, Hood thought. Nearly time for those exercises.

"That's the other problem," Ormerod said. "If a cabinet minister's working for the East, God knows who else is. West German intelligence, not to mention the rest of the NATO governments, are sieves when it comes to security. If it is Diercks, and he's got friends, the investigation could take months. The BND might not get him at all."

"Could we?"

Ormerod bit at a thumbnail. "We could help the BND along if it looked as though they were being stalled. Not noticeably, of course."

"How long can we wait for the BND to do something?" asked Hood. "Today's the twentieth."

"A week to ten days, at the outside. The Pact exercises will start in early August. They usually get into place around the twelfth."

"Alright," Hood said. "I'd like to give the Germans ten days. If nothing's going forward by then, we'll have to help it along." He looked at Ormerod. "Can you get set up in that time?"

"No problem."

"What about going up an additional NATO alert level?" asked Martin. "At the beginning of August. We could find some pretext. We normally take alerting precautions when the Pact exercises start."

"Nothing out of the ordinary," Hood said. "The Russians are probably worried enough as it is. It's a risk, but I think we need to take it."

"Okay."

"That's all, then," Hood said. "Let's keep our fingers crossed."

The others began to get up, except Chalmers. "Suppose," he asked suddenly, looking off somewhere in the direction of the tall windows of the Oval Office, "that the poor bastard's innocent. That the Kremlin's arranged all this?"

"If they have," Hood said tiredly, "we should accept it in the spirit with which it was offered. Rudel has got to go."

Bonn
July 22

IT WAS A DIFFERENT SAFE HOUSE, west of the Rhine this time, and in the evening as before. Diercks sat and worried, as he had before; one meeting with the Russian was bad enough, but a second was a courtship of disaster. What were they thinking of?

For the first time he was feeling doubt about the ability of his controllers. Decades of the least contact possible, and now this.

Diercks exhaled slowly, levered himself out of the armchair, and crossed to the curtained window (so much like the previous one), bumping his shin against the coffee table as he went. Although the summer evening sun was still strong, little of it filtered into the living room; the drapes were almost opaque.

KGB curtains, Diercks thought, studying their folds from a dozen centimeters away. No light through these. Who is out on the street? If anyone?

He had been told, as before, not to look out the window. He tilted his wrist so that the faint light illuminated the face of the Cartier watch. The Russian was late, very late.

To hell with them, Diercks thought. A glance, no more.

With great care he moved the right edge of the curtain away from the frame, opening a gap of less than a centimeter. Across the way the windows of the facing building were blank, empty. Down in the street, pulled up to the curb, were three parked cars: an Opel and two Volkswagens. A blond woman was pushing a baby carriage past one of the Volkswagens. Next to a lamp post, a few meters to the south of her, two young men were sitting on the curb, passing a bottle of beer back and forth. They were very dark, guest workers, Diercks thought, probably Turks. One of them said something to the woman pushing the baby carriage and she began to walk faster, staying as far away from the curb as she could manage.

Animals, Diercks thought. Rudel's doing one good thing, getting rid of the foreigners. Proletarian solidarity is all very well, but until they've been educated in Marx and Lenin they shouldn't be allowed to mix with us. They don't understand us, and it's bad for them, they're like children, they need teaching before they can become a useful part of the revolution. And until they're taught, they should stay at home.

The driver's door of the Opel was swinging open.

Diercks knew he should draw the curtain, but did not. How long has that car been down there? he wondered. He could not remember if it had been at the curbside when he arrived at the safe house.

A man got out of the Opel, locked it, and began to cross the street. It was Anton. Very slowly, Diercks let the curtain drift back to the windowframe.

When the Russian entered the flat, Diercks was sitting in the armchair, hoping the movement of the drapes had gone unnoticed. Again there was the Lufthansa bag, the check for listening devices, revealing nothing, and again Anton sat in the chair facing Diercks.

"Well," he said, and smiled.

Diercks was not mollified. "Well, what, Anton?" he snapped. His throat was so dry that his voice broke momentarily. "Why have you dragged me out again? Even to another house, doesn't Berlin know—"

Anton put up a hand. "Berlin knows very well it's dangerous," he said. "But it's very important. We need to know the result of Rudel's meeting with the French president. You haven't sent anything at all."

"There was nothing to send," Diercks said angrily, sitting straighter in the chair. "Except what I already have. Paris is interested in expanding its nuclear forces, and would like to explore the question of Franco-German cooperation further. That's as far as it's gone. If there had been anything more, I would have told you."

"Nothing?" Anton persisted. "No unofficial communications, not a thing? Nothing you might have" — a fractional pause — "overlooked?"

"Nothing, nothing at all." The Russian's tone carried an inflection that made the back of Diercks' neck tingle. "God in heaven, you don't think I'm lying, do you? You don't think I've been turned, do you? Where would you *get* such an idea?"

"No, no, nothing like that at all," Anton said hastily. "It's just that — well, there are questions being asked. You were to ensure that policies like Rudel's were never executed, and here they are being carried out. I'm on your side, I know where your loyalties are. But people who haven't met you, the bureaucrats back there — you know how they can be."

"There's no question about my loyalties," Diercks said hotly. "They've always been to Berlin. And the Soviet Union."

"Of course, yes, that's always been assumed. Herr Raus," Anton went on weightily, "you've served the SSD and the KGB well for many years. That can't be forgotten. We just want more hard material."

"That's not what you said last time, Anton."

"Last time Rudel didn't have the bit between his teeth. Now we need more explicit action."

"What?"

"Tomorrow, when you go back to work, I'd like you to make one copy of all the *in camera* cabinet meetings for the past two weeks, particularly anything concerning the French. Don't do anything with the copies after you've made them, just put them in a safe place. We'll be in touch as to how to move them."

"Copies of everything? Do you know how much *paper* that is?"

"Well, use your judgment. Obviously we're not interested in anything that'll be made public soon. But anything referring to the French, include."

"Alright," Diercks said with resignation, "I'll do it." I suppose I could keep it in the safe at home, he thought. For that length of time. Call them working papers, if the worst came.

"Fine." Anton was zipping the Lufthansa bag, standing up. "Leave in about ten minutes. You're quite secure."

"Good," Diercks said. "Pardon me for saying so, but I hope I don't see you again soon."

"I hope not too," said Anton.

Across the street, behind the curtains of a second-story window facing the HVA safehouse, the man running the BND surveillance team said, without removing his eye from the camera viewfinder, "The control's coming out."

The camera with its long lens had been strategically placed just behind an irregular tear in the drapes. The drapes were a dull burgundy color, not lined; the tear was very difficult to see from the outside. There was always a risk of reflection off the lens, so the camera was kept well back in the room unless needed; there was a lens hood to block reflections, but it was preferable not to take chances.

"Spotted," said a voice in his earphone. The Mercedes camera van was parked half a block to the north. A battered and heavily curtained Volkswagen camper sat an equal distance southward.

"How were the pictures?" said the man in the apartment.

"Good. Very good." The scrambling on the radiotelephone made the voice tinny and muffled at the same time; the watcher in the Mercedes sounded as though she were at the other end of a poor long-distance link.

"That'll do, then," said the man in the apartment. "Don't follow him, the photos may give us the make. Wait for the other one. "

"Yes."

"Couldn't get bugger-all through those curtains over there," said the other man in the apartment, after a few minutes' silence. He had possession of his own tear in the drapes, and was peering through a lowlight camera, adjusting its focus on the front step of the SSD house. The man in charge of the team refocused a little, to sharpen up the image of the front door.

"He's been had cold, anyway," said the tape technician. "If he makes those copies, he's cut his throat."

"Anybody recognize him?" asked the man in charge.

"Which one?"

"The sloppy one. The one who opened the curtains."

"No. He kept his hat down when he went in. Couldn't get a clear sight. The mobile cameras probably got a better one, he was on their level."

The man in charge considered calling one of the mobile units for a tentative identification, but decided against it. They'd know soon enough, anyway.

"He's pretty high up," said the tape technician. "To be able to talk that way. *In camera* cabinet minutes, my God."

For a moment the three of them contemplated what they were doing. Then the man with the low-light camera said, "Another fucking scandal. These politicals ought to be investigated back to their grandmother's navels and if they don't come out clean they should be chucked. How could an asshole like this get away with it for so long? We need the whole government cleaned up."

"Why don't you express your opinions to Chancellor Rudel personally?" the man in charge said, with more than a trace of acid. "I'm sure he'd agree with them."

"You wait," said the cameraman. "Give him a chance, he'll clean things out."

"Smarten up," said the tape technician. "This is the Federal Republic, not Weimar."

They had been in the flat with little to eat or drink for eighteen hours, and they were all irritable. The normal political differences among the three men had been accentuated under the stress; the technician a democrat to the core, with a shading of idealism left; the man in charge twelve years older, cynical but despite himself rather frightened by the treason that had flowed into the tapes; and the cameraman, somewhere between the other two in age, convinced that Rudel could drive back the sea.

"What's the matter?" asked the cameraman. "You got a Turkish girlfriend?"

"Piss off," said the technician. "Look smart. He's moving."

The audio monitor carried the sound of footsteps, receding from the couch in the living room across the street. A click, then another one: the apartment door opening and closing. There was a silence in the monitor, that of an empty room.

"Anytime now," said the technician. He had carefully noted the number of seconds required to go up or down stairs in the HVA building.

"Front door's opening," said the man in charge. "Good. He's left his hat off." He began clicking the shutter, vaguely aware of the buzz of the lowlight camera off to his left.

"He's moving off on foot," said the Volkswagen mobile. "Got a good frame, but he keeps putting his hand in front of his face."

"Keep taping," said the man in charge. "He's just worried." Christ, it can't be, he thought. "Alpha, follow him. But carefully. Lose him rather than scare him." He tracked the camera right, following the target's back, the lens pushing against the tear in the drapes.

"Going to lose him," he said. "The film is almost gone anyway. I've got enough, though." He turned away from the viewfinder. "That shit," he said.

"What?" said the tape technician.

"That," said the man in charge, "was our revered foreign minister, Franz Diercks."

A short silence. Then the technician said, "Are you sure?"

"Wait," said the man in charge. He pressed a button on the communications console. "Beta. Did you get him?"

A pause. "Yes. He went right by. The tape's good."

"Who was it?"

Another pause. Then: "It looked like Minister Diercks."

"Don't use that name again," said the man in charge. "Not even scrambled. Pick up on Alpha, but no scares. Just track him to his next destination."

"Repeat, please?" The scrambler circuits were buzzing with some kind of interference.

The man in charge said it again and got an acknowledgment. "Crap," he said. "The miracles of modern technology. We can hardly hear each other." He started putting his shoes on, getting ready to leave. Looking up from a knot, he noticed that the tape technician was studying his machinery, wearing a troubled expression. He tugged futilely at the knot and said, "What's the matter?"

"I don't like it," the technician said. "That Russian swept the whole apartment. I know these bugs are good, but . . . that machine of his didn't sound like it was doing anything. As though it were dead. Bad batteries, or something."

"That stuff isn't supposed to be found by sweeps," said the man in charge, defeating the knot and beginning to tie the shoe. I really ought to polish these things, he thought. He looked up again. "Are you sure he swept?"

"Yes," the technician said. "We always get an indication when there's a sweep. But this time it was just a few beeps and pops, nothing regular, not like a real sweep signature."

"Maybe his stuff wasn't working properly. Be thankful for small mercies. We've got tapes and pictures, that's all we need."

"Yes," the technician said. He sounded faintly doubtful.

"Just stay put," said the man in charge. "I've got to see some people."

Bonn
July 24

A STONE'S THROW AWAY from the pedestrian precincts of the old city, in the grounds of the Villa Hammerschmidt, Hans Stahl, the president of the Federal Republic, was hosting a garden party. Above the lawns and flowering shrubs, the white facade of the president's official residence rose in austere grace towards a threatening sky: tall arched windows, delicate cornices, long balustrades, a porch whose roof floated on the capitals of Doric and Corinthian columns. Perhaps twenty meters from the foot of the porch steps, to the other side of the gravelled drive, a marquee had been erected. Stahl's guests, a hundred or so of them, had formed several clumps, one on the porch steps, another on the porch itself under the portico, the third orbiting the marquee, and the fourth, which had discovered the bar, inside the marquee itself.

Rudel was with the group under the portico, talking with the cultural attaché from the French embassy. He had only half an ear for the woman's words; he was much less interested in French cultural exports than he was in Paris' response to his suggestion for nuclear-weapons cooperation. Moreover, he was decidedly worried about the political crisis stalking him in the shape of Foreign Minister Franz Diercks, who was standing by the marquee with a drink in his hand, the perfection of innocence. A few meters away from Rudel, President Stahl himself was holding court with a clutch of diplomats; although his office was almost purely a ceremonial one, the Bundespraesident carried a considerable amount of unofficial weight in Bonn, and cultivating him could do no one any harm.

"—would be of great benefit, both to Paris and to Bonn," the Frenchwoman was saying. She spoke German with an annoying burble, as though through soft mud. Rudel produced an expression of interest, looking past her shoulder across the lawn. In a few minutes he would know. He noticed the tall blond American trade secretary again, hovering a few meters away from Diercks, as Washington's people were always doing these days, hoping to pry a little more information out of the foreign minister.

The Frenchwoman had stopped talking. Rudel jerked his attention back to her face: patrician, overtanned, expectant. She wanted a response to whatever she had been saying. He looked out at the lawn again, wondering what that had been.

Beyond the columns at the far corner of the porch he saw them, dressed in dark gray suits, not out of place, but not belonging, either. Like a pair of prostitutes at a wedding, he thought. "Excuse me," he said to the Frenchwoman. "Could we continue in a few minutes? I have some boring but unavoidable business."

He barely noticed her answer as he turned and walked unhurriedly down the steps onto the gravelled drive, smiling at Stahl as he passed. Somewhere behind him he sensed the presence of his bodyguards, a necessity he disliked, but endured. The guards maintained a careful six meters' separation as he left the drive and walked slowly towards the marquee and the two men waiting a little way to its east, under one of the oaks that dotted the lawn. Eyes followed him, including Stahl's, but no one approached: Rudel was known to value his privacy. A few meters away from the pair Rudel gestured for his bodyguards to wait behind.

The two intruders were clearly uncomfortable. Wolfgang Bach, the head of the BND, rarely had personal contact with the chancellor, and never in a social setting. The other man, Staatsminister Helmut Kempf, was in charge of the Chancellor's Office, and was official watchdog over the BND.

"Well?" Rudel said to Kempf. "I hope you're going to tell me there was nothing to this."

Kempf grimaced and passed a hand through his short graying hair. "I wish I could, Chancellor. But there's no doubt any more. Unfortunately for all concerned."

"Yes," said Rudel. He felt a moment of corroding despair, then drove it back. "Go over it for me, exactly what happened. There may be an explanation."

"Wolfgang," Kempf said. "You've got the details."

"I'll try to be brief, Chancellor," said Bach. "I gather you've already been informed of the allegations made by the SSD defector in Berlin, named Ewald?"

"Yes."

"About two weeks before the defection," Bach said, "we spotted an HVA safe house. They were very careless, but we didn't want to look a gift horse in the mouth, so we put in monitors. We were just about to give up on the place — nothing had happened, and we thought they'd detected us — when they opened the house up again. We don't know who the first man was, we're still working on an identification."

"That was two days ago," put in Kempf. Rudel nodded.

"We put in a full team immediately," Bach went on. "Then . . . Minister Diercks entered the safe house. A little while later another man arrived, and they had a conversation."

"The tape you played me last night," Rudel said to Kempf. Kempf inclined his head, as though reluctant to admit it. "Go on," Rudel said to Bach.

"Diercks referred to the contact, twice, as Anton. His name is actually Dmitri Alexeyevitch Klimanov. He's one of the economic staff at the Soviet embassy, been here for several years, but until now we thought he was one of the few embassy personnel who was what the diplomatic list said he was. He has never engaged in anything untoward at all, but the photos from outside the safe house were positive identification."

"And Minister Diercks promised to give Klimanov copies of minutes of the secret cabinet meetings," said Rudel, without expression.

"Yes," Bach said. "The voiceprint on the tape is the minister's. And there is film of him leaving the safe house. If the Chancellor wishes to see the film—"

"No," Rudel snapped. "The tape was quite enough. Did he

provide the minutes as the Russian requested?" He put out a hand and rested it on the trunk of the oak tree, the old bark rough and dry under his palm.

"Not yet. He hasn't made any contacts with the Russian, and has not appeared to use a dead drop or a brush contact. The copied documents are either at his home or still in his office. To be sure we would have to have authorization to search those places." He paused. "That sort of authorization is difficult to obtain."

"Yes," Rudel said. And then: "How sure are you?"

"Very," said Kempf. "I wish we were not, but we are."

"Wait," Rudel said. He turned and walked across the green lawn towards the marquee. A few spatters of rain flicked at his cheeks; President Stahl and his corona of guests were beginning to move into shelter.

Just inside the marquee he found Diercks, talking at great speed to the Danish ambassador. Rudel touched Diercks' arm. The foreign minister looked around, smiling.

"Excuse me," Diercks said to the Dane. "I'll rejoin you."

"Refill your glass," Rudel suggested to Diercks. "This might take a little while."

He waited while the foreign minister made his way to the bar, thinking, I have waited so long, and now this fool may bring ruin on my head. Possibly, though, I can weather it. What was he thinking of, to be caught like this?

"You won't have a glass?" Diercks asked, rejoining him.

"Not just now. Come outside with me."

They walked around to the back of the marquee. The spatters of rain had ceased, leaving in the air a heavy moist stillness. "Yes?" Diercks said expectantly.

"Franz," Rudel said gently, "We know about it now. You, and Anton, and the safe house. You can stop pretending."

From the shelter of the oak tree Bach and Kempf watched as the foreign minister emptied his glass, handed it to Rudel, and began to walk towards them.

Approximately one hour later, the head of the CIA station in Bonn received a telephone call in his office at the United States embassy. The call was placed by the blond trade secretary, who had only just managed to excuse himself from President Stahl's garden party.

"Anything?" asked the station chief.

"The gentleman had to leave abruptly. I don't think he'll be back."

"That's too bad," said the station chief. "That really messes life up. Alright. Check in as soon as you can. There's some other contingencies riding on this."

"Okay."

The station chief sighed, pressed down the receiver cradle, and began dialing the number of a prominent freelance journalist.

West Berlin
July 27

"IT LOOKS AS THOUGH you didn't need to worry," Brand said. "They didn't waste any time at all."

"It went like shit through a goose," Kastner agreed. The two men were in the BND Opel, rolling through the streets of the Charlottenberg District. It was ten in the evening.

"What did they say after you got Ewald to Pullach?"

"Not much. Horstmann turned him over to Schell. Schell didn't look happy to see us."

"No wonder, dropping that load on his plate." Brand steadied himself, one hand on the Opel's dash, as Kastner braked viciously for a red light. "Are you worried about something?" he asked the German suddenly.

"It was *too* damned quick, for my money," Kastner said. "We must have nailed Diercks good and proper, almost as soon as Ewald started spilling his guts in Pullach. That means Diercks put a foot wrong. Now, I ask you, if he's been happily tunnelling away in our garden for the past God knows how many years, without anybody so much as looking at him sideways, how come he got so careless all of a sudden?" Kastner engaged the clutch with a jerk. "Immediately after Ewald drops over the Wall with a sackful of goodies. I'd have been happier if it had taken a couple of months to catch Diercks with his fingers in the till, the way it usually does."

"You do get coincidences in this business," Brand pointed out. "Real ones."

"I suppose," Kastner said. He slowed the Opel for a right turn into Gatowerstrasse. "You notice," he said, "the press didn't waste any time, either. The stuff they printed they didn't get from Bach, I can tell you."

Brand looked down at Kastner's copy of *Berliner Morgenpost* lying on the seat between them. A streetlamp cast a fleeting band of light over the headlines:

FOREIGN MINISTER DIERCKS ARRESTED ON
SUSPICION OF ESPIONAGE: WAS LEAKING
CABINET SECRETS TO EAST, SOURCES ALLEGE

"I wonder exactly who those sources were?" Brand said.

"God knows. Your people in Bonn, the Russians, the SSD, somebody working for any of them in the BND. Maybe even Washington." Kastner paused significantly; Brand didn't respond. Kastner was not so naive as to think Brand wouldn't have passed the information along, but neither of them wanted to pursue the implications of that.

"Anyway, we'll never find out," Kastner went on. The Opel's engine misfired, coughed twice, and then resumed its mutter. "Dammit," the German said. "This thing needs new plugs. You don't suppose," he continued, "that somebody on the other side of the Wall *wanted* this to happen? They're making the usual diplomatic row, but they would anyway, to keep up appearances."

"You mean Diercks is innocent and they set him up?"

"No, not that. I mean Diercks is guilty, *and* they set him up. They threw one of their best to the wolves, to force Rudel to resign. Willy Brandt, all over again. Rudel's going to have his hands full in the Bundestag tomorrow. It might work."

"The thought had occurred to me," Brand said. It had also occurred to him that Moscow and Washington were united, for once, in their attitude to the German chancellor, although for different reasons. "But the SSD and the KGB don't usually work like that. They try to take care of their own. They'd have to be desperate."

"Hell," Kastner said. "I don't know. Either they did or they didn't. Either way it's the same for Rudel."

"Could be," Brand said.

"Anyway," Kastner said, "what I wanted to see you about, apart from the routine stuff earlier, was this. Could you just pretend you never heard that tape? I suppose I panicked. Tell your people everything's under control. No, don't tell them, they already know. Thanks anyway."

"No problem," Brand said. "Maybe someday I'll need you to pull my chestnuts out of the fire."

"For your sake I hope not," Kastner said. "I'll take you back to your car."

As the brown Opel slowed for a turn into a sidestreet, the man in the blue Volkswagen behind it eased back on the accelerator to maintain his discreet sixty meters' separation. He was an expert; he had several times chanced losing the Opel rather than risk detection, but the night helped. And the BND man didn't seem suspicious, not the way he had the previous week. That meant the defector was out of the city, and nobody even now had any idea of where he had been kept while he was still in West Berlin. Like it or not, the BND safe house was still safe. The surveillance would likely be dropped in a day or two: too little profit for too much risk.

The Volkswagen, following the Opel, turned into the sidestreet.

"Shit," said the driver. The BND car was stopped not twenty meters ahead, with Kastner's passenger getting out of it. There was no option but to drive by at a good clip and hope the Volkswagen attracted no undue attention. The Opel slipped by on the right, dome light on. Good, harder for them to see out.

At the next intersection the driver slowed and looked in the rearview mirror. Kastner's passenger was out of the car now, walking towards the intersection in the pool of light from a streetlamp. The Opel stood motionless at the curb.

The driver of the Volkswagen made a quick decision. Kastner was likely going to go home, and there wasn't much point in following him just to see that. His companion, however . . . the German had never picked up a passenger before.

He turned right, coasted into a puddle of darkness by the

curb, turned off the engine and lights, and waited. Kastner had collected his passenger from the sidewalk a couple of blocks to the east; with luck and human nature he'd have dropped him closer to his car than that.

A minute later the Opel rolled straight through the intersection, northbound. Moments after that Kastner's passenger left the sidestreet, crossed the road, turned right, and walked sixty meters past the yellow-lit windows of the drab postwar apartments to a silver BMW. A few seconds later the car's headlights came on and the BMW pulled out into the street, momentarily blinding the man in the Volkswagen. He turned his head away as the BMW passed and then, fumbling to get the top off his pen, twisted to look at its rear license plate. He freed the pen and scribbled the license number on the top margin of his newspaper. Then he sat for a moment, considering: follow the BMW or go to Kastner's apartment block?

He was supposed to be watching Kastner. They could find out who the driver was from the license number. Deciding, he started the Volkswagen and set out for the BND man's home.

THE NEW YORK TIMES
West German Chancellor Refuses to Resign in Espionage Scandal

BONN, July 29 (UPI) — West German Chancellor Ernst Rudel announced today that he would not resign from the government in the wake of the espionage scandal which erupted last week with arrest of the West German Foreign Minister, Franz Diercks. While details of the case have not been released, sources close to the government allege that Diercks, a longtime ally of Rudel in the Christian Socialist Party, was an agent of East German intelligence. As a cabinet minister, Diercks had access to high-level information about the political and military affairs of both West Germany and other NATO governments.

In Washington, a State Department spokesman refused comment, stating that while the White House and Pentagon were concerned about potential damage to NATO security, charges against Diercks were purely an internal matter for the German government. It is the most serious espionage scandal in West Germany since the arrest in 1974 of a senior aide to then chancellor Willy Brandt, which later resulted in Brandt's resignation.

Moscow
July 29

"So," NIKOLAYEV SAID, in a voice heavy with fatigue and depression, "it didn't work. We have lost one of our best people, to no good end."

"Rudel may yet have to resign," said Foreign Minister Kamenev. No one around the long table in the Politburo conference room appeared particularly convinced by his remark.

"I don't think he's going to," said KGB Chairman Minkov. He glanced at the defense minister. "How long do we have before must decide irrevocably on military action?"

"Not long," answered Fedashkin. "We have to choose one way or the other before midnight August 14. After that the exercises will have moved the forward echelon away from the optimum startlines. Deciding to go ahead after that will cause severe movement difficulties. Prohibitive ones, in the view of the General Staff."

"We have three options," Ivanov said impatiently. "First, to do nothing and accept the long-term decline of our strength and the eventual breakup of the Warsaw Pact. Second, to execute Barbarossa Red with an excellent chance of success. Third, attempt to dispose of Rudel physically. I can see no other paths open to us. Can anyone else?"

A long silence, which was broken by Nikolayev. "Assassination of a foreign head of state is not an activity we want to be known for. There would be all kinds of repercussions. And reprisals."

"There are enough disaffected groups in West Germany to deflect any suspicion," Minkov pointed out. "Even if a group which carried out such an operation were linked to our foreign activities, we could plausibly deny that we endorsed or suggested such an atrocity." He paused. "I also have reports which show that the Americans are just as angry with Rudel as we are. The First Directorate is certain the Americans leaked the news of Diercks' arrest to the press, in far more detail than Bonn or the BND would have liked." He gave a brief ironic smile. "We were about to do the same, but the Americans saved us the trouble."

"Have *they* got a cabinet minister in their pocket as well?" asked Kamenev, with a trace of acidity.

Minkov looked thoughtful. "Not as far as we can tell. But we *are* trying to find out how they discovered so much so fast. A high level CIA informant in the BND, most likely. The fact remains that Washington might not be too displeased if Rudel abruptly exited the international scene. They would make loud public noises, of course, as we would, but the tone behind closed doors in the State Department and the Pentagon would be rather different."

Nikolayev emitted a sigh which was audible only to himself. Rudel's refusal to resign had been infuriating; it could do nothing but strengthen Ivanov and the neo-Stalinist faction, a faction which was beginning to exert more and more influence on those who had so far supported Nikolayev. It was like stepping into quicksand; once you started to sink, you were likely going to go all the way down, unless someone threw you a rope. But anyone doing so risked being dragged down himself; most thought twice before inviting political oblivion. Nikolayev would in fact have preferred to wait, in the hope that domestic and foreign pressure would force Rudel's resignation after all, but if that failed to happen, and if the deadline for military intervention had passed, he could be finished as general secretary. Pensioned off to a fourth-rate dacha somewhere on the Crimean coast, at best. Not that, never that; he had grown too used to power.

"Is the mechanism in place for such an attempt?" he asked Minkov.

"Yes. We can put it into effect within a week, with minimal risk to ourselves."

Now that he had made the decision, Nikolayev felt a wash of relief. No Rudel, no pressure for war. That would disappoint Ivanov, probably Minkov and several of the others as well. Fedashkin remained an enigma. The defense minister, while obviously willing to carry out the attack in the west, had so far shown no particular enthusiasm for it beyond what his position and rank demanded.

"It's a drastic option," said Nikolayev, "but if it averts the need for military intervention, I believe it to be justified."

Within five minutes Minkov had the authority to proceed with the operation, which for reasons known only to himself he had codenamed PRIMROSE.

Bonn
August 6

THE METAL SHADE of the terrace lamp was somewhat corroded, which made the bolts securing it to its mounting difficult to turn. After two or three minutes of careful effort — he did not want to strip the bolt threads or shear the heads off — the man in the coveralls managed to loosen the shade and slide it off the retaining stem. He was setting the shade carefully on the tool platform of his stepladder when a voice below and behind him said:

"What're you doing up there?"

The repairman half turned and looked down. Staring up at him was a broad meaty face adorned with an unfashionably short haircut.

One of Rudel's security people, the man on the ladder thought. "Changing the bulb," he said. "It's shot."

"Let's see your work order and identification."

The repairman fumbled in his coveralls and presented his clearance card. "The work order's in the toolbox," he said. "You find it, I'm busy."

The crewcut security officer allowed himself an expression of irritation, and then rummaged in the green metal box at the foot of the ladder. Eventually he unearthed a smudged rectangle of paper, which he read carefully. Then he dropped it pointedly on the paving beside the toolbox. Luckily there was no wind. "You going to be long?"

"Fifteen minutes," said the man on the ladder.

"Make it ten," said the security officer. "We'll be clearing the plaza."

"Alright." Bugger off, the repairman thought.

The security man hesitated and then stalked away along the plaza towards the flight of wide shallow steps leading down to the concourse along Streseman Boulevard. Beyond the boulevard and the river wall the Rhine flowed intense blue-green in the morning sun. Above the plaza where the repairman worked on his ladder, the long rear facade of the Bundeshaus, the Parliament Building of West Germany, rose austere and white, its disciplined rows of windows reflecting the sunlight back into the east.

The repairman glanced over his shoulder; the security officer was disappearing at the bottom of the plaza. They'd be clearing the river approaches to the Bundeshaus in a few minutes, just before Rudel came.

The repairman removed the big frosted glass bowl from the lamp base and unscrewed the bulb, which was perfectly good. He then reached inside his coveralls and removed a packet wrapped in brown paper. The packet was crescent-shaped, about twenty-five centimeters across the horns, and ten centimeters thick. Inside the waxed paper, fixed on the outer rim of the explosive which formed the bulk of the crescent, was a band made up of scores of small steel darts. Sunk in the inner curve of the crescent was a small radio receiver wired to an electrical detonator. When the detonator was triggered by a signal from a remote transmitter the exploding crescent would form a blade of superheated gas and steel flechettes slashing across the plaza, lethal out to a range of fifty meters. The crescent did, however, have to be positioned so that the plane of the explosion was a meter and a half above the pavement where the plaza steps leading to the concourse began. This took the repairman perhaps three minutes and the help of a small template and spirit level, and a couple of lumps of modelling clay. When he had adjusted the mine to his satisfaction he replaced the glass bowl of the lamp, fitting it carefully over the crescent of explosive, and then bolted the metal shade back onto its bracket. The bulb he slipped into his coveralls.

At the bottom of the ladder he paused for a moment to

survey his handiwork, and then folded up the ladder and closed the toolbox. After lighting a cigarette he picked up the box and the ladder and walked north to a small stand of poplars decorating the northeastern corner of the Bundeshaus. Out on the Rhine, across the midmorning traffic of Streseman Boulevard, a large motor launch with a high pilothouse was proceeding south, at no more than a walking pace. The repairman put his ladder and toolbox on the grass, extracted a small black plastic box from his coveralls, and clicked a button on it twice. After a moment a light gleamed briefly, no more than a reflection off bright metal, from the launch. He nodded, satisfied, collected his ladder and toolbox, and walked down to the boulevard.

Rudel was tired. He slumped in the rear seat of the Mercedes, watching the Rhine slide by the window. He wished he could spend an hour just walking along the river wall alone. But he could not; he was chancellor of Germany, and it was too dangerous.

Franz, Franz, he thought, watching the river with its tugs and barges and long pleasure craft, Franz, you idiot. Now I have to clean up after you. We can keep our majority by an edge, if nothing goes wrong this morning. If it does, we'll be licking the boots of the Americans again. But I won't have to put up with it. I'll be gone.

The Mercedes and its motorcycle escort were drawing up at the curb in front of the Rhine facade of the Bundeshaus. A dozen plainclothes security men hovered anxiously among the potted trees and the flowerbeds, watching.

One of the security detail was opening the Mercedes' door. Rudel got slowly out of the car. We could be great again, he thought. Not in the old way, but strong and unified, the central power of Western Europe, perhaps someday of all Europe. There has to be reunification; if we don't move toward it soon it will go glimmering, like so many other lost chances.

The plaza with its rows of lamp standards was just above him. Two security guards preceded him up the stairs. Two followed him.

Halfway up he slipped and stumbled, falling heavily to his

knees. One of the guards behind him bent down and grasped his arm.

Out on the Rhine, in the motor launch with the high pilot-house, the man looking through the fieldglasses said, "Now." His companion at the chart table pressed a white button in the center of a brown metal box.

The mine in the lamp exploded.

Munich - Washington - Berlin
August 7

THE BEER HALL in Neuhauserstrasse was packed with bodies, sweltering, and so smoky that from its rear tables the three-meter wide television projection screen seemed to hang suspended in a blue haze. The hall was abnormally quiet except for the amplified voice booming from the tall speakers below the projection screen. The chancellor was finishing his speech.

"As I mentioned when I began," Rudel's image said to the ranks of laborers, silent at the long tables, "I am very fortunate to be able to speak to you tonight." He gave the trace of a smile. "It seems that a small stumble is not always a bad thing. If I had not slipped on the steps of the Bundeshaus, you would be hearing my obituary, not me."

The smile vanished. "I am speaking to you now," he said, "to tell you that I am perfectly well, and to tell you that I shall continue to carry out the responsibilities of the chancellorship as I always have. The misguided ones among us who carried out this attack *will* be found, and when they are they will be given all the rights to which they are entitled under German law, no matter whether they came from, West or East. But we should remember that, if such people as these were ever to come to power, they would make haste to deprive us all of those same protections. They take advantage, willingly, of our commitment to freedom and the rule of law, intending to destroy both. Expecting mercy for themselves, they would offer none to others." Rudel's face had become somber. The audience sat transfixed; cigarettes burned themselves away in the tin ashtrays, the tendrils of smoke ascending into the dimness above.

"That is one thing we must not forget," Rudel said, after a fractional pause, "no matter how such people hide their desires behind slogans and ideology. *This* Germany is free, and will remain so, if we remember what we once were and what we can become again." He smiled. "And now I must leave you. Good night, and sleep well."

The screen faded to black. There was a momentary silence. Into it, a voice shouted in the accents of Prussia, "*Deutschland erwache!* "

"When you think about it," Secretary of State Chalmers said, "it's surprising nobody's taken a shot at him before this. He's made more than enough enemies in the lunatic fringe."

"Is there any possibility the Russians were behind it?" asked Hood, from behind the great Oval Office desk. He looked at the CIA director.

"It's always possible," said Blake Ormerod. "But there's absolutely nothing to go on so far, no group's claimed any responsibility. Interpol's suggesting a foreign worker organization linked to the West German extreme left. If there's a connection to the Kremlin, nobody's going to be able to prove it. We've got nothing at all."

"You know what this is going to do," Chalmers said, as though stating the last line of a logical proposition. "Remember how Reagan's popularity shot up after what's-his-name tried to kill him? It'll have the same effect for Rudel. He took a beating after the Diercks business. This will put him right back on top. In Germany, at least."

"In Germany, maybe," Ormerod said. "We all know what people in other places will be thinking."

"What?" asked Hood. "Enlighten us."

"It's too bad he slipped," Ormerod said.

Lotte von Veltheim lay on the beige corduroy sofa in the second-floor sitting room, the back of one hand resting across her eyes.

Although it was still early evening, she had closed the curtains and turned on the lamps so that the room looked as it had when Rudel had last been there, except that the fireplace now contained only a heap of soft gray ash. The sitting room was Lotte's private retreat; the cleaning staff did not enter it.

She was still sick and dizzy over the news from Bonn. So close, it had been so close. If he had not slipped on the Bundestag steps . . .

She put the thought away and sat up on the couch, elbows on knees, chin on her clasped hands. It had not, after all, happened; she would not have to face the aftermath. He was still alive, very much so; when she had telephoned him in midafternoon after his television appearance he had sounded elated, almost euphoric, as though he had escaped death by some providential dispensation.

If Bismarck hadn't taken the title for other reasons, she thought, history might remember him as the Iron Chancellor. Indestructible, or nearly so.

Whatever group had attempted Rudel's killing had not identified itself, but the press was speculating on a connection between the radical Left and a hypothetical Turkish extremist organization. That did, indeed, make more sense than anything else. On the other hand . . .

Not the Russians, she thought. It could not possibly be them. No matter what factions are at each others' throats in the Kremlin. This is the one thing they would not do. It would cost them too much.

The nausea would not go away. She dragged herself off the couch and walked to the fireplace, looking up at the old photograph of the Berlin garrison above it. Her head barely reached the mantelpiece. How I used to wish I were tall, she thought. And beautiful. Back then. Would it have made any difference? Not to be imprisoned in this short dumpy body, with this mind? Not mayor of West Berlin, perhaps, but a housewife, out there somewhere in Reinickendorf or Wedding or in the West, two or three children, a husband in an office or a factory, all those things?

"Old," she said, to the images of the young men so long

gone under the earth, or to the clock ticking softly on the mantel. "Too old now, anyway."

I cannot ever remember feeling like this, she thought, turning away from the fireplace. So sick of it, and so tired, finally, of it all: the compromises, the betrayals, the manipulation, the endless vigilance, never able to rest, always an adversary for tomorrow. All to serve Germany, I told myself thirty years ago, when I was strong enough not to think. A lie. It was power I wanted, because I could have nothing else with this body and this mind. Power, that sweet addiction, that snare. Betraying me. How I've paid for it, for my pride in my ability, for my professionalism, like Hitler's generals. How I wish I could escape.

And Ernst, what is he doing? And why, so quickly? He frightens me, now. What would have happened if they'd killed him? Would I have been expected to carry on with his plans? I had no idea they'd gone so far.

But I helped him become what he is, the German chancellor. Whatever happens, I cannot call myself innocent.

How I wish I were innocent again.

She stood in the center of the room, in the warm light of the lamps, and wept for the first time in thirty years.

Moscow Military District
Maneuver Area
August 7

THE MIL-3 LIAISON HELICOPTER flared for its landing just to the west of a low hill, the downblast of its rotors thrashing up plumes of dust and vegetation from the dry tawny thatch of grass and weeds. Defense Minister Fedashkin sweltered under the helicopter's canopy; beads of perspiration tickled his hair and skin underneath the earphones. As the rotors slowed he gratefully detached the headset, wiped the back of his neck with his hand, and levered himself out of the seat. One of the Mil-3's crew was opening the fuselage door; Fedashkin scrambled out of the machine, feeling the last of the downwash as a cooling breeze across his face. A colonel wearing Guards insignia was waiting for him just outside the diameter of the rotor blades. Fedashkin stalked up to him. The colonel saluted.

"Colonel Mygakov, sir," the officer said. "Second Guards Motorized Divisional Staff. If you'd care to follow me, Marshal Besedin is at the observation bunker."

"Well, get on," Fedashkin said, returning the ghost of a salute. "Be quick about it." The anxiety nagged at him as it had for days, like the whine of a mosquito in a dark bedroom.

Colonel Mygakov set off hurriedly towards the crest of the hill, Fedashkin close behind. A hundred meters from the helicopter, at the summit of the rise, was a grove of larch trees with a dozen staff and communications vehicles scattered around it. Their dull green surfaces shimmered in the heat. As Fedashkin neared the larch grove and the vehicles, he thought: I should have cancelled this visit, so should Besedin. Stupid to be out here at a time like this. Necessary, though, have to keep to routine, lull any watchers, let them sleep, thinking they know what we're doing. Only forty minutes to Moscow, anyway.

The command bunker was a low concrete structure sunk into the side of the hill on the far side of the larches. It was permanent, being the main headquarters for the military staff and inspection teams responsible for monitoring the District exercises. Just outside the bunker entrance Marshal Viktor Besedin, chief of the Soviet General Staff, was talking rapidly to a small group of senior officers of the Second Guards. The staff officers looked nervous. While the presence of the chief of the General Staff and the minister of defense meant great honor, it could also mean professional disaster if the exercises were not properly executed. The Second Guards, moreover, was one of the most senior formations in the Red Army; with its sister, the Guards Kantemirov Tank Division, it supplied most of the tanks and vehicles for the great May Day parades in Moscow. The Second Guards was also one of the few Category A divisions on Russian soil, with a full complement of men, fighting vehicles, and transport, and theoretically at least was among the most effective formations in the Soviet ground forces. In the days of Brezhnev, Andropov and Chernenko, however, the unit spent so much time in preparing for its ceremonial occasions that its actual combat power had been drastically eroded. Its new commander, whom Besedin had personally selected, had been ordered to correct this. He had been given six months to do the job, and now appeared confident enough to invite both Fedashkin and Besedin to view the results. If he had done what he had been ordered to do he would be promoted and sent to the Kiev Military District to repeat the performance. And the Kiev Military District command was the next to last step on the road to the rank of marshal of the Soviet Union. The commander of the Second Guards would be regarding his guests' reactions to the exercise with leechlike attention.

As Fedashkin rounded the larch grove, Besedin saw him and turned away from the staff officers by the door of the bunker. Colonel Mygakov saluted as the two senior men exchanged formal greetings, and then absented himself as quickly as decently possible. Fedashkin and Besedin barely saw him go.

"Hello, Viktor," said Fedashkin after they had exchanged the obligatory salutes. The two men had known each other for nearly twenty years, had gotten drunk together, and did not usually bother with formalities. "How does it look?"

Besedin shrugged. "Alright so far. They'll be starting in twenty minutes." He grinned, displaying a rank of teeth which had been perfectly capped in East Germany. "They'd *better* start in twenty minutes. Or the whole divisional staff's going to be serving on the Amur River, out there staring at the Chinese. I think they'll get going on time."

"What're they doing?"

"Simulated prepared attack on a fortified position." He looked up at the sun. "They're putting a battalion down by helicopter in the Green Force rear areas. The airborne component should be along a few minutes before zero."

"Is there anything to drink? My throat's a desert."

"Down by the OP. Kedrov's got a table set up."

They walked back to the group of divisional staff. General Kedrov, commander of the Second Guards, snapped to attention with his officers. Fedashkin returned the salute and said, "Well, General Kedrov, I'll be able to pay more attention to what you can do after I have something cold inside of me. Marshal Besedin agrees, I think."

"Right this way, Comrade Minister," Kedrov said. If he were nervous, the ease of his manner concealed it perfectly. He led the two senior men to a long table set up in the shade of the larches; the day was very hot. On the table, nestled in beds of ice, were platters of caviar, hors d'ouevres, and pastries. Bottles of vodka and Crimean champagne, their necks wrapped in white cloths, protruded from frosted silver buckets. Fedashkin nodded appreciatively and accepted a glass of vodka and a plate heaped with caviar from the white-coated enlisted man behind the table. Besedin took a glass of champagne. Only when Fedashkin was loading the fish roe onto an imported water biscuit did Kedrov help himself to a pastry. The other officers maintained a wary distance. There were only five of them; the rest of the staff would be at their operational posts, in the bunker or down on the rolling plain under camouflage, waiting. With them would be the officers of the inspection team sent out from Moscow, also waiting. Fedashkin spared a glance from his plate for the long slope leading down to the plain with its bands of wood and scrubland and meadow, dusty green or tawny in the early afternoon heat. The camouflage was good, he had to admit that. There was nearly a regiment tucked away in the fields and under the trees within his line of sight, but he couldn't see a trace of fighting vehicles, men or guns.

"I hope," he said to Kedrov, "that your staff hasn't been tempted by the idea of preparing the men *too* well." He was referring to the practice of giving tank and gun crews and platoons of soldiers exact information about where and when an "enemy" was to appear, so that there would be no surprises to make an exercise go wrong and damage the reputations of unit officers. Such choreography made for an impressive performance on exercises, but the Americans and Germans were hardly about to oblige with exact details of their forces and intentions.

"No, Comrade Minister," General Kedrov said, apparently undisturbed by the question. "It happens, certainly, but not in my command. You won't see any Bolshoi Ballet here. I would respectfully request that you remember this if events today don't follow the ideal course. Some of the men will have surprises, some won't, plans will inevitably go wrong. My junior officers are required to show initiative when that happens. Some of them will make incorrect decisions. Those are the ones I'm going to replace."

Fedashkin nodded with satisfaction. Kedrov seemed to have understood the conditions of his promotion: put an end to the "Bolshoi Ballet," as he so aptly described it, in the Second Guards. If it worked even reasonably well the experiment would be repeated in other formations.

Kedrov looked at his watch. "With your permission, I should return to my post."

Fedashkin nodded. "Go ahead. We'll be joining you shortly."

They saluted and Kedrov herded the five staff officers

towards the command bunker. They had the self-discipline not to stare wistfully back at the loaded table.

Besedin finished his champagne and put the glass down. "Is there any word yet?"

"Not yet," said Fedashkin. "I told the Poliburo the deadline. There is a little while yet before we have to make a final decision."

"If it happens, we'll win," Besedin said confidently.

"I expect so. Provided we can do it quickly enough, and the Americans don't panic."

"I assume the Foreign Ministry and the propaganda organs have that under control."

"We have to assume it," Fedashkin said. "Anyway, the Americans won't be eager to commit suicide on behalf of the West Germans. We can flatten North America, and Washington knows it. But it won't come to that."

"Helicopters," said Besedin suddenly. He shaded his eyes, looking out to the southwest past the larch grove. Fedashkin followed hs gaze. Along the horizon was a scattering of dots, evanescent in the heat waves shimmering up from the plain. Rapidly the dots hardened and expanded, transforming themselves into a great gaggle of Mil-24 gunships and Mil-8 assault helicopters. The pounding of the rotors and the whine of turbines combined into one great solid block of sound that vibrated against Fedashkin's skull.

The big machines were on a northwest course, flying towards the Green positions. Over there the umpires would be observing the defenders, calculating how many of the helicopters they might expect to shoot down if the conflict were real. In an actual attack the positions would have been pounded with artillery and airstrikes, and perhaps with gas. The later analysis of the exercise and the umpires' decisions would take this into account in determining who had won and who had lost.

The helicopters were receding into the northwest. Fedashkin and Besedin found that they could hear again, faintly. A dozen meters away Colonel Mygakov was hurrying towards them. Despite the fading beat of the helicopter assault wave, he still had to shout to be audible.

"Comrade Minister, sir, there's an urgent call for you."

"Who?"

"It's Moscow."

Fedashkin and Besedin exchanged glances, and then hurried after Mygakov. Inside the bunker field telephones buzzed, radios crackled and hummed, one of the new Ryad battlefield computers rippled arcane symbols across a pair of terminals, and in one corner a teleprinter gave a fair imitation of a heavy machine gun. At a big table in the center of the room Kedrov and his staff leaned over a map, grease pencils busy.

"Here's the Moscow line, Comrade Minister."

Fedashkin took the receiver. The noise inside the bunker made it difficult to hear. He stopped his left ear with his index finger. "Hello? *Hello?* Fedashkin here."

"This is Chairman Minkov, Minister. I am giving you advance warning. The arrangement did not work out. We got the word an hour ago. Rudel made an appearance on West German television at noon, their time. Secretary Nikolayev has called an emergency meeting of the Defense Council at four this afternoon. The usual place."

Fedashkin looked at a clock on the wall. He would make it easily. "Alright," he said. "I'll be there. Goodbye."

"Goodbye."

Fedashkin replaced the receiver in its cradle, very carefully. After a moment he became aware that Besedin was looking at him with a peculiar expression on his face: apprehension mixed with anticipation and a strange kind of relief.

"You'd better come back to Moscow with me," Fedashkin said. "I think we are going to have a great deal of work to do."

Zossen, East Germany
August 12

"REMEMBER," SAID MARSHAL PYOTR LESIOVSKY, commander-in-chief of the Group of Soviet Forces Germany, "the eyes of the socialist and capitalist worlds are upon you. Any shirking of duty will be detected instantly, to the shame of the incompetent, that of his brother officers, and that of the soldiers who trust to him for their welfare and success. I urge you to give the utmost sacrifice to make these Suvorov exercises an example to the world of the capabilities and the dedication of the fraternal socialist nations."

Lesiovsky sipped at his glass of water, put it back beside the microphone, and stepped down from the podium. The sixty-odd senior staff officers, both German and Russian, combined in an exuberant burst of applause that reverberated off the mustard-yellow walls of the long room until the C-in-C had left by the side door, whereupon the clapping stopped abruptly.

As the applause died, Colonel Vedenin, who was sitting in the second row in front of Harpe, half turned and said, "I've got to have a word with the boss. Go on ahead and save me a seat at the briefing."

Harpe nodded and got up to leave. The other officers crowded around the exits from the long room, in a low hum of conversation. Harpe avoided talk and went down the long concrete corridor and to the stairs that led to the suite of rooms code-named Crossbow Central. The suite was the planning headquarters for the deception and electronic warfare operations of the Warsaw Pact forces in Northern Europe, and lay underneath one of the long concrete blockhouses that formed the hard core of the Zossen headquarters. In peace Zossen controlled the Group of Soviet Forces, Germany: a score of Soviet armored and mechanized infantry divisions, six East German divisions, hundred of ground attack aircraft and assault helicopters, and vast quantities of artillery and tactical rockets. In a war alert, Zossen would be transformed into the headquarters of the Western Theater of Operations, heavily reinforced, and assigned to overrun Western Europe from the Austrian border to the northern tip of Denmark. While that happened, the 20th Guards Army, for whose deception and electronic warfare measures Harpe and Vedenin were responsible, would finally lance the political abscess that West Berlin had represented since 1945.

Harpe showed his identification to the guard at the door of the Crossbow Central installation — it was a high-security area; you had to show papers even if the guard had seen you coming and going for weeks — and went in. Beyond the vestibule, which was monitored by a closed-circuit television camera, was the big room where most of the department's routine work was carried out. In the room were a dozen desks, four computer terminals, rows of file cabinets, and a pair of teleprinters; on the walls were ground glass screens on which maps could be displayed, including those showing American surveillance satellite tracks and the frequencies with which they passed over central Europe; a couple of posters exhorting socialist dedication; and a photograph of Secretary Nikolayev flanked on one side by a portrait of Lenin and on the other by one of Marx. On a metal table in one corner stood a tea urn and a chipped white saucer containing three slices of dessicated lemon. The office staff was hard at work preparing the hundreds of documents required for the Suvorov exercise.

Harpe went on through the office into the dank meeting room. It was floored with grimy white linoleum and smelled of damp concrete and lime. The roughly finished cement walls were unpanelled. Acoustic ceiling tiles had never been installed and above the fluorescent lights a tangle of pipes and air ducts lay exposed. In the center of the narrow room was a table made of thin plywood supported by a metal frame. Gray-green folding steel chairs stood around the table and against the walls. Sitting stiffly on the chairs at the table were the chiefs of staff of the tank and mechanized infantry and support forces that made up the 20th Guards Army. They nodded politely as Harpe entered; he didn't have seniority over all of them, but he worked at the Zossen headquarters which was worth a couple of grades of rank.

Harpe found a seat, and placed his uniform cap on the chair next to it to hold it for Vedenin. Nobody spoke. The silence began to grow awkward.

The door opened and General Gresko, commander of 20th Guards Army, barged in. Behind Gresko came Vedenin and a clerk struggling with a pile of documents, each a centimeter thick and bound in green cardboard: the Operational Directives for the Suvorov exercise. The clerk deposited the pile on the table with a thump and then made a hasty exit. Gresko was obviously not in a good mood. "Pass these around," he said, shoving the pile of ODs towards the nearest staff officer. "They're labelled for each of your formations, don't get the wrong one. Sign the receipt sheet as you take it. Let's get started. Colonel Vedenin: Please instruct these officers in the electronic intelligence and deception measures to be practised."

Vedenin waited for a moment until everyone had a copy of the ODs and said, "We'll start on page three." Rustling of pages turning. "These are the radar disciplines. *Everything* except the deception radars will be turned off starting at 1800 hours on the fourteenth, that's Saturday evening. The shutdown schedule for each of your formations starts on page four. There's a lot in it; go through it carefully. By 2100 hours there shouldn't be anything on the air except for the deception stations. The same goes for radio transmissions; that starts in section four of the directives. No unit is to transmit anything after the shutdown has been completed, so if any of your people screw up the monitors will know about it. I want to get through the schedule in detail, so are there any questions before we start?"

"Colonel Vedenin?" It was one of the East German officers. "Yes?"

"We're shutting down on the evening of the fourteenth. I

understood the exercises were to start early Monday morning. Does that mean we stay in position all through Sunday?"

"I'll answer that," Gresko said. "There have been some changes. The exercises still begin Monday, but the 20th has been ordered to experiment with a full-scale night march under radio silence. That's Saturday night into Sunday morning."

"I see. Thank you, Comrade General."

"Anything else?" Vedenin asked, looking pensive. There was nothing else. The Russian went on.

The briefing on the electronic measures alone required a full hour. The Operational Directives for the exercise were unusually elaborate, specifying the use of all electronic equipment down to the last detail: radio nets from company level upwards; gunnery, antiaircraft, flank surveillance and early warning radar; position beacons; active infra-red detection systems; divisional and army level jammers and other electronic countermeasures and support devices. As the various equipments began their phased shutdown, their signals would be partially duplicated by carefully positioned deception stations, so that a listening enemy would think the 20th Guards was settling in for the night. As the divisional radio nets and radars went off the air, the masses of men and fighting vehicles and tanks would begin their movements toward battalion assembly areas, fifteen kilometers from the perimeter of West Berlin. They would remain there during the following day, Sunday, and that night experiment with a battle approach to within three kilometers of the city. After that they were to withdraw to their original assembly areas. The inspection teams would judge 20th Guards' competence by the execution of the deception operations, the speed with which the combat formations moved, and whether they maintained their organization properly in doing so. Night marches under radio silence were notoriously difficult to control; if march discipline were not followed to the letter, a column which started out in impeccable order could reach its destination in disarray, and reach it late in the bargain.

Vedenin finally ended. Harpe was feeling a pronounced unease, which had actually begun some time before this morning, when he and the Russian and the Crossbow staff had been putting the final touches on the procedures. Someone, somewhere up in the Soviet hierarchy, had been fiddling with the Suvorov plans; in the original outline Harpe and Vedenin had received back in June, the 20th Guards never approached the West Berlin perimeter closer than twenty kilometers. Moreover, the divisional frontages had not, to begin with, run parallel to the city's boundaries, but had been oriented eastward. The changes had come down from Plans only two nights previously, and the Crossbow staff had worked twenty hours a day to modify the ODs appropriately. Harpe's eyes were dry and gritty with fatigue.

"There's one other thing," Gresko said. The others, who had been slipping the ODs and their pages of notes into their document cases, paused. "It's not in the Directives," the Russian said, when he had their undivided attention, "but I've been authorized to tell you verbally. At any time, your divisional or formation commander may receive a code word, which you don't have to know, to disregard the electronic restart schedule and switch everything on at once, radar, radios, beacons, the lot. We want to see how good you are at responding to unforeseen circumstances. If he gives that order, don't wave these ODs in his face, he's not suddenly working for the Americans. Just do it."

A scatter of nods and murmurs of agreement. There had been rumors that the Soviets were suddenly trying to make their command responses more flexible.

Harpe sat quite still, not permitting the slightest change in his face. He had known nothing of what Gresko had just said; it was driven home again just how little the Russians really trusted their allies.

Then, like a rush of freezing water, the implications of the Russian's words hit him.

God in heaven, Harpe thought, they're not going to stop three kilometers from the Wall. That's why Romanov and Vedenin were called back to Moscow; it was for a secret briefing. Sunday night the 20th Guards are just going to keep on moving, right into Berlin.

West Berlin
August 13

BRAND WAS SITTING ON THE TERRACE, reading a day-old copy of the *New York Times*, when the telephone rang in the kitchen. For a moment he had difficulty separating its buzz from the hum of the dishwasher and David's sandbox experiments with a wooden stick and a metal pail. Alison was sitting on the swing, reading *The House at Pooh Corner*. "Jenny," he called, "can you get that?" He had reached the middle of a column on the assassination attempt on Rudel and was trying to follow the columnist's argument that the Soviets would not be so stupid as to try to remove the German chancellor by force. The writer favored a Turkish dissident group as the offending organization.

"Hardly," she called from the bedroom window above his head. "I'm putting the wash away."

"Sorry," Brand said. He went into the kitchen and picked up the telephone. Alison trailed after him, book in hand.

It was Anderson. They exchanged pleasantries for a moment. Then Anderson said, "Paul, would you mind if I dropped over for a few minutes?"

"Sure," Brand said. Alison was prancing by the kitchen table, trying to get his attention, whispering sibilantly. He gestured violently at her, without noticeable result, and added, "I'm almost out of scotch, you'll have to put up with beer or cognac."

"No problem. See you in a few."

"Okay." Brand rang off. Alison now was tugging at his shirt. "Daddy," she said, "I asked you politely, two times."

"I was on the telephone," Brand said, irritation rising, "as you could very well see. How often have I told you to behave when I'm on the phone? Once more, and it's no television for *three days*."

"But, Daddy—"

A wail from outside, barely audible over the dishwasher. From somewhere upstairs Jennifer called, "Paul! David's whacked his head on the sandbox. I thought you were watching him."

"Shit," Brand said, and went out onto the terrace. David was picking himself up from the grass beside the sandbox, a pink crescent over his right eyebrow. He found his feet and trotted towards his father, small features screwed up into one large agony. Brand caught him up, drawing the thick brown hair back from the scrape. David snivelled.

"You're okay, short stuff," Brand said, inspecting the mark. The skin wasn't cut. "You'll live."

Jennifer appeared at the back door. "Is he alright?"

"A scrape."

"Bring him in, I was going to give him a bath. He could use one."

Brand deposited David in the kitchen with his mother and then went back to the terrace where Alison sat in a sullen heap in one of the chairs, pretending to read. "What's the matter?" Brand asked.

"You like David more than me."

"Don't give me that, Alison, you know it's not true. Come over here and let's read."

She emitted a long sigh, climbed out of the chair, and brought the book to her father. Brand began to read.

They had nearly finished the third chapter when the doorbell chimed. "Sorry," Brand said. "We'll have to finish it tomorrow."

Alison inspected pages. "But it's only five more paragraphs."

"Sorry." Brand got out of the chair, sliding his daughter to the ground, feeling guilty. "It'll still be there tomorrow. I have to see Uncle Walt about some things."

She stood in front of him, angry, adamant. "You're *always* seeing people about things. Why can't you be home at night all the time like Gudrun's father?"

Jennifer appeared in the doorway to the house. "Upstairs," she said. "We haven't time for that, anyway it's bedtime." To Brand she said, "Who is it?"

"Walt."

"I'll put her to bed. You owe me one, it was your turn."

"Okay." He got up hurriedly and went to the front door. Anderson stepped over the threshold, looking dishevelled. "Hello," he said, swinging his briefcase awkwardly. "Sorry to come over on such short notice."

"Doesn't matter. Drink?"

"Not now, thanks. I've got something for you."

"Come on up."

They mounted the stairs to the upper hall. At the back of the house was Brand's personal office, which he had furnished to his own taste, rather than that of his wife: pegged oak flooring, white plaster walls on which hung two Chambers prints and a tapestry from Turkestan, and a large teak desk with an IBM microcomputer and terminal on it. A laser printer sat on a low table to the left of the desk, and on its right was a tall stand containing a bank of music equipment and a videocassette recorder. In shelves on the window wall was an extensive tape and record collection.

"Music?" said Brand. "Anything in particular?"

"Doesn't matter."

Brand selected a tape at random from the shelf and inserted it into the deck. Music flooded from the speakers: Bach's Cantata 131, the delicate oboe melodic line with its ornaments of strings and harpsichord. Anderson took a small box from his briefcase and proceeded around the room with it, searching.

"No bugs," he said as the cello chimed into the music. He put the sweep away and lowered himself into the slingback chair next to the bookcase.

"I'll turn it off," Brand suggested.

"Alright. Can we have some Mozart? Never liked Bach really, he dances around too much."

Brand installed Mozart's 21st piano concerto in the deck. "What?" he asked as the first movement began.

"Harpe," Anderson said. "He wants to come over."

"Oh." Brand looked out the window at the oak tree. Its foliage, driven by an evening breeze, rippled gently in the fading light. "For good?"

"Yes. It was in the last drop. He says he's through."

"He thinks they're onto him, then. How much time has he got?"

"All he said was, as soon as possible. Tomorrow night, at the latest." Anderson paused. "There's something else worrying him. He's been passing data on the 20th Guards exercises. Apparently some of the exercise instructions were changed at the last minute. Tuesday. He got the information into the pipeline Thursday afternoon, we received it late this morning. The combat elements of the exercise are going to be within a dozen kilometers of West Berlin on Saturday night, and there's a lot of electronic deception laid on. Sunday night they come as close as three kilometers, then go back to their staging areas for the start of the main exercise on Monday."

A cold finger touched Brand at the nape of his neck and glided down his spine. "What in hell are they up to?"

"Langley and NSA are trying to figure it out. There's damn-all out of the ordinary going on anywhere else, as far as we can tell. It's always a little antsy when the Pact's holding those big exercises, but I gather Washington doesn't think the political situation suggests any military action. There's nothing unusual going on in the Soviet sector of the city, either, no military preparations at all."

The cold finger on Brand's spine warmed a little. "They wouldn't start on a Sunday night, anyway," Brand said. "That would put them over the frontier early Monday morning. Better to move twenty-four hours earlier, catch us early Sunday morning. Does Harpe think that's what they're going to do?"

"He didn't say," Anderson said. Then he went on thoughtfully, "Or it might be a double bluff. They know we think they'd most likely hit us on a Sunday, so they wait till Monday. Tuesday, even."

"Maybe," Brand said. "But like you said, the political situation . . . maybe it's a prod at Rudel."

"Yes. Maybe. At least, that's what home would like to believe."

The strings glided into silence and the piano began, delicate, dispassionate. "Rudel's not paying much attention to prods these days," Brand said. "Why is Joachim so hot to come over all of a sudden? Does he know something he's not telling us?"

"It's possible," said Anderson. He rubbed his eyebrows. "If there is something in the wind, he might be worried that we'll want to keep him in place as long as possible. Until it's too late."

"We agreed we'd pull him out whenever he wanted it, no questions aked," Brand reminded Anderson.

"Yeah. I know. Langley's said it'll keep the agreement."

The two men contemplated the music for a moment.

"Walt," Brand said abruptly, "do you think the Russians are finally going to do it?"

Anderson thought, chin on hand. "They'd be stupid to," he said finally. "They've got a new detente, Bonn's determined to pull out of NATO, which should suit the Kremlin right down to the ground, and the Sunday-Monday timing's wrong. Either Harpe's got cold feet or the SSD is onto him."

"You're going to pull him out?"

"Have to wait for instructions. I—"

The telephone on Brand's desk chimed. He answered it. "It's for you," he said.

Anderson leaned over and took the extended receiver. "Walt here." A pause. "Yes. Alright." He handed the instrument back to Brand and rubbed his eyes with a thumb and forefinger. "Shit," he said. "Maybe I'll have that drink now."

"Cognac? The ice is all downstairs."

"Sure."

Brand got the drinks out of the liquor cabinet and handed Anderson the snifter. Anderson was wearing an expression of equal parts exasperation and worry.

"Anything I should know?" Brand asked, sitting back down at the desk.

"Yeah. Very definitely yeah. Langley says bring him out. Posthaste. By tomorrow night at the latest." Anderson drank half the cognac at a gulp. "Goddamn. That gives us no more than enough time."

"Can you do it?" Brand asked. He had a sudden vision of Joachim hanging on the barbed wire of the Wall, deserted.

"We've got enough time," Anderson said. "Just about

everything's in place. If necessary we could delay twelve hours."

"Langley's moving awfully fast," Brand said. "Unless they're worried Harpe's got hard evidence they need in a hurry. Has he?"

"Not as far as I know." Anderson absentmindedly bit at a thumbnail. "Maybe. Maybe he does, by now. The big question at home is, why would the Pact screw up now just when they've got so much going for them? That's what's bugging Langley, I think. They want to pick Harpe's brains. Also they're not sure they want to keep him in place any more. It's only a matter of time until he gets nailed, they always do at his level, and there are going to be more talks on the balanced-force reduction treaty. Apparently the White House has said it doesn't want anything, repeat anything, to screw up the talks. They don't want one of our people caught with his fingers in the cashbox at Zossen."

"That's goddamned stupid," Brand said. "He could be invaluable where he is."

"Not if he wants to get out. He might clam up, and then we've got the worst of both worlds. Him there, and no data coming out."

"Alright," Brand said tiredly. "He comes out. Then what?"

Anderson shifted uncomfortably in his chair. "There's something else. I was going to tell you this weekend. The BND is kicking up dust, probably because of Rudel's influence. I won't go into details, but there's been a new agreement. If any major East German defector comes over the frontier, he's jointly debriefed, no matter who's been running him. If it's us — I don't know about the Brits — there has to be parallel debriefing, CIA and BND."

"That's crazy," Brand said, in disbelief. "We can't operate like that. Not with the leaks they've had."

"Yeah." Anderson made an angry gesture. "You'd think after their security screw ups . . . anyway, we're operating on their turf. So when Harpe comes over, he goes through the mill twice. At least."

"So Kastner and I have to take Joachim to Pullach. Erich for the BND, me for the CIA."

"You got the first part right. But he's going to Bonn, this time."

"What for?"

"He's being taken seriously enough that they want him to talk directly to Staatsminister Kempf, the head of the Chancellery Office, the guy that breathes down the neck of the BND to keep it on the straight and narrow. When you get to Bonn there'll be a raft of people who want pieces of the poor bastard. Kempf, like I said. Anton Schell, the BND counterespionage chief, and Dietrich, the guy that runs the BFV domestic operations. Not to mention Bundeswehr military intelligence. Also two people from Langley."

"Are they printing tickets?" Brand asked. "Performance of the week? They'll drive Joachim nuts."

"They all want to know everything fast," Anderson said. "Times like these, nobody wants to wait."

"He'll want to defect back," Brand said. "He's uptight as it is. Do we have to do all that?"

"That's what's coming down," Anderson said. "Sorry."

Brand listened to the Mozart for a moment, knowing he could do nothing for Joachim, and then said, "What about me and Erich?"

"You can come back here as soon as the Langley people arrive. What Kastner does is up to his people."

There was a soft knock at the door. "Jenny?" said Brand.

She opened the door perhaps ten centimeters and said, "They're off to bed. Can you spare them a moment?"

"Okay. Scoot them in."

Alison and David trooped in, smelling of soap and toothpaste. Brand hugged them both tightly. "Good night, you two," he said. "See you in the morning. Say goodnight to Uncle Walt."

They did, and were gone, the door closing gently behind them and their mother. Anderson contemplated his cognac. "Does she know?" he asked.

"I've never told her," Brand said. "But she knows."

"Yeah," Anderson said. "Same here." He emptied his glass. "So you'll nursemaid Joachim for a couple of days, eh? Get him settled in Bonn."

"Yes," said Brand, remembering Harpe's lonely, exhausted face in the drizzling gray light of the Alexanderplatz. "I'll do it. But after that, Walt, we're going to have to talk. I'm going to have to pack it in. No hard feelings. Just . . . things."

"Okay," Anderson said. He looked for a long thirty seconds at the Chambers prints on the wall. Then he said, almost as an afterthought, "No problem. We'll talk about it. You got any more of that cognac?"

East Berlin — Zossen
4:00 P.M. - 10:00 P.M., August 14

HARPE OFTEN SPENT Saturday afternoons working at the Amt 16 headquarters, which was located on the eastern outskirts of the Soviet sector of the city, near Vogelsdorf. It was the same habit that had contributed materially to his divorce, twelve years previously, from his (then) wife of three years. Even in those days, before his infatuation with the West and his internal love affair with the armies of the old Wehrmacht, he had been subject to the compulsion to WORK, in capital letters: he understood, without liking it, the joke about Saxons:

"*Mutti*, now that grandfather has died, will we bury his ashes?"

"*Nein, Junge*. Grandfather's ashes must go in the hourglass on the mantelpiece. Grandfather must work; all we Saxons must work."

Harpe took his Saxon profile to work at the Vogelsdorf electronic intelligence complex, which consisted of three low and carefully nondescript red-brick buildings with hardly anything to distinguish them from Agriculture Ministry office blocks but the festoon of aerials and parabolic dish antennae projecting from the roof of the central building. The antennae monitored all of West Berlin's military and civilian electronic traffic. Underground, shielded data lines carried a torrent of electronic intercepts and raw intelligence from the other listening posts studded across the Democratic Republic into the primary and secondary signal processors. The processed output was fed into the banks of decryption and frequency analysis computers installed in and under the northernmost of the three buildings.

The third block, south of the building which bore the corona of antennae, consisted of offices, where the analysis staff worked. Harpe's office was on the second floor; it had a small window about the size of a suitcase stood on end. The glass was whorled, so that no one could see in (or out) and it was additionally shielded by a louvered blind reputed to prevent eavesdropping by laser-based surveillance devices.

Harpe sat at his desk, trying to decide whether an odd new electronics signature from the British sector of Berlin reflected a change in cryptographic techniques, or whether it was merely a test transmission or even the product of a piece of faulty equipment. There wasn't anything else like it floating around; Harpe suspected it to be a test transmission. Or perhaps the British garrison was playing games again. They knew about Amt 16 and its listening posts, and would occasionally transmit long heavily encrypted messages which burned up a lot of computer time to decode, if they could be decoded. When they were, the plain language text would be passages from obscure and boring novels (or worse, 19th century Church of England sermons), nursery rhymes, or other inconsequentials. Once they had sent the entire text of the Helsinki agreements concerning freedom of travel and association, which had caused a minor flap among the department's senior staff when the translation landed on their desks.

There was nothing else to be done with the intercepted signal until they got at least one other match. Harpe closed the file and picked up the top magazine from the stack in his incoming mail tray. It was an American electronics trade publication dealing with leading-edge communications technology; Harpe consumed reams of such material in a month, all in English. He read the language, especially when it was technically oriented, much better than he spoke it. He was actually more fluent in spoken Russian than in English, a fact which annoyed him when he happened to think of it.

He began turning pages, looking for nuggets of information that might be cross-referred to others gleaned from similar sources. It was startling how much information a trained professional could harvest from material openly available in the West; it was as though they didn't care how deeply they compromised processes and devices that would, east of the frontier, be treated as state secrets. Perhaps it was a mark of their confidence, their conviction of invulnerability; or perhaps of their innocence. Whatever it was, it made life much easier for intelligence officers in the East.

He turned another page, and then realized that he had not retained a fraction of what he had read. His concentration was gone. Trying again, he found himself staring at the glossy page (such high quality paper, they throw it away over there, he thought) without seeing it.

How much longer before they contact me? he worried. I cannot wait until they refer the problem, and my survival, all the way to America.

He leafed through the glossy pages of the magazine, avoiding the other thought. It came anyway.

Perhaps they won't let me come over.

No, not that, he told himself, Paul wouldn't let that happen. But when are they going to make contact, tell me how to get out? I have to leave before the Russians do whatever it is they're going to do. Perhaps they're doing nothing. I'll look like a fool, with all these warnings. Do they believe me, over there? Not likely, not right away, they'll want confirmation from their machines, the Americans like machines. They'll wait.

He worked through the stack of periodicals, trying to find useful morsels. Nothing seemed important. Finally, he rearranged the whole stack precisely on the desk, and tried to think clearly.

He had to get out tonight. They hadn't contacted him in the morning, before he left his flat, although he had waited by the telephone until nearly noon. But there were ways they could find him, even here at Amt 16. Perhaps they were having difficulty getting the exit documents in place.

The Russians are going to strike, Harpe thought. I could feel it at Zossen, the way they acted. But I have to know more. Anything at all.

He made a sudden, and knowingly irrational, decision. He picked up the telephone and dialled on the internal net.

"Switchboard."

"This is Colonel Harpe. I'm going out for two hours. Hold any messages at your desk."

"Yes, Colonel."

Ten minutes later, after logging out at the security desk, he was in his Wartburg sedan driving along the ringroad leading around the eastern edge of Berlin, heading for Zossen. He had no clear idea of what he was going to look for when he arrived at the Soviet Army HQ, except to try to find Vedenin and try to extract some information from the Russian colonel, at whatever risk was reasonable. But there was no certainty that Vedenin would even be there, and there was, unfortunately, no very good reason for Harpe to be at Zossen. When the main exercises began early Monday morning, Harpe was supposed to be up at Eberswald, with the 20th Guards Army headquarters, monitoring ESM and electronic intercept procedures. A preliminary exercise was scheduled for Sunday afternoon, but that was to take place at Eberswald as well.

He should think of some excuse to turn up at Zossen. Perhaps he had left something behind when the Suvorov briefing ended? Too weak, far too weak. A problem with the operational orders, that was better, at least good enough, perhaps, to get him past the gates. Then he could try to find Vedenin. If the Russian wasn't there . . .

Maybe it's all mirages, Harpe thought after a few kilometers, just before turning off the autobahn onto the secondary road leading to Zossen. It doesn't matter, I'm getting out anyway. I'd better. They'll catch up with me sooner or later, I've got to go, no matter what happens out here.

He thought there was more military traffic on the road than usual, mostly supply transport and staff cars. At the heavily guarded gate to the Zossen complex, Harpe showed his Grade Six pass (good to the end of August) and his NVA identification. The Russian sentry waved him through.

Half a kilometer along the access road he had to stop at the second set of gates. The security check was much more thorough this time. A Russian captain — Harpe hadn't seen him before, the guard rotations had been frequent over the last few days — scrutinized the papers microscopically. Then he went into the guardhouse. Harpe could see the Russian talking on the telephone; sweat gathered under his capband. He looked, despite himself, at the briefcase on the seat beside him. The contents were legitimately in his possession, the papers were a good excuse for him to be at the headquarters complex, but even so . . .

Inside the guardhouse the Russian captain was nodding, hanging up the telephone at last, moving towards the door. Here I go, Harpe thought, off to the cellars of the Magdalenenstrasse.

The Russian leaned into the window of the Wartburg. His uniform smelled faintly of cabbage. "What's the purpose of your visit? Your name's not on the access list."

What access list? Harpe thought. "I wasn't expected," he said. "I have business at Block F."

"With whom?"

Harpe took a chance. "That's not your concern," he said. "Don't you know what's going on? Do you want Colonel Romanov asking why I was delayed to no purpose? That's a Grade Six pass you're looking at. Doesn't that mean anything to you?"

The captain stiffened; Germans, even colonels, did not speak so to Soviet officers. After a moment of consideration he said, "I'll have to telephone ahead to Block F."

"Do so," said Harpe. The sweatband of his cap was drenched; the interior of the Wartburg felt incandescent, even in the westering sun of early evening.

After perhaps two minutes the captain returned from the guardhouse. "Alright," he said. "You can go on. Only to Block F. Check at the security desk within ten minutes or there'll be people out after you."

"I know how it's done," Harpe said irritably. He returned the captain's gesture of a salute, the barrier rose, and he drove on into the complex of formed-concrete bunkers and cement-block surface buildings that was the headquarters of the Group of Soviet Forces, Germany. The Russian captain's behavior niggled at him; Harpe did not normally have trouble at the access controls. He wanted to put it down to a newly assigned guard captain, determined not to flex from the letter of army orders, but the incident worried him.

He pulled the Wartburg up on the flaking concrete parking pad of Block F and looked around for other German uniforms. He couldn't see any. He went inside the block, identified himself at the security desk, and asked for Vedenin. The lieutenant behind the desk rang Vedenin's local, listened, and hung up. "The Colonel isn't available," he said.

"I was supposed to meet him," Harpe said. "He's here somewhere?"

"Yes." Uninformative, with latent Slavic suspicion.

"Where can I locate him?"

"He is at the HQ block, but he is in a meeting."

Patiently Harpe asked, "When is the meeting over?"

"I have no information on that."

"Colonel Romanov, then."

"Colonel Romanov is also in a meeting."

"Oh." After a pause Harpe said, "Can you arrange to have a message taken to Colonel Vedenin?"

"No, Colonel." The lieutenant was on the bare edge of civility, even for a Russian. Another of the German-haters, Harpe thought. "No one there is to be disturbed," the Russian said.

"I see," said Harpe. He turned to go and then asked, "Where're the German officers meeting?"

A flicker of surprise crossed the lieutenant's face. "There is no such meeting," he said, and then looked as though he could have bitten his tongue off.

"I'll check with Colonel Vedenin tomorrow," Harpe said, and went back out to the Wartburg. He sat for a moment behind the wheel, thinking. After a moment he decided on one more try; there was nothing to be lost by driving past the HQ block on his way out. He started the engine and drove deeper into the Zossen complex.

As the Wartburg rounded the corner by the main communications building with its hedge of aerials, Harpe saw them: a dozen staff cars drawn up outside the General Headquarters block. The staff drivers were nowhere to be seen. The guards at the HQ entrance eyed Harpe's car suspiciously as it rolled past. He was careful to keep looking straight ahead, nonchalant.

Who's in there? he thought as he turned the west corner, away from the eyes of the guards. That's an awful lot of staff cars, all alone. And where are the drivers? Don't tell me a bunch of senior types drove themselves over here with their own lily white hands. I hope getting out's easier than getting in was. Left again now, towards the main gate, don't get lost around here today. God in heaven, what a waste of time, noting conclusive to pay for the danger, just hints and surmises, nothing more.

He reached the inner gate. On its far side a big Volga staff car was drawn up, the guard captain at the driver's window. As Harpe slowed for the checkout point the barrier flew up, and the Volga accelerated rapidly into the headquarters complex. As it flashed past Harpe thought: Whoever's in that car is late for something.

For a moment the face of the man behind the wheel did not register, although Harpe had seen it recently, a very senior officer's. He ransacked his memory, finally put a name to the face. It was that of one of the men attending Marshal Lesiovsky's speech at Zossen, about the importance of the Suvorov exercises: Colonel-General Demichev, commander of the First Guards Tank Army up north, the one targeted on the West German city of Kassel.

What is Demichev doing at Zossen? Harpe thought. He should be up in his headquarters at Dresden, getting ready for Suvorov.

The guard captain was giving the Wartburg a cursory inspection, waving Harpe through, the red and white stripes of the barrier rising.

There aren't going to be any exercises, Harpe thought. Demichev is here for another briefing. Not for Suvorov. For the real one.

In the Magdalenenstrasse headquarters of the SSD, Major Gustav Klemm was working late. He had been away from his desk for two days with stomach flu, and an Everest of paper had accumulated in his absence. Klemm's office was part of the Trade Contacts Division of the SSD's Directorate for Surveillance; the division was responsible for monitoring the behavior of Western businessmen who had regular contact with the assorted foreign trade organizations of the German Democratic Republic. There were a lot of businessmen, and a lot of monitoring reports. As if that were not enough, the HVA added to the torrent of documents by forwarding "observations of interest" made in the Federal Republic or in West Berlin. There was an intimidating stack of such observations on the major's desk.

Klemm pulled the next file folder from the pile. It had been logged in two hours previously, with a Grade 3E priority. Klemm, after he had begun to read the observation report, frowned; it should have been sent with a higher priority than 3E, probably 2A from his first look at the contents. He would have to light another fire under the distribution clerks.

He went on into the file. It was a positive-identification signal from the HVA civilian surveillance station in West Berlin, originating from a contact two or three days previously; the document, for some indeterminate security reason, failed to state when the observation had been made. One of the watchers had picked up a meeting between Erich Kastner, who as far as was known was head of BND Berlin border surveillance, and an unidentified individual, male, Caucasian. The latter had been driving a silver BMW 320i; the car was traced through the plate registration to the ownership of a Paul Brand, an American businessman in West Berlin. Details of his organization followed, with a detailed addendum describing Brand's parent company in the United States.

Major Klemm continued through the rest of the report with mounting concern. When he finished the paragraph detailing Brand's dealings with the Ministry of Trade he swore under his breath and reached for the telephone.

Harpe had almost reached the turnoff from the Berlin-Zossen road onto the autobahn leading back to Vogelsdorf when he decided not to go back to his office. Instead he continued straight on, past the Schoenefeld airport, north towards the Kopenick District and his apartment building. The traffic was heavy, for East Berlin: day trippers returning from the country. Harpe cursed the driver of one of the ubiquitous two-cylinder Trabant sedans as it cut in front of him, sounding like an overgrown motorcycle. He tramped hard on the brake pedal, making the Wartburg's tires screech unnecessarily.

Control yourself, Harpe thought as the Trabant pulled away in a cloud of blue oil smoke. You can't stop the Russians by bending the car. If they're going to attack, the best you can do is get to the West and give them some kind of warning. If the West has even six hours it will help, they can be alert at least; if the Russians spot an alert, maybe they'll call the whole operation off. They'd have to have surprise, starting like this, from maneuvers. But will Brand's people take it seriously? What have I got? Not much, a peculiar meeting, no Germans in it, could be nothing. But I don't think it's nothing, there's more there . . .

He had to stop for a red light at the next intersection. His heart was pounding. Harpe took several deep slow breaths, willing himself into calm. He would never pass the checkpoint if he were feeling like this. He wouldn't pass the checkpoint if the documents hadn't turned up, either.

His apartment was only a few blocks away but Harpe decided not to go there either; he did not think there was an alert out for him, but if there were, his home would be where they'd start. Instead he began looking for a telephone kiosk. After a few minutes' search he found one, just off Hultschnerstrasse. There was also, wonder of wonders, a place to park the Wartburg.

The kiosk was still stifling from the residual heat of the day. Harpe dialed the Amt 16 switchboard number. While it rang he glanced at his watch: twenty past eight. He had thought it was later than that. He wondered, briefly, if the watch had stopped running and then started again.

"Switchboard," said a voice in his ear.

"This is Colonel Harpe," Harpe said. "Are there any messages for me?"

"Control," said the voice, warningly.

Harpe ransacked his memory for the day's clearance code. "Emerald."

"One moment, please, Colonel." A pause. A bead of perspiration edged down Harpe's upper lip; it tickled. "Yes, Colonel

Harpe. Just one. Vehicle maintenance called to say they have obtained new spark plugs for your car."

"Good." Harpe hung up, lightheaded with relief. He brushed the sweat from his lip and hurried back to the Wartburg.

Major Klemm was having difficulty obtaining information from the Trade Ministry; no one in the Technology Office worked this late on a Saturday, and the official who specialized in dealing with American electronics firms was out of the city for the weekend. Klemm finally pried the man's country number out of the Trade Ministry switchboard and then called SSD Records, again, to tell the clerks to hurry up. He wanted a list of everyone who worked, or had worked, with the Technology Office in the past two years, and who had had contact with Americans on a routine basis. The clerks were to search specifically for references to Paul Brand.

They promised, again, to hurry. Major Klemm dialed an outside line and called the country number the Ministry had given him. After fifteen rings he gave up; there was no one there. Reluctantly, he decided to inform his superior, Lieutenant-Colonel Schramm, that they might have a problem; perhaps a large problem.

Harpe parked the Wartburg near the Treptower S-Bahn station, bought a newspaper at one of the kiosks near the station entrance, and then began his stroll along Puschkin Allee towards Treptower Park. Out on the Spree River one of the White Fleet excursion boats was sliding away from the river port, bound southwards. Ahead and to Harpe's right across a vast carpet of grass rose the low mound of the Hill of Honor, with the Russian war memorial crowning it, the mausoleum and its huge statue of a Soviet soldier reddish-gold in the waning light.

I should have parked at the other end, Harpe thought. I may not have much time.

After a few minutes he had passed the Memorial. Turning into the section of the park called the Rose Garden, he began to look for the bench and the dead drop. The bench was on the path that led past the pond on the Memorial's southern side. Harpe had only used the drop once before; he hoped no one had taken up residence on the bench. It would have been better if the switchboard message had been about carburetor parts; that drop was behind a toilet tank in one of the public restrooms up at Alexanderplatz. There would have been a shorter trip to the border.

I suppose the Americans know what they're doing, Harpe thought. Ahead he could see the bench, vacant under the shadow of a lime tree. He slowed. A few people were on the path, couples mostly, walking in the last of the soft fading evening light. Harpe unfolded the newspaper, glancing at the headline — more about the Soviet Baikonur-Amur railroad opening — and sat down on the bench. His left hand hidden in the folds of the paper, he began to read the lead article with great interest.

After three minutes or so he looked up. No one was nearby except a blond couple, arms about each other's waists, walking slowly away from him under the deepening shadows of the trees. Harpe jiggled the paper and moved his left hand to slide his fingers under the seat of the bench.

For a dreadful moment he thought it wasn't there. Then he felt it: the sharp corner of an envelope. It was secured to the underside of the bench with double-sided tape. Harpe pried gently, feeling the envelope separate stickily from the warm metal seat.

Careful now, don't drop it.

The envelope pulled free. Harpe slipped it from beneath the bench and pressed the tape against the newspaper's underside. Then he rearranged the paper so that the envelope was folded out of sight.

The light was fading rapidly. Harpe got up, put the newspaper under his arm, and left the Rose Garden for the last time.

Major Klemm at last had received some of the files he had ordered from Records. He began scanning them, searching for the most likely candidates for recruitment by the West through the American named Brand. Klemm wanted a short list of suspect individuals by the time Colonel Schramm reached

Magdalenenstrasse; the colonel had been decidedly annoyed at being disturbed at home. He had also vetoed any further attempts by Klemm to contact the head of the American division of the Technology Office. Suppose, Schramm had pointed out tersely, the man was the one Brand was running, if the American were indeed running anyone. Do you want *that* on your record?

Klemm, who had merely wanted a shortcut to finding out which Ministry employees were in regular contact with Brand, realized he had put a foot into quicksand. He agreed hastily, and then redoubled his persecution of the clerks in Records.

The summer darkness was almost complete when Harpe returned from the park. He looked up and down the dimly lit street, more or less unobtrusively, as he unlocked the Wartburg. No one loitered, no men sat in cars down the curb trying to read newspapers by the light of the streetlamps.

My people wouldn't be that sloppy, anyway, Harpe thought. The SSD is far better than the KGB could dream of being, here.

He opened the door and got into the Wartburg. An S-Bahn train was entering the Treptower station up the street, its brakes squealing intermittently. Harpe removed the envelope from the newspaper and slit the flap with a thumbnail; he had some trouble since the nail was bitten almost to the quick. Inside was a wad of documents: identification papers in the name of Gerhardt Fritsch, complete with Harpe's photograph; a currency exchange permit; a document allowing him leave from his work at the Omega optics factory (he was a quality control supervisor); and an authorization for the bearer "Gerhardt Uwe Fritsch, with transit number 102016" to spend twenty-four hours in West Berlin for compassionate reasons, to wit, the terminal illness of his grandmother. His grandmother's married and maiden names as well as her address and the hospital of her treatment were also recorded. Harpe had no doubt that if the control post at the Friedrichstrasse U-Bahn transborder station contacted the Koenigen-Luise Hospital, they would be informed that Anna-Marie Fritsch, aged eighty-two, was at the point of death from pancreatitis, and that she was expecting, hourly, a visit from her grandson, Gerhardt Uwe.

The Americans are good at it, Harpe thought. Much better than anyone gives them credit for. And they do it under the noses of the BND, since the West Germans can't keep their own house clean.

There was one more document, with a scrap of rice paper clipped to it. On the rice paper was written: ONLY IF YOU NEED IT. Harpe crumpled the note into a ball and dropped it on the floor of the car; his mouth was already dry and if they caught him it wouldn't matter if he had choked down the rice paper or not.

The document was an HVA passage authorization, signed by General Markus Ott himself. The signature had to be a forgery but the form appeared absolutely authentic, down to the intricate web of the paper whose striations gave a moiré effect in the light of the streetlamps. Harpe slipped the HVA pass into his tunic with the other papers, thinking: They've got a document source over here. That bit of paper wasn't made in the West.

He tucked the empty envelope under the seat, started the Wartburg, and drove northeast along the banks of the Spree to Stralauer Platz, where he tucked the car away in a sidestreet near the Ostbahnhof railway station. The station was on the perimeter of an industrial area, and the street was quiet; the late shift would not start for a little while yet.

Perhaps I am going to be lucky, Harpe thought, getting out of his car and locking it carefully. He regretted, in a rather sentimental way, leaving the little vehicle behind; he had acquired it just four years ago, and it had been one of his most prized possessions.

Never mind, he thought, opening the trunk and removing the briefcase he had put there that morning in preparation. Perhaps in the West I'll be able to get another car. A Mercedes, perhaps. Or even an American car, a Lincoln or a Cadillac. Something big, shiny.

He managed a smile at the fantasy. If he were right about what the Russians were intending, the Americans would soon have more on their minds than big shiny cars for Colonel Joachim Harpe.

* * *

SSD Major Klemm was finally beginning to make some progress, which was just as well, since Lieutenant-Colonel Schramm had been breathing down the major's neck ever since arriving at Magdalenenstrasse. Schramm was up for promotion to full colonel, and the successful apprehension of an American agent in contact with the Trade Ministry would do him a great deal of good. Klemm still had a problem, however.

"This last one," Schramm said irritably, jabbing at the list of names on his desk. Klemm stood uncomfortably, not quite at attention, in front of the desk, hands clasped behind his back. The obligatory portrait of Erich Honecker, secretary of the Communist Party of the German Democratic Peoples' Republic, stared fixedly back at him from the mustard-yellow wall behind Schramm. "This last one," Schramm repeated. "Joachim Harpe. What's the matter there?"

"We don't have that file," Klemm said awkwardly. He had drunk too much coffee and badly needed to relieve his bladder. Honecker's expression seemed to acquire a disapproving cast. "Harpe's not a civilian. Special assignment from Military Intelligence Amt 16."

"The intelligence crew, eh?" said Schramm ruminatively. "The Military-Political Directorate's got his dossier, then. Have you called them?"

"No," Klemm said. The relationship between his own Surveillance Directorate and the sister organization responsible for monitoring the political loyalty of the armed forces was a delicate and prickly one. The head of each directorate felt that his organization should have control over the surveillance of military personnel, and the two jurisdictions had never been defined to anyone's satisfaction. Klemm was not about to jump willingly into that bearpit. "I preferred to wait for your authorization," he added.

Schramm nodded at one of the ugly green chairs, studded with tarnished brass tacks, in front of the desk. "Sit down," he said. Klemm sat. The vinyl upholstery of the chair squeaked and hissed under his buttocks, as if in protest at his presence. "Brand," Schramm muttered. He had already read the file on the American. "The identification was positive? He was in the car with the BND man, Kastner?"

"I called Pivka in HVA," Klemm said. "He told me there wasn't any doubt."

Schramm appeared to be thinking. After a moment he opened Brand's file again, and began to leaf through it. Klemm waited. After perhaps four minutes Schramm closed the file. "So Amt 16 was trying to arrange for Brand's cooperation. That's why there's a stay-away flag on his dossier. Amt 16 was working through the Trade Ministry, like they sometimes do. Do you suppose they had any luck with Brand?"

"I don't know," Klemm said.

"It's beginning to appear that the result might have been the other way around," Schramm said, with a tinge of satisfaction. The independent data collection and surveillance activities of military intelligence had always been an annoyance to the SSD, particularly when certain individuals were put off-limits to the men in Magdalenenstrasse, as Brand and Harpe had been. A good solid defection from military intelligence to the West would suit the SSD's organizational interests very nicely, as well as Schramm's personal ones.

"Fine," Schramm said, sitting up abruptly from the slouched position he had assumed behind his desk. "Locate Harpe, right away. I'll try to get his file out of the Military-Political Directorate, or at least a photograph of the bastard." He paused. "I'll also arrange for a stop order under his own name at the border checkpoints. If he spots us looking for him, he might run. Make collecting him easier." He paused for a moment. "And if Brand sticks his head through the Wall for one second, I want him. Do what you have to."

U-Bahn line Number 6 begins at the northern boundary of West Berlin, runs southeast until it reaches the edge of the Soviet sector, and then continues through six stations until it re-emerges in the western half of the city. Of the six stations five are closed, empty, and guarded. The sixth is Friedrichstrasse, and there one can board a train, if one is East German and has the correct papers, for the West.

Harpe, as far as he knew, had the correct papers, and there were now only three people ahead of him at the last set of steel barriers before the station platform itself. The control officer seemed uncommonly conscientious, unfortunately, checking every set of papers with micrometer precision. Harpe adjusted the civilian hat a little, hoping the gray suit would not attract attention by its wrinkles. It had been in the briefcase all day; he had tried unsuccessfully to shake out the worst of the creases in the toilet cubicle in the Ostbahnhof station, just before stuffing his uniform — oh, the finality of that — into the toilet reservoir. After some internal debate he had put his army identification into the tank in a different cubicle; if he were checked at random he might be able to talk his way out with the help of the SSD authorization, but not if he were found to be carrying army papers in a second name.

The short line now shortened by a third; the middle-aged couple ahead of him at the control point were obviously, from their speech and clothes, West Germans. The officer behind the glass inspected their papers with great care. The West Germans fidgeted.

"Visiting relatives here?" asked the officer. He was about thirty, with washed-out blue eyes set a little too closely together.

"Yes," the man said. "My cousins," he added unnecessarily.

The officer nodded and handed the papers back. The West Germans went through the barrier as quickly as dignity allowed. Harpe found himself face to face with the control officer, who studied him without apparent interest. Harpe pushed his permits and identification under the glass, trying to exhibit the correct proportions of nervousness and anticipation that would be expected of an East German about to spend a night and a day in the West.

The control officer read the documents, and, without looking up, said, "How long has she been sick?"

"About ten days," Harpe said. "Pancreatitis. It says there."

"How are you going to get to Lichterfelde Hospital tonight?"

"My grandmother's at Koenigen-Luise Hospital," Harpe said, exhibiting surprise. "I'm going there tomorrow."

"You've got somewhere to stay?"

"Yes. Relatives. My uncle." This was dangerous ground.

The control officer recorded Harpe's identification and time of crossing in the transit ledger, then pushed the documents back. Harpe tucked them away in his suit. "Go on," said the officer.

Harpe turned towards the barrier and took a step. He was two meters from the West.

"Just a minute."

Harpe turned around. The consternation on his face was not manufactured. "What?" he said, thinking, I'll have to use the SSD identification, God knows what complications . . .

"You're due back through here before eight tomorrow," the officer said. "You've already wasted two hours. Don't try to make them up."

"I won't be late," Harpe said. "I'll be here well before eight."

The electrical lock on the barrier clicked, and he was through.

Berlin - Bonn
2:30 A.M., August 15

THE TEMPELHOF AIR TERMINAL was almost deserted, except for a clutch of US army officers awaiting a MAC flight back to the States. All traffic through the old Berlin airfield was military now, the civilian airlines using the newer facilities of Tegel airport in the north of the city.

"We'll go up to the VIP lounge," Anderson said, as they passed the group of officers, three of whom were playing a languid game of poker on the top of a suitcase. "The security's better up there."

Brand nodded and glanced around at Kastner to see if he'd heard. "Good," Kastner said. "When will the plane be ready?" Harpe, trailing along behind the BND man, was looking somewhat nervous; there were dark semicircles under his eyes.

"It should have been ready by now," Anderson said. They went through a metal door and up a flight of stairs to the lounge. "Some technical problem or other."

"I hope it isn't much longer," Harpe ventured as they entered the lounge, a long room with several sofas and chairs and low tables and a bar along one wall. "They are looking for me already. I am sure of it."

"Don't worry," Anderson said. He went to the windows that looked out onto the airfield and made sure the curtains were tightly closed. "They can't get near you here, even if they know you're gone. There's plenty of security. Herr Kastner's people, as well as some of our own."

Harpe nodded and flopped into a chair. The three-hour initial debriefing at the US consulate had drained a good deal from him. Brand sat down across from Harpe and said reassuringly, "We'll be out soon." Privately he was filled with apprehension. Both he and Anderson had hoped the East German would bring with him some definite information about the reality or unlikelihood of an impending Russian attack, but all he could offer was the peculiar behavior of the Soviet staff out at Zossen the previous afternoon. Anderson and Kastner had been on the telephone half a dozen times during the debriefing, trying to persuade both Pullach and Langley that Harpe's fears should be taken seriously, but they did not seem to have made much progress. Both the West German defense minister and his deputy were in Brussels at a NATO conference, and the head of the BND was on a week's vacation. Kastner had taken the radical step of asking Horstmann to contact Bundeswehr intelligence, but the military had no indications of Soviet aggression and were unwilling to advise an alert on an unconfirmed report. As for Langley, the CIA computers had swallowed Anderson's long priority message, but had apparently not decided what to do about it.

Joachim might just be overreacting, Brand thought. After all, NATO monitors hundreds of critical indicators that are supposed to warn us of a surprise attack in the making. And there are all kinds of troop and aircraft movements going on over there anyway, for the Suvorov maneuvers. How much does that confuse the indicators, I wonder? Joachim's information's certainly vague enough; if nothing happens, we won't be able to fault him for it, and he'll be out of the East. Although Langley was willing enough to withdraw him anyway. With the force reduction talks coming up, they'd rather be taking in a defector than running a CIA man in the Soviet GHQ.

"There's nothing to drink, dammit," Anderson said, surfacing from behind the bar where he had been rummaging about hopefully. "By God, I could use one."

"So could I," said Kastner.

"I'm going to check on the plane," Anderson said, and left the lounge. Brand watched the door swing closed behind him. He wondered if he should phone Jenny.

* * *

"You're going to *Bonn?*" she had said, slamming the cupboard door shut, rattling the glasses. "Tonight? Just like that?"

"I'm sorry," he said. "It came up all of a sudden. Walt asked me to do it as a favor."

"Why in hell," she said, "can't Walt go to Bonn himself?" She had overlooked a coffee cup when putting the dishes away and picked it up with quick, angry movements. She put in the cupboard, this time without slamming the door. "We were supposed to go out to Grunewald tomorrow afternoon. You were going to teach Alison how to sail. When are you going to be back?"

"Monday," Brand said. "Maybe Tuesday."

She leaned back against the kitchen counter. Brand could not remember when he had last seen her so angry. It was a shock; she was normally understanding about his absences.

"Monday," she said. "Or Tuesday. Goddamn it, Paul, I know you have to travel on business. I don't mind so much when it really is business. This isn't. You've been nervous as a cat these last few days, snapping at the kids. It's the other thing, isn't it? What you're doing for Walt."

"What other thing? Jenny—"

"Wait till I've finished. I'm not blind. You used to be an intelligence officer, and I know damn well you still are. How naive do you think I am? Walt doesn't spend any more of his time than he has to thinking up ways to sell more gadgetry to the East Germans. Trade attaché, hell, he's a CIA man and you are too, even if your name's not on their payroll. I've put up with it ever since we came to Germany, and I'm sick of it. Every time you cross the Wall I wonder if you'll make a mistake, if you'll end up in an East German prison for ten years. Or when you go out in the evening, whether they'll find you in the Spree next morning with a faceful of cyanide. I don't know how I'm going to stand it much longer."

"Jenny," he said, and reached out. "Look—"

She pushed his hand away. "Stop it. Go to Bonn. But when you come back, we're going to have to talk this out. I have to tell you, I've been thinking of a separation."

Brand let his hand drop to his side. "Oh," he said. He felt as though someone had kicked him in the throat.

"Paul, I still love you. Maybe I'm not a good CIA wife. But I can't stand this any more."

"I was going to pull out," Brand said. "Very soon. As soon as this business in Bonn is over, I'm going to tell Walt I'm resigning. We'll go back to the States, somebody else from Mitex can take over here. It's time. The children need to go home."

She looked at him doubtfully. "Are you sure?"

"Yes," Brand said. "I've been intending to make the move for some time." He rubbed his eyes. "I'm sorry I took so long."

"So am I." She was still angry. "Why didn't you think about how I felt?"

"I didn't know you knew."

"Men," she said.

He wished the air had been cleared before he left. The day he got back from Bonn he was going to call Alex in Boston and ask for an immediate replacement to be sent out. Then tell Anderson he was through. If the SSD linked him to Harpe, he would no longer be able to set foot in the East. He had made his last journey across the Wall.

"Joachim," he said to Harpe. "Are they really going to attack?"

"No one believes me," Harpe said, with some bitterness. "I am not even sure why I believe it myself. But I think they're coming, if not today then tomorrow."

Anderson came back into the lounge. "The plane's ready," he said. "You'd better hop."

"You're not coming?" Harpe asked.

"No. There'll be a debriefing team coming in from the States this afternoon, they'll work with the BND people, and military intelligence." Anderson looked at his watch. "Colonel Harpe, you'd better try to get some sleep on the plane. You've got a long day ahead of you."

Harpe nodded, a morose expression on his face. Everybody got up and trooped towards the door. Brand decided, suddenly: there was a telephone on the bar.

"I'll catch up," he said. "I want to give Jenny a call."

Anderson looked at him quizzically for a moment, then nodded. "The plane's out in front of the terminal," he said. "A Beech C12 utility transport. You know the type?"

"Yes. Thanks."

Anderson nodded again, and was gone.

She answered on the third ring. Brand imagined her, tousled, leaning on one elbow, holding the bedside telephone in the dim light of the blue pottery lamp she had always liked so much. "Hello?" Blurred with sleep.

"Jenny, it's me. I'm still in Berlin, leaving in a couple of minutes."

"Oh." He could sense her awakening completely. "Is anything wrong?"

"I don't know. There might be. Listen, I want you to get the kids up right away. Book the earliest flight you can out of Berlin. To England at least. If you can get one to the States, do that. Take all the cash out of the safe in the office there, don't forget your passport." He paused. "If you can't get a plane out of Europe right away, go to Bonn. Check with the embassy; I'll call them and tell them where I'm staying. They'll tell you."

"Will they do that?"

"Remember who I work for?"

"Alright. Paul — is it going to happen this time?"

"It might be. I don't know, I may look very foolish this time next week. I hope so."

"I'll call Pan Am right away." She was thoroughly awake now.

"Good. Contact your father as soon as you know where you're going. I'll contact him from Bonn, if I can't raise you in Berlin." He paused again. "I love you."

"I love you," she said. "Keep yourself safe."

He rang off and hurried out of the lounge.

STAVKA - Kalinin
3:10 A.M., August 15

WELL TO THE NORTH OF MOSCOW, perhaps thirty minutes' drive south of the outskirts of Kalinin, there was a restricted zone of some tens of square kilometers. At the center of the zone, protected by antiaircraft guns and missile batteries and two full regiments of KGB security troops, was the STAVKA complex, the new operational headquarters of the Soviet General Staff.

The complex had been built, with Byzantine security precautions, over the previous two years; there was little to see on the surface of the zone but a triple barbed-wire fence with watchtowers, two heavy-duty asphalt access roads, and a scattering of low concrete structures topped by mazes of aerials and parabolic receiving antennae. To the ever-present American satellites orbiting far above, the installation appeared to be only one more of the enigmatic communications complexes the Russians built to deal with the torrent of information pouring down from their own orbital surveillance systems.

Ninety percent of the headquarters was underground, protected by monstrous slabs of steel-reinforced concrete sunk into the earth. Despite this protection, however, the complex was not intended to be the central military command location if there were nuclear war; that was reserved to the Zhiguli Supreme Command Post, under a granite plateau on the Volga River near Kuibyshev. The Kalinin installation had been built for use in lower-level conflicts, to centralize and replace the aging and cramped facilities in Moscow. The General Staff was confident that it would have enough warning of a strategic nuclear attack to evacuate key personnel to Zhiguli; in fact, full activation of the latter complex in the present circumstances was politically unwise since Moscow wanted to convince the United States that there was no danger of a nuclear first strike. To move the military and political leaders, lock, stock and barrel to Zhiguli would indicate precisely the opposite.

The main bunker of the Kalinin installation was referred to, unofficially, as the Lenin Bunker. On its lowest level were conference and communications facilities for the senior officers of the General Staff, and for its superior body, the Defense Council, which consisted of Nikolayev, Ivanov, Fedashkin, KGB Chairman Minkov, and Secretary Yakov D. Lensky.

At this particluar meeting of the Council, two other men were present: Marshal Viktor Besedin, chief of the General Staff, and Colonel-General Vasili Tsarev, head of the General Staff Directorate of Military Intelligence, the GRU. Besedin and Tsarev were looking decidedly anxious, the latter more so. Glasses of tea sat untouched in front of them on the polished oak table.

"What do you mean, the operation may have been compromised?" asked Nikolayev. He was very angry; they had risked so much, on the assumption of secrecy, and now this.

"It is by no means certain," Besedin said. "It is only possible. Our monitoring of NATO communications indicates that if there was a warning, they haven't taken it seriously."

"Explain how this happened," Fedashkin said in a brittle voice.

"General Tsarev can explain it best," Besedin said. "The GRU was indirectly involved, unfortunately." Besedin glanced at Minkov, who was gazing abstractedly into space.

Tsarev cleared his throat and began to speak. "We maintain liaison with the East German Military Intelligence Service, as you know. One of these liaison officers, a German, worked with the section of the GRU Sixth Directorate — electronic intelligence — that is based at Zossen headquarters. Last night the SSD decided to pick him up as a security risk. I won't bore you with the details, but East German military intelligence had also been running him as an agent collecting Western electronic secrets under Trade Ministry cover. We were aware of this; the officer was extremely useful at Zossen because of his work with Westerners. At any rate, SSD decided to question the man. They couldn't find him. About 11 P.M. yesterday it was discovered that a male of his description had crossed into West Berlin about an hour previously, on false papers. The SSD contacted military intelligence, who called Zossen. The man had been out at Zossen yesterday afternoon, looking for his Russian liaison, who naturally was at the Barbarossa Red briefing. The German wasn't seen again before he made the crossing."

"Is there any chance," asked Nikolayev, "that he found out what was going on at that briefing?"

"They're doing damage assessment at Zossen right now," said Tsarev. "In addition to everything else, the German is a trained intelligence officer. It is possible he guessed something." Tsarev was pale and sweating. If Barbarossa Red had to be called off, after all the preparations and the attendant risks, his punishment would be dreadful.

"But you say," said Ivanov to Besedin, "that there is no special NATO alert."

"That's correct. Only the normal precautions they take when we are on a major exercise."

"What would happen," asked Lensky, "if we gave a halt order now?"

Fedashkin looked at the clock on the wall above the big illuminated map of Europe. "It would cause catastrophic problems. The lead elements of the first ground echelon began moving west at 0200. They will be crossing the border at first light, just before five. A halt order would throw everything into confusion because the movement timetables are extremely complex. We would have forty-kilometer traffic jams which would not be cleared until well after first light. American satellite surveillance would leave Washington in no doubt as to our intentions. The Americans by now have noticed our troop movements, but their knowledge is clouded by the cover of the exercises. The infra-red trackers up there will give them some indication of our approach to the border, but interpretation of that sort of data is difficult, it won't be conclusive. They will need at least ninety minutes to decide that the IR traces are showing a major move to the frontier. But if we are caught in daylight there will be no doubt. They will see the tanks and the infantry columns with no difficulty."

"In short," said Ivanov, "we cannot stop."

"That's right," Fedashkin said. "Unless we are willing to suffer the consequences. First of all, the Americans and the West Europeans will be frightened out of their wits, and after that we will look like fools. They may decide that we had determined to go through with the attack, but were too incompetent to carry it out with the surprise we needed for success. I need hardly state the implications of *that*, both for American aggressiveness and the loyalty of the Pact nations. To both it will seem that we are incapable of effective military action."

"What if NATO goes on alert, say, in the next five minutes?" asked Minkov. He did not appear to be excessively worried.

"They have little reaction time," Besedin interposed. "Most of their heavy formations are scores of miles from the frontier, it's early Sunday morning with many officers and personnel away from their units, and their alerting procedures, at least for the ground formations, are very poor. Their air component has better alert routines, but Barbarossa Red is intended to suppress most of the initial NATO air reaction by heliborne attack on the forward airfields, use of incapacitant gases, and air strikes at first light on their rear bases."

Nikolayev studied the wall map for a moment. "They have their nuclear reaction force out there," he said. "The planes, what do they call them?"

"Quick reaction aircraft," Tsarev supplied, unprompted. "QRA."

"What are those planes going to do when our helicopters fly over the border?"

"Nothing," said Besedin. "The NATO governments won't release them on unconfirmed reports, or even when we move over the frontier. The QRA planes are intended to respond to a sudden nuclear strike, and we aren't doing that. They'll be in the air, as soon as the first alert is out, but Brussels will withdraw them to secure bases in the Benelux countries as soon as they realize we're attacking conventionally. The West won't want to escalate to theater nuclear war at the beginning."

"NATO cannot do a great deal in the next two hours," Fedashkin added. "Their QRA aircraft are not an issue. In any case, our assault helicopters are scheduled to overfly the border at 0330." He looked at the wall clock. "That is only a few minutes from now."

"There is no choice, then," Nikolayev said.

"No, Secretary," said Fedashkin. "Not militarily."

"And the East German spy has not been able to raise an alarm."

"If they had believed him four hours ago," said Besedin, "and gone on alert, we would have detected their decision in time to countermand the start orders. After one o'clock this morning it was too late."

Nikolayev looked again at the wall map, and then at the immobile faces of his advisors.

"There will be no halt order," he said, knowing the decision had already been taken from him. "Give the codes for Barbarossa Red."

NATO Headquarters, Brussels
3:20 - 4:08 A.M., August 15

THE HEADQUARTERS of the North Atlantic Treaty Organization resembled a termite nest broken open by a bear: officers, diplomats, civilian staff scurrying about unshaven, hollow-eyed from interrupted sleep, wishing for coffee for which there was no time. In the Situation Center, which housed the NATO-wide communications and computer resources used both for routine operations and crisis management, the tension had been growing since 0240, when satellite surveillance began to transmit infra-red signatures indicating large-scale Soviet vehicle movements. Brussels knew that the Warsaw Pact was intending to carry out extensive night exercises, but the scale of the activity was surprising. As well, a great deal of unusual air traffic had been detected on the eastern edge of the maneuver areas: this bore the earmarks of large concentrations of helicopters.

At 0245 the Military Committee had been called into session as a precautionary measure, and some of its members — those who were available on this summer weekend — had reached SHAPE military headquarters at Casteau, Belgium, by 0310. Fevered communications began among the committee members and their respective governments, as soon as London, Bonn, Rome and the other capitals could be awakened, and Washington. NATO's secretary-general in London was alerted, and issued orders for the NATO Council — the governing body of the organization — to meet at the Brussels headquarters within two hours, shortly after dawn. Five minutes after he issued the summons, Casteau HQ received computer analyses suggesting very large Soviet troop movements not far east of the frontier, but the conviction at the headquarters still was that the activity was no more than night exercises on an unprecedented scale. This sentiment was strengthened by the fact that the Warsaw Pact liaison had told Brussels that the Suvorov maneuvers were to be more than usually elaborate. Moreover, none of the non-Russian Pact formations had moved, except for some rather heavy vehicle traffic around Berlin which could be no more than supply convoys testing their ability to supply the Warsaw Pact forward echelon. Finally, the signals traffic that NATO electronic intelligence was collecting from the Russian command net appeared to be absolutely normal for a night exercise.

At 0325 the Military Committee in Casteau, on the advice of the secretary-general and those of the NATO Council who were available up the road in Brussels, decided that NATO forces should take no immediate action until the Situation Center had more time to draw conclusions from the confusing flood of information pouring in over the computer and communications nets.

While it was left more or less unsaid, the council feared that a major NATO alert would frighten the Russians into assuming that Western forces planned to attack the Soviet formations in their assembly areas, while they presented agreeably concentrated targets for nuclear weapons. The American and British representatives on the council argued bitterly against the refusal to take some kind of action, which was supported by Denmark, Spain, Holland, Belgium and, somewhat oddly, by Bonn, where Rudel was maintaining an open line from the Chancellery. The major bone of contention was that a general war alert would require dispersal of nuclear warheads from the storage centers — "igloos," the Americans called them — to operational units or temporary munitions dumps. If this were to happen, the Russians might be forgiven for assuming the worst, especially if they really were engaged in nothing more than troop exercises. On both sides of the frontier it was generally accepted that dispersal of nuclear devices meant one of two things: either the dispersing power expected an attack, and was protecting its retaliatory ability, or it was planning one, and was placing the warheads with the forces that were to deliver them.

As usual, the French observers at the Brussels HQ held their tongues, and spoke only to Paris.

President Hood, who had been first alerted at the White House at 2120 Washington time, did in fact take some measures: he ordered an "immediate exercise alert" for the American ready reserves, and had the Current Action Center under the Pentagon alerted for his arrival.

The suspicions Harpe had brought over the Wall six hours previously were still being digested by CIA and NSA computers, where they had joined a mass of other unsubstantiated information. The CIA Berlin cipher office had flagged Harpe's report, accidentally, as Grade Nine, although Anderson had submitted it as Grade One. Moreover, the priority code had been corrupted in transmission and the Langley communications officer who had received the despatch had downgraded it because he could not make sense of the designation. He was supposed to query the originating station if this happened; however, he was within two minutes of going off watch, and decided to leave the query for his relief. Unfortunately, his relief arrived at the station several minutes late, and in his irritation the watch officer neglected to mention the corrupted priority. The message, with its already downgraded Nine designation, began to work its way through the silicon intricacies of CIA computers.

At 0328 the forward radar stations along the German frontier reported that they were experiencing intense electronic countermeasures. Three minutes after that two of the installations, equipped with more advanced signal processors, informed Brussels that they were picking up the signatures of "many" low-flying aircraft, probably, because of their speed and altitude, helicopters. The machines were flying due west, and almost at the frontier. Six minutes later a priority call from NATO Northern Army Group headquarters at Monchen-Gladbach reported that an unknown number of helicopters had crossed the border and were flying at minimal altitude and maximum speed into the Federal Republic. The radar stations apparently had reported them so late because of the electronic countermeasures, and because the machines were flying almost in the treetops; in fact, most of the crossing reports had been sent by ground troops of the *Bundesgrenzschutz*, the German light infantry formations responsible for slowing an attack until the heavy NATO forces could deploy into battle order.

The Brussels Situation Center immediately began trying to contact the forward radar stations and border guard posts directly, to find out exactly what was happening. Even at this point there was concern in Brussels and Casteau that the Russian helicopters might be no more than a large-scale training mission that had lost its way and strayed accidentally over the border; there was no indication of attack by ground troops, although the infra-red sensors on the satellites far above indicated increasing vehicle traffic now less than forty kilometers from the frontier.

A direct link with the radar at Wolfsburg was established at 0340. The officer in the Situation Center exchanged perhaps three words with the station, when a high screech erupted from the receiver and the line went dead.

Almost simultaneously, the NATO headquarters building vibrated, and all the lights went out.

Bonn
4:15 - 5:00 A.M., August 15

THE BEECH TRANSPORT AIRCRAFT carrying Brand, Harpe and Kastner banked into its landing approach to the small military airfield near Siegburg, twelve kilometers northeast of Bonn. Harpe was sprawled in his seat, head back against the rest, mouth open a little, sound asleep in the cabin's dim light. Brand glanced across the aisle to make sure the East German's seatbelt was fastened; it was. Kastner was hunched over in the seat ahead of Harpe's, chin on hand, staring out the window at the occasional speckle of light below: village streetlamps, gasoline stations, the yellow windows of early risers.

The curtain separating the flight deck from the cabin was drawn abruptly aside and the copilot emerged. He closed the curtain and made his way towards Brand, holding the seatbacks to steady himself against the Beech's incline. He looked worried. Brand felt a tickle of apprehension.

"Colonel Brand?" The copilot had to raise his voice to be heard over the hum of the twin turboprops. Harpe stirred a little.

"Something the matter?" asked Brand.

"We think so. About twenty minutes ago we got a partial transmission about a lot of air traffic near the border. We started monitoring some of the military frequencies. It looks as though there's a partial alert on."

"Only partial? Did you check with Siegburg control?"

"They don't know any more than we do. There's something wrong with communications."

"Any military formations based at Siegburg?" Brand asked.

"No. It's used mainly for in-country VIP flights and some training. It's pretty small."

"No trouble getting down?"

"No."

Kastner had been following this as well as his English allowed. "You mean they're leaving on the lights of the runway?" he said.

"Apparently," the copilot said, turning to go back to the flight deck. "We'll be down in just a few minutes, sit tight."

"Idiots," Kastner said in German. He peered out the window. Past his head Brand could see streaks of light outlining the runway; the Beech was banked well over, about to go on final approach. "An open invitation."

"What?" asked Harpe, sitting up abruptly. His eyes lacked focus.

"There's a partial alert on," Brand told him. "Something's happened." My God, Jenny and the kids, he thought. Where are they?

Harpe opened his mouth as if to speak, and then closed it, shrugging fatalistically. He slumped back in his seat, staring at nothing.

Brand heard thumps as the landing gear went down and locked. The Beech's engines hummed steadily; the aircraft bumped a little as it passed through a patch of turbulence. The outer marker lights slid underneath. The Beech sank a little and the landing gear rumbled on the runway; after a second or two the engines howled in reverse thrust, then settled to a low buzz. The aircraft trundled towards the terminal, rocking gently on its undercarriage. Brand, staring out the window, thought he could see a streak of gray on the eastern horizon.

"I hope that car's here to meet us," Kastner said, unbuckling his seatbelt. "I don't want to be stuck on an airbase if the Russians have suddenly gone mad."

Brand got his travel bag from under the seat, got up stiffly, and joined the two Germans at the C12's door. Eventually the plane drew to a halt a hundred meters from the airfield's control building. On the roof of the control tower, a beacon swept the night. The Beech's twin propellors whined to a stop. The copilot came back from the flight deck, opened the door and let down the steps. "Anything else?" Brand asked the copilot as the Germans left the plane.

"No. I'm not hot to go back to Berlin, though. We were supposed to turn right around."

"Maybe you should.wait half an hour," Brand suggested. The copilot looked at him sharply, then nodded. Brand went down the steps and joined the others as they walked towards the glass doors of the control building. His left shoulder ached. He shifted the travel bag to the other one, which was no better. When they reached the doors he lowered the bag to the pavement; Kastner did the same with his. Harpe had no luggage at all. Brand had bought him some shaving equipment, underwear, and a couple of shirts, and had stuffed them into his own bag.

"Where's that bastard car?" Kastner said. The tarmac was brightly lit but deserted except for a Luftwaffe C130, a light liaison helicopter, and the Beech. A service vehicle was parked next to the C130 but no groundcrew were visible. High above, the control tower beacon strobed against the stars. A light breeze was blowing out of the east; dawn was coming.

The three men stood uncertainly. "I'd better find a phone," Kastner said after a moment. "They might have thought—"

"What's that?" said Harpe suddenly.

They listened. Brand heard a faint steady drumbeat from the direction of the eastern horizon, now just visible. After only a few seconds the noise became distinctly louder.

"Somebody coming in low," said Kastner.

"More than one," Brand said. "Helicopters. A lot of them."

The airfield lights suddenly went out, the tower beacon with them. Without the glare of the fluorescents the eastern horizon was immediately more defined. Behind the three men the Beech's starters began to whine.

"You guys!" The copilot was standing in the C12's doorway, his face a pale oval in the dawnlight. "Get on board, quick. There's a whole fucking battalion of Soviet choppers coming. *Move it.*"

"Jesus," Brand said. He half turned for the plane. My God, he thought, how did they manage to surprise us so?

"Wait," Kastner said. Yellow light splashed across the tarmac at the corner of the control building. A black Mercedes followed the light, moving slowly, unconcernedly, past the C130 towards them. The beat of the approaching helicopters was very loud now. The copilot was shouting something from the Beech, Brand couldn't hear what.

Kastner sprinted for the Mercedes, followed by Harpe. Brand, with a despairing glance over his shoulder at the Beech, followed, his luggage forgotten on the pavement beside Kastner's. The C12's door was already half closed and the little plane was beginning to move. The Americans were going to try to get out.

Kastner wrenched open the Mercedes' door, shouting something at the driver. One of the Russian helicopters pounded right overhead, travelling west. Brand looked up involuntarily. There was just enough illumination from the Mercedes' headlights to identify it as a Mil-24 ground support helicopter, painted in splotches of tan and dark green, a red star outlined in white on the fuselage belly, the stub wings jagged with rocket pods and gun capsules.

The Mercedes' headlights went out. Flares exploded out on the airfield, throwing the C130, the liaison helicopter, and the control building into stark relief. Red and green tracer began to flow out of the eastern sky.

Brand piled into the back of the Mercedes, falling on top of Harpe. The big car accelerated and turned suddenly, almost throwing Brand out the still-open door. He managed to grab the armrest and slam the door shut. Kastner was in the front seat, yelling at the driver.

"—to the bridges before—"

The liaison helicopter absorbed a stream of tracer and blew up. Brand felt a blast of heat on his face. Bright sparks flickered all over the Luftwaffe C130 as cannon shells struck the fuselage and tail. In the flares' light, Brand saw the Beech out on the taxiway, gaining speed, trying to reach the runway. Suddenly it turned into a blinding balloon of orange and yellow flame.

The Mercedes was travelling fast now, slewing around the corner of the control building, heading for the airport access road. Ahead and above the car the dark shapes of two more helicopters were settling towards the ground. They weren't putting down any gunfire.

The troop transports, Brand thought as the Mercedes howled down the access road right under the huge descending Mil-6 helicopter. They'll put troops down to grab the landing strips and hang on until the Russians can send planes to land more men and heavy equipment. Then they'll dig in and fight until the ground forces link up with them. Are they really expecting to get all the way to Bonn on the ground?

Jenny, Jenny, where are you?

West of the Siegburg airfield, across the Rhine in Bonn, Rudel was hurrying out of the Chancellery. He had been awake since ten minutes to three, when Brussels had contacted him about the threatening developments across the frontier. He had immediately called the Federal Security Council to the Chancellery, as well as those members of the cabinet who were available. Both the defense minister and his deputy were, unfortunately, out of the country, the latter in Paris and the former, as luck would have it, in Brussels. The defense minister arranged an open line from NATO HQ to the Chancellery, and Rudel and his staff followed developments over that for forty minutes, until the line suddenly failed. Contact was not reestablished for another quarter of an hour, and even then the connection was very poor. Apparently several key telephone exchanges in Belgium had been sabotaged, and the main power line to the Brussels HQ had been cut for half an hour just after 3:30 A.M., the result of another bomb attack. Casteau battle headquarters was having difficulty reestablishing communication with the Northern Army Group at Monchen-Gladbach. Technicians in Brussels managed to get a line open to the Central Army Group operations headquarters at Seckenheim at 0415; that HQ had also experienced communications sabotage and reported that it had been attacked by helicopter-borne troops around 0345. These had been driven off after half an hour of bitter fighting.

By 0430 the Chancellery, through contact with Brussels and its links to various Bundeswehr commands, had begun to form an idea of the weight and direction of the Soviet attack. It was at this point that a large force of low-flying helicopters was reported by a militia post about twenty kilometers to the east of Bonn; the machines were moving directly towards the capital. Emergency plans existed to move key government personnel out of Bonn to Freiburg near the French border if the capital were about to be overrun, but the plans had assumed at least twelve hours' warning. The only air transport immediately available was a Luftwaffe helicopter that had flown down from Cologne airport shortly after the start of the emergency and was now waiting, engines warmed, on the Chancellery grounds near the *Kanzlerbungalow*, Rudel's official residence.

Several valuable minutes were wasted while Rudel and the members of his Security Council tried to decide whether to remain and risk the possibility of capture, or flee the capital and try to pick up the reins of government from Freiburg. But nothing was ready in the alternate capital; Rudel decided to leave the Chancellery temporarily for the relative safety of the Bundeswehr Third Corps headquarters, south of Bonn at Koblenz.

So now Rudel was trotting down the Chancellery steps, followed by the members of the Security Council, and a couple of aides hoping for a place on the helicopter. He had called his residence and told Anna-Marie to go directly to the aircraft and wait for him there. She had sounded frightened but in control when he told her the Russians were on the way; she remembered the stories of 1945.

The little group was perhaps a hundred meters from the helicopter when they heard the beat of the Russian Mil-24. The sound seemed all around them, reflected and re-reflected by the trees of the park; it was impossible to pinpoint the direction from which the machine was coming. Ahead, on the lawn, the Luftwaffe helicopter was running up its engines, its rotor blades spinning at near liftoff speed.

And then, a hundred meters above it to the right, the city's glow reflecting dully in its dun-and-green finish, was an enormous helicopter with a red star on its belly.

West Berlin
4:20 - 5:00 A.M., August 15

THE EARLIEST FLIGHT Jennifer Brand had been able to book was an Air France airbus for Frankfurt, leaving Tegel airport at ten to five. There was a British Air connecting flight out of Frankfurt to London at 7:30; after some internal debate, she had decided to leave the city immediately rather than wait for a direct flight.

Now she sat in the departure lounge, numb with fatigue and apprehension, Alison leaning against her, half asleep, David on her other side staring glazedly into space. Both children, thank God, were behaving themselves; awakened at three in the morning, they had sensed their mother's distress and had been subdued and quiet ever since. All Jennifer had told them was that they were on their way for a surprise visit to grandfather in England.

David squirmed. "Mommy?"

"Yes?" Jennifer looked at her watch; ten minutes until boarding.

"I'm thirsty."

"I'm thirsty, too," Alison said, straightening. Her small face, like her brother's, was pinched and pale with fatigue.

"You'll have to have water. I haven't any change for the drink machines."

"That's awright."

They really must be thirsty, she thought, holding David up

to the water fountain, or they'd be campaigning for soft drinks. Ten thousand dollars in my purse and I haven't any change. I never realized Paul kept that kind of cash around the house. Thank God he did.

For no particular reason she thought of the red Audi 6000, her own car, down in the parking bays of the airport. She didn't like leaving the car there for any length of time, especially the Audi. They were preferred targets for professional thieves.

She sat down again, David on her lap, and thought: If Paul's warning comes true, I'll never see the car again anyway. I wonder what's happening out there, in the dark beyond the Wall.

An attendant in an Air France uniform appeared and opened the door to the passenger ramp leading out to the aircraft. The twenty or so travellers in the departure lounge stirred sleepily, reaching for sweaters and cabin luggage. Jennifer put her son down and began helping Alison with her yellow nylon jacket. When she looked up again another man, also Air France, older than the first, was standing at the exit door next to the first attendant. They were talking quietly, worried expressions on their faces. Jennifer's stomach turned over.

After a moment the older man turned to the passengers in the lounge and said, in French-accented German, "Please excuse me, ladies and gentlemen. Your flight is about to leave, but there is some information you ought to have first. About an hour ago a large number of helicopters flew from East Germany into the Federal Republic, and began making landings there. There have been reports of fighting in West Germany, but as yet there have been no hostile acts against this city. We do not know exactly what this all means, or how serious the situation actually is."

He paused and took a deep breath. Under the hard fluorescent light he looked pale and strained. "Our flight crew has agreed to attempt to fly out before the situation becomes worse. The aircraft will go directly to Paris, not to Frankfurt. We will leave it to you to decide whether or not to board. It is possible there will be some risk."

A blond man wearing glasses started to ask a question. The Air France official held up a hand and repeated the announcement in his own tongue. As he spoke, Jennifer stood quite still, paralyzed with indecision. Stay, and risk the Russians, or go, and risk death on the way to Paris?

Paul told me to get out, she thought. But he didn't tell me I'd be faced with this.

She knew enough about modern warfare to realize that if the NATO garrison of West Berlin resisted to the bitter end, the city would be devastated. It could go on for days, no water and no electricity and no food towards the end, no medicines, the hospitals overflowing, no help from outside. And when the Russians took the city, what would they do with the Americans who had been trapped there? Especially with women?

Damn you, Paul, she thought, fury rising in her, for leaving me with this. How much do you really care?

Alison was tugging at her sleeve. "*Mommy*, what's the matter? Are we having a war?"

I can't keep them here, she thought. Risks either way.

She slung the flight bag over her shoulder, took the two children by the hand, and started for the boarding ramp. A dozen people, mostly men, were clustered around the Air France official, gesticulating, questioning. He kept shaking his head and saying in French and German, "No, no, I've told you everything, that's all I know, that's all anyone knows—"

Idiots, she thought, pushing around them. Either they go or stay, whatever they know won't make any difference, just pick one or the other.

In the airbus the cabin crew's smiles were conspicuous by their absence. They were all frightened. No sooner had Jennifer gotten the children into their seats and buckled in than she heard the thumps of the doors closing and a whine as the engines started. Two stewards, clinging to routine, came down the aisle, distributing pillows, blankets and magazines. Jennifer took bedding for the two children and a *Paris-Match* for herself, although she knew she would not read it.

"Mommy," Alison said, "I have to go to the bathroom."

"Me too," said David.

For a moment she wanted to strike them both. Then she thought: Hold on to yourself, you're all they've got for a little, it's not their fault we're caught in a war. "The pilot won't let us get out of our seats until the airplane's flying," she said, forcing calm reasonableness into her voice. "As soon as he says it's alright, you can go to the bathroom."

"But—"

"Alison," Jennifer said in a warning voice. "I can't do anything about it. You'll have to wait."

Alison sighed theatrically. David had lost interest in the proceedings and was looking out the airbus window. "Mommy," Alison said after a moment, "you didn't answer me back there. Are we having a war?"

"Maybe," Jennifer said. The airbus was moving slowly out onto the taxiway, rocking gently on its undercarriage. Dawn had to be near but because of the cabin lights the outside still appeared quite dark. "But we're going to see Grandpa Drury in England, so we'll be quite safe."

"Won't they have a war in England?"

"No, of course not." She looked past the children again, out the cabin window. The airbus was turning onto one of the main runways. By craning her neck she could see part of the eastern horizon ahead. It seemed a little paler than the rest of the sky.

The plane stopped. Jennifer looked at her watch; a quarter to five. Come on, she thought. We can be out of East German airspace in twenty minutes.

The engines began to spool up. After a few seconds the pilot released the brakes and the airbus began to accelerate down the runway, flaps and leading edge slots extended, beacon lights winking rhythmically. Then the cabin floor tipped sharply upwards. Jennifer, who had flown a good deal, thought: He's not wasting any time. Alison, in the window seat, had her nose glued to the porthole. David was peering around her.

The vibration of tires against pavement ceased. Thumps as the landing gear came up, whine of slots and flaps retracting. The engines hummed at full takeoff power. Jennifer looked past Alison's head, watching for the start of the aircraft's turn to the west.

The northern horizon flickered with lightning. A storm, Jennifer thought. Did I close all the windows, oh damn, I didn't check the one in Paul's study.

The flicker was continuous, steady. But, she thought, when

we came out of the house there was a quarter moon. There wasn't a storm in the forecast last evening.

Then she realized that she was watching, not the glow of distant summer lightning, but the gun flashes of an immense artillery barrage.

Washington
11 P.M., Eastern Daylight Time, August 14

THERE GOES THE ELECTION, Hood thought irrelevantly, striding with his secret service bodyguards and military and civilian aides through the Current Action Center towards the Emergency Conference Room. The CAC, a two-story room at the center of the Pentagon, looked like nothing so much as a modern office in a large insurance corporation: loose-leaf binders, stacks of papers and forms, styrofoam coffee cups full and empty, rows of desks and computer terminals and ranks of telephones. Except that employees in large insurance companies did not wear uniforms; the CAC was part of the National Military Command Center, the core of the United States' vast defense computer and communications system.

"Defense Secretary Martin is already here, Mr. President," said the colonel who had met Hood and his entourage outside the CAC. There was a line from the CAC to the White House Situation Room, but Hood preferred not to insert that extra link into the command structure. He had come directly from Pennsylvania Avenue as soon as it had become clear, about half an hour previously, that there was very serious trouble in Western Europe. How serious, no one on this side of the Atlantic knew yet; communications with Brussels and Casteau, and with AFCENT headquarters in Holland, were very poor, and none of them seemed to have a clear idea of exactly what the Russians were doing.

"Thank you," Hood said to the colonel. "Has there been anything on the Molink?"

"No, sir. Moscow's still sending the routine test messages. So are we."

"Alright." The fact that Nikolayev hadn't yet been on the Moscow Link, otherwise known as the Hotline, didn't surprise Hood; the Russian would prefer not to tip his hand too early.

They were out of the CAC in the corridor leading to the Emergency Conference Room. "Is the chairman of the Joint Chiefs here yet?"

"General Bentley arrived five minutes ago, sir. So have the rest of the Joint Chiefs. Here we are, Mr. President."

Hood entered, followed only by the major carrying the Football, the satchel which contained the authorization codes for the release of American strategic nuclear weapons. Hood hoped briefly that he wouldn't have to open the satchel. Inside the ECR were already present Defense Secretary Thatcher Martin, Chairman of the Joint Chiefs of Staff General Bentley, and the Joint Chiefs themselves. As well there were several senior military officers, and four civilian advisors. They were sitting in the blue plush chairs around a large conference table on which were several telephones. Above the table and dominating the room were large glass wall screens on which could be displayed maps, data transmitted by satellite, computer displays, or film. A readiness board gave the alert level of the various American combat commands. Normally they were at Defense Condition Five, except for Strategic Air Command and the Pacific Command, whose usual level was Defcon Four. Now all commands were at level four, still a peacetime one, but of increased vigilance.

"Just exactly what is going on over there?" Hood asked, slipping into the chair reserved for him at the table's head. The major with the Football went and sat on a small sofa at the far end of the room. His rather young face was perfectly expressionless.

"It's difficult to tell yet," said Thatcher Martin. "At 3:30 A.M. European time — about half-past nine in the evening over here — a hell of a lot of Russian helicopters crossed the German border. So far there have been reports of fighting between airborne troops and NATO garrisons from the frontier radar posts right back to Bonn." He raised his voice slightly. "Can we have the NORTHAG and CENTAG displays, please?"

One of the screens above the table flickered and a map of Europe from the northern tip of Denmark to the Alps appeared on it. On the map were displayed, in blue, American troop and aircraft dispositions; those of the NATO allies were various other colors, and the Warsaw Pact forces were red. There were several red parachute symbols in the Federal Republic, from Frankfurt north to the Danish border. As Hood watched, another red parachute popped into existence near Kassel.

"That's another confirmed report," said Bentley. "That's one of the Luftwaffe airbases in Central Army Group."

"Does that mean they control it?" Hood asked. Presented with the situation in this manner, so that you could actually see the enemy airborne forces in the act of invasion, was vastly different from verbal or printed information. It was uncomfortably reminiscent of a very elaborate computer game.

"No, Mr. President. It only means that we now have a confirmed report of Warsaw Pact airborne forces in combat at that position."

"Where's this information coming from?" Hood asked.

"The Milstar satellite net. Uplinks from the data fusion centers at Monchen-Gladbach and Heidelberg are supplying it as it comes into them. It's also being combined with IR imaging data and DISCUS 3 satellite information before it's displayed."

"There's supposed to be a data fusion facility at Casteau, isn't there?" asked Hood. "Isn't that functioning?"

Bentley rubbed his jaw; he hadn't shaved. "There is one. But it's out due to a power failure. Probably sabotage on the ground. CENTAG HQ is having a lot of communications difficulty over there. It's likely for the same reason."

Jesus, Hood thought. If they foul up our communications we're fighting with our heads in a sack. He looked up at the readiness board. SAC had gone to Defcon Three. As he watched, Pacific Area and North American Air Defense joined SAC. "Why is European Command still down at level four?"

As he watched the alert level on the European Command status panel changed to a 3. "What's slowing them down?"

"Communications difficulties," said Thatcher Martin. Hood waited for him to go on, but he didn't.

"They're not touching our satellites, though," said the Air Force chief of staff. "That may mean that whatever they're trying to do, they're not going for broke. And as far as we can tell they haven't put their Strategic Rocket Force on advanced alert. Just enough to preclude a first strike."

"Submarines?" asked Hood.

"Normal patrolling, usual percentage in port," Bentley said. "I—"

The conference room door opened suddenly. "What is it?" said Hood.

"Excuse me, Mr. President," said the colonel who had shown Hood to the ECR. "But there's some very recent information that isn't on the board yet."

"Let's have it."

"CENTAG reports heavy artillery and rocket fire on West German border positions. Warsaw Pact ground forces are definitely crossing the frontier in several places. They've overrun several of the German blocking positions, linked up with the helicopter troops that came in earlier. We've also identified a major air attack shaping up."

"Major conventional attack from exercise positions," Bentley said, as though reading a chapter heading from a textbook in a lecture hall at West Point. "Anything from NORTHAG?"

"Not yet, sir."

"Alright." The colonel left hurriedly. "It'll be coming up on the display any minute," Bentley said. "We'd better confirm."

After perhaps twenty seconds, a fog of red dots appeared east of the frontier and began to drift across it. As the computers analysed their headings the fog began to coalesce into blobs: large formations of aircraft on specific headings. At the border itself, a red rectangle shifted position westward.

"That's part of Third Shock Army," Bentley said. "There's no doubt about it now. They're coming."

"The bastards," somebody said. Hood looked down the room at the young man carrying the Football. The major gazed back at him, expressionless. Not yet, Hood thought.

"What's happening exactly?" he asked.

"We think it's the surprise option," Martin said. "They're going to try to grab as much of Western Europe as they can before we can react effectively. They're banking on us having to consult with NATO every step of the way before we decide to use tactical nuclears. Forty-eight to seventy-two hours. That's the window of opportunity they're looking at. They'll use surprise to deal with our conventional forces in the meantime. Moscow will get moving diplomatically any time now."

On the big screen the red blots had progressed farther west, and several more red rectangles had crossed the border or were inching towards it from the east.

"We'd better go to full alert," said Bentley.

"Alright," Hood said. He was thinking rapidly. "Wait. Hold SAC and NORAD at Defcon Three. Everything else, all the way up. Full engagement permission for conventional arms in Europe."

"But—" began the secretary of defense.

"Do it. They've not used tactical nukes, and they're holding off on strategic readiness. We'd better show them we'll do the same. We've got to keep the lid on this until we can start talking to the Kremlin."

"Yes, Mr. President," Thatcher Martin said stonily. Hood went on, "What's the status on the QRA aircraft?"

"As far as we know," Martin said, "they are still on the ground. There has been no indication of tactical nuclear usage by the Pact." He swallowed. "We suspect some of the German airfields they were based at have been overrun by airborne troops. Some of those may have gotten off the ground. But Casteau didn't issue any of the go-codes, fortunately."

Thank God for small mercies, Hood thought. All we need is a couple of QRA pilots flying around Europe with blood in their eye and armed nuclears on board. Even if Casteau didn't issue the codes. Jesus, we don't *know* enough. "Can you get me through to SACEUR? I want confirmation on that."

SACEUR was Supreme Allied Commander, Europe, at the Casteau military headquarters; if the go-codes had been or were about to be issued, General May would have done it.

"General May isn't at the headquarters," Bentley said

heavily. "His deputy, General Charteris, is filling in for him. May was in an accident on the way to Casteau. A truck hit his car."

"More sabotage?"

"We don't know yet."

"Has Charteris ordered dispersal?" Hood said tightly, thinking: If it's a major attack we'll have to follow doctrine, disperse the warheads and the bombs out of their storage igloos to the units that will fire them. And we've never even practised dispersal, it was always too provocative, it means we expect an attack and could mean, over there, that we are getting ready to preempt it . . . and by that invite an attack by the Russians. War by accident, the old nightmare.

"*Have* they been dispersed?" he repeated, after a few moments of silence.

"No," Thatcher Martin said. "There hasn't been time. A number of the weapons storage sites were overrun by helicopter troops. We're waiting for details."

"Any predelegations?" Hood asked.

"No," Bentley said. "The situation's too confused at the moment. Nothing below SACEUR level."

A small mercy for us all, Hood thought. If Casteau and Brussels start losing their communications, they'll delegate nuclear strike authorizations down to the military headquarters, with predelegated launch codes. If there's no control at all we could have battalion majors firing Pershings at Moscow. And, God help us, we planned it that way, so that there'd be a nuclear deterrent even if our command structure was wiped out, so that there'd be so many triggers for nuclear war that the Russians would never risk it. And now they have, anyway. Do they know how close we are to going out of control?

One of the telephones, a white one with a direct line to the State Department, chirred softly. Hood picked it up, nearly dropping the receiver; his palms were slippery. "Hood."

"Chalmers, Mr. President. We've had a communication from the Soviet ambassador. Has Nikolayev been on the Molink yet?"

"Not yet."

A sigh in the president's ear. "This is the message that's

going out all over, apparently. The rest of the staff might want to hear it." The secretary of state's voice was flat, expressionless. Hood pressed the button on the phone base marked AUDIO. "Give it to me verbatim," he said.

"Alright," Chalmers said, his voice metallic over the loudspeaker in the base of the white telephone. "Point one. 'The Soviet Union and its allies have undertaken the current police action in the Federal Republic of Germany to eliminate the growing danger of nuclear war in Europe which could be precipitated by the irresponsible and criminal actions and policies of the West German chancellor and his government. Chancellor Rudel by his behavior has shown himself an implacable enemy of the fraternal socialist nations, to wit, by his pursuit of the possession of nuclear arms, his militarist expansion of the German armed forces, and the reestablishment of the fascist General Staff, as well as by his subversive attempts to undermine the peaceloving governments of the Warsaw Treaty.'

"Point two. 'Warsaw Pact occupation of the Federal Republic will be temporary, and the policing forces will be withdrawn to the normal frontiers as soon as the West accepts and negotiates for a demilitarized and nuclear-free zone in Central Europe.'

"Point three. 'Agreement to the above plan may result in much more extensive treaties in the field of disarmament, beginning a millennium of peace which has always been the ultimate purpose of socialist diplomacy.'

"Point four. 'The fraternal socialist nations will not be the first to use nuclear weapons, but if any NATO member states do so, the Soviet Union will respond with appropriate measures up to and including national annihilation.'

"Point five. 'The fraternal socialist nations guarantee that the territorial integrity of France will be respected and that no attacks against French troops in West Germany will occur, provided they refrain from involvement in the conflict, and provided that France refrains from assisting NATO forces by any overt or covert means whatsoever.'

"Point six. 'No Warsaw Pact ground forces will advance into the Benelux nations, into Denmark, Norway, Greece, Italy or Turkey, nor will their territories come under air attack, although forces of any NATO nations in West Germany will be dealt with appropriately should they engage in the conflict in support of the neo-fascist German regime.'

"Point seven. 'Cancellation of existing military pacts and the total withdrawal from Europe of non-European troops is essential for the success of negotiations.'

"Point eight. 'The Warsaw pact nations urge the NATO countries to open these negotiations at the earliest possible moment, so as to avoid unnecessary destruction and loss of life, and to reduce the possibility of escalation to a nuclear level.' That's all."

The silence in the room seemed endless. Finally Chalmers' voice, thin and metallic over the audio connection, said, "Mr. President? Are you still there?"

"Yes," Hood said. "We're still here."

"Those bastards," said Bentley. "Those lying sons of bitches. They set us up. They were planning this, all the way. They never wanted a peace. They wanted Europe."

"Alan," Hood said. His throat seemed to have closed. Rage, he thought clinically, somewhere in the back of his mind. "Is that all they want?"

"That's all they've stated," Chalmers said. "God knows it's enough. The assholes suckered us."

Hood looked along the room to the young major with his satchel of release codes, the Football. There it is, he thought, and I'm angry enough. I could do it. There would hardly be any argument, just now. We could try the first strike, we're as ready as we ever can be.

"Mr. President?" Chalmer's voice.

I cannot do it, Hood thought. Not yet. He forced calm into his voice and said, "The military situation's unpredictable. I don't want to act until I talk to Nikolayev."

"With all due respect," Bentley said, "that may be too late."

"I know," said Hood. "But I'm going to wait anyway. Tell me what we've got on the ground over there."

West German Airspace
5:28 A.M., August 15

BOTH CHILDREN were asleep, lying back in their seats, Alison with her mouth open. A strand of fair hair, blown by the airstream from the ventilation nozzle overhead, drifted across her eyes; she grimaced. Jennifer reached up quickly and adjusted the nozzle to blow more gently. She was trying to think.

The Air France pilot must have seen the artillery barrage open, because he had put the airbus into the steepest climb Jennifer had ever experienced, the cabin floor tilting like a drawbridge. Then he had turned sharply right, the engines howling, swinging towards the west. As the aircraft pulled out of the turn Jennifer could see, well away to the south, more flickering, and clusters of sparks and flashes on the ground that were probably shellbursts. They had seemed thickest around the Teltow Canal, where the Americans' Andrews and McNair barracks were located. Then the airbus had passed through a thin layer of scattered cloud, and the city below was visible only intermittently. But the liner had continued to climb, still at full power.

He wants to get out of the way of the shells, Jennifer had thought. They could be all around us.

The two children were looking out the window. Alison wanted to know what the shell flashes were.

"Just some fireworks," Jennifer had said. "Or maybe some houses on fire." Kevin's down there somewhere, she thought. What chance does he have? None, he always said, if there were a big war West Berlin would go in days. Dead or prisoner. There won't be any help from the West. What will the Russians do to their prisoners?

A little while after that the airbus levelled out, but the seatbelt and no smoking signs remained on. A stewardess came down the aisle. She looked as frightened as Jennifer felt. Jennifer asked if the children could use the bathroom.

"Yes. But be quick, please. The captain may have to change course suddenly."

"Yes. We'll hurry."

They had just returned to their seats when the cabin loud-speakers crackled. "This is Captain Barre," a voice said. Jennifer strained to follow the French. "Please remain seated and observe the no smoking and seatbelt signs. You may have noticed that we have gained altitude rather quickly. This is because . . . there are indications of an attack on West Berlin, and we are removing ourselves from the area as quickly as possible." A pause, throat being cleared. "As you know, our destination was to be Frankfurt. However, it is reported that Frankfurt is receiving no incoming flights. Accordingly we will fly directly to Paris. Air France will make every attempt to assist Frankfurt-bound passengers to their destinations, and to accommodate those with connecting flights onward. Thank you."

And that had been all.

Jennifer looked at her watch. They must be close to the French-German border by now. After that, not long to Paris and some kind of safety. For a while, at least. Until someone became too frightened, and exploded a nuclear weapon, it didn't matter who, or why, or even where. From there it would simply go on, inevitable.

Folly and fear, she thought. The two horsemen who lead the other four.

The airbus was banking. From the angle of the dawn sun she thought the plane was swinging towards the southwest.

Something gray went by the window, very quickly. The airliner jolted.

Oh God, she thought, not now.

Some of the other passengers on the port side of the plane —

not many had braved the flight — had seen it as well. She could hear exclamations in a mixture of languages.

David stirred, opening his eyes. "Mommy. Are we going to be there soon?"

"Soon," she said. "In a—"

It inched into her field of view, just beyond the port wingtip: black conical nose tipped with a spike, sleek cockpit canopy, huge air intakes, sharply swept wings studded with long rockets. It was all dove-gray, except for the nose and the red stars and the big yellow 36 on the fuselage beneath the canopy. She could see the pilot, helmeted and visored, insectoid.

He can't want to kill us, she thought, we can't hurt him. Why can't he just let us go?

David was sitting up, looking out the window. "Mommy, Alison, look at the airplane! Why's he looking at us? Maybe it's Uncle Kevin—"

The Russian interceptor abruptly flipped one wing over the other and rocketed out of sight. The airbus bumped again and the cabin floor tilted downward. The whine of the engines rose. The cabin loudpeakers crackled, went silent, then came on again. A woman's voice said, "Please tighten your seatbelts as much as you can, move your seats to the upright position, remove your shoes and any eyeglasses. We are making an emergency descent. Please remain calm; this is a routine measure."

Jennifer leaned over and jerked off David's shoes without untying them, thinking, A routine emergency? I suppose better that than scream over the PA.

Alison was waking up, finally. Jennifer couldn't get the child's sandals unbuckled.

"Mommy, what are you *doing?* "

"The airplane is going down very quickly," Jennifer said. "So we have to take our shoes off." She gave up on the buckles and tugged. One sandal came off, then the other. Jennifer fumbled for the catches and got the seats upright. Somewhere forward in the cabin a woman was crying. The chidren's belts were fastened but she tightened them some more anyway.

The airbus was going down very quickly now. Jennifer's ears popped. Alison grimaced suddenly. "My ear hurts. How come the ground's leaning over so much?"

He's just trying to get down in a hurry, Jennifer told herself. They're not really trying to shoot us down.

She looked, against her will, out the window. The green and brown earth was very much nearer. As she watched, a long gray slab of metal slid out of the trailing edge of the airbus' wing.

Flaps, she thought. He's trying to slow down. But we're too high for a landing approach. What in the name of God is happening out there?

Oberleutnant Horst Genscher's Tornado interceptor was one of a few that had survived the helicopter-borne attack on the Luftwaffe airfield near Warburg just before dawn, and the airstrike that had followed it at first light. His aircraft and five others had managed to get off the ground after a nearby Bundeswehr reconnaissance unit drove the Soviet assault troops away from the airfield, and no more than five minutes after takeoff Genscher and his wingman had run into a flock of Mig23s providing top cover for at least a squadron of ground-strike aircraft. In the swirling combat that followed, the German planes had been separated. Genscher was fairly sure he had destroyed two Migs, but he was afraid his wingman had been lost. Viktor Marcks, the radar intercept officer in the seat behind Genscher's, was also unable to contact the ground control station that was supposed to handle the squadron's battle deployment; the signal was there somewhere, but it was being heavily jammed.

Genscher looked at his gauges. Enough fuel for another thirty minutes. The sky, to the eyes alone, appeared empty.

"What've you got?" he asked Marcks.

The RIO, hunched over his screens in the rear cockpit, said, "There's stuff all over the place. Computer says most of it's hostile."

"Anything close enough to hurt us?"

"Not for the moment."

They would get an alarm from the warning systems, if something locked onto their aircraft, but you couldn't be too careful. "Vector us on the nearest target," Genscher said. The oxygen rasped harsh in his throat. "We've got to stop some of these assholes."

Marcks gave him a heading and target altitude. Genscher put the throttles to full military power, without afterburners. The Tornado howled through the morning sky, thirteen thousand meters above the earth.

"It's thick out there," Marcks said after a moment. "ECM all up and down the bands. Just a minute. I've got a large target, it's not emitting. Turn to 060, it's thirty-four kilometers off . . . it's descending . . . speed about 800 . . . funny, there's another target approaching it from the rear, signature shows hostile. Second target is smaller."

"Maybe the big one's a troop transport," said Genscher. Nothing would give him more pleasure than to chop down a planeload of Russian paratroops. "Support for the helicopters that came in this morning."

"It's squawking now," said Marcks. "Oh, shit, it's civilian. What's he doing up here?"

"Caught like we were," Genscher said. "Let's look."

"He's at 6000 meters, descending more slowly now, slowing down, too. Bear 055."

The Tornado went into a dive, accelerating rapidly. A few moments passed.

"The small target's formated on the big one," said Marcks. "Now he's ascending, dropping back. He's slowed to 600. You should have a visual on the big one, ahead and crossing to the left. The hostile's backed right off . . . now it's approaching again. *He's starting a firing pass!*"

"I have it," said Genscher. The large target was visible ahead to the left, a skewed cruciform as it banked, diving.

"Get the other one," Marcks said. "Quick."

Genscher put in the afterburners. The Tornado leaped forward.

The airbus was tipped right over, shuddering in every rib. Jennifer could look almost straight down along the wing, at a loop of river, woods, a scatter of farms, roads. The earth, so safe, so unreachable. Alison was crying with fear, David looking at her with round terrified eyes.

A tremendous BANG from the front of the cabin. The airbus wrenched sideways, shaking violently. A howling gale swept through the cabin, dragging dust, blankets, pillows and magazines towards the ragged hole that had suddenly appeared in the roof above the fourth row of seats. The overhead panel popped open and oxygen masks fell out. Jennifer groped for them. Her lungs burned, her head felt as though it would explode. David was screaming, barely audible above the shriek of the escaping pressurized air. Jennifer was vaguely aware that the airbus was in an even steeper dive.

Genscher pulled the Tornado around behind the Mig23, just as it completed its firing pass at the airliner. He couldn't see whether the civilian plane had been hit; it had slowed suddenly and dropped on one wing out of his field of view.

The pilot of the Mig, intent on the airliner, had neglected his attack alarm, or it wasn't working properly. Genscher was too close to use a missile; he put a two-second burst from the twin Mauser cannon into the Mig's starboard wing root, and the Russian plane blew up.

Jennifer regained consciousness as the airbus passed through 2000 meters. The airliner was still shaking, its streamlining badly affected by the single cannon shell that had struck it at the beginning of the Mig's firing pass. If the French pilot had not turned the airliner when he did, the Russian's gunfire would have ripped the fuselage from end to end.

The noise of the slipstream screaming past and through the hole in the cabin roof was deafening. The oxygen masks whipped back and forth in the violent gusts. Half-aware of what she was doing, Jennifer grabbed two of them. The children were still unconscious, faces pinched and blue. She managed to put the masks over their noses, one hand for each child. Outside the ground was sliding closer and closer, but she could see the horizon. The airliner seemed, somehow, to be under control.

It banked. She saw that the flaps were still down. Just at the wing's trailing edge the curve of a tire was visible.

Landing? she thought. Dear God, let us get down, let my children get down.

A built-up area slipped into sight, suburbs. They looked

peaceful. Then expanses of grass, brown from the August heat. Banking less now. A huge black patch in the brown grass, centered on a burned-out helicopter. Red and white markers. Only a few meters up now.

The airbus slammed down with a tremendous thud, harder than Jennifer had ever landed. She waited for the engines to reverse thrust. Nothing.

What is he waiting for?

The reverse came on. The margin of the runway was flashing by. Out on the airfield lay two more wrecked helicopters, burning vehicles, columns of smoke, fires. The airbus raced along the runway, slowing bit by bit, swinging violently onto a taxiway. The engines, even throttled back, howled deafeningly through the hole in the fuselage.

The children were waking up, groggily. Jennifer let the masks go and put her arm around them, holding tight.

The airbus finally slowed. The terminal building came into view outside the window. Jennifer could see military trucks, jeeps, an armored car. After a perhaps another minute the liner stopped, the engines shutting down. Jennifer's ears began to recover from the howl of the turbines. As it became possible to hear again, the cabin address clicked on. "This is Captain Barre. Please remove your seatbelts and leave the aircraft immediately, by the rear exit." Jennifer heard a thump as the hatch at the plane's tail opened. "We are at Cologne airport. This airport has been attacked by Russian forces but is safe for the moment. For your own safety go directly into the terminal building. I am sorry that Air France cannot assist you further, but all air traffic in and out of Cologne has been suspended."

If he says he hopes we've had a pleasant flight, Jennifer thought, I'll die laughing.

The address clicked off. Through the hole on the cabin roof she could hear sirens, and very faintly, the staccato tattoo of automatic weapons.

Bonn
6:00 A.M., August 15

IT WAS FULL EARLY MORNING, sky the color of a robin's egg, unbroken by the palest wisp of cloud. Brand, Kastner and Harpe crouched at the rear of the Mercedes, which lay angled across the curb on Rheinaustrasse, a few hundred meters from the Kennedy Bridge. Near the bridge, half a dozen columns of brownish-black smoke befouled the warm air. Across the bridge the west bank of the Rhine lay white and gray and green under the early sky, safe, unattainable.

The Mercedes' driver was still in the car, flopped against the wheel, the crown of his head blown away by bullets from the Russian position at the east end of the bridge. The street was empty; the civilians who had been on their doorsteps a few minutes earlier had all fled indoors. Above Brand's head a blue-checked curtain fluttered delicately from an open window.

The Mercedes had nearly made it to the Kennedy Bridge, after a wild ride from the Siegburg airfield into Bonn, as the light strengthened. Along the streets, Brand had seen men and women at windows, wakened by the beat of the Russian helicopters, peering at the sky. A few had been more perceptive, or quicker to turn on their radios: Volkswagen minibuses and Fiats and Opels and Audis were being loaded hurriedly in suburban driveways, surprised and barely awakened children being strapped tightly in the rear seats, late, much too late: the Russian troops had taken the passages over the Rhine.

There were very few refugees yet, but the torrent of terrified civilians would be coming soon, the dispossessed fleeing on the roads of Europe once more, piling up against the dam of the Russian paratroops trying to hold the northern length of the Rhine until they were linked with the tanks of the Guards and Shock armies, or were reinforced from the air by men flown into captured airfields by the huge Antonov-22 troop transports. Until the isolated Russians on the banks of the Rhine at Bonn were defeated or relieved, they would take no chances and give no mercy. The vehicles under the smoke columns at the eastern approaches to Kennedy Bridge were not troop carriers or self-propelled guns or Leopard tanks but small family sedans, Volkswagen campers, light trucks, rusty bakers' vans, bright Mercedes. The Russians at the bridgehead had fired on them all.

Brand and the others had reached the northernmost of the three Rhine bridges, the Friedrich-Ebert Bridge, half an hour previously. The Russians were already there. Kastner had thought the Kennedy Bridge, closer to the center of the city, might still be open, so they had turned south amid the slowly growing stream of refugee traffic. It had been a forlorn hope; the Russians were defending the bridge approaches from well forward, having overrun the river police station. They were now firmly established behind the station's walls, and in barricaded positions on the bridge itself. One of them had put a burst through the windshield of the BND Mercedes as it approached, killing the driver. Brand still hadn't decided why the Russians hadn't shot the rest of them as they were tumbling out of the car. Conserving ammunition against the inevitable German counterattack, likely.

"They're SPETSNAZ," Harpe said from his crouched position at the rear bumper. "At least a battalion. Maybe a whole brigade."

"Why?" asked Kastner. The SPETSNAZ were specialist long-range diversionary troops, GRU-controlled, trained for insertion behind enemy lines to attack airbases, nuclear storage depots, major military headquarters, port installations, or even national capitals and their government apparatus. A SPETSNAZ battalion fielded about four hundred carefully trained professional killers.

"Doctrine," Harpe said. "The doctrine they drummed into

us at Zossen was that to win, we had to paralyze the Western command apparatus. For Bonn, the Russians would use the best they've got, the SPETSNAZ. They've probably got half your government in the bag over there on the other side of the river."

"This won't get us anywhere," Brand said. The breeze from the river carried the smell of burning oil, explosives, and the sweetish odor of blood from the dead driver of the Mercedes. "We have to get across the goddamned Rhine. Somehow."

"Boat?" said Harpe. "Are there boats near here?"

"Don't know," Brand said. "Erich?"

Kastner looked perplexed. "I don't know this part of Bonn. There might be, if the Russians haven't got to them. But if there's only a brigade, they can't have hit everything."

"What weapons have we got?" Brand said. He was leaning on the Mercedes' rear bumper; the bright chrome was warming slowly in the sun.

"Nothing," Harpe said.

Kastner grimaced and pulled his jacket back to expose a 9mm P38 pistol. "Not much more."

"Sorry," Brand said. "Me neither. Did the driver have anything?"

"Probably," said Kastner irritably. "You want to go and look for it?"

"If they're SPETSNAZ," Brand said to Harpe, "what're they likely to do if they see me?"

Harpe frowned. "They're trained to shoot quickly. But at the moment they're probably only worried about moving vehicles. Also the officers will want to save ammunition."

"Alright," Brand said. "I'll try for it." The old intoxication was coming back, the heightened sense of reality, every color and line alive and direct. The rush.

"If they start shooting," Kastner offered, "I'll try to put their heads down."

"No," Brand said, almost absentmindedly. "The range is too long for a pistol. And they'd cut us to pieces if they noticed. Wait."

Kastner nodded. "Break a leg," he said, for luck.

The Mercedes was lying half over the curb with its front

bumper perhaps three meters from a lamp standard. The angle between the car's right side and the buildings along the sidewalk formed a shallow dead zone. Brand left his position at the rear bumper and crawled along the concete to the front passenger door. It was ajar, left open when Kastner flung himself out of the Mercedes. Brand fitted his fingers around the door's edge and pulled. The door moved easily. Brand waited.

Either the Russian sentries on the bridge didn't see the movement, or didn't want to waste ammunition. Brand crawled over the doorsill onto the car floor, keeping as low as he could. Above him the shattered windshield shimmered, a bright crystalline web. Drying blood and fragments of bone and brain tissue spattered the leather of the seat, like some kind of exotic pâté. Brand reached out and fumbled at the driver's belt. Nothing. Try farther up, under the jacket. Found it, in a shoulder holster. Brand extracted the weapon carefully: another P38, better than nothing.

Trying not to think about the Russian sentries up on the bridge, he slid out of the car, then slithered back to the dead zone at its rear. "Anything?" asked Kastner.

"P38," Brand said. "How I'd like an M16."

"I'd settle for a HK-MP2," Kastner said. "We're going to have to get across without either. You want to try for the boats?"

Ahead, beyond the Mercedes, a Russian AKM crackled. The flat, dry explosions were followed by the pop of a light mortar. Brand peered around the car's flank.

A bright flash in front of the police station, then another. Several chunks of brick tumbled off the station's front wall. From beyond the bridge appproaches and out of sight came the pop-pop-pop of detonating mortar shells. In the pause following Brand could hear sirens across the river, and from some undeterminable direction the rhythmic snap of German automatic weapons.

"Hello?"

Brand looked up. Above them, framed in the blue-check curtains at the window, a red-haired woman had appeared. Brand waved at her to get back. Misunderstanding the gesture, she leaned farther over the sill, winding the casement wide open.

"Shit," Kastner said, seeing her. "Go back in," he shouted. *"Get in."*

"What's happening?" she called down, regardless. "Are they gone? Can we get across the—"

The SPETSNAZ sniper was alert; to him the woman in the window must have looked like a spotter or a German of his own profession. The 7.62mm bullet from the bridge took her throat out rather horribly, and continued on to shatter the opened casement window and gouge a channel in the brick of the building wall. The woman folded over the windowsill, as though tired beyond endurance, a bright scarlet flood cascading down the wall beneath the window. In the room behind her a child began to wail.

"Stupid *bitch*," Kastner snarled helplessly. "Where in Christ's name is her husband? That kid—"

It could have been Alison, or David, in the room behind the blue curtains. Brand tore his eyes away from the dead woman and said, "We can't get up there, they're watching us. Nothing we can do, anyway."

"If only she'd listened," Kastner said. He was white around the lips and eyes.

From the street behind them came a characteristic metallic clatter, the aircooled rattle of a Volkswagen engine. Harpe, kneeling, said, "Are your civilians all mad? Don't they know what to do in a war?"

"It hasn't sunk in yet," Brand said. "Your people were too fast."

A blue VW camper rounded the corner from Marienstrasse and began proceeding slowly northwards, towards the Mercedes. Brand waved furiously at the driver, trying to warn him; Kastner shouted something incomprehensible in gutter Berlinese. The camper didn't slow down but maintained its erratic weave.

"The stupid shit's drunk," Kastner said in a hoarse voice. For some reason the Russians hadn't fired on the VW, perhaps because of its slow indeterminate progress up the street.

"Are we staying here forever?" Harpe said. "Can we try for the boats?"

"Wait," Brand said. The camper's weaving had some kind of purpose.

The VW was within ten meters of the Mercedes when the Russians on the bridge changed their minds and began firing. The vehicle swerved sharply, turned almost sideways to the axis of the street, and ran up on the curb behind the BND car. Its windshield starred suddenly, but there was no one behind the glass. The gunfire from the bridge ended.

Brand heard the cargo door on the far side of the camper rumble open; somebody had survived. Next to him Harpe said, "We have to go. We're running out of time."

A helmeted head peered around the VW's front bumper. Below the helmet was the white grim face of a man in his late twenties. "Hey," he said, crawling towards them in the dead ground behind the Mercedes. He was wearing a mottled camouflage smock and combat boots besides the helmet, and had a Heckler-Koch G3 assault rifle clutched in his right hand. Three more men, a little younger, crawled after him. The third carried a field radio strapped to his back.

"*Heimatschutzkommandos*," Kastner said. "Thank God there's somebody around here." The HSK were West German territorial forces, meant for rear area security, screening, and a general reserve, rather like the US National Guard. They were equivalent in fighting power to light infantry and had trucks and a moderate number of second-line armored fighting vehicles. "Morning, Oberleutnant," Kastner said to the officer. Above them the dead woman dripped. The child inside the apartment was still wailing.

Brand suddenly realized that he was looking straight down the barrel of the G3. The other soldiers, except the radio man, were covering Harpe and Kastner. "We've had enough troubles with saboteurs already. Who are you? Quick!" ordered the lieutenant.

"Can I get my wallet out?" Kastner asked.

"Carefully."

Kastner extracted his BND papers. "There. Satisfied?"

The lieutenant inspected them carefully and then nodded, as though the Russians couldn't forge BND identification cards. "Alright. We've got to watch our backs every minute, you understand. You're not the only ones trying to get across the Rhine. An hour from now it'll be a madhouse down here." He looked up at the slaughtered woman. "Snipers?"

"On the bridge," Brand said. "They're very quick."

"What unit are you?" asked Kastner.

"Second battalion, Nordrheim Westfalen HSK," said the lieutenant. "Or we're supposed to be. Everything's buggered up. The battalion was on maneuvers east of here when the Russians came in. They must have got the defense district HQ because we haven't had any orders, either that or the phones are all out. The major was trying to move us to the west bank when we ran into the Reds at the bridges. We're trying to pry the fuckers off the approaches right now. You probably heard the mortars."

"Yes," Brand said.

"Where did you lot come from, anyway?" the lieutenant asked. "You aren't civilians."

"Siegberg airfield," Kastner said. "In from West Berlin."

The radio crackled angrily. The soldier carrying it slipped out of his straps and did something complicated with the knobs on its front panel. Then he passed the handset to the lieutenant. The lieutenant muttered into the mouthpiece for a moment, in some kind of German army communications jargon. For a moment Brand felt himself back in Central America, although he could not follow the radio discipline.

"We're supposed to be reconnoitering down here," the lieutenant said, passing the handset back to the radio man. "The major's going to try to try to clear the Russians off this end of the bridge. This is a deathtrap, though, we can't use it, they can shoot right down the street." He glanced up at the dead woman again. The child above, for some reason, had stopped crying. "What are you going to do?"

"Try for a boat," Kastner said.

"There's a mooring jetty at the foot of Steinerstrasse," the lieutenant said. "The street's a block south." He checked the clip of the G3. "We're going to try to find a better approach. Good luck."

"Pinch them out?" Brand asked.

"Try to," the lieutenant said. "We're going to hit them from three sides at once, if we can find the cover. Push them back on the bridge where we can mortar them." He turned and began crawling away, followed by the other HSK men, the radio man struggling with the straps of his equipment.

"Be careful," Brand said. "They're tough bastards."

"Yes," answered the lieutenant, without looking back.

The German soldiers disappeared around the VW. A few seconds later Brand heard their bootheels pounding on the pavement, off towards the south. A desultory shot from the bridge snapped out, apparently without result.

"Now what?" Kastner said. "You want to see if there's a boat at Steinerstrasse, or hope the HSK manages to clear the bridge?"

"Let's look for a boat," said Brand.

Fifteen minutes later they were at the river end of Steinerstrasse, having scuttled away from the Mercedes as though the devil himself were after them. The Russians on the bridge hadn't fired, probably because they were running into problems of their own; from the western bank of the Rhine the rumble of heavy weapons was intermittently audible. Somebody over there was putting the SPETSNAZ troops under pressure.

They came much too far, Brand thought as the three men trotted across the riverside pavement towards the boat jetty. Why did they try to take Bonn with no more than a brigade, maybe no more than a battalion? They'll be doing well to hold the bridges until evening, this far from ground support. And the planes haven't put in an appearance at all. It's as though they didn't intend success.

Maybe they were only after Rudel and the government. Shoot them all, then wait for a ceasefire?

"Shitheaded son of a cocksucking whore," Kastner said. "There's nothing here. Not a fucking paddle."

Brand stopped thinking about the vagaries of Soviet tactics and looked at the jetty. It stretched, T-shaped, out into the green Rhine water, its moorings naked of boats. Across the river the trees of the Stadtgarten and the placid bulk of the Colegium Albertum lay as they always had lain, as though nothing were happening. At the end of the jetty a man in green bathing trunks pumped furiously at a yellow inflatable raft, watched by a frail blond woman holding a baby. Half a dozen other people regarded the raft with varying degrees of cupidity.

These are the first, Brand thought. Only a matter of time, a few hours, before it gets worse, much worse. At the moment they still have some sense of order. By noon they'll be killing each other for a boat like that, unless the bridges are opened.

"We'd better go back," he said. "The bridge is the only way, unless you want to try downstream, or swim."

"I can't swim well enough to get across that," Kastner said. "I might as well jump in and drown myself."

In his mind's eye Brand saw the Grunewald and the banks of the Havel, David arising, soaked, muddy, and furious from the river's edge, the heavy beads of water sliding from his hair along the fine brows and the delicate child's skin; Alison gliding on the swing under the oak, the warmth of her thin child's back under his hands as he pushed, her shadow moving across the lawn as the night drew in; Jennifer kneading bread under her strong hands at the kitchen table, the smell of yeast and hot milk and butter in the encroaching dusk.

"We have to go back," Harpe said, decisive. "Your people may be able to take the bridge."

"Paul?" Kastner said. "What's the matter?"

"Jennifer and the children were leaving Berlin this morning," Brand said. "I told them to get out." His eyes were burning. "I left it too late."

"Don't think about it," Kastner said. "It'll slow you down."

"That's right," Harpe said seriously. "Just now we have to survive."

"You two are the soldiers," said Kastner. "What do we do now?"

"Joachim's right," Brand said after a moment. "The HSK may get the bridge back. There was shooting at the other end. The Russians aren't having it all their own way." And what do we do after we're across? he asked himself. Joachim's information isn't worth anything now.

Never mind. Just get to the other bank, go to the embassy, find out what's happening in Berlin, if anybody got out. Start that way.

They retraced their steps to Rheinaustrasse. The weight of the pistol dragged at Brand's jacket. He realized, suddenly, that he had been awake for nearly twenty-four hours. He glanced at the other two, hoping he did not look as unshaven and unkempt and red-eyed as they did. Harpe was worst of all; he had had the strain of the border crossing in addition to everything else.

A traffic jam had arisen out of nowhere in the Rheinaustrasse; Brand heard the blare of horns well before they reached its intersection with the road to the river. In the north-south avenue leading to the bridge approaches, a long column of civilian vehicles had sagged to a halt; to make matters worse, a large van had tried to bypass the stalled cars by driving on the sidewalk but had been cut off by a green Audi with a flat tire. The two drivers stood toe to toe, screaming at each other. Horns blatted and blared. The sidewalk where the van blocked it was clotted with men and women and children, walking or pushing bicycles, dragging suitcases, pulling red children's wagons heaped with hastily collected belongings.

Brand and Kastner and Harpe pushed through the crowd, making sure the P38s were well hidden, but ready. The mass around them was at the point of mindless panic.

"Where the devil are the police?" Kastner shouted at him over the din.

"Ahead," Brand called back. "I see some. They've got a roadblock."

The column of fleeing vehicles had been halted by a police and militia barricade at Marienstrasse. The distracted officers at the block were trying to divert the traffic away to the east, to avoid the Russians at the bridge. The refugees, despite the evidence of the smoke columns on the bridge approaches, did not want to turn away from the west and the river. Every driver protested, causing the traffic behind to slow even further.

Brand was no more than a dozen meters from the barricade when the driver of a red VW Jetta suddenly gunned his motor, jinked between the barriers, and shot up the street towards the bridge, accelerating all the way. For a few very long moments nothing happened, the small red car rocketing past the disabled BND Mercedes and the HSK Volkswagen camper.

The balustrade of the bridge sparkled for a moment. Twenty meters past the Mercedes the Jetta swerved suddenly, its front tires shot out, and then slid diagonally across the street. It hit the curb, bounced, and turned over twice, landing on its wheels. From the bridge there were more sparks. One of the tracers found the car's fuel tank. Brand heard a small soft thump, like a doll being dropped in another room, and the Jetta's rear half disappeared in a hot tongue of flame. Nobody tried to get out. A moment later the rest of the car took fire.

"Stupid bastard," Kastner said.

The death of the Jetta's passengers had an immediate effect; the drivers arguing with the police and soldiers at the barricade stopped suddenly and both the refugees on foot and those in cars began moving away up the Marienstrasse.

"*You!* Where are you going?" One of the policemen at the barricade, a lieutenant, was staring at Harpe. "Where do you think you're going?" The East German, exhausted and disoriented, had walked right up to the barrier, instead of moving off to the east.

"BND," Kastner said, coming up behind Harpe.

"Stop right there," the lieutenant said. "Identification."

"It's in my jacket," Kastner said, carefully. The police officer's pistol was out, although not pointing anywhere in particular.

Kastner moved with extreme care. Behind the policeman the HSK troops watched, their G3s unslung, loosely cradled. Germans, Brand thought. Ready for war, instinctively. They always seem to know what to do.

The lieutenant inspected Kastner's papers carefully. "Alright," he said, handing them back. "These other two as well? BND?"

"No. But they're with me. BND business."

"Keep going, then."

"We need to get to that Mercedes up the street," Kastner said. "It's our only transport."

"Sorry," the lieutenant said. "Nobody goes past." He gestured at the burning Jetta. "You saw that."

"The HSK is going to hit the Russians soon," Brand said, as though he knew for certain. "We can get the car out."

"Nobody passes," the lieutenant said. "Not even BND."

Brand heard a faint howl from southwards. The sound rose to an earsplitting shriek and a pair of Alpha jets, the black Luftwaffe crosses stark on the wings, shot over the intersection and screamed towards the bridge. Mixed with the engines' howl was a sound like tearing canvas: aircraft cannon. Brand instinctively threw himself flat on the ground. Harpe did the same.

The jets were gone as quickly as they had come. Gouts of smoke and flame suddenly obscured the bridge approaches: the Alphas had been loaded with rockets. Brand got up on one knee. Most of the policemen and the militia were still on their feet, slow to react, looking north towards the Kennedy Bridge.

Brand grabbed Harpe by one arm and dragged him up. Kastner was getting to his feet. "Come on," Brand said. "The car. Quick."

They began running for the Mercedes. The Alphas howled in for another firing pass. The noise was deafening. Time stopped; Brand's legs pumped and pumped but the Mercedes seemed to draw no nearer. Then, suddenly, he was throwing himself to the pavement behind the car's bumper, Kastner and Harpe beside him.

"Back where we started," Kastner wheezed. "How I'd like a beer."

Brand felt nothing of the kind. He was nauseated with fatigue. The Alphas were now a diminishing scream to the northwest.

"Where are the Migs?" he said. "Why aren't they supporting the bridgehead?"

Harpe, gasping for breath, nevertheless managed to look puzzled. "I don't know. They ought to be. Maybe it isn't all working right."

"Mortars," Kastner said. They listened, watching carefully around the flanks of the Mercedes. Puffs of smoke were rising around the end of the bridge. Brand heard a heavy machine gun begin to fire, then another.

"The HSK's going to try," Kastner said.

The battle for the east end of the Kennedy Bridge went on for most of the morning. Around ten o'clock, Brand and Kastner managed to drag the dead driver out of the Mercedes and lay him in some kind of repose on the sidewalk. As far as they could tell by peering under the car the engine and transmission and radiator weren't damaged: no oil or water on the pavement. Behind the car, Harpe actually managed to take a nap. Brand tried to, while Kastner kept watch, but images of Jennifer and Alison and David kept floating against the reddish-brown of his closed eyelids. Finally he gave up.

The Alpha jets came back at a quarter to eleven; twenty minutes after the planes left Brand heard the flat heavy crack of a tank gun. The bridge end was now totally obscured in smoke and dust, and from their postion it was impossible to tell who was winning, or whether the fight had reached a stalemate. All three men, by this time, were very thirsty.

Towards noon the firing began to die off. A wind from the southwest sprang up, and slowly the smoke and dust blew away from the bridge. The pale concrete of the long shallow arches was blackened and smeared; chunks of concrete had been blown out of the abutments, and the balustrades gaped like broken teeth. Brand could see the upper part of a vehicle on the bridge roadway, half obscured by something burning on the river shore. The vehicle was moving slowly west, across the bridge. The smoke ebbed a little, exposing a long dark bar protruding from the machine's front. A tank turret.

"We've got tanks on the bridge," Brand said. "Look."

Kastner looked. "Let's try it," he said.

They piled into the Mercedes, trying to avoid scraps of the driver, and the flies. Kastner turned the ignition key. The starter ground. And ground.

"*Scheisse*," Kastner said. "You bitch. *Start.*"

The engine caught, banged twice, and then settled into a steady hum. Kastner reversed the Mercedes off the sidewalk and started up the Rheinaustrasse towards the bridge, past the black and still-smoldering Jetta with its curious odor of burnt pork.

Zossen - West Berlin
1:00 P.M., August 15

MARSHAL PYOTR LESIOVSKY, commander-in-chief of the Soviet Western Theater of Operations, was allowing himself a cautious optimism, which was shared by the senior staff officers around the long table. There had always been the back-of-the-mind concern that, when and if the armies of the Warsaw Pact rolled over the frontiers, the operation would founder in a swamp of traffic jams and misdirected formations. This had almost happened in the police action in Czechoslovakia in 1968, and might have occurred several years later if the fraternal socialist armies had had to intervene in the Polish crisis of the early '80s. The dismal traffic control and mobilization mechanisms exposed at those two times had been taken to heart by the General Staff, and it appeared that the remedies had, at least so far, been effective. Even the reorganization of command from a peace to a war footing had gone fairly smoothly.

The big map projected on the wall screen in the Western Theater headquarters at Zossen showed the results of all these efforts. During the afternoon of August 13, Zossen had transformed itself from the HQ of the Group of Soviet Forces in Germany into the GHQ of the Western Theater of Operations by the simple expedient of flying in three command staffs from the Byelorussian and Kiev Military Districts to assume control of the apparently random collection of combat formations in East Germany and Czechoslovakia. The Western Theater, after this long-prepared reorganization, now consisted of three Fronts, or groups of armies: the First West Front, comprised of the ten divisions and three independent armored brigades of 2nd Guards Tank Army and 3rd Shock Army; the Second West Front, with the eleven divisions and three independent brigades of 1st Guards Tank Army and 8th Guards Army; and the Central Front, which was to secure the southern flank of the Warsaw Pact advance without carrying on major offensive operations of its own. The Central Front forces were politically sensitive: of its eight full-strength divisions only two were Russian, the rest Czech, and the Czechs were not to be trusted in major combat operations outside their own borders, especially against American troops.

Behind this first echelon, well back in Poland and Czecho-slovakia, lay the second: 28th Army, 4th and 5th Guards Tanks, 41st Army, totalling another twenty divisions. To support the first echelon were the Migs and Sukhoi fighters and bombers and ground-attack aircraft of 1st, 16th, and 29th Air Armies, nearly four thousand combat planes. Attached to each Front and Army were brigades of surface-to-surface rocket launchers, whose missiles could transport conventional or nuclear or chemical warheads for scores of kilometers; there were whole divisions and regiments of artillery, swarms of ZSU antiaircraft vehicles with their four-barrelled radar-controlled guns, bridge layers like monstrous insects, squat BMP troop carriers, and tanks, thousands of tanks, in kilometer-wide bands on divisional attack frontages or in small wedges of half a dozen or a score, probing into the uncertainties of the West.

Farther back yet, in Russia, were the mobilizing divisions of the third echelon and the reserves. They could not reach the combat zones before the 72-hour deadline to end Barbarossa Red, so they had to be left out of Lesiovsky's calculations as far as the immediate fighting was concerned. But when they arrived, if they were indeed needed, and if the war could continue for more than three days without turning into holocaust, they would add scores more formations to the tremendous weight of men and machines already battering at the defenses of the West.

It is a limited war, Lesiovsky reminded himself, again. The Greeks and the Turks and the Italians are not to be touched, and

Austrian neutrality is to be observed. Now if Paris and London and Washington will just keep their senses . . .

"Let's have a look at 20th Guards," he said, putting his imagination back where it belonged. If there were any immediate problem, it was with the attack on West Berlin. "If we don't put down their artillery by 1700 hours the supply transport's going to run into interdiction fire, especially from those damned British long-range guns."

The strategic map promptly disappeared from the wall screen and was replaced by an irregular multicolored blob, a map of the city with reference overlays and color coding to show the extent of Soviet and NATO-held territory. NATO territory was in blue. There was still far too much of it for Lesiovsky's taste.

"What's wrong with those 20th Guards HQ idiots at Eberswald?" he said, allowing irritation to creep into his voice. His staff, already uncomfortable in the metal chairs surrounding the table, went quite still. "They've had since five this morning," Lesiovsky went on. "This was supposed to be a surprise operation, or was I misinformed? Half the city should be overrun by now, and the 19th Guards Division still can't take Gatow airport. We can't feed the East Germans in except as support, and 6th Guards is still frigging about up in the French sector. *I want those long-range guns!* "

"Marshal Lesiovsky, sir?"

"What?"

The speaker was Lieutenant-General Mistischenko, in charge of liaison with 20th Guards Army. "Begging your pardon, Comrade Marshal, but the information on the screen is out of date. We have the Foch Barracks, and the French have collapsed along the northern perimeter. Also, the 19th took the Gatow air terminal half an hour ago. The Brook Barracks in the British sector has been taken, and we believe we will have control of the McNair Barracks in the American zone before early evening." Mistischenko gestured at the map. "The whole perimeter should be adjusted inward, as much as half a kilometer in some cases."

"Very good," Lesiovsky said acidly, somewhat relieved, although he was careful not to show it. He turned to his chief of staff. "Find out why the displays are being updated late and fix it.

Now," he said to Mistischenko, "give me a time for the neutralization of those long-range guns. The plan was for no later than 1700 hours."

"We'll have the positions by 1900," Mistischenko said promptly. "Provided that, when they're located exactly, we can use army-level artillery concentrations."

Lesiovsky frowned. Redirecting the fire support of the artillery away from the infantry advance into the city could reduce the pressure on the NATO garrison, leaving them with time to regroup and perhaps even mount counterattacks. On the other hand, leaving the NATO artillery intact could mean unacceptable delays in the movement of the supply columns westwards. Lesiovsky would likely be relieved of his post if that happened.

Wars are made up of difficult decisions, he thought. "Tell 20th Guards to take whatever measures are necessary as far as artillery usage is concerned," he said. "Starting now, their priority is detection and neutralization of NATO heavy weapons. Existing ground-attack plans will be carried out, whether artillery support is available or not. Is that understood?"

"Yes, Comrade Marshal," said Mistischenko emphatically. "If the Marshal will excuse me—"

"Go on," Lesiovsky said. Mistischenko hurriedly left the map room, to give 20th Guards their new priorities.

"Let's have the situation at the front," Lesiovsky said.

Two generals stood up and walked to the map screen, which had flashed to a representation of the European front from the tip of Denmark to the Austrian border. The two officers were a study in contrasting physique. Kuznetsov, the taller, was still quite young and had a strong square jaw and blue eyes above Slavic cheekbones. He was Lesiovsky's chief of intelligence.

The other man's name was Sergei Yanovich Vlasov. He was short, almost as broad as he was tall, and quite remarkably ugly, with an enormous blunt nose and slitted eyes, the genetic relic of some Mongol incursion into the west of old pre-Czarist Russia. Vlasov was head of the Operational Directorate of the GRU, Soviet military intelligence, and he had come to Zossen straight from Moscow. His Operational Directorate was charged with the collection, analysis and distribution throughout the Soviet war machine of all militarily significant information, and his presence at Zossen was both a vote of confidence from Moscow and a warning against failure. Vlasov had extremely powerful friends in the General Staff.

Lesiovsky wished wholeheartedly that Vlasov were still back where he belonged, in Moscow. He was still surprised that the GRU man had been sent out to Zossen; it could mean there was something in the wind, perhaps an intelligence coup of some sort was to be announced.

Unless something had gone badly wrong with the military estimates of NATO strength. Lesiovsky didn't want to think about that. The Warsaw Pact at the moment only slightly outnumbered the Western forces in immediately available divisions, and if it had not been for the speed and surprise of their attack they would have had little chance of achieving their objectives.

Kuznetsov was unfolding a metal pointer, clearing his throat. The staff officers in the long bunker room rearranged themselves with a rattle and scrape of metal chair legs.

"We have been extremely successful," Kuznetsov said without preamble, "in interfering with NATO communications and mobilization while preserving our own. On balance, we have achieved the surprise demanded for Barbarossa Red."

A flutter of relief in the long room. Vlasov, leaning against the cold concrete wall of the bunker, stared impassively at the map. Kuznetsov glanced at him and went on. "This is the current military situation. It is now seven hours since the lead echelon crossed the frontier, and we have advanced, in three major thrusts, between thirty and seventy kilometers. The deepest penetrations have been made by the heavy reconnaissance units. You can see our dispositions here." He tapped the upper quadrant of the map with his pointer. "On the northernmost axis of the advance, 2nd Guards Tank has engaged scattered units of the West German 6th Panzergrenadier Division to the east of Hamburg, and screen units of 3rd Panzer outside Luneberg. These attacks have been very successful, and we anticipate the isolation of Hamburg by nightfall. SPETSNAZ units have eliminated resistance at four of the six nuclear storage sites near Hamburg, and have also managed to eliminate the commander of 6th Panzergrenadiers and several of his staff." He smiled for a fraction of a second. "Similar attacks have taken place elsewhere. They will delay the West German reaction considerably.

"Farther south," Kuznetsov went on, clicking the pointer against the screen's glass, "3rd Shock Army has overrun much of the 1st Panzergrenadier Division heavy elements barracked at Hannover, and has bypassed 3rd Panzer in order to reach the bridges over the Weser River before nightfall. The Weser is the last major geographical obstacle before the North German plain, so we must secure it to maintain the speed of our advance.

"Farther south, the right wing of Second West Front is positioning itself to form a pincer around Kassel and defeat in detail the German 2nd Jaeger Division. Their deployment was severely hampered by the airborne detachments we landed at first light. Once the Kassel area is cleared the way will be open for a rapid advance into the forest strip to the city's northwest, and beyond that forest is our objective, the Ruhr."

He looked around the room, as though expecting questions. There were none. "The third axis of advance consists of the 8th Guards Army of Second West Front, which is now fifty kilometers west of the border and is advancing on Frankfurt. As you can see, there are three powerful American divisions in the area, as well as 5th Panzer; the 8th Guards is to pin these forces down rather than attempt to destroy them, in accordance with the political directives. Frankfurt is to be bypassed initially, and taken only after the east bank of the Rhine is secured at Wiesbaden. At that point the Front's left wing will halt and prepare to repel any US-German counterattacks from the American 5th and 7th Corps."

Kuznetsov paused again, coughed huskily, and then resumed. "Army Olomuc and Army Boleslav, the primarily Czech formations, have advanced to secure the southern flank from the Austrian border northwest past Regensburg and Nuremburg, and are progressing satisfactorily. No major offensive operations are planned in that sector, as you know."

Kuznetsov collapsed his pointer with a series of sharp clicks and finished, "The air attacks have been successful. We estimate that between three and four hundred NATO aircraft of various types have been destroyed on the ground and in the air, with many more damaged. Our losses have been in the neighborhood of a hundred and fifty, from all causes. So far, NATO air opposition has been weak and disorganized, owing to sabotage, helicopter-borne assault on the command centers, and battle losses. Finally, our decision to use gas on critical targets has doubled the rate of advance in some cases, and severely hampered both NATO ground and air operations."

Kuznetsov fiddled with his pointer for a moment, as though expecting a barrage of questions, but everyone was looking at Vlasov. After a moment Kuznetsov returned to his seat.

Vlasov walked to the center of the platform in front of the map. He didn't bother looking at it. "Let me congratulate you first," he said, "on a brilliant beginning to Barbarossa Red." His voice was deep and mellow, at odds with his appearance. "General Kuznetsov's appreciation of the situation is very accurate, *as of the present time*." Vlasov emphasized the last words. "I would warn you, however, that the present happy situation may not continue. NATO command is not populated exclusively by fools" — here a sardonic smile — "although it does have a number of individuals whose first loyalty is to us. Unfortunately, the reporting facilities we have in the West, and which have given us precise information about our targets, are going to be less accessible now that fighting has begun. This means that when NATO begins to reorganize, and it will, we will be more in the dark than usual about their intentions. Therefore the Supreme Command and the Politburo regard as essential the success of Barbarossa Red within seventy-two hours. That is all the time we have before NATO can decide on the use of nuclear weapons in Europe. One minute longer, comrades, and we risk holocaust. I cannot tell you how we know this, but we know it. Thank you for your kind attention."

Vlasov lumbered off the platform and sat down, like a bear lowering itself onto its haunches. Lesiovsky hurriedly stood up and started for the platform himself, thinking with disbelief: They sent him here from Moscow to tell us that? But how can he be so sure of the seventy-two hours?

Because we have someone to tell us when NATO decides to go nuclear? That would be no surprise, Vlasov wouldn't have to come here himself.

Lesiovsky was on the platform now, turning to the generals and colonels of his staff.

Holy Mother Russia, he thought suddenly. It's not that at all. Of course Vlasov had to come here to tell us, you could never put it in writing or on a Telex line.

There's somebody in the West who can delay the NATO decision.

Somehow, he got through the rest of the briefing.

Twenty minutes later, as the staff officers were leaving for their posts, Vlasov shot Lesiovsky a significant look. The marshal stepped down off the platform and went over to the GRU man.

"Could I speak to your chief of intelligence?" Vlasov said. "It's of some importance."

"By all means," Lesiovsky said. "Kuznetsov. Come here a moment."

Kuznetsov hurried over to them, looking anxious. "General Vlasov wants a word with you," said Lesiovsky.

"With both of you," Vlasov said. "I am passing along an urgent request from GRU Second Direction." Second Direction carried out all GRU intelligence operations in the two Berlins. "They are very anxious to locate a certain person. She's likely in West Berlin, but they've lost track of her. I want your GRU people to put in one of the reserve SPETSNAZ teams to locate her. It's essential she be found as soon as possible, and removed, intact and unhurt. She should be brought here. Someone from the Direction should see her as soon as she arrives. I'll give you his name and how to reach him."

"Arrange it immediately," Lesiovsky said to Kuznetsov.

"Yes, Marshal. Comrade General Vlasov, are there photographs available of the target?"

"Oh, yes," said Vlasov. "There won't be any trouble with that. Second Direction wants Lotte von Veltheim, you know, the mayor of West Berlin? The one they call the Iron Maiden."

Current Action Center, the Pentagon
7:20 A.M., Eastern Daylight Time, August 15

AT PRECISELY the same time Vlasov delivered his request to Lesiovsky, President James Hood began an intelligence briefing by the heads of the CIA, the National Security Agency, and the Joint Military Intelligence Staff. The news was almost all bad, as bad as any of them could have conceived twelve hours earlier, except that neither side had yet resorted to nuclear weapons.

Pearl Harbor again, Hood thought. Despite everything we tried to do to prevent it. How could we, how could I, have been so stupid? Moscow planned this from the beginning, the IALT treaty, the force reductions, all of it. All they needed was a reason, like Rudel. And I thought Nikolayev could be trusted, not greatly, but enough. How I would like to smash them, those stupidities, those betrayers of reason.

He knew the anger was partly due to fatigue, and that he did not make rational decisions when he was fatigued. Nevertheless, the primitive urge remained: destroy the invaders. The fight or flight reaction, adrenalin streaming through the blood.

Another thought, almost an aside, flitted through Hood's mind: Curious they didn't wait longer, until more American forces were gone. A year or two would have been all they really needed. Nikolayev. What is he thinking now?

He had been trying to reach the Russian for hours. The Molink was still silent, except for the test messages.

"Congress," Hood said, and drank from the glass of water he

was holding. The rim of the glass was a bright spectral circle, reflecting the varicolored lights of the situation map on the screens above the conference table. Because of communications problems the data on the maps was as much as forty minutes behind reality.

"The members are trickling in," said Chalmers. He had come over from the State Department around four in the morning, unshaven, in a rumpled polo shirt and baggy corduroy trousers. His hair sagged messily over his eyebrows. "Some of them aren't very happy to come. Neither House is going to be anything like full, nobody's keen to be here if the situation really heats up."

Conceivably, Hood could ask Congress to declare war on the Soviet Union, provided Washington had not been incinerated in a thermonuclear fireball before he had time to do so. But in the present situation there was no point in such a declaration; it would commit the United States to a political and military stance half a century out of date. Full-scale war was not now the long process of mobilization, conversion of civilian factories to produce weapons, and eventually combat, but a series of codes whose transmission would erase two thousand years of painfully constructed civilization from the northern hemisphere.

"Alright," Hood said. "We declare a national emergency. Drafts, the rest of it. There's just a chance this might go on for some time, if we can keep it conventional and if we can stabilize the front in Germany." He stopped, looking at the Joint Chiefs chairman. "Can we do that?"

"We're starting the Reforger lifts," Bentley said. Reforger was the plan for the air transport of men and light equipment into Europe, where their heavy weapons were prepositioned in vast supply dumps. "There's been no Soviet air or naval interference with the lifts yet, so it looks as though they're not worried about our reinforcement capability. That means they're gambling they can reach their objectives before we can put more men and weapons in the field." He stopped, and passed a hand over his forehead. "Unfortunately, as you heard from the CIA and NSA reports, there were Soviet airborne attacks at the Reforger dumps at dawn, and then airstrikes. We don't have a good idea of how much of the prepositioned material we've lost."

"The long and the short of it is," Hood said, "is that we don't know if the men are going to have anything to fight with once they get there, if they do."

"Yes," Bentley said. "We've been asking AFCENT and SHAPE for several hours how much damage has been done, but their communications are so bad over there that they're not much help." He gestured. "What we know about the ground war at the moment is up there on the screens. There are a couple of bright spots, though. Our forces down on the southern flank of the Pact advance haven't been heavily attacked, which indicates the Soviets are trying a smash-and-grab raid to the west, maybe as far as the Rhine. They'll use what they take as bargaining counters in the negotiations after they stop their advance. But if they leave us alone on that flank of theirs, we might be able to mount a counterattack to cut their suppply lines. Maybe even get behind the leading formations heading for Frankfurt. A lot of their flank protection appears to be Czech and East German. They'd crack faster than the Russians."

"Is that a reasonable prospect?" asked Chalmers.

"We'll need more information than we've got at the moment," Bentley said. "But communications are improving, a little. We're watching the situation as well as we can. Seventh Corps has been told to keep an eye out for a weak point."

"Let's have the bottom line then," Hood said. "How far have they come, and what have we got to stop them with?"

Everyone around the table looked at Mahon, the director of the National Security Agency. Mahon steepled his fingers and said in a matter-of-fact tone, "We're starting to see the pattern of their advance now. The axes of main thrust are against the Hamburg area, towards the Weser River stopline at Hanover, against Kassel, and southwest towards Frankfurt. Some of their reconnaissance formations have been detected as much as sixty kilometers west of the border, and the lead elements of some of their main units are only fifteen kilometers behind those. They're accepting open flanks and endangered communication lines, which means they're going for broke. They'll advance as far as they can with the fuel and ammunition they're carrying in the first echelon, and worry about consolidation later. Their tactical doctrine is to punch a hole in our defense perimeter, expand it, and then pour as many tanks and troops and guns as they can lay hands on into our rear areas in order to disrupt command and communications. Technique of the expanding torrent."

He stopped, looked up at the maps for a moment, and then went on: "The roads on our side of the frontier are clogged with refugees. They're slowing down the Germans and the British in the north and center to something like half the planned rates of advance. That means we're not going to be able to put forces at the stoplines on schedule. The West Germans and the British — we're starting to get satellite photographs through now — are having to move the refugees off the roads, or go around them, all of which takes time. The Russians aren't bothering with that. They just keep going. We've had several indications of Soviet tanks driving right over refugees, if they can't get out of the way in time."

There was a short silence. "They're using gas as well," added Thatcher Martin.

"That too. They've put persistent lethal gases on a lot of air-fields, and on barracks and the vehicle parks the airborne troops didn't hit. They've also used non-lethal incapacitant gases on refugee columns and at choke points, so that the roads are blocked even more than they might be. The Bundeswehr vehicles either have to move the casualties off the roads, or drive over them, like the Russians seem to be doing."

"What's the Soviet alert status?" asked Hood.

"High, but their ICBM submarine movements are close to normal. The've got most of their strategic aircraft up, on rotation, but none of them have left Russian airspace. We're listening to what we can of their strategic rocket forces command traffic, but analysis says they're not planning a first strike. As far as we can tell, they haven't gone to launch-on-warning."

"Make sure none of those B52s and B1s go an inch outside their holding orbits," Hood said to Bentley. The long-range bombers of Strategic Air Command had been flying patterns over North America for several hours, waiting for the codes that would send them towards their targets, from Leningrad to Moscow to Vladivostok: the burning of Russia. Bentley had been arguing over the last hour for an American launch-on-warning alert, but Hood had vetoed it. The idea of firing the Minuteman ICBMs from their silos out in the American heartland, on no more than a computer threat analysis, was more than he could stomach.

"Yes, Mr. President," Bentley said formally. "They've already had those orders."

Hood ignored the implied rebuke and asked Mahon, "What else are the Russians doing conventionally?"

"They're mobilizing the western military districts — Baltic, Byelorussian, Carpathian — for the reserve echelon, but they're not doing the same farther back. There's been no mobilization in the Moscow Military District, for example. Same conclusion we reached before. They want a short war, with no big buildup on either side." He paused. "One other thing's happened, though. We have some evidence that they may have dispersed their theater nuclear weapons in Europe. Probably under cover of the Suvorov exercises."

"Are they going to use them?" Hood asked.

"Under the circumstances," said Mahon, "it looks more like a precautionary measure. If we decide to go nuclear, they want their warheads dispersed." He cleared his throat. "I think Nikolayev is sending us a very clear message. He doesn't want this to turn into a theater nuclear engagement. He's willing to risk some things to achieve that. For example, we thought Soviet doctrine for an attack on Western Europe demanded at least conventional airstrikes against England and the Benelux countries, maybe even on France, and definitely a vigorous attempt to prevent reinforcements from North America. Nikolayev isn't doing those things. That means the Kremlin thinks it can finish this very quickly and leave us with the decision of either accepting the result, or starting a nuclear war in Europe."

"Any bright spots at all?" Hood asked.

"Not many," Mahon said. "There are a few satellite pictures that show the Russians are having problems, though. Their traffic control's broken down in a few places, particularly near Wurtzburg at the join between 8th Guards and the Czech and Russian divisions guarding the south flank. That's why we think we might get a useful counterattack down there. We've also intercepted a lot of demands for additional issues of ammunition and fuel. They may have underestimated their requirements, which means the rate of advance might slow down in the next day. We think some units have also gone where they weren't supposed to, taken the wrong objectives. Those are just straws in the wind at the moment, though. They're still moving west, and at the moment we can't stop them."

"How soon can the secretary-general convene the NATO Council?" asked Hood. "We've got to get a consensus on the Europeans' position on nuclear release."

"Not before three this afternoon, our time," Chalmers said. "The members are scattered all over Europe. Holidays, out in the country on a Sunday, you name it. He's been trying to get them together since dawn over there, but it's taking a lot of time."

"We have to go unilateral," Bentley said. "Mr. President, we can't wait for the Europeans. We have to disperse those warheads, the ones the Russians haven't neutralized, or we risk being disarmed over there. We can't wait for the NATO Council to endorse the decision. We may have lost half of our nuclear assets already. We *have* to disperse the weapons in Holland and Belgium, and we have to do it now."

Hood looked up at the status board. All the readouts now said DEFENSE CONDITION ONE: troops deploying for combat, all leaves cancelled; the aircraft carriers, submarines, cruisers, destroyers and frigates at full alert, weapons loaded and manned; the B52 and B1 and F111 bombers airborne in their holding patterns; the Minuteman ICBMs ready in their silos, the young air force officers with their ignition keys seventy feet underground in the missile control cabs, waiting in front of the firing consoles.

"Order SHAPE to start dispersal," Hood said. Damn Nikolayev, he thought, for the hundredth time that morning. Why won't he get on the Molink and talk to us? We can't go on working through the old diplomatic apparatus. What in hell does he think he's doing?

Playing the waiting game, of course. He wants to see how well the Pact is doing, how we respond, before he talks beyond what was in that set of demands. We have to disperse, if nothing else to show them we won't collapse at the first push, and just in case Moscow decides to go nuclear after all. A poker game.

"Mr. President," Bentley said, putting down the green telephone, the satellite link to SHAPE, "the dispersal order's gone through. I—"

"Be quiet a moment," Hood said. "I want to think."

So it was done, the first American unilateral action over the depoloyment of nuclear weapons. The Europeans would be even more frightened, soon, than they were now. Hood began running through his mental list of the official positions of the NATO and nonaligned governments.

London: committed to the last, as he had expected. The prime minister had always held the view that the Russians would back away from a confrontation if they were met by force.

Brussels: frightened and confused, overtly committed to a stand-fast policy, but all too aware of the nuclear weapons based on Belgian soil.

The Hague: Holland stood in much the same position as Belgium.

Norway and Denmark: tacitly in favor of negotiations. Neither had ever allowed nuclear weapons within their borders.

The Italians, Greeks and Turks, being well removed from the current fighting, had endorsed the official NATO doctrine of vigorous defense, but had also indicated that negotiations should not be rejected, especially if the choice lay between that and nuclear war. The Canadian government held, for similar reasons, the same opinion.

The neutral Austrians were bluntly in favor of considering the Soviet proposals. Austria would receive a large dose of radioactive fallout if bombs detonated to her west. Vienna's opinion was shared by a large number of other states, from Argentina to Japan, none of whom wanted to suffer the consequences of a war in which they were not involved and which they had had no part in beginning.

Paris was dilatory. Moscow's announcement that France would suffer no harm if she stayed out of the conflict was causing the Elysee Palace to consider long and deeply. If Paris declared for neutrality, the American air and sea lifts would not be allowed to use French ports or airfields. NATO reinforcement of the Central Front in Germany would be crippled.

Finally, and most important, West Germany. Bonn had been virtually incommunicado during the first hours of the morning, because of the Russian heliborne attacks. The Soviet specialist troops had managed to bag most of Rudel's Federal Defense Council as they were leaving the Chancellery for the escape helicopter to the German Third Corps HQ at Koblenz, a few miles south of the capital. Rudel, miraculously, had managed to get away to the Federal president's residence northwards across the park, turning up on the steps of the Villa Hammerschmidt as the Mil-6 helicopters drummed way into the east with their cargo of West Germany's most experienced military administrators. The Federal president, shattered by the news of the invasion and Rudel's flight to his front door, had gone into seclusion.

By late morning, the Russian special troops had either escaped in their helicopters or been disposed of by HSK and militia units around the capital. Rudel had returned to the Chancellery with what military and government staff he could scrape together. Hood had spoken directly to the German chancellor only once, around noon European time, to confirm his escape. Rudel, as expected, had sounded distracted and preoccupied. He had refused to consider immediate use of tactical nuclear weapons, pointing out that the Soviet lead units were so deep into Federal territory that a nuclear explosion would do more harm to German civilians than it would to Russian tanks. You might as well, he had said to Hood, burn down the house to get rid of the termites. There had been no reasonable answer the president could make to that. They had agreed to consult later, when the Russian dispositions became clearer.

But the alliance is beginning to crack, Hood told himself, chin in hands, as he stared up at the luminous maps with their red and blue and white symbols. If we had seen the war coming, if we had been able to progress through the alert stages from one to another, if we had been able to deploy as we always planned . . . then we might have had the confidence to hold together. It's been too fast, out of the blue, the mental shock the Kremlin planned. What's left to do?

Reinforce and try to fight a conventional war? Too late. None of the reinforcements will reach the battle before the

Kremlin's grabbed what it wants. We have to fight with what we've got over there, what did somebody call it once? The come-as-you-are war.

Or launch theater nuclear war? First a warning shot, on one of the Soviet tank reserves, for example, to show the Kremlin that a further advance would bring down a rain of tactical nuclear weapons? Such a decision was supposed to be taken by a plenary session of the NATO Council, but there was no guarantee that the member states would endorse the United States' desires. During the debate the Russians would advance many kilometers farther west, eating deeper into the heart of Germany. And Hood was by no means certain that the Russians would back away after a demonstration attack. Nikolayev and his marshals might bet, with reason, that the United States would not actually precipitate full-scale nuclear war in Europe, that the Americans would not, as Rudel had put it, burn down the house to kill the termites. The Russian tank spearhead would go on, secure in the belief that the West would not finally resort to atomic weapons.

That left either negotiation, or the ultimate sanction: a first strike with all available strategic weapons against the heartland of the Soviet Union itself. But such an act would not save Europe, nor anything else. In any case, the preconditions for a successful first strike were hours gone. There could be no surprise now for either side.

And the buck, Hood thought, as Harry Truman said, stops here. Nowhere is there anything in all the studies that tells me what to do now. The Russians must have always suspected that, that we would be undecided long enough to let them do what they wanted to in Europe, if the conditions were right. Now they've taken the chance, and pretty soon they're going to find out if they *were* right. How Nikolayev must be sweating over there. But the bottom line, as they say, is that our deterrence is failing. Dispersal is its last gasp, and I'm not sure that will convince the Russians to stop. Our strategy's collapsed at the the first brush with reality, a mirage the Russians could have walked through anytime they had the nerve. Unless we use the dreadful things.

"I beg your pardon, Mr. President?" Chalmers said. "What's dreadful?"

He had not been aware of speaking the last words aloud. He looked down the long table, past its end, to the couch where the major waited with the satchel of release codes. A solution of a kind, hovering.

"I — " he began; but whatever he had been about to say was lost with the twitter of the white telephone next to the Molink teleprinter under the screen of Europe. After a moment's pause Chalmers stood up, went to the console, and picked up the receiver.

He listened for a few seconds and then said, "Mr. President, Secretary Nikolayev wants to speak to you."

Bonn
4:00 P.M., August 15

THE SPETSNAZ ATTACK of the early morning had had one fortuitously positive result; it had temporarily emptied the hotels near the government district. Brand had booked two adjoining rooms at the Steigenberge, right near the Chancellery on the Bundeskanzlerplatz. The hotel was short-staffed, the desk clerk had informed Brand apologetically, as Kastner and Harpe signed the register; because of the morning's "disturbances" a number of employees had not shown up for work. Brand had nodded sympathetically. Then there had been some trouble over Harpe's East German papers, which was solved by Kastner's BND identification. The three men had finally reached their rooms at two in the afternoon, the adrenalin wearing off, leaving them almost too exhausted to speak. Nevertheless Kastner got onto the telephone, trying to find out what to do with Harpe. After a score of attempts he finally reached Staatsminister Kempf's office at the Chancellery. The office would not say where Kempf was, nor how he could be reached, nor when he would be available. And no, Herr Schell of the BND had not arrived from Munich. No one had arrived from Munich.

"Damnation," Kastner said, replacing the receiver, while Harpe looked on anxiously. "Schell didn't turn up, and the Staatsminister's not available."

"Try the Bundeswehr regional headquarters," Brand suggested. "Maybe their military intelligence people will know what to do." Kastner nodded and began dialing again. Brand went into the other bedroom to use the telephone there. The hard lump of fear and worry under his breastbone was expanding moment by moment, now that he had reached relative safety. Jenny and the children. Still in Berlin, or in England, or dead somewhere in a wrecked airliner in the fields of Germany?

He tried the US embassy, once, twice, ten times. Busy, always. He thought about giving up and sleeping for an hour and trying again, but didn't. A line had to be open sooner or later. Numbly, he kept dialing.

Somewhere around the fortieth attempt he got the ring tone instead of a busy signal. After fifteen rings a man answered. Brand could hear voices in the background, a lot of them.

"United States Embassy. Matthews."

"My name's Paul Brand. I'm an American citizen. Can you check and tell me if my wife has arrived there? She—"

Matthews cut in, his voice edged with anger and frustration. "Mr. Brand, we have several hundred people here, all looking for someone or trying to get out of the country or God knows what else. We can't check for individuals at the moment. Are you in Bonn?"

"Yes."

"You'd better come over here and look for yourself."

"Listen," Brand said, "I'm with the CIA."

A bark of laughter, humorless. "Half the people calling here are saying something like that. Is there anyone here who knows you?"

"I was working through . . ." Brand began, and then stopped. Not on an open line, not with Walt still back in Berlin. "I'll come down there."

"Alright. Excuse me, I'm very busy."

"Goodbye," Brand said, but Matthews was gone.

Kastner came in through the connecting door, Harpe following. Seeing Brand sitting slouched on the bed, the receiver still in his hand, Kastner said, "Any luck?"

"No. I'll have to go to the embassy. What's happened with Joachim?"

"The Bundeswehr people are sending a car."

"How much can you tell them?" Brand asked Harpe. Now that the East German was about to disappear into the maw of the Federal German intelligence machine, Brand realized that he was going to miss the thin, intense soldier. He had been Harpe's lifeline to the West for nearly two years, his protector and confidant, and he knew that he might not see Joachim again for months, if ever. "How much that would help us immediately, that is."

Harpe shrugged. He appeared at the point of exhausted collapse. "I'll give them everything I know. It might help a little. It would have helped a great deal a few days ago. Now . . ." He shrugged again.

"How are you getting to the embassy?" Kastner asked.

"Rent a car. Taxi."

"There won't be a rental car available for love nor money," Kastner pointed out. "They've all disappeared west by now. And anybody with a taxi's going to be saving his own skin. The subways aren't running at the moment, either, according to the Bundeswehr people. I'd like to drop you off, but it's the wrong way and they want Colonel Harpe immediately."

"I'll take the Mercedes," Brand said with an inward shudder of disgust. "The only thing is, the police may stop me with that broken windshield."

"There's likely a BND registration in the car," Kastner said. "I think the police have other things to deal with than broken windshields." He scribbled on a sheet of hotel stationery. "If they do stop you, call me at this number."

"Thanks," Brand said. "I hope I don't need to."

I should have slept before trying to drive down here, he thought. Twice as he drove down the Rheinufer, the boulevard that ran along the river's west bank, he had almost dozed off. Fortunately, the wind through the Mercedes' smashed windshield helped keep him awake, although he had to keep his speed down because the rush of air made his eyes water. The wind also kept the car from smelling too much of blood. He had put a hotel bedsheet over the seat to cover the worst of the stains.

The police weren't interested in him, either, despite the

damaged car, either because they had already seen plenty of shot-up vehicles, or because they had other matters to worry about, such as loose remnants of the Russian airborne attack. The Soviet troops hadn't seemed very serious about holding on to their positions in Bonn; it appeared to have been a raid against government personnel rather than an attempt to seize the bridges for the ground troops. It had probably been a separate force that attacked the Siegburg airfield. Bad luck for the Russians in Bonn that the HSK unit was near their landing zones, already activated.

There was much less traffic on the north-south boulevard than he had expected. The traffic jams of westbound vehicles were all on the east bank, at the bridge approaches. There wasn't much military traffic, either: a few trucks carrying HSK men, a pair of Marder armored infantry carriers, a Faun artillery tractor towing a 155mm gun. The West German military machine, at least in the rear areas, didn't seem to be pulling itself together very quickly.

Brand fiddled with the Mercedes' radio. It popped and clicked, then delivered Beethoven's Third Symphony. Across the dial the programming was exclusively classical music, except for a Belgian station that drifted in and out, unintelligible. Occasional faint bursts of jamming leaked through the music. Brand gave up and switched off; he was nearly at the embassy, anyway. He swung the Mercedes into Austrasse, and immediately stood on the brakes. There was a roadblock just ahead, police manning it, backed up by soldiers. A logjam of vehicles had collected at the barricade.

He didn't want to try conclusions at the block, not with blood all over the Mercedes' seat, despite the phone number Kastner had given him. He turned left into a sidestreet, hoping the police would be too busy with frantic civilians to notice him. Half a block along he pulled over in a no-parking zone and switched off the engine. After a moment's thought he got out of the Mercedes, opened the hood, and removed the ignition control module which he put in his pocket.

The P38 was still in his jacket. He debated taking it with him through the barricade. Too dangerous. He locked it in the trunk instead, and set off up the street.

At the barricade he had less trouble than he had expected. One of the policemen studied his American passport, patted him for weapons, and let him go through. They weren't passing cars or anyone except Americans. Brand found himself walking beside a gaunt middle-aged man accompanied by a very short dark-haired woman wearing sunglasses, and two girls in late adolescence. They all carried suitcases and looked apprehensive.

"You're American?" asked the gaunt man.

"Yes," Brand said. "Are they letting anybody else through?"

"Only if they're married to Americans." A southern accent, North Carolina maybe. "We've got a rental car but they wouldn't let us bring it through. Waited for an hour in the lineup before we found out, goddamn it." He hefted the suitcase. "You alright, Nancy?"

"I can manage," said the short dark woman, breathless. Brand felt he should offer to carry her suitcase, but didn't. He was too tired.

"We've got tickets back home for the end of the month," the man said. "I tried to rebook this morning, but the airport at, where is it, Cologne, is shut down. We thought we'd better come here." The man was frightened, Brand realized, wanting reassurance, even from a stranger. "You think the embassy can get us out?"

"Maybe," Brand said, although he couldn't think of any realistic way for it to do so. One of the girls was looking at him oddly. He was abruptly conscious of his dirty clothes, his growth of beard, and the fact that he needed a bath. "Maybe," he repeated.

"Is it true the Russians attacked?" Nancy asked. "We heard shooting this morning. And sirens."

"I'm afraid so," Brand said. He didn't want to talk any more.

"Hell's bells," said the man. "Look at that."

Ahead, in front of the embassy building, the driveway ran around a broad oval of grass. Across the oval, and on the lawns byond it, spread a dense crowd of men, women, and children, standing, sitting, lying. More were on the embassy steps, under the hot afternoon sun. A single ambulance was parked in front of the steps.

"My god," Nancy said. "We'll never get out of here."

Brand forced himself into a trot. The crowd seemed to come nearer very slowly, as though approached in a dream. He searched for a woman accompanied by two children. Many like that, no one with Jenny's bright hair. It isn't a noisy crowd, he realized as he reached the oval. It's quiet, scared quiet.

He reached the embassy steps and started up. Two Marine guards stood at the main doors, weapons slung. Their faces were impassive. "My name's Paul Brand," he said. "I'm here to see Matthews."

"Sorry, Mr. Brand," said one of the Marines. "The embassy's temporarily closed. No entry without a pass."

"Corporal," Brand said in his best officer's voice, "I'm a retired colonel in the US army and I work for the CIA. I've just flown out of West Berlin. I need to talk to your resident. Now if you won't let me in, find someone who *will*."

After a moment's hesitation the Marine unclipped a radio from his belt and spoke into it. Somebody at the other end answered. The Marine listened, the instrument clamped to his ear. After a moment he said, "Somebody'll be out in a minute. You'd better be sure of your facts, Mr. Brand. If you're not, you'd better go back down those steps."

Brand ignored him. After perhaps three minutes' wait a gray-haired man wearing glasses with thick black rims appeared at the doorway. He wore a suit the same color as his hair, but the suit needed pressing. The man opened the door and said, "You're Mr. Brand?"

"Yes."

"We had a signal yesterday that you were coming through from Berlin. That was before all this happened, of course. My name's Bob Faulkner. Come in."

The embassy lobby was full, mostly women and children, not tourists like those outside. Families of embassy staffers, Brand guessed. The Dip corps takes care of its own.

"We'll go along to my office," Faulkner said. "They're —"

"Wait a minute, please," Brand said. "I have to find out if my wife and children are here. Two kids, six and four, my wife's name's Jennifer. She was —" He stopped.

Faulkner had halted and was looking at him with surprise. "Didn't you call?" he asked. "I left instructions at the switchboard to tell you if you called. Your wife and children have been here since eleven o'clock this morning."

Berlin - Southern Germany
6:00 - 10:00 A.M., August 16

KEVIN DRURY lay behind a rough barricade of broken bricks and thought about Christina Mellors, wondering how she would react if she could see him in the dusty rubble of the Wavell Barracks, the butt of a Sterling submachine gun clamped under his arm.

Badly, he decided with some bitterness. She never liked mess.

He raised his head a fraction, peering through a crevice in the brick mound that had once been a wall. Well to the other side of the mound, from the shattered buildings on the barrack perimeter, he could hear the rumble of engines. They were getting ready again.

Somebody was crawling up the mound beside him. Kevin looked over his shoulder: Hewitt, a sergeant from the Green Howards. The units were all mixed up now, Parachute Regiment officers like Kevin fighting beside the men of the Royal Scots Dragoon Guards, the Welsh Guards, the Artillery, and the Royal Anglians, the remnants of the doomed Berlin Brigade. There was no armor left, not even the Saracen light fighting vehicles, and precious little truck transport. Ammunition was in short supply, and there were few men left to use what remained.

"What?" Kevin asked.

"Colonel Villiers says they're getting ready, sir," Hewitt said in a rush. "He's sending a MILAN section up here. When the ammunition's gone we're to withdraw across the Heerstrasse Bridge to the east bank of the Havel. We're to set up positions there, as quick as we can. The MILAN section will go the same route, there're supposed to be reloads over there."

"Does Colonel Villiers know the Russians are all over the east bank?" Kevin said, disbelieving. "They came down through the French sector this morning. They'll slaughter us on the bridge."

Hewitt rubbed a hand over his forehead, leaving pale streaks in the soot and dust coating his skin. "The MILANs are coming sir, You'll have to decide."

Decide what? Kevin wondered, trying to force his numbed brain to work. Decide to stay and be overrun, or decide to be shot to pieces on the bridge? What good's a MILAN team going to do here? They haven't any reloads to speak of, and the ammunition seems to be on the other side of the river. The Russians won't even blink at us. If we'd been able to get the men into position yesterday morning . . .

On that morning there had hardly been time to breathe. The Soviet engineers had blown corridors in their own minefields and border fortifications, and the 19th Mechanized Division had poured through the gaps, supported by a vicious and precise artillery barrage which caused dreadful casualties at the Brooke and Wavell and Montgomery barracks. Two hours passed before the surviving British troops were able to form some kind of organized resistance, and by that time the Russians were well inside the outer defenses. By noon, Gatow airfield had been overrun and the Russians were regrouping for a thrust north along the Havel to pocket the British garrison near its barracks. To the north the French were under heavy attack, losing the Foch Barracks and much of their ammunition stocks and vehicle park in the first three hours of the assault. As far as Kevin could tell, the Americans were as badly off; great plumes of blue-black smoke still rose from the southern part of the city, over the oil tanks in Lankwitz near the McNair and Andrews barracks.

We should have had just a little time, he thought, lying on the bricks, his tongue gritty with mortar dust. We could have put up a better fight, even with three or four hours' warning. Surely somebody must have known something. Why weren't we told?

Hewitt had been gone for two or three minutes. Kevin half

turned to look to the rear. A head poked from a doorway in one of the ruined buildings behind him, in a line with the battalion command post in the ruined barracks administration block. Kevin tensed, then saw the British helmets and mottled battle-dress. A soldier scuttled into the open, stumbling on the broken masonry underfoot, the 25-kilogram bulk of the MILAN antitank missile pressing him down. Kevin waved, urging him forward. A second soldier emerged from the building, a larger man, less clumsy with his load.

That'll slow the BMPs down a bit, Kevin thought. I hope the Yanks are keeping the Russians tied up down south. Jenny and her kids are down there, likely.

He felt a pang of guilt. He had not had the slightest oppor-tunity, realistically, to contact his sister and tell her to take shelter or get out of Berlin or give her other useless advice, but he still felt that somehow he should have been able to do something for her. Maybe Paul, with his connections, had been able to get them out, although Kevin doubted it.

The MILAN team was only fifteen meters away, straining under the load of the launcher and the missile. Kevin was raising his arm to direct them into position when the Russian 160mm mortars concealed beyond the barracks' perimeter dropped a neat pattern of shells precisely on top of them. The mortar bursts detonated the MILAN warhead and the shockwave blew Kevin's legs off and threw the rest of him clear over the mound of bricks into the open.

For some reason or other he was still conscious, although he could not move. In the bright early sunlight he saw a line of Rus-sian troops advance out of their positions to the northwest, behind them the low-turreted BMP personnel carriers grinding forward in support.

I ought to shoot at them, he thought. Can't find the Sterling, damn it. Dead. I'm dead. Can't find my legs either, it should hurt more. Darkening in the sky. Should go home to bed, tired. Never you mind, it'll be better in the morning. Pick me up, Dad, like you did at the fair. Can I have the bear, the blue one. Tired. All gone now. Good night, sleep tight, cuddle down now. Now.

* * *

Far to the south, in the M557 command vehicle that was serving as the combat HQ of the 2nd Brigade of the US 1st Armored Division, Colonel Charles Brand was studying his situation maps. The brigade chief of staff, Robert Fitzpatrick, marked a suspected Soviet artillery concentration on the plastic overlay, put the grease pencil down, and said, "I can't understand it. They should be all over us by now. Why're they giving us time to pull ourselves together?"

"Don't know," Charles said. He was desperately short of sleep — they all were, the only saving grace was that the Russians would be in the same condition, if not worse — and he found it difficult to concentrate on the map. Fitzpatrick with his voluble worries didn't help. "You think they've stopped?" he asked Major Langham. Langham was chief of brigade intelligence.

"It's starting to look that way," said the major. He was a redhead, and the paleness of his beard made him look as though he were the only one in the command post who had bothered to shave. He picked up the pencil Fitzpatrick had discarded and used it to trace the thrust lines of the Warsaw Pact armor. "They came through the Hof Gap yesterday morning like a ton of bricks, over in the 4th Panzer sector. Those troops were mostly Czech, with a corsetting of Russians. They wouldn't have got through so fast if they hadn't had surprise. But I'm still wondering why the Czechs were trusted enough to be put in the first echelon. The only reason I can see is that the Russians aren't going to advance the Czechs any farther into Germany than they already have. They're probably there to secure the extreme Soviet flank along towards Austria. Not as a major invasion force."

He paused and bit at the end of the grease pencil, a thoughtful expression flitting across his face. "Our division's sitting right on a seam between two of their major formations. Look. Army Boleslav east of us, to our right, 8th Guards Army on our left, to the west and Wurzburg. The only 8th Guards formation near us is an East German division; all the Russian units are in the heavy fighting to the west. I'd bet the 8th Guards Army boundary is right here." He traced a line on the map with the grease pencil.

"The seam's right along Highway 279, then," said Charles.

"Russians and East Germans to the west, Czech and two Russian divisions to the east." He was thinking hard. Where formations commanded by different headquarters adjoined — the "seam" — there was always a vulnerable point, because of the tendency of each HQ to assume that an attack at the join was the other's responsibility. As well, coordinating movements between two large forces was difficult; one might withdraw or advance before the other did, thereby leaving a flank open to envelopment by an astute enemy. "Is that what divisional intelligence says?" Charles asked.

"Yeah," said Langham. "They've passed the appreciation on to Corps HQ at Stuttgart. What they'll do with it is anybody's guess."

"The Soviets aren't pushing us at all, though," Fitzpatrick reiterated. "That still doesn't make any sense. 8th Guards is pounding away at the Germans north of Wurzburg, but in front of us the Pact's just sitting still. What do they think they're doing?"

Charles looked down at the map again. The Soviets' behavior seemed irrational, militarily. At the beginning they had gone by the book: sabotage, communications attacked by airborne units, bridges blown, fuel and munitions dumps hit to the rear, then waves of aircraft to strike at the NATO airbases. Rumor had it that scores of American jets had been destroyed in the first twenty minutes after dawn, while still on the ground. Whether that were true or not, the sky had been almost empty over the brigade's positions since noon the previous day. Even most of the Russian planes had gone, and whatever was left of NATO airpower in the region seemed to have been drawn off to the west, where by all accounts the fighting was bloody. According to the maps, and the latest information from Division, the Pact had driven ten to thirty kilometers deep into West German territory from Wurzburg east to Regensburg, and then had stopped dead.

"How are the Germans doing at Wurzburg?" Charles asked Langham.

"12th Panzer's holding north of the city. The weight of the Russian attack is west of them, towards Frankfurt. Our 3rd Mechanized is supporting the Germans, but we're being pulled east, away from the Rhine, to do it. If the 3rd's dragged too far this way, there'll be a clear run for 8th Guards right to Darmstadt on the Rhine." Langham looked at his colonel. "I'll bet my retirement pay that's what's going on. They want to reach Darmstadt and seal off our supply lines against the French border. We're pocketed, then. They can let us wither on the vine. No need to risk attacking us with the Czechs or the East Germans at all, and Zossen can use the divisions it trusts, the Russians, where the fighting's toughest."

"Sense," Charles said. "It does make sense. Politically. They want to deal with the Germans, not us. If they leave us alone they'll be less likely to get a nuclear reaction from Washington. And we'll be bargaining chips if there are negotiations."

"If it goes on that long without somebody pushing the button."

Charles whistled tunelessly between his teeth. "Any more on weapons dispersal?" Around 0400 the brigade had been alerted by Division HQ to prepare to receive nuclear shells for the M109A2 self-propelled howitzers of the artillery support battalion, but the devices hadn't arrived yet.

"No. I talked to Benedict half an hour ago. He didn't know whether Corps had got the predesignations yet or not."

"Alright. Any idea where the West German reserves are?"

"Benedict said 10th Panzer left Ulm around midnight. Part of it should be here this evening if Russian air leaves it alone. 4th Panzergrenadiers is trying to sideslip this way, so as to mask Nuremburg if Army Boleslav does advance. No timeline on that one. 1st Mountain is supposedly moving up from the south towards Regensburg. They're too far away to do us any good at the moment."

"Yeah," said Charles absently. He was wondering whether Division were looking at their maps as he was looking at his. They might be able to concentrate two full armored divisions, his own and 10th Panzer, maybe parts of two more, into a counterattack position on the flank of the Soviet drive on Frankfurt.

Right opposite that seam.

* * *

By midmorning on Monday, August 16, the great wave of the Warsaw Pact invasion had flooded deep into the Federal Republic, from Kiel on the Baltic coast all the way south to Frankfurt where the Russians were trying to force the passages of the River Main against bitter resistance from the US 8th Infantry Division. The advance was still grinding forward; nowhere yet had the Pact armies been driven back.

In Zossen, however, Marshal Lesiovsky was not quite as optimistic as he had been twenty hours earlier. At several points his troops were behind schedule, most seriously on the Weser River, where attempts to expand the bridgehead on the south bank were going very slowly. The other sore points were the delay of 3rd Shock Army, which was still tied down by West German units around Hanover, and the fact that 7th Panzer had finally gotten on the road from its barracks near Dortmund and was moving towards the battle area.

Worse still, NATO airpower was showing a resurgence. The combat reports of the Soviet pilots after the first strikes had been overly optimistic; more Western aircraft had survived than Zossen had hoped. As a result the Warsaw Pact interceptors and fighter-bombers had still not achieved air superiority over the battle areas. Combat losses and serviceability problems were reducing the sortie rate of the Migs and Sukhois, and the pilots and ground crew were tired and dropping in efficiency. Moreover, some of the forward airstrips had been attacked by Dutch and Belgian-based Tornado strike planes flying in at low level; the Soviet air armies were now beginning to pay the price of the political decision not to attack NATO airfields in the Benelux countries. Attacks against Dutch and Belgian bases were now being mounted, but getting at them was proving very expensive in planes and aircrew.

Several other incipient problems were troubling Lesiovsky and his staff. As NATO resistance stiffened, the advance had slowed, causing severe traffic jams behind the battle areas. Ammunition and fuel consumption had been nearly double that predicted, and while each unit theoretically carried with it enough combat supplies for six days' heavy fighting, it was becoming clear that the first echelon would begin to run out of essentials by the end of the third day of high-intensity warfare. Preparations for moving supplies by air and road had to be accelerated, and this was causing further movement problems. The tank breakdown rate was also well above that predicted.

Finally, and possibly worst, some units were starting to lose their way as the advance continued, attack the wrong objectives and bypass ones they should have taken, or simply cross the line of march of another unit and spend several hours disentangling the resultant traffic jam. These hours were precious, and could not be made up. The seventy-two hour deadline loomed nearer and nearer.

On balance, though, Lesiovsky still felt that he could achieve the majority of his objectives within the time allowed, even with his supply problems. NATO did not have the reserves to maintain its present resistance everywhere; sooner or later the front would crack. It had to.

The Russian marshal would perhaps have been less optimistic if he had know that because of map reading errors, a spate of traffic control difficulties, and the unexpectedly strong resistance of 12th Panzer north of Wurzburg, a gap was opening between the flanks of 8th Guards Army and Army Boleslav. Charles Brand's seam was becoming a tear.

Bonn
10:00 A.M., August 16

SOMEWHERE CLOSE BY, a telephone was ringing. Brand sat on the terrace at the rear of his house, watching Alison and David play in the sandbox. The sky was very bright, painfully bright, not blue at all; the swing and the oak tree and the children cast vivid ebony shadows on the lawn's dry grass.

The ring again. Brand thought: It's the red telephone, it's come. He looked at the grass. The blades, one by one, very slowly, were beginning to shrivel. Tendrils of smoke coiled delicately. Alison was looking at him, her mouth open in a wide O. They didn't give her time to grow up, Brand thought. He tried to rise.

And found himself sitting upright in bed in the hotel room, the sheet around his waist chill with perspiration. The telephone on the bedside table was beginning, possibly, its third ring. A bar of sunlight fell through the join between the thick drapes at the tall windows; he could hear traffic noises from the Bundes-kanzlerplatz. He grabbed at the telephone.

"Paul Brand. Hello."

"Paul." It was a woman's voice. It was familiar, but he couldn't place it. "This is Lotte."

His brain wouldn't work properly. Did he know a Lotte? "I beg your pardon?"

A sigh of exasperation from the receiver. "Lotte. I showed you some photographs in May, remember? At my house."

He was instantly awake. "Lotte. Where are you?"

"I need to see you," she said. "It is very important." She spoke the words in a flat tone that put him immediately on his guard.

"Yes," he said. "Where?" He looked down at Jennifer curled beneath the sheet beside him. She was still asleep, eyelids fluttering in a dream.

"May I come there?"

"Jennifer and the children are here," he said reluctantly. Alison and David were still asleep in the adjoining room; Kastner and Harpe had not come back yet. By this time Brand thought they probably wouldn't.

"I'm sorry."

"You know where I am. Could we use the restaurant downstairs?"

"I would prefer not to. Paul, I am becoming desperate."

"Alright," he said. "Come. Room 516." At her end Brand could hear the engine of a heavy vehicle; she was calling from a telephone booth.

"Within twenty minutes. I'm not far away."

"See you then."

She rang off without saying goodbye. Goddamn, Brand thought, replacing the receiver. Now what? The mayor of West Berlin calling me from a phone booth in Bonn? The world's gone crazy.

He looked down at Jennifer; she was stirring, opening her eyes. For a moment they were confused and frightened, then cleared. "Paul? Were you just on the phone?"

"It was Lotte von Veltheim," he said. "She's coming up here in about twenty minutes."

"She's *what*?"

"She wants to talk to me."

She struggled upright in the bed against the drag of the sheet. "You invited her up here? With the children still asleep? What for? After what we went through yesterday? What in the name of Christ *for?* "

"Jenny," he said helplessly. The relief they had felt at finding each other at the embassy the previous afternoon had begun to fray not long after they had reached the hotel; whatever else she wished to feel, Jennifer Brand was furious at what she saw as her husband's desertion of her in Berlin. He could hardly blame her for it. From her viewpoint he had left her and their children in a city about to fall under siege, when he might have warned her earlier, and she and Alison and David had almost died in the air under the guns of the Russian fighter. At Cologne airport she had moved heaven and earth to find a way to Bonn, a few kilometers down the road. David, for twenty desperate minutes, had managed to lose himself while she was doing so; she had finally located him wandering down a boarding ramp that ended in open air twenty feet above the tarmac.

The cash she had brought from the house in Berlin saved her. She had waved a fistful of American dollars at a cab driver who was already besieged by desperate travellers trying to escape the airport. He had shoved Jennifer and the luggage and the children into the car and driven off with less affluent petitioners hanging, almost, from the door handles. The ride to Bonn and the embassy had cost her two and a half thousand dollars; Brand considered it cheap. He would not have begrudged all the money she had been carrying. The remaining cash, however, would be useful. He was uncertain how much longer his American Express card would be of any use, and in a few days West German marks might well be worthless, if there weren't some sign by then that the Federal Republic would survive. The clothes and razor and soap he had bought the previous afternoon to replace those lost at Siegburg airfield had already doubled in price.

At least the Belgian frontier's not far away, he thought. We should leave for there in the Mercedes this afternoon, if there's no sign the front's stabilized.

"Sorry," he said, uselessly.

"It doesn't matter," she said, throwing off the sheet and standing up in her green nightdress, rubbing her eyes. "It doesn't matter now, any of it. Berlin's gone. So's Kevin, likely. And our house. And most of our friends." She would not look at him.

"There's something wrong with Lotte," he said. He rubbed at a bruise on his shin, collected somewhere between Siegburg airfield and the Kennedy Bridge. "She ought to be at the

Chancellery, broadcasting to Berlin, or something. Helping Rudel."

"I'm going into the other bedroom. I'll sleep on the couch," she said. "Try not to wake the children."

He nodded, wordless. He wanted to say: Don't do this, I need a little help, I was nearly killed yesterday myself. I'm not doing these things because I want to.

At the connecting door she stopped and turned to look at him. "When we get out," she said, "if we do, we're going to have to talk about this. Your behavior. You've put me, yourself, and the children into danger. Especially it's the children. You can't go on doing it. Not if you still want us."

A burst of anger seized him. "Hasn't it occurred to you there's a war on? I can't help what my orders are."

"I know there's a war on," she said, the connecting door closing behind her, quietly, so as not to waken the children. "A Russian pilot nearly killed us yesterday."

He had finished shaving by the time Lotte arrived, as well as having bribed the hotel's room service to deliver sausage, milk, bread and butter, fruit and coffee, enough for six people. As a slight afterthought he had added a bottle of Hennessey cognac. The hotel had been reluctant to give up the food from its kitchens; it was expecting deliveries to be interrupted because of the fighting, and did not want to be caught short. Brand's promise to the service manager of a hefty surcharge "for prompt service" had finally brought a loaded trolley to the door, after which five hundred American dollars had changed hands. Brand felt only slightly guilty; the children would be ravenous when they woke up.

He opened the door almost before she finished knocking. Outside it, a denim purse slung over her shoulder, stood the mayor of West Berlin, dressed in a dirty brown leather jacket and blue jeans, dirt-stained and spotted with rusty smears that might have been dried blood. A dark green kerchief was drawn over her hair and knotted at the back. In the dull light from the suite's curtained windows her face was ashen, ancient. If he had passed her on the street he would not have known her.

"Jesus, Lotte," he said. "Come in, quick."

She gave him a trace of a smile and said, with a remnant of the old grace, "Thank you, Paul. I'm sorry to come to your doorstep like this. Are Jenny and the children safe?"

"They got out of the city just in time." He closed the door behind her, putting the security lock across. "They're in the next room. Sleeping. I've got food and coffee and cognac. You need some of each, I think."

"Yes. Some of each, if you don't mind."

He made her a plate of bread and sausage, then poured coffee and cognac for each of them. Out of some lingering sense of propriety he left the liquor alone until he had eaten nearly half a roll and butter; by that time Lotte had consumed two of the sausage links and her own roll and was leaning back in the chair, coffee cup in one hand, cognac glass in the other.

"You have no idea what that feels like," she said. "I have not been so hungry since I was a little girl in Berlin, just after the war. There was nothing to eat in Berlin, then." She drank coffee, then cognac. "As, I suppose, there is nothing there now. Or won't be, soon. The Russians will have the place, and they won't give much to the West Berliners. If anything at all. They always hated us. We were always what they couldn't be. Not because we were Westerners, but because we were Germans. And free of them. Showing what we could do if we were free."

She was rambling a little, perhaps because of exhaustion, perhaps because of the cognac, or both. Brand said:

"Lotte, what are you doing in Bonn?"

She leaned her head against the high back of the chair, closing her eyes. "There was to be a conference of city mayors beginning yesterday in Frankfurt. I was invited, naturally enough. I arrived late Saturday night. Early Sunday morning the Russians attacked Frankfurt airport with helicopters and then airstrikes. I knew what was coming. The airport was closed so I took one of the Frankfurt mayor's Mercedes and started driving north. It should have taken two hours at the most, city to city. Then I ran into the refugees, ten kilometers north of Frankfurt. They'd heard the Russians were coming again. A lot of people were walking, even. Pushing baby carriages, children on their

backs, pulling toy wagons with suitcases on them, even wheel-
barrows stuffed with bits and pieces, old clocks, antiques they
didn't want to leave, grandfather's ashes, I don't know. It was
1945 and the Russians all over again, the roads clogged, even the
Bundeswehr units couldn't clear them, they had to go around
into the fields. The tanks went right over cattle and sheep, they
were in such a hurry. I tried the B roads, they were nearly as bad.
Then I ran out of gas." She shrugged. "I found some more. I had
gold with me. At sundown there were air attacks. I saw Luftwaffe
planes, but not enough of them. Like the last time. I had to
sleep, so I pulled off in a lane. This morning the roads were a
little better. I reached Bonn about an hour ago. I found you
through your embassy." She gave a faint smile. "I am still, for
what it's worth, the mayor of West Berlin."

Outside the window a heavy tracked vehicle roared and
clanked along the Bundeskanzlerplatz. Not the Russians yet, he
thought. Not for a while.

"What's happened?" he said.

She had put the coffee cup down and was balancing the
cognac glass carefully on the arm of her chair. "Paul. I need your
help. I've come to you because you're both German and
American, and I need the Americans just now. I know you know
many people in the United States. I don't want to go to my own
people, because I don't trust them enough."

"With what?" Brand said. He wanted to go back to sleep. He
wished the embassy had refused to tell Lotte where he was.

"This." She lifted the cognac glass and drank, then put it on
the bedside table with a tiny clink. "Paul, I am a colonel in the
GRU. And I want to defect."

At first he could only look at her. She gazed steadily back at
him.

"I can't believe it," he said. "You?"

"Yes." She held out her glass. "Give me some cognac."

He refilled her glass and said, "For a long time?"

"Yes."

"Why now? After so much time?"

She shrugged, an uncharacteristic gesture. "I was recruited in
1958. You might remember how my father ended, in one of

Hitler's camps. I was ripe, in those days, like a lot of others. I wanted Germany whole again. Under a decent government, but not one dictated to by the Americans and the British and the French. And I was young then, it was before the Wall, before 1962. I was in university, in political science, in Munich. I'd become a Marxist, not a communist, I told myself, but a Marxist. Some of us had a discussion group. We thought the best way to reunite the country was to get rid of the Americans and the British and the French, declare a neutral West Germany, and turn it into a socialist state. Then, we thought, the Russians would let East Germany join us.

"There was a graduate student in the group, older than the rest of us. He was violently anti-American. His name was Fritz Heinemann. I started sleeping with him. At the time I was working a few hours a week in the CSU office in Munich. After a couple of months, Fritz asked me to get him some CSU membership and contribution lists. He said they were for a businessman friend of his, to help him find customers with money. I shouldn't have done it, but I did."

Brand nodded. It was the classic beginning to an entrapment.

"I haven't time to go into the details of what happened after that. Eventually Fritz went on his way, but I went on supplying information to people he'd introduced me to, all Germans. By then I knew it was going to East Berlin, but I had convinced myself I was working for a Germany free of foreign domination, and that the CSU was no more than a tool of the Americans and West German big business. And I was beginning to make a mark locally in the CSU. I was good at organization, at convincing people of things.

"Then came 1962 and the Wall. I was appalled, I couldn't see how the East Germans, Marxists, could do such a thing. I told my contact I was going to leave politics altogether. He told me I couldn't. It was then that I discovered I was working, not for Germans, but for the GRU. They told me things I wanted to hear. They promised to help my political career, said I could help both Germanies by continuing to work for them. It was that or exposure, trial, prison. And I still believed, and I still wanted power. Despite the Wall. The GRU is very good."

"It was the GRU," Brand said, wanting to be sure. "Not the KGB."

"I know the difference," she said, and put her lips to the glass again. "But the KGB has never known about me."

"Oh," Brand said innocently. "I thought the GRU and the KGB worked hand-in-glove."

"Not always," she said. "Let me tell you a story." She drank again, watching him.

"Go on," Brand said.

"I am not sure of the specific details, but it was something like this. You know the Russian power structure is a triad, of the secret police, the army, and the Party. Whenever one of them becomes too strong, the other two combine to bring it under control. Beria, the secret police chief under Stalin, tried to become general secretary. The army and the Party were afraid of him, and arranged his arrest and execution. Then the Party managed to get rid of Marshal Zhukov, the man who led the Russian armies to victory over Hitler. They pensioned him off, more or less, in a Politburo vote while he was on an inspection tour in Europe. The Party had control again."

"I know all this," Brand said. He was beginning to lose patience.

"I know you know," she said equably. "Let me tell you something else. In 1963 I was told to drop all my information-gathering activity, and do nothing more than watch a certain man. What he thought, how he acted. It wasn't hard, because he was in the same political spectrum I was. I had no way of being sure, but at that time, and much later, I believed he was with the KGB."

"A long-term agent," Brand said. "A mole, a termite."

"Yes. Very evocative. But it was clear from some of the instructions I was given that the individual was to have no idea that I was observing him. I was a cross-check for the GRU on a KGB agent. It's uncommon, but it happens. The two organizations work together, but they are somewhat short on trust, at least at the operational levels."

"How did the GRU know in the first place that your target

was KGB?" Brand asked. "Dzerzhinsky Square would hardly have told the GRU."

"I think it goes back a long way," she said. "To Stalin's time, just after the war. I think the Praesidium, as they called it then, decided that Germany had to be eliminated once and for all from the Western orbit, even if doing so took half a century. Stalin was very afraid of Germany even then, remember. So he put out some orders, to the GRU and the secret police, they were called the NKVD in those days, to start looking for a final solution to Germany. They worked out how to do it, but then Stalin died." She paused, poured the last of the coffee into her cup, and added Hennessey. "You understand I do not know all of this for certain. But I am not a politician for nothing, and I have had information that even your CIA has never known. Also, I understand the Russians."

She drank at the mixture in her cup, and went on. "But the mechanism the NKVD — the KGB, by then — and the GRU had started together was still running. The difficulty, after the fall of Beria and Zhukov's disgrace, was whether the secret police and the army should share the knowledge with the Party. The project gave Dzerzhinsky Square and the military a great long-term advantage, as far as the destruction of West Germany was concerned, but at the same time the effort was a political time bomb. I think they finally decided to share the knowledge, but only as necessary. Krushchev never knew, I am certain. Brezhnev and Andropov did, without doubt. About Chernenko I am not certain. But I would bet my life that Nikolayev has not been told. I believe the military and the KGB do not think he is the leader for Russia."

Brand's cognac was almost gone. He poured a little more into his glass and said, "You mean that the GRU of the Soviet General Staff and the KGB have been running a major agent in West Germany since the sixties, and that the Party has not always been told about it?"

"Yes," she said. "I think so."

"And the GRU wanted to guard their flanks by using you to watch him in case the project went wrong, so that they would have enough warning to dissociate themselves from it?"

"Probably." She produced a small shrug. "Now you are describing motivations I can only guess at. Remember, because of Beria and Zhukov the KGB and the military have a common interest against the Party. They will not try to overthrow it because it gives them their legitimacy, but they always want to reduce its power."

"Lotte," he said, "why did you choose me to tell these things to?" Heavy vehicles, perhaps a truck convoy, were passing in the street outside.

She gave the shrug again. "I always wondered about you, Paul, although I never told my control anything. Even when you first arrived in Berlin. Lots of money, a good military background, solid business connections, all of it, even the German blood relationships. And your friends, the Andersons. I thought you were CIA from the first time you walked through my front door."

"Why didn't you tell your people?"

"Because I thought I might need you, somewhere down the road. As I have."

There was a long silence. Finally, Brand said, "Why have you come over now? I would have thought the war was what you were working towards."

Her head sagged; she pressed fingertips to her temples. "I was always told there was to be no war," she said. "In Frankfurt I heard about the invasion. It was enough. I was tired of them all, their constant lies. My own lies. I am a German. There was not supposed to be a war."

"Did the GRU tell you to leave Berlin?"

"No. I was supposed to stay there. I left under false papers." She gave a small dry smile. "They were made by the Russians."

"If there hadn't been an invasion they would have found out where you'd gone," he pointed out. "Frankfurt. To the conference you weren't supposed to be attending."

"If there had been no invasion," she said, "I was going to defect anyway."

Brand was not a trained interrogator, but he thought they had been away from the main point for long enough. "You mentioned the man you were supposed to watch all these years," he said. "Why was it Franz Diercks was caught so easily? Did the Kremlin decide to throw him away simply to destroy Rudel?"

She looked at him, surprise giving away to amusement. "Innocent," she said. "Of course they threw poor Franz Diercks away. Probably Nikolayev wanted Rudel gone, and the KGB and the GRU obliged. Except that it didn't work. It wasn't intended to. Neither was the assassination at the Bundeshaus."

He stared at her, unbelieving. He could hear Alison talking in her sleep, or waking, in the other bedroom. Outside, to the north, there were sirens.

"Rudel," he said.

"Yes," said Lotte. "Rudel. He's theirs. He always has been."

Current Action Center, the Pentagon 10:00 A.M., Eastern Daylight Time, August 16

THE WAR was thirty-four hours old. In that time Hood had managed a total of four hours sleep, in fits and starts. He had showered once, just before going on television to reassure the country that the situation in Europe was under control, and that Soviet adventurism would be dealt with in any necessary manner. Judging from recent reports on the commercial networks, he had not been notably successful; there had been a run on gun shops and food outlets, and there was an expanding exodus of urbanites into the countryside, as well as a few medium-sized riots in California and the northern Midwest, accompanied by looting. The National Guard had already been called out because of the state of emergency, and the riots had been suppressed quickly. Hood avoided contemplating the results of an admitted American defeat in Europe.

Twice he had been on the Molink to speak to Nikolayev; both times the Russian leader had done no more than reiterate the Kremlin's original demands. Nikolayev was clearly aware of the impossible situation in which Hood found himself, and unless something dramatic happened to change the military situation in Europe, at least some of those demands would have to be accepted. The alternative was tactical nuclear war, the ruin of Europe, and quite probably the end of the two superpowers in a deluge of thermonuclear warheads.

The tension in the emergency conference room, high from

the beginning, had grown steadily. Both Thatcher Martin and the Joint Chiefs had been pressing Hood, since dawn, to leave Washington and take to the air in the National Emergency Airborne Command Post, a Boeing 747 derivative packed with computers and communications equipment. So far he had resisted; when the Russians found out he had left the capital, especially after ordering the weapons dispersal, they would assume the worst. And Nikolayev was still in the Kremlin; he had even received the American ambassador there two hours previously. That meeting had had no useful results, either, but it did indicate that the Russian leader was anxious to defuse American suspicions of a first strike.

Hood was in the washroom attached to the emergency conference room, shaving for the first time since his television appearance, when Chalmers put his head in. "Mr. President," he said formally, "CIA Director Ormerod is here. Something very serious has come up."

"What's he doing away from Langley, dammit?" Hood snapped. His temper was wearing very thin. It was not a good state of mind for a man in his position. "He's supposed to be staying on top of things over there."

"There's some critical information. Blake said he had to bring it himself," said Chalmers.

"I'll be right there."

Hood finished rinsing his face, first in warm, then in cold water. As he did so he thought: Politics is merely a set of decisions you have to make between the merely unpalatable and the catastrophic. Murphy's law.

He dried his face and returned along the short corridor to the emergency conference room. Blake Ormerod, Director of the Central Intelligence Agency, was slumped in one of the blue chairs, muttering to Chalmers. Bentley was on one of the telephones, voice hushed, urgent. The others around the table shuffled computer printouts or gazed up at the wall screens, where the unit symbols glowed on the maps like icons lit by altar candles.

"What've you got, Blake?" Hood asked, sliding into the chair at the table's head. "I hope it's good. Not much else is right now."

"This," Ormerod said, sliding a file folder along the polished surface of the table towards the president. "We started getting the transmission from the Bonn embassy three hours ago. It took an hour to complete it, it's almost verbatim. When we had all of it off the printer I had a précis made and came over here."

Hood left the file closed. "Good or bad?"

"It depends," said Ormerod. "It depends on how we handle it."

Hood studied Ormerod's face for a moment, then opened the folder, and began to read.

Even the précis took him nearly five minutes. When he had finished he skimmed the verbatim transmission, sensing the others watching him even as they worked.

Finally he looked up from the dossier. Chalmers met his gaze, then Bentley. Ormerod remained slumped, hands behind his head, looking up at the luminous icons, which moved so slowly that they seemed not to move at all. Like the hour hand of a watch approaching midnight.

"Secure the room," Hood said. "No one in here but us."

A major carrying a stack of photographs shot a startled glance at Hood, put the stack down with a thump, and hurriedly left. Chalmers closed the conference room door behind him and locked it. The room fell silent.

"I have here," Hood said flatly, "an allegation that Rudel is working for the Russians. Blake, tell them."

Ormerod took his hands from behind his head and put them on the arms of his chair. "We received a transmission from the CIA station chief in Bonn," he said. "A defector turned up there early this morning, their time. She says Rudel is a Russian plant. We would have put it down to disinformation, the Soviets still trying to get rid of the chancellor, except for one thing. The defector says she's a lieutenant-colonel in the GRU, and she happens also to be the mayor of West Berlin. Her Honor Lotte von Veltheim."

"*Rudel?*" said Chalmers. "That's . . ." He stopped, perhaps for the first time in his professional life at a loss for words.

"Rudel," Ormerod said. "Apparently, according to von Veltheim, the whole Soviet operation is the result of a long-term scenario. Rudel's behaved as he has simply to give the Kremlin a reason to eliminate West Germany."

"That's absolutely crazy," said Thatcher Martin. "Not even the KGB would be that crazy. Never mind the GRU and the Politburo."

"It gets better," said Ormerod. "The mayor says Nikolayev probably doesn't know anything about Rudel's real loyalties. The army, and the GRU and the KGB have never got around to telling him. Intentionally."

"They set him up to do this?" said Chalmers. "Because they didn't like IALT, or the force reduction talks? Because Nikolayev cut the military allocations?"

"I don't know," Ormerod said wearily. "All I have at the moment is what's in that file. The problem is verification. Veltheim may be what she says she is, but she may, as I said, be another KGB-GRU maneuver to suck the ground out from under Rudel. They've tried twice already, according to her. Diercks was the first attempt, a political solution. The other was the assassination shot. Neither, she says, was meant to succeed. They wanted Rudel as safe as possible. No matter what the Party had in mind."

"You said the problem was verification," Hood said. He was trying to fathom the complexities of what lay in Ormerod's file. Perhaps, only perhaps, it could be a way to salvage a little from the wreck. If it were true.

"Yes," Ormerod said. "Verification. It's very tricky, but we might be able to be sure Rudel's working for the East. According to Veltheim, Rudel will sue for peace, unilaterally, giving the Russians everything they want, in the third day of the war. Pleading the need to spare Germany and everyone else from going nuclear. The population over there's so scared now they'd love him to give their country away, if it means they can save their skins. Collapsing NATO along with the surrender, of course. The British and the Benelux countries won't want to continue if Germany's quit. They'll all have to come to terms with Moscow. So will France, eventually. They've got us by the balls, and there's no way we can make them let go, unless we either go nuclear or turn the conventional war around. Or try a first strike."

"What're the chances in the south of Germany?" Hood asked Bentley.

The chairman of the Joint Chiefs looked up at the wall screens. "We may be able to do something there," he said. "There is a gap opening between their 8th Guards Army and the Boleslav units. How they haven't spotted it I don't know, maybe they have but the units on the ground aren't responding to orders. The chance won't last a lot longer. I think we should throw everything we've got in the region into that gap. If we can get thirty kilometers through the enemy perimeter, we'll be right behind the Russian units that are putting pressure on Frankfurt. They'll have to turn around to meet us. We might even be able to pocket them, if we can pull the German 10th Panzer up from the south quickly enough."

"It won't be enough to stop them up in the north of Germany, though, will it?" Hood said.

"Unfortunately, no. But it'll do two things, if we succeed. Frankfurt will be relieved, and our men in the south of Germany won't be cut off from supplies."

"But no decisive military victory."

"No," Bentley said. "Not if you mean throwing them back to their borders. We don't have the ability to do that."

"Let's do as much in the south as we can," Hood said. "Anything to mess up the Russian plan will help. If we put even a small military success with a political one . . ." He looked at Ormerod. "Maybe we have the makings of a political solution. If Rudel sues for peace before another thirty-six hours are gone, we'll have to give a lot more credibility to the German woman's evidence." He poured water from a carafe into his glass, the small cubes of ice tinkling gently. "Let's think about what we're going to do if Rudel tries to hand over Germany to Moscow." He turned to Ormerod. "Where's Lotte von Veltheim?"

"At our embassy in Bonn. No one except our people know she's there."

"Who have you got on the ground?"

Ormerod grimaced. "Hardly anyone. The man who brought her in was attached to the West Berlin station. The same people who sent that report about the Soviet meeting at Zossen."

And that got lost in a computer, Hood thought. It could have given us at least a few hours, but Langley said it couldn't have been confirmed at the time, anyway. Blake, your people have a lot to answer for. But later.

"Can he work with the Germans?" Hood asked.

"He knows the mayor personally. He also has liaison with the West German security people. In Berlin, but it should still work."

"Right," Hood said. "This is what we're going to do. First, we will not make any public accusations against Rudel. And I want Lotte von Veltheim kept under lock and key in the embassy over there. Your man who brought her in, what's his name?"

"Brand," Ormerod said, reluctantly, unwilling even now to expose identities. "Paul Brand."

"Keep him there," Hood said. "We may need him. Next. General Bentley, release the predelegation codes to 7th Corps. If we're going up against the Russians on their south flank, I want everything ready. Our people already have the warheads, haven't they?"

"Yes," Bentley said. "The 7th Corps weapons were dispersed nine hours ago."

"Alright." Hood took a deep breath. "I am going to assume, for the moment, that the German woman is telling the truth. And I am going to call the general secretary, and tell him that we have found out about Rudel."

A long silence, while the maps flickered overhead. "Mr. President," Chalmers said finally, "you can't be serious. He'll laugh in our faces."

"Yes," Hood said. "He may. But I am also going to tell Nikolayev that if Rudel proves himself a Russian agent by offering unilateral, unconditional peace, we will refuse to observe it, or enter negotiations with the Kremlin, and that we will consider the covert actions of the Soviet Union as just cause for a major war. Either Nikolayev knows about Rudel, or he doesn't. If he does, what I just said still goes. If he doesn't, he may start taking a hard look at what his army and secret police have committed him to. After he's done that, he might talk a little more softly." Hood looked at Bentley. "Especially if we can manage a successful counterattack in the south."

"Suppose Rudel doesn't make the offer?" Ormerod said. "That the woman's a plant?"

"We're no worse off than we are now," Hood pointed out. "Another Soviet attempt to destroy the chancellor went wrong, that's all."

"How far," asked Thatcher Martin, "do we go if Rudel makes that offer?"

Hood regarded the defense secretary soberly and said, "We'll cross that bridge when we come to it."

Bonn
8:00 P.M., August 16

HIS FAMILY was gone, now, and Brand thought it more than likely that he would never see them again. He sat with his head in his hands in the small office on the top floor of the American Embassy, in a black fury at Lotte for having involved him in Rudel's treachery, and for having caused the president of the United States, no less, to require his services in Bonn.

Brand had taken Lotte to the embassy in her own car, as soon as she had finished her confession. Before leaving he had gone into the adjoining suite to tell Jennifer where he was going, and why. She stopped him with an upraised hand. "I heard," she whispered, so as not to wake the children, who were still lying in exhausted sleep in the double bed by the window. "You're going now?"

"Her people will be looking for her, if they find out she's not in Berlin," Brand said. "I have to get her out of here."

"You're coming right back? We have to get out soon, Paul. I want to go today. We've got to get to France. The airports there are still open."

"I'll get back as soon as I can," Brand had said. "Faulkner is going to have to talk to her."

"Paul," she said, "I'm only going to say this once. I don't want to be alone with the children, even in America, if this gets completely out of control. I want you with us. Can you promise that?"

He wanted to say yes. "I'll do what I can."

She studied him for a moment, then lay back on the couch, drawing the light coverlet around her. "Go and do what you have to do," she said.

So he had taken Lotte to the embassy. Faulkner, whom Brand now knew to be head of the Bonn CIA station, had interrogated her himself. He would not let Brand leave; he felt Brand's presence would keep Lotte at ease, and talking. At the beginning Faulkner was particularly anxious about her motives; he was half-convinced that she was acting under Russian orders to attempt, again, the destruction of the German chancellor. By the end of the preliminary interrogation he had changed his mind. There would be no particular purpose served now if Rudel were forced out of office, and if he were indeed a Soviet agent the last thing the Kremlin would want would be his exposure. Faulkner had a transcript prepared for transmission to Washington. Lotte was put under Marine guard in one of the embassy's guest rooms, and Brand tried again to leave. By that time it was two in the afternoon; he knew Jennifer would be half-frantic at his absence. They should have left for the border by twelve.

Then Faulkner had asked him to wait until the response from Washington came in. Reluctantly, Brand agreed. He drove back to the hotel in Lotte's Mercedes, to find Jennifer and the children packed and ready to go. The confrontation had been dreadful, the more so because of the presence of the children.

"Can't you wait for an hour?" he said to his wife. "There might be an answer from Washington by then."

"What's the answer going to be?" she said bitterly. "Either they tell you to stay, or they let you go. If they're going to let you go, fine. If they tell you to stay, you're going to to decide once and for all where your loyalties are. To us, or to whatever's keeping you here. Every minute the planes out of France back to the States are filling up. If we can't get out of Europe because of your delays, you can count me out of your life. And the children with me."

David was clinging with both arms to his mother's leg, eyes wide. Alison sat on the bed, pale still with fatigue, too distraught to speak. "Come back to the embassy with me," Brand had said. "They'll know how to get us out."

She had agreed to that. They reached the embassy perhaps half an hour before Washington's reaction to Lotte's information arrived; they had waited in the same office Brand was sitting in now.

Faulkner summoned him at about a quarter to five. No action was to be taken for the moment, but . . . President Hood wanted Brand to stay on the spot; Brand already knew about the situation and could help in resolving it. It would not do to spread the knowledge to more people than absolutely necessary.

Was the president making a request or giving an order? Brand had wanted to know.

"It's not an order, but it's pretty close to one. Remember you're a CIA officer and you were a colonel in the army. You'd better stay put."

"Then you'll have to make arrangements to get my family out of Europe before the end of the day."

Faulkner pulled strings somewhere. At seven o'clock a civilian helicopter was waiting on the embassy's rear lawn to take Jennifer and the children into Belgium. They would be put on the first available Military Airlift Command back to the United States. Alison had hysterics. David was withdrawn and impassive, Jennifer icy. Her lips when she kissed him goodbye were immobile, like a statue's.

Damn Lotte anyway, Brand thought. Involving me. Damn Hood.

He wondered for a moment where Harpe and Kastner were. He hadn't seen either of them since he had left the hotel for the first time the day before. Maybe Harpe would pull some rabbit out of the hat that would help NATO derail the Russian plans, but Brand doubted it. Nobody at the embassy seemed to know exactly what was happening to the east, or even how close the Russians were. The refugees were still streaming through Bonn, fleeing west, spreading rumors that ranged from the ridiculous to the plausible: Munich overrun (highly unlikely), Hamburg and Kassel in flames (all too likely), Russian aircraft attacking refugee columns with guns and rockets and dropping gas canisters (known to be true). What the devastation was like where the Russian advance had passed Brand could only imagine, but he knew that his imagination could hardly match the reality. Modern weapons, even conventional ones, were far more destructive than their Second World War counterparts. Whatever the outcome of this war — it hadn't even been given a name yet — the rebuilding of the devastated zones would take years, even if no nuclear weapons were used. Bonn so far, except for the fighting of the previous morning, had been spared attack; the skies were clear of Soviet planes. But then the capital was not an immediate military objective. It would not need to be, if Lotte's story were true. Rudel would hand it to the Russians.

I wonder if we're winning or losing? Brand thought. I think probably we're losing. What is Hood going to do about Rudel?

Moscow
2:00 - 4:00 A.M., August 17

THEY WOULD BE ARRIVING SOON. Alexei Sergeyevitch Nikolayev, general secretary of the Communist Party of the Soviet Union, strode along the red-carpeted corridor on the third floor of the old Kremlin Arsenal. The wall sconces gleamed dully, shedding distorted oblongs of pinkish-yellow light on the white walls and the strips of polished floor on each side of the carpet. For security reasons the Politburo and Secretariat meetings were now being held in the Kremlin, rather than at the Staraya Square Central Committe building; telephone and computer lines led from the suite of Arsenal conference rooms out to the STAVKA command complex near Kalinin. Down the hall from the conference suite was a communications center and next to that a small room containing a round table and several chairs. In this room was installed a special telephone with attached amplifier and speaker. At the other end of the telephone was Washington; it, and the teleprinter in the communications center next door, were the Russian end of what the Americans called the Molink. Adjoining the Molink room was Nikolayev's temporary office, which contained a large austere desk with a standard lamp on it, two chairs upholstered in red plush, a safe, a table next to the desk on which sat five telephones, and a portrait of Lenin on one white plaster wall. One of the telephones on the table was also connected into the Molink, so that Nikolayev could use the line without needing to leave his office. This telephone did not have a speaker attached to it. Normally any calls to or from Washington were listened to by a group consisting of at least Nikolayev, Fedashkin, Kamenev and Ivanov, out in the Molink room.

But when Hood had called not an hour ago, Fedashkin was out at STAVKA, and Ivanov had gone to Staraya Square on some unspecified business. As soon as the call came through Nikolayev summoned Kamenev, the only senior Politburo member still in the Arsenal, to the Molink room. The two men had the inestimable advantage of speaking English, which was not shared by the other members of the Politburo; consequently, they were able to dispense with the services of the simultaneous translators. As it turned out, this was a very good thing: one set fewer ears to hear what the American president had to say.

Nikolayev had expected another attempt to moderate Soviet peace conditions, which had been all that had come out of the first two discussions with Hood. Hood was very clearly trapped in an impossible situation, and it appeared both to STAVKA and to the Politburo that their estimate of American resolve had been correct. Washington would not resort to nuclear war in the face of conventional attack, even if their European allies were going to be defeated. And France, one of the major STAVKA worries, had shown no signs of supporting the Americans and the Germans; Paris would likely continue to avoid commitment, since the French had nothing to gain and everything to lose by involving themselves.

But the third call had been different. Holy Mother Russia, Nikolayev thought as he hurried down the corridor, what if Hood is telling the truth?

He could not be. And yet what he had said made sense of most of Rudel's mad policies: the new General Staff, the pressure on the guest workers, the rearmament proposals, the advances to the French regarding nuclear weapons. Only the Germans could have listened to him.

On the line to Washington, when Hood had given him the details, Nikolayev had scoffed. He had to, since Kamenev was listening to the conversation on the speakerphone. But when the conversation ended, with Hood's semi-ultimatum regarding Rudel, Nikolayev had replaced the receiver very carefully and said to Kamenev:

"Come into my office."

They went in, Nikolayev closing the door firmly behind them. Kamenev sat on one of the red chairs. Nikolayev leaned against the desk. The desk lamp, the only one lit, cast irregular shadows on the walls and on the portrait of Lenin.

"Hood said his accusations will be proven by Rudel's plea for peace," he said. "Have you heard anything of such a proposal?"

"No," Kamenev said. "Nothing at all."

"Could the KGB and the army and the GRU have done this?"

Kamenev considered. "It's remotely possible," he said finally. "Ever since Brezhnev died the armed forces and the KGB have been exerting pressure on the Party. I need hardly point out that ex-KGB chairman Andropov took the general secretaryship against the Party's wishes, with army and KGB support. He died too soon, perhaps, for them to consolidate their position. In any case Chernenko, who was a Party man, became secretary. But he was old. Perhaps they drew back a little to take a larger step forward."

Nikolayev studied the shadows on the walls. He thought perhaps he could trust Kamenev; the man had been a committed member of the Party ever since Nikolayev had met him, long ago in Leningrad. He had few military or KGB connections, and was fundamentally a Party ideologue, although more pragmatic than most. He also owed Nikolayev his post; Nikolayev had supported him over a number of others in the Central Committee when the position of foreign minister was being filled two years ago.

As for the others . . . assume the worst, for the moment, that Hood was telling the truth. Minkov, of the KGB. At the center of it. He would have to know everything, so that Rudel could be kept safe even if the Party wished otherwise.

Fedashkin. It was possible he did not know, although Nikolayev doubted it. For something like the Rudel plot to succeed, the defense minister would almost have to know, unless he were a strong Party man, which Fedashkin was not. He had been a captain in the defense of Leningrad against the Nazis, and after that a major with Rokossovsky's troops at the taking of Berlin in 1945. Surviving the postwar purges and Marshal Zukhov's disgrace at the hands of the Party, he had worked his way up the military hierarchy to become chief of the Kiev Military District, then to an advisory post on the Defense Council under Brezhnev, then to a position on the General Staff . . . deputy head of the Intelligence Directorate. The GRU.

"Secretary—" said Kamenev.

"Wait," Nikolayev told him. The catalogue was nearly complete.

Viktor Besedin, chief of the General Staff. If Fedashkin knew, he had to as well. Vasily Tsarev, head of the GRU. A certainty, like Minkov. A military background, as well, like Fedashkin's.

"I think," he said to Kamenev, "that we had better take some measures to defend ourselves."

So now he strode along the Arsenal corridor in the light of the wall sconces, towards the Politburo conference room; and all the others, by now, were on their way to the Kremlin. For, as they supposed, an emergency meeting of the Politburo. It was indeed an emergency, but not the military one most of them would be expecting.

He entered the conference room, feeling as though he were walking awake in the Party's oldest nightmare, one that had begun with Trotsky and had never really gone away since: an alliance of the secret police and the military to reduce the Party to a figurehead for their power. Beria, Stalin's NKVD head, had tried to assume the general secretary's chair after the old dictator's death, but the army, remembering Stalin's purge of the officer corps before the war, had joined the Party to remove and then execute him. But the KGB had become more civilized since Beria, and the military was no longer so frightened of Dzerzhinsky Square. What both organizations resented now was strong civilian control, in the particular persons of Nikolayev and his supporters in the Secretariat, the Central Committee and the Politburo. The military, in particular, had become used to having its way under Andropov and Chernenko and during the long period of Brezhnev's last illness.

I should have been more suspicious when Fedashkin was so willing to slow the pace of weapons production, Nikolayev thought, leaning on the back of one of the chairs, staring at the portrait of Lenin on the end wall. He and the others threw sand in my eyes, with this talk of more advanced military technology. As if we could ever hope to match the Americans.

He looked at his watch. He had perhaps twenty minutes before Kamenev joined him.

The problem, he thought, walking slowly up the length of the table to his chair at its head, is to find out whether the KGB and the military have used Rudel to precipitate a war without the Party's knowledge and consent. I hope confrontation is the right course, but there is no time for anything else. I think Kamenev and I have covered all the eventualities. . . . If Hood is talking nonsense, Minkov and the others will deny that the plan ever existed, and we can decide what actions to take if Hood tries to accuse us publicly.

But we must not forget that even if Hood has been given false information, he may believe it to be true. And if Washington thinks the war began because of a KGB plot . . . There is no predicting how the Americans may react. We are in very great danger if Hood does not keep his head.

On the other hand, Nikolayev thought, lowering himself tiredly into his chair, if Hood is speaking the truth, the conspirators will have the choice of denying their actions, and be exposed later when Rudel does exactly what Hood says he will; or admitting what they have done and attempt to represent it as being in the best interests of the Party. We must not allow them to make a case for that. We have the advantage of surprise, and if we act quickly, we can dispose of them before they can rally support. The Party organs will have to ratify my actions later, but faced with a *fait accompli*, and the evidence of treason, they will vote in my favor.

He sat in the empty conference room with its portrait of Lenin and the red and gold flag of the Revolution, going over the plan once again, reviewing his forces, the Politburo members who would be loyal to him. Kamenev was calling them now, warning them of an impending political crisis in which the Party would need their full support. He was also to contact Andrei Krysin, the minister of Internal Affairs, who controlled the internal security troops of the MVD. Nikolayev did not want to trust KGB men or army soldiers in this.

The door opened and Kamenev came in. The foreign minister slumped into a chair midway along the table. "Everything is arranged," he said.

"Krysin?"

"He's sending eight men and a major from MVD headquarters. I gave personal orders to the KGB post at the Nikolsky Gate to give them Arsenal passes. They're to wait in the east stairwell until I call them."

"What did you tell Krysin?"

"That an unnamed personage here needed an escort to Khodinka airfield, and that the men were to be put under my orders. That for special reasons the KGB was not to provide the escort."

Nikolayev rubbed his jaw. The reason was thin, but it would do. Krysin, in any case, did not get along with the KGB chairman; there was a constant rivalry between the MVD and the KGB for resources and men. Krysin would keep silent for as long as Nikolayev needed.

"We have about an hour," Kamenev said. "Can we go over it once more?"

They filtered in, one by one. In addition to the Politburo members there were present also Colonel-General Vasili Tsarev, head of the GRU, and Marshal Viktor Besedin, chief of the General Staff. These latter two appeared somewhat mystified by their summons, and rather put out at being dragged from their posts at STAVKA. Besedin, in addition, exuded a faint air of worry, as though he had matters on his mind that required immediate attention but for which he could not quite find time.

There's something troubling Besedin, Nikolayev thought, as Chairman of the Council of Ministers Dmitri Gorlenko, last to arrive and late as usual, slid into his chair at the far end of the table. The green baize of the tabletop was neatly arranged with pads of lined paper and carefully sharpened pencils; Besedin selected one of the pencils and began to making diagrams on the pad in front of him, lips pursed. Nikolayev studied the chief of the General Staff intently. There is something wrong out at STAVKA, he thought. What? What else am I not being told?

Nikolayev smiled in the broad comfortable way that had

deceived so many enemies. "This meeting must be hurried," he said, "as we all have other things to do. I spoke with President Hood shortly after midnight, and I am happy to report that he is still in the noose we have tied for him. He has made no threats of nuclear retaliation, and I believe such an action can be discounted in the time before we reach our objectives and our deadline. The neutrality of France, in addition, virtually assures our success. We owe Comrade Foreign Minister Kamenev our thanks for this achievement."

Kamenev inclined his head modestly. A congratulatory mutter rounded the table.

"The end is in sight," Niklolayev went on. Softly, softly. "We especially owe thanks for their socialist commitment and careful preparation to the GRU, the KGB, the General Staff. When we have achieved victory, as we soon will, the United States will be exposed as an empty shell. They cannot even protect their friends, much less defeat those they have made their enemies. The power of America will be broken forever."

He paused, looking around the table. The members Kamenev had warned all wore expressions of polite attention, despite the fact that Nikolayev's words did not seem to reflect a crisis; but they had learned in a hard school to conceal their thoughts. Of the others, Ivanov looked impatient, Tsarev and Besedin remained impassive under the rain of praise, Sereda and Lensky wore noncommittal expressions. Minkov was studying his fingernails.

Fedashkin, on the other hand, was watching Nikolayev intently. Behind the gaze was the thought: Why, Secretary, have you called us here to listen to this pap? Why does the Party interfere with my business in this pointless manner? Leave us to go on with our war.

Nikolayev smiled again and said, "As I mentioned, President Hood has been in contact with myself and Minister Kamenev. It is a pity more of you were not here to listen to what he had to say. He has made nonsensical allegations, but we should consider precautionary measures in case he decides to act on them.

"He says that a German woman, the mayor of West Berlin,

in fact, has confessed to being a GRU agent. She has told the American president that Chancellor Ernst Rudel is also an agent, controlled jointly by the KGB and the GRU for the past thirty years. That Rudel, sometime in the next twelve hours, is going to sue unilaterally for peace, meeting all our conditions for the Federal Republic."

Dead silence. Now Fedashkin, like Minkov, was studying his fingernails.

"That is balderdash," said Ivanov. "What can Hood hope to gain by such contortions?"

"If it were true," Nikolayev said, "it is an intelligence coup of the highest order. To my knowledge no security force has ever succeeded in placing one of its own people in the leadership of a foreign country." He assumed an air of faint disappointment. "Unfortunately, the German chancellor will not be so agreeable in reality. But we must decide what to do if Hood tries to salvage his foreign policy with ridiculous accusations. Assuming the German woman was lying, of course. If she wasn't, we'll know later today, when Rudel speaks to us."

"General Secretary," Minkov said.

Nikolayev, who had picked up a pencil and scribbled the date at the top of his pad, looked up. "Yes?"

"Rudel will be asking for peace. Unilaterally. Before tomorrow morning."

Nikolayev put the pencil down very slowly. Tsarev looked extremely angry, as did Fedashkin and Besedin. They did not want me to know, Nikolayev thought.

"Do you mean," Nikolayev said, "that Hood has been told the truth? By this GRU agent, this defector?"

"Substantially, yes," said Minkov. "I should point out, however, that the existence of this GRU person was not known to the KGB. If she had been—" He gestured dismissively. His meaning hung in the air: if we had known, this defection would never have occurred.

"Crosschecking is normal procedure in joint operations," Tsarev said. He didn't say anything else; there was nothing he could. His organization had been grossly negligent.

"So you were aware of this," Nikolayev said to Tsarev.

"Chairman Minkov, so were you. Minister Fedashkin, Marshal Besedin, you too?"

Nods. "Secretary Ivanov?"

"No."

"Anyone else?"

It was impossible, from Nikolayev's tone, to tell whether to expect praise or blame. But the atmosphere in the long room had altered subtly. No one else admitted to knowledge.

Nikolayev continued to smile. "In short," he said, "you four took it upon yourselves to make the highest policy decisions without the direction of the Party. You have, in fact, behaved as though you *were* the Party."

"Secretary Andropov knew of Rudel," Fedashkin said angrily. "We did not bypass the Party."

"No? Was this matter ever discussed in the Secretariat? Or in *this* Politburo? Or in Chernenko's? I cannot recall any such discussions. What you had was the general secretary's endorsement, not the Party's. *Why did you not inform me?*" The smile was gone.

"The operation was coming to fruition," Minkov said. "We judged it preferable that you be able to issue a plausible denial if something" — he glanced at Tsarev — "went wrong. I—"

"You arranged among you for the defection of Diercks to have no result," said Nikolayev. "For that, and the failure of the assassination attempt on Rudel, you are guilty of intentional failure to carry out the Party's directives."

Fedashkin began, with a certain desperation, "That was not—"

Nikolayev slammed his palm flat on the table with a crack only slightly muffled by the baize surface. "You maneuvered this country into war by deceiving the Party. Because you thought you knew better than the Party. Thanks to you we have risked the Union's destruction in a war which was not necessary. And then you let the Americans find out. *Who are you working for*, us or them?"

He stopped. The faces around the table were uniformly white, with either anger or fear.

"I move that Fedashkin and Minkov be stripped of their

Politburo membership and that their posts in the Central Committee be reviewed," Nikolayev said. "Vote."

Slowly the hands went up, five, then six, Gorlenko's, Lensky's, even, finally, Ivanov's.

"Done," said Nikolayev. Fedashkin and Minkov sat very still, their faces the color of putty. Kamenev got up quietly and left the room. "In addition," Nikolayev said, "I propose that these four men be charged with treason. For the reasons I have already stated." He had to get them physically out of the way and replace them with solid Party men; he was courting disaster if he allowed them loose to drum up support in the military and intelligence organizations. "Is there any disagreement with this?"

No one, seeing which way the wind was blowing, disagreed. After another moment Kamenev reappeared at the door. Behind him were the MVD major and eight soldiers. "Those four," Kamenev said, pointing. "Take them to the MVD headquarters. Lock them up and do not allow them to speak with anyone unless you have a directive from Minister Krysin or myself."

A moment later Fedashkin and the others had stumbled out, Kamenev following to make sure they left the Kremlin without interference. Nikolayev felt a surge of relief. It had worked; he had not been sure it would, less sure than he had let Kamenev believe.

"We must arrange for the immediate replacement of those people," he said. "The Party is still in danger. We need men who are utterly loyal."

They began to work on it, as though Minkov and the others had never existed. Names were proposed, rejected. Finally, they had a short list. The men were to be appointed the next day, without the usual procedures; there was a war to be fought.

They were finishing when Kamenev returned from his shepherding mission. "Secretary," he said, from the doorway, "there's an urgent message from STAVKA."

Nikolayev got up hurriedly and followed Kamenev out of the room. On the way to the communications suite he said, "There is still one factor I can't account for. We had better try to get some more information out of those four. If the Germans and the Americans are not totally crushed, surely Washington wouldn't let Rudel surrender? How could he make such an act acceptable? His own government or the Americans would remove him."

They were entering the communications room. "I'm not sure," said Kamenev.

The duty officer said, "Comrade Secretary, STAVKA is on the direct line."

Nikolayev picked up the receiver, glancing at his watch as he did so. Four o'clock in the morning. He would have to catch a nap in the room behind his office, on the couch there, before the 6:00 A.M. military briefing. "Nikolayev here."

"Secretary," said a voice in his ear, tinny because of the scrambling, "this is Deputy Defense Minister Mikhalin. I am sorry to be calling you, but the minister is unavailable. We have bad news from the Second West Front. An hour ago the Americans and Germans started at least a two-division attack into the flank of 8th Guards Army, from the south near Wurzburg."

"What of it?" Nikolayev said. "I fail to see why this is so alarming. We expected a flank attack at that location."

"Yes, Secretary." The voice, even with the distortion, took on a nervous tone. "But our formations there have gotten out of position. They thought they were in the right places, but they weren't, and there's a big gap. There's nothing between the Americans and the Germans and the rear of 8th Guards but five or six infantry companies and a tank brigade." He paused; the line to STAVKA hissed quietly. "Also," said Mikhalin, "it is now certain that the Americans are dispersing their nuclear weapons."

West Germany
6:50 A.M., August 17

THE SPECIALIST UNIT manning the Zil-135 launch vehicle and its accompanying pair of trucks — one mounting a radar dish, the other the antenna arrays of a mobile command post — had been readying the missile for perhaps half an hour. The launcher had been concealed in a grove of beech trees ten kilometers west of the town of Nienburg, well behind the forward edge of the battle area which was now pressing up against the interchange of Highways 214 and 69 near Diepholz. The unit commander, a lieutenant-colonel, was uneasy about moving the Zil out of cover, but the missile, an SS21 short-range tactical weapon, had to be fired from an open area.

His men had done all the preliminary adjustment and testing possible before the Zil moved out of cover, and now the big four-axled launch vehicle was slowly elevating the weapon to firing position. The colonel, eyes narrowed against the early morning light spilling under the beeches from the glade beyond, watched from beside the command truck as the SS21 tilted. The men of the unit were trained to an extreme pitch, but with weapons like these, accidents and preparation errors came easily.

The SS21 stopped moving. Technicians clustered around its tail, setting the speed brakes, then trotted back with the Zil's crew to the firing point ten meters from the command truck. The colonel could hear birds, finches perhaps, up in the leaves somewhere, just audible over the rumble of gunfire to the west. In the other direction, over Nienburg, great columns of grayish-black smoke bubbled slowly into the sky, like a volcano erupting in slow motion. A West German infantry battalion supported by a few British antitank units had been holding the town the previous day; Nienburg was a road intersection needed to speed up the advance, so it couldn't be bypassed and pinched out later. Two divisional artillery regiments had knocked the town into its own cellars, with most of the defenders and probably half the population. Unfortunately the streets had been so choked with rubble after the bombardment that the tracked infantry carriers and the tanks had to go around the place anyway. There had been a heavy rain during the night, and the roads and fields were chewed up so badly by the tracks of the fighting vehicles that a lot of the wheeled transport got stuck or broke down with snapped axles or flat tires, for which there were unaccountably few spares.

The colonel's unit was an independent one, subject for movement purposes to STAVKA's direct control, so the colonel had had little opportunity to exchange battlefield rumors with other officers. In fact he was not supposed to talk to them at all, except to make sure they did not interfere with his movements, and he had the written and command radio frequency clearances to make sure this happened. But what the colonel could not find out from other officers, he was seeing for himself, and what he saw made him uneasy.

He had received his movement orders from STAVKA the previous morning, and had driven west across the pre-liberation frontier into a landscape out of a nightmare: burned villages, smashed farms with the bodies of cattle and horses and pigs stiff-legged and bloated in the fields, groves of splintered trees, wrecked military trucks and civilian vehicles and fighting machines of every description: tanks, BMP personnel carriers, NATO infantry combat vehicles the colonel did not recognize, self-propelled guns with tracks ripped off and draped over the hulls like funeral crepe, towed artillery with splinter shields crumpled like tinfoil, barrels twisted, tires burned from their rims. And everywhere bodies lying in the warm kiss of the August sun: soldiers, male civilians, women, children, young girls and adolescent boys, under a pall of their own reek and the stench of burning.

As the SS21 unit moved farther west, the number of disabled Soviet fighting and transport vehicles increased steadily. At first most had been abandoned because of battle damage, but towards Nienburg the colonel noted that a rising proportion had simply broken down or run out of fuel. In some cases control had collapsed, often at crossroads where groups of officers screamed at each other, waving creased and dirty maps, and enormous traffic jams stretched eastwards out of sight. Some of these tempting and immobile targets had been attacked by NATO aircraft, which had prompted the colonel to drive across country in the Zil, using it to tow the trucks if they got stuck. He had had the impression that enemy airpower had been effectively destroyed in the war's first hours, but plainly this was not so. As well, there were fewer Soviet planes and helicopters overhead than there had been. And the troops he saw on the roads were hungry, thirsty and exhausted, and sometimes lacking in organization. One distraught tank commander, who had asked the colonel for directions (which the colonel had refused) told him that his entire tank battalion, except for three T80s, had been destroyed in an unprepared attack against German tank killer units dug in along a sunken road. The Russian reserve had overrun the defenders at last, but their losses had been crippling too.

It was not, the colonel considered, that the NATO forces were gaining strength; from the debris and wreckage and bodies it was plain that they were suffering bitterly. The problem was that the Warsaw Pact offensive was flagging. He had expected to see enormous columns of reserves grinding along the roads from the east into the Federal Republic, but what should have been a torrent was no more than a brook. Obviously the second strategic echelon, moving in from Poland and the military districts on the Russian border, was behind schedule. The columns of trucks supplying the first echelon were sparser than he thought they should be, and they stood broken down by the side of the road in increasing numbers as the colonel's unit approached its destination. Nienburg was actually its alternate firing position, the primary one being at a map reference still on the NATO side of the battle area. By this the colonel knew the advance was behind schedule; how badly, he was not sure.

The unit's deputy commander, a major, left the technicians around the firing point and walked through the dappled shade to the command truck. "Reporting weapon ready for firing, Comrade Colonel," he said.

The colonel nodded and took off his helmet to wipe his forehead. Under the beeches the air was already very warm. He looked over at the technicians; even in their summer uniforms they were perspiring heavily, patches of sweat darkening the dull green army tunics.

The army uniforms were a deception. The technicians were KGB specialists normally responsible for the custody, maintenance, and targeting of nuclear weapons. The other soldiers of the unit, who drove the Zil and the trucks and manned the radar were also KGB, drawn from the KGB Border Guards Directorate. The Border Guards divisions, several of which were at least equal to army units in strength and equipment, possessed aircraft, armor, artillery and, conveniently, Zil-135 launch vehicles and SS21 missiles. Where the warhead had come from the colonel did not know (nor did he want to) but he did know that KGB internal security troops were responsible for nuclear weapons stockpiles. Once or twice he had wondered, on the drive west, exactly what his orders were meant to achieve, but he had quickly shut off the thoughts; they were unconstructive, and they were dangerous.

He climbed into the back of the command truck. The radioman sat by his transceiver, hunched over, earphones clamped to his head. The quartz-driven chronometer bolted to the communications console indicated 06:58:50. If the display reached 07:00:00 and there had been no countermanding order, the colonel would give the order to fire the SS21. He wondered for a moment whether STAVKA were frantically trying to reach him, to tell him to abort the launch, but was unable to do so because of jamming. The super-high-frequency satellite frequency he had been given was supposed to be impossible to jam, though. In any case, the intent of fixed planning like this was to ensure that orders — any orders — would be executed even if the command structure were destroyed or out of contact with its units. The colonel supposed the Americans did the same thing, when it came to nuclear weapons. A deterrent would be useless if you could neutralize it by wiping out a few headquarters.

He tapped the radioman on the shoulder. "Anything?"

"No signal, no jamming, no interference, colonel." The radioman had repeated the same formula dozens of times since the unit had reached the firing position.

The colonel climbed out of the truck and stood where he could see both the radioman and the major at the firing point. The finches, or whatever they were, were still twittering. Out in the glade the sun struck heat ripples off the dull metal of the Zil's cab.

The radioman took off his headset and said, "We are on zero. No signal, no jamming, no interference."

The colonel raised his hand and called out to the firing point, "Launch."

Four minutes later a Soviet two-kiloton nuclear weapon detonated at six hundred meters altitude just northeast of Lindern. It was really a demonstration shot, since there were no important fixed military installations within its lethal radius, but it did manage to catch the remnants of a British tank battalion withdrawn outside the town for resupply. The battalion was reduced from a remnant to a wraith. There were also a great many civilian casualties, primarily refugees making for the Belgian frontier.

The signature of the Soviet nuclear strike was detected instantly by a Vela II surveillance satellite orbiting far above Lindern. Twenty minutes later President Hood, having heard nothing from Nikolayev since the Molink call regarding Rudel, made the most difficult decision of his life. To support the NATO attack into the rear of the Soviet 8th Guards Army east of Frankfurt, he unilaterally authorized the expenditure of one nuclear device of not more than two-kiloton yield "on an appropriate military target." In a major sense the act was more political than military, since Hood was now convinced that he had to show the Kremlin that the United States would, in fact, use nuclear weapons in Europe's defense.

The target selected by the American commander at 7th Corps HQ was a concentration of Russian tank and artillery reserve formations moving down from the northwest to reinforce the East German 4th Motor Rifle Division. The 4th had been taken in its left flank a few minutes after dawn, when 10th Panzer, the US 1st Armored, and 12th Panzergrenadier divisions attacked into the gap between the 8th Guards and Army Boleslav, with the objective of splitting the two Warsaw Pact formations and striking the rear of the Russians to the west. The East German resistance had been crumbling since early morning, partly because of the relentless pressure of 10th Panzer, and partly because the Warsaw Pact troops were not showing great determination in resisting their Western cousins. The Russian tanks and guns coming down from the northwest were intended to stop the rot, if only by their presence.

The American nuclear strike, which was carried out by one of the self-propelled guns of Charles Brand's armored brigade, had two immediate results, one as expected, the other wildly unpredictable. The first was that the Russian reserve was stopped in its tracks, and badly damaged. The second was that the front line of the East German division broke completely. When the Russian officers and KGB police units attached to the formation tried to drive the men back into battle, the soldiers attacked them. The divisional second echelon was ordered forward. Led by junior East German officers and NCOs, it also turned on the Russian cadres. By noon the entire 4th Division was either surrendering to Bundeswehr troops, or was in open revolt against the Russians. The division's headquarter's transmitters had been taken over by the rebels who were broadcasting appeals for support to the Czechs of Army Boleslav, to other East German formations, to the West Germans, and to the Americans. 10th Panzer, the resistance in front of it evaporating, roared towards the rear of the Russian 8th Guards.

Bonn
12:20 P.M., August 17

BRAND HAD BEEN IN THE CIA Communications Center on the embassy's top floor when the news of the Russian and the retaliatory American nuclear strikes came in. The large square room with its dozen or so communications and operational personnel had become quite silent with Faulkner's announcement of each attack; then they had returned to their arcane tasks at the transmitters and computer consoles, surrounded by the intermittent chirr of telephones and the buzz of printers.

He sat at an unused desk in one corner of the room, waiting, as he had since the previous evening, and watching Faulkner leaf through a stack of decoded intercepts. The CIA station chief's face was unshaven, stubbled silver, and his hair was dishevelled. He had been awake most of the night. Brand had been, too, although not for the same reasons.

Kastner was perched on one corner of the desk, drinking coffee out of a paper cup, with his eyes half closed. He had turned up at the embassy early that morning, looking even more frayed and lined than usual, to tell Brand that the debriefing team was finished with Harpe. The East German had been put into protective custody, to be flown out of the country if circumstances required it. Kastner had tried to return to Pullach for reassignment, but had been unable to find air transportation. Brand took a chance and asked whether the German could be added to the group who knew about Lotte, pointing out that

Kastner's knowledge of and contacts in the BND could be useful. With some reluctance, Faulkner had agreed, with the stipulation that Kastner not be informed of Rudel's alleged treachery until, and if, he needed to know about it. The BND man did know that Lotte was in the embassy, and that she had information about a Soviet intelligence ploy, but nothing more.

Faulkner put the intercepts down and walked slowly to Brand's desk. Kastner opened his eyes and absentmindedly swirled the coffee in the paper cup. "Are we all going to live until sunset?" he asked in his heavily accented English.

Faulkner shrugged. "There's no word of another exchange. Something else is going on, though. 7th Corps reports that an East German division down there has revolted, or collapsed, or both. No more details yet. But the Russians at Frankfurt are in trouble if that's happened. They'll be pocketed."

"Stalingrad in reverse?" Brand suggested.

"Not much hope of anything that complete. But the Russians will have to try to turn around to fight off the threat to their rear. That'll take the pressure off our people around Frankfurt. It'll also make a mess of the Russian timetable. And we know that some of their units up north are in rough shape. Not as rough as ours, but bad enough. They banked too much on everything going exactly right. You'd think they'd have known."

"The Russians always were too rigid," Kastner observed. "Always plans. When the plan didn't work, they made another one. Now they cannot do that. Not enough time."

"They've gambled," Faulkner said. "They might still pull it off, if they're willing to settle for less than the whole pie. If it doesn't escalate any more." He paused. "But it always did, in the simulations."

Brand didn't want to pursue that line of thought. He looked at his watch. "Three minutes until Rudel comes on the air," he said.

"I wonder if he does it?" said Faulkner.

"If he does," Brand said, "how's he going to formalize it? The whole Soviet embassy staff's interned."

"He'll manage, I'm sure," Faulkner said.

Kastner looked swiftly from Brand to Faulkner and back

again. "The speech that was announced this morning? You know what he is going to say?"

"We might," Faulkner said, without expression.

"Washington monitoring it?" asked Brand.

"You want to believe it," Faulkner said. "Direct satellite feed from here. They want to know yesterday."

The idioms left Kastner in the dust. Faulkner said, "Let's have a look at him." Brand and the German followed him to the console monitoring the West German radio and television stations.

"Forty seconds," said the console operator.

On the monitor screen was the familiar countenance of a broadcaster; he was ending a segment on civil defense measures. The television and radio networks were carrying mostly public service programming now, and had been since Sunday morning, as well as a great many news reports. The reports were studiously innocuous, so as not to incite panic or cause rumors: a losing battle.

The commentator faded out, to be replaced by the network identification. After perhaps five seconds Rudel's face appeared on the screen. His blue eyes stared directly into the camera; there were deep lines around his mouth and over his eyes; he looked wan, but the charisma was still there.

"Citizens of the Federal Republic," he began. "I wish I could bring you reassurance and news of victory, but I cannot. I have to tell you now that a nuclear weapon belonging to the Soviet Union has exploded on Federal territory, that an American atomic bomb has been used in retaliation against Soviet troops on our soil, and that this government is now faced with a dreadful choice.

"We have considered asking NATO to respond in force, as the Americans have already done unilaterally. But this would be to invite the destruction of our country, probably that of Europe, and perhaps that of the human race itself. This is an action which we, as civilized human beings, cannot undertake.

"Accordingly, I shall instruct our Foreign Ministry to make immediate contact with the governments of the Warsaw Pact, and inform them that the government of the Federal Republic will accept, as early as possible, their conditions for peace. We do this to spare our nation, and the others of the world, from the horror of nuclear war. The cost to us will be great, but not as great as that of a global holocaust. In time we will regain all that we have lost, and more besides.

"You can well imagine my feelings at this moment. I ask you all to remain calm, to accept courageously the misfortune which has befallen our country, and commit yourselves to the rebuilding of Germany in the difficult times which lie ahead.

"I will be speaking to you again in the near future. Thank you, and for the moment, farewell."

The screen went blue-gray. "The bastard," Faulkner said after a long silence. "He did it. It's still hard to believe."

"What now?" asked Brand.

"We wait for Washington to call. They won't be long, I can tell you. Herr Kastner, you'd better prepare yourself to hear some evil news."

Moscow
1:15 P.M., August 17

"THERE'S NO DOUBT?" said Nikolayev. "None?" The Politburo, or what remained of it after the arrests of the morning, had taken up residence in the room with the Molink speakerphone in the Kremlin Arsenal.

"None," said Kamenev. "I questioned Minkov myself. He didn't need any coercion. He was in fact proud that the plan continued despite our counteractions. The nuclear strike early this morning was launched by a specialist KGB unit reporting directly to STAVKA. They were using army cover."

"What in hell for?" said Ivanov. He was pallid; the treachery of the army and the KGB had shaken him badly.

"Because, according to Minkov, the conspirators thought Rudel would need a credible reason to ask for peace while NATO was still resisting strongly. He had one assignment other than that: to delay any use of Western nuclear weapons past the seventy-two hour limit, to allow our forces to achieve their major objectives. Obviously he failed in that, now that the Americans have retaliated. Also, they have dispersed their warheads. They do not appear ready to negotiate. And as we have heard, Hood will not accept Rudel's surrender. The Americans now know he was one of ours." He grimaced. "I am not sure why they have not attacked us in strength in Europe already."

"I have to contact Hood as soon as possible," said Nikolayev urgently. "Events are already almost out of control. What is the military situation on the West Front?"

"I have the report from the deputy defense minister," Lensky said. In the aftermath of the purge he had more or less taken Fedashkin's place. "Early this morning, before his removal, Fedashkin was concealing the reality of the situation. We have reached seventy percent of our objectives, but our tank and infantry divisions are exhausted and reinforcements and resupply are moving far more slowly than we need. Fedashkin must have hoped that Rudel's action and the consequent later surrender of the West German armed forces would arrive before the offensive stalled completely.

"The second strategic echelon from Poland and Byelorussia is twenty-four to thirty-six hours behind schedule. The only consolation is that the NATO troops on most of the West Front are as exhausted as our own. That is unfortunately not the case in the Frankfurt area." He stopped for a moment, looking around the table. "The West German penetration behind 8th Guards Army is not being held. There is no doubt now that the East German 4th Division is in revolt, or is surrendering. The formation on the east side of the penetration is Czech, and it is not fighting well. We are in danger of collapse along a third of the Central Front, either by Czech and East German disinclination to fight, by surrender, or by open rebellion. NATO does not have enough reserves to exploit such a collapse fully, but we cannot afford it politically. As it is we may have more East German formations turning against us at any time. If we appear to be suddenly in a vulnerable position, with many of our troops committed in the west, I cannot answer for the loyalty of the Poles either."

"In short," Nikolayev said, "we have failed. Or the KGB and the military have failed the Party. Betrayed it, rather."

"That's correct," Lensky said. "Barbarossa Red is not succeeding. According to the deputy minister, we cannot now take all our objectives. Not conventionally."

"Yes. And the Americans have dispersed their weapons," Nikolayev said. "We have always taken that to be an indicator of readiness. We cannot surprise them now."

"And also," Lensky went on, "we have the threat of widespread revolt in the rear of our first echelon, and our second echelon, most of it, is not in a position to react, since it is so late.

We could lose the entire Group of Forces in Germany. That threat will not be eliminated by nuclear strikes against NATO. We could, if utterly necessary, use nuclear strikes against the Poles and Czechs and East Germans, but we would be also doing NATO's work for it by smashing up our own supply lines. Not to mention the problems with the Warsaw Pact afterwards."

"Can we deal with the NATO counterattack?" asked Kamenev.

"To do so we will have to abandon the attack on Frankfurt," Lensky said. "But it will be very difficult to disengage, and turning the 8th Guards divisions around to fight the West Germans and the Americans in their rear will leave us extremely vulnerable. In its present battered state the 8th Guards might disintegrate, if the NATO units west of Frankfurt go over to the offensive so that the 8th is caught between two attackers."

For a moment Nikolayev was engulfed by a wave of fear and rage and despair. Issue the launch orders, he thought, try the first strike against the United States, resolve this at a blow, one way or the other. The relief of an irrevocable act, not this agony of uncertainty and doubt. If you do not know which act is the right one, any act will do.

He drove the emotion back into the abyss from which it had emerged. "We cannot politically afford a major military setback," he said. "Not now. I must talk to Hood. We must come to some resolution, and soon. If Zossen believes 8th Guards is going to collapse, Marshal Lesiovsky may initiate tactical nuclear strikes without referring to STAVKA. He has that authorization, remember."

"Cancel it," suggested Kamenev.

"Absolutely not," snapped Ivanov. "If the Americans and the Germans pre-empt him, he cannot waste time contacting STAVKA. He might have lost his communications, anyway."

"Secretary Ivanov is right," said Nikolayev. "We cannot rescind Lesiovsky's authorization."

"What are we to propose to Hood?" asked Kamenev.

"We have to secure the Warsaw Pact," said Nikolayev. "Nothing else is as important as that. If NATO elects to help the East Germans or the others, we are facing catastrophe. I will propose to Hood that we offer to withdraw to the prewar frontier if he guarantees not to support rebellious Warsaw Pact forces."

"You are throwing away everything we've gained," Ivanov said bitterly. "Better to go down fighting than this . . . *retreat*."

"You heard the report from STAVKA," Nikolayev said. "We cannot handle both NATO and a revolt in the Pact. Our armies in Europe do not have the strength."

"There's another solution," Kamenev said. "One which may provide a good ostensible reason for us to withdraw, without losing our reputation completely."

"What?" asked Nikolayev.

"Rudel's removal from the chancellorship. If that happens, we can pull out on the grounds that the fascist government in Bonn has fallen, and that we have no territorial ambitions in Western Europe in any case. Remember, our attack has frightened the world. They expect us to remain, to absorb the Federal Republic. We can no longer do that, as we originally intended. If we withdraw we will be in a somewhat better diplomatic position. We were doing nothing more than defending ourselves against a dangerous madman."

"And if the Americans cannot get rid of Rudel?" asked Ivanov.

"They have to," Kamenev said. "With all respect to Secretary Nikolayev, we cannot pull back to the frontier if Rudel is still in power. It is too much of a defeat. But remember, Hood wants Rudel gone too, for obvious reasons."

"Would Rudel resign without orders from us?" asked Nikolayev. "Remember, he has no idea he has been exposed. He may decide to bluff if they confront him. They have no documented proof, only the German woman's accusation. What could they do if he simply refused?"

"Tell Hood," said Ivanov, "that we will withdraw only if Rudel is disposed of. Otherwise we will take any appropriate action to ensure the survival of our forces. We cannot be perceived as suffering a military defeat."

"Very well," Nikolayev said wearily. "That is what I will tell him. That our withdrawal is contingent upon Rudel's . . . disposal." His hand drifted towards the telephone.

"Before you call," said Kamenev, "there is one other thing that might help. Minkov told me. Barbarossa Red was more than the invasion plan. It is also Rudel's code name. A little joke of Fedashkin's. Tell Hood that. If Rudel is confronted with it, he will have to concede that he is vulnerable."

"Very well," said Nikolayev again, and lifted the receiver.

Bonn
5:00 P.M., August 17

THERE WERE FIVE OF THEM in the embassy Lincoln, driving north along the Adenauerallee. Faulkner was behind the wheel, Brand next to him. In the rear seat, in uncomfortable proximity, sat Lotte, Kastner and the United States Ambassador, Lane Coburn. Coburn, a lean elegant man with a precisely controlled tan and extremely white hair, had worn an expression of extreme distaste ever since they had left the embassy.

"I see the necessity for this," he said, looking out the car window at the Landeszentral Bank as it slid by on the right, "but I am not certain whether it's going to work."

Faulkner slowed a trifle and then pulled out to pass an HSK truck towing an elderly antitank gun. "You see that?" he said, gesturing at the long barrel of the weapon. "The Germans are running out of everything they need to fight with. From Frankfurt north they're bleeding white, and the British and the Belgians and some of our units aren't much better off. We've got a ghost of a chance in the south, but there're no reserves to exploit any success. And the Russians are running out of steam too. There'll be a stalemate pretty soon, and then either we or they will have to try to break it with nuclear weapons. Unless there are some negotiations. We don't have much time. The Russians have demanded a resolution here by half-past five. The president says they won't wait any longer than that."

"What will they do?" asked Brand. He shifted in the deep

leather seat; the Walther P38 in his jacket was digging into his ribs. He was not much more optimistic than Coburn; they had no documents, nothing except Lotte's evidence and a scrap of a code word the Russians had provided; perhaps for reasons of their own. There was no reason for Rudel to do other than deny everything, if he kept his wits about him. If he did that . . .

"The president didn't indicate that," said Coburn. "Except that they wouldn't withdraw. Fundamentally, they want Rudel gone to save face." He was clearly displeased at Faulkner's direct contact with Hood.

"Also," Faulkner added, "the Russians want to keep the pressure on NATO. The conventional battle, like I said, looks like becoming a stalemate somewhere in the middle of West Germany. The Russians haven't got all they wanted, but we've lost a hell of a lot. Sooner or later some commander's going to find himself in a tight spot and ask for launch authorization. The way things have been going, he might get it; 7th Corps has already been issued with predelegation codes."

We're trying to stop on both sides, Brand thought. But it's slipping out of control. Too many things going wrong in too many places at the same time. Too many mistakes.

"The Germans are going to detest this, if it turns out to be true," said Coburn.

"Do you think it's not true, Mr. Ambassador?" asked Faulkner. "Rudel didn't consult anyone on that peace initative, not even his own cabinet, as far as we can tell. He just did it. Nikolayev blamed Rudel on the KGB and the military, which may or may not be true, but the Kremlin's willing to pull back if Rudel's no longer chancellor. And Fraulein von Veltheim is not exactly a suspect witness."

Kastner spoke for the first time during the drive north. "When I spoke with Staatsminister Kempf after . . . I was given the evidence, I told him that the chancellor was a possible security risk. He was extremely reluctant to believe it, even with Fraulein von Veltheim's testimony. But when your president phoned the deputy chancellor with the Russian withdrawal offer, and their admission . . . But I think it was Rudel's peace proposal that finally convinced him. The Staatsminister and the deputy chancellor could not believe Rudel had done it, without consultation, even after the bombs were used, not while we were counterattacking in the south. Not while we are still fighting."

"So the Germans want him gone too," Coburn said.

Ahead of the Lincoln, Brand could see the antitank barricades of the new Chancellery defenses. Behind the barricades were two Leopard tanks, a scattering of armored personnel carriers, and a cordon of heavily armed soldiers.

"That's right," Faulkner said, as he slowed the big car. "Rudel has to resign."

"Wait," Kempf said. Brand and Kastner and Lotte halted obediently. The fluorescents flickered overhead. The chancellor's outer office was vacant, the chairs neatly placed under the two desks, the typewriters and terminals turned on but unattended. Outside the long windows the late afternoon sun lay rose and gold along the roofs of Bonn.

"The deputy chancellor is waiting downstairs for the outcome," Kempf said. "Herr Kastner, you and Mayor von Veltheim had better be right about this. I would never have believed you but for that offer for peace. Even President Hood's persuasiveness would not have convinced me. Nor what Nikolayev said."

"Not even that?" Brand asked.

"Not without corroborating evidence. If the chancellor had waited until we had no hope . . . Then, perhaps, I would have agreed with his offer. But not yet." He looked at his watch. "We have only a little time before the Russian deadline. Go on."

Lotte walked slowly toward the heavy door to the Rudel's inner office. She knocked three times, once more, and then opened it a little. "Ernst. It's me, Lotte."

Through the gap Brand could see Rudel at a great rosewood desk, with a communications console behind his chair. An expression of disbelief spread across the chancellor's face. It was strange to see; Brand had never really believed that Rudel could be startled.

"Lotte," he said in that light resonant voice Brand remembered from the reception in Berlin. The eyes were the same intense blue, only far more tired. "I thought we had lost you." He began to stand up.

She stepped through the door. "Ernst," she said, "there are three people here who need to talk to you. Would you mind?"

Rudel had moved around the end of the desk, so that he was invisible behind the door. The Walther dragged at Brand's jacket.

If she can't move him, Faulkner had said, you'll have to kill him. He cannot be allowed to live, no matter what Coburn has been told. No matter what the Germans think. If he is not gone by the deadline, in one way or another, the Russians will likely use nuclear weapons to save their 8th Guards Army. Coburn doesn't know that yet, but it's what Hood told me. We'll get you out if you have to do it.

"Bring them in," Rudel said after a barely noticeable hesitation.

Kastner and Brand and Kempf followed Lotte through the door. Lotte closed the heavy soundproof slab behind them. The three men stood for a moment while Rudel surveyed them with curiosity. After a moment he said, "Ah, Herr Brand. I know you. I met you in March, in West Berlin." He switched that intense gaze past Kempf to Kastner. "I'm afraid I've not had the pleasure."

"Ernst Kastner. BND, Berlin station."

"I see," Rudel said. He retired to stand behind the great desk. "Please find somewhere comfortable to sit. Lotte, I'm sorry, but I can spare you only a few minutes. I am expecting the Soviets to respond to the peace offer at any moment. There is a great deal of preparation to be done. Staatsminister Kempf, have the senior Russians been returned to their embassy building yet?"

"Yes," Kempf said.

"I would have thought," Lotte said, "that you would have heard from the Kremlin by now. As far as I know the fighting is still going on, and the Russians have not answered. Is it possible they are not interested?"

Rudel closed his eyes momentarily, as though in pain. "It's unlikely. Although I did expect an answer before now. We must resolve this before . . ." He trailed off and said, "Lotte, how in the name of God did you get out of Berlin? I had given you up for lost."

"Ernst," she said, "The Americans know what you've done.

So do we. It's not going to happen as we thought."

Rudel lowered himself, very slowly, into the black leather. chair behind the rosewood desk. His face was devoid of expression. "I don't understand you. Who thought?"

"The Russians have given you up," she said. "The Party did not know about you. You were part of an operation by the KGB and the Soviet army. Secretary Nikolayev wants an accommodation with the West. He has repudiated you."

"What nonsense is this?" said Rudel.

"I was GRU," Lotte said. "I have been watching you for them for more than twenty years."

"Ah," said Rudel. He looked at Kastner, then Brand. "That is why the BND is here. And you, I suppose," he added, "are the CIA representative."

Brand nodded.

"You are Barbarossa Red," said Lotte. "The Russians themselves gave us your code name. Nikolayev is desperate to end the war."

Rudel looked at Kastner. "You intend to arrest me on these grounds?"

"No," Kempf said. "Resignation would be preferable."

"Preferable," repeated Rudel. "And you, my friend," he said, turning the dark blue eyes on Brand, "why are you here? To make sure for Washington?"

"I'm just here," Brand said.

"Lotte," Rudel said. "What happened? Why did you tell them?"

"Because you gave us another war. That was not in the plan. Not in the one I was told."

"No one is told everything," Rudel said. "I thought as you did, until very recently. That there was not to be a war. I was to withdraw from NATO, proclaim neutrality, announce that Germany was strengthening her armed forces, attempting nuclear agreements with the French. But the last two were only to convince the Americans that Germany was still their bulwark against the East. The measures were never intended to take place."

"And the General Staff?" asked Kempf. His voice shook slightly, from anger or grief, Brand could not tell which.

"That was real," Rudel admitted. "But what actual influence could it have had?" He shrugged. "I was duped long ago, when I was recruited. I wanted Germany reunited. There was never any chance of that while we were still part of NATO. As a neutral there was a chance that we could be one again." He studied Lotte for a moment. "As I said, the goal I worked towards did not include war. Then I was instructed differently."

"How?" asked Kempf.

"There were several prepared contingency plans. This was one of them. The idea was that once I had asked for peace, popular pressure and fear would make it impossible to retract. So I spoke without consulting the cabinet."

"You would have let us fall under Russian rule?" said Kempf.

Again the shrug. "The Russians, over time, might have allowed reunification, if West Germany were no longer a military threat to them. No empire lasts forever. In five centuries, who will care who was loyal to whom?" He coughed, briefly, carefully, behind his hand. "What must I do now? Do I have a choice?"

"You must resign," Kempf said.

"No," said Rudel. "I will not do that. Not to go through what will happen after."

"We will have to place you under arrest," Kempf warned.

"Really?" said Rudel, looking at Kastner with a faint smile. "What will you do with me? Put me on trial? The Russians will not thank you for exposing them. It might endanger your negotiations. I do not see what you can do."

No, Brand thought. I cannot. He looked at Lotte. He was startled to see tears running down her cheeks. She opened her denim bag, searching for a handkerchief. Brand's hand began to drift, against his will, to the Walther.

Lotte's hand was deep in the denim bag. Rudel said "Lotte—"

There was a flat dry crack. Lotte's right arm jerked slightly. Blood suddenly appeared at Rudel's throat. She fired again, and once more, round dark-edged holes appearing in the blue denim. The two bullets struck Rudel in the center of the chest. He tried to get up, and could not.

"Lotte," he said, in a choked voice. Blood came out of his mouth. He fell back in the chair, eyes widening.

Brand had the Walther in his hand, too late. Lotte's pistol was out of her bag and she was was pointing it at him. "No, Paul," she said. "Put it down."

He did so, very carefully, on the floor beside his chair.

"We both believed it, once," she said, put the muzzle to her breast, and pulled the trigger.

Current Action Center, the Pentagon
August 17

"SO HE'S GONE," Hood said. He was looking up at the wall screens, where the lights glowed. The orders had gone out from NATO half an hour ago: suspend all offensive operations in the south, assume defensive positions. In a few hours the firing all along the battle line from Austria to the North Sea would be dying away. Soon after that the Russian withdrawal, assuming Nikolayev kept his word, would begin. Hood thought the Russian leader would not risk doing otherwise. The president did not believe the Kremlin's troubles with the Warsaw Pact were finished yet.

"Yes," said Blake Ormerod. "I wasn't sure he would confess."

"Neither was I," said Hood. "If he hadn't . . ." He folded his hands and rested his chin on them. He looked very old. "We were fortunate Brand knew Lotte von Weltheim. We could never have gotten somebody else close to Rudel in the time we had. Even if we didn't use him, finally."

"Thank God a German killed Rudel," Ormerod said. "I would have hated to disown Brand. But politically it would have been the only choice."

"Yes," said Hood, looking up at the maps where the lights glimmered. "Mr. Brand is a very lucky man."

THE NEW YORK TIMES
Ceasefire Holding, Withdrawal Announced

BONN, August 19 (Reuters) — The temporary ceasefire in the European war, officially concluded late yesterday, appears strengthened by a Soviet announcement that their forces will begin to withdraw to the prewar frontiers within forty-eight hours. Ironically, the ceasefire was agreed only hours after the West German Chancellor, Ernst Rudel, died unexpectedly in Bonn. Cause of death, according to a West German government spokesman, was massive heart failure.

In Washington, Secretary of State Chalmers said he was encouraged by the Russian move, and that it indicated that the defensive posture of NATO had been totally successful. In the same press conference, Defense Secretary Thatcher Martin called the strong Western resistance to the Soviet attack "a great victory for the cause of peace."

Author's Note

THE PENETRATION of both NATO and the West German government by eastern intelligence services has occurred time and again since the end of the Second World War, the establishment of NATO and the rebirth of the West German armed forces. Sometimes these agents have occupied positions of trust at the highest levels. A few have been:

– Alfred Frenzel, a Social Democrat member of the Bundestag.

– Gunther Guillame, senior aide to the West German Chancellor, Willy Brandt.

– Otto John, head of the BFV, the West German domestic intelligence service.

– Heinz Felfe, head of the Soviet section of the BND, the West German foreign intelligence service.

– Peter Fuhrmann, a West German expert in military secrets, and a senior civil servant in the Defense Department.

– West German Rear Admiral Luebke, chief of NATO's logistics division. (A few days after being confronted with the evidence of his treachery, he either committed suicide or was murdered.)

– BND deputy chief Major Horst Wendland. (Wendland killed himself on the same day Admiral Luebke died, perhaps for personal reasons.)

– George Paques, deputy director of the press and information agency of NATO.

    – Nahat Imre, financial comptroller of the NATO international staff.

The actual penetration of a West European cabinet or, in the most extreme case, of the recruitment of a head of state, has apparently not yet occurred. It would be difficult, but for the KGB and its sister services, probably not impossible.

    It is, after all, the final step.

QUANTITY SALES

Most General Paperbacks books are available at special quantity discounts when purchased in bulk by corporations, organizations, and special-interest groups. Custom imprinting or excerpting can also be done to fit special needs. For details write: General Paperbacks, 34 Lesmill Road, Don Mills, Ontario M3B 2T6, Attn: Special Sales Dept., or phone (416) 445-3333

INDIVIDUAL SALES

Are there any General Paperbacks books you want but cannot find in your local stores? If so, you can order them directly from us. You can get any General Paperbacks book in print. Simply include the book's title, author, and ISBN number, if you have it, along with a cheque or money order (no cash can be accepted) for the full retail price plus 75¢ per copy to cover shipping and handling. Mail to: General Paperbacks, 34 Lesmill Road, Don Mills, Ontario M3B 2T6.